What the hell, he thought, rereading the note again. He pulled down the duct tape from the fence as he noticed two blood-stained thumbs attached to the tape. He yelled and dropped them to the ground, then whirled around looking in every direction. *Was someone watching him?* Suddenly he was sweating, saliva ran down the side of his mouth. *Someone is after me! What does it mean...You're next?"*

Running back to the golf cart he jumped in and hit the starter. It sputtered then stopped. "Got damn, come on, dammit!" He tried the starter again. Nothing! The motor was dead.

He had to get back to the safety of the trailer. Beating on the dash he jumped out and ran back up the lane but almost immediately slowed to a trot. He was grossly out of shape. Not even thirty yards up the lane he was out of breath. Bending over he placed his hands on his knees as he panted heavily. He felt like he was going to be sick. He realized that he needed to calm down. Looking back down the lane he whispered to himself, "God, whose thumbs were those?"

Starting up the lane once again he tried to compose himself, but then he saw something that shouldn't have been there—something underneath the rusted bumper of an old Buick. He approached the odd looking object slowly, but then much to his horror he discovered what it was. The mangled remains of a body lying in a pool of dried black blood, the face half eaten away, one of the arms missing. He couldn't believe what he was seeing. He wanted to scream but nothing came out of his mouth. Then he remembered. *The dogs! That's why they were bloody. They had torn the body apart.* Backing away from the body, he knew this was the first time his dogs had ever killed anyone. He turned and ran up the lane all the while thinking, *How did the person get in? Were they put inside the fence? The note said I'm going to be next!*

SEASONS OF DEATH
THE SMOKY MOUNTAINS MURDERS

To Terry!

Gary M Yeagle

MARLENE MITCHELL GARY YEAGLE

a BlackWyrm book
Louisville, Kentucky

SEASONS OF DEATH: THE SMOKY MOUNTAINS MURDERS

A BlackWyrm Book
BlackWyrm Publishing
10307 Chimney Ridge Ct, Louisville, KY 40299

Printed in the United States of America.

ISBN: 978-0-9820067-5-7
LCCN: 2010941569
Cover photograph by John Schneider

First edition: December 2010
Second edition: April 2011

CHAPTER ONE

THE FIRST THING HE NOTICED as his eyes slowly focused on the early spring morning was the wall of dark green trees that stood directly in front of him. The morning sun had just begun the age-old process of penetrating the deep forest and burning off the blue mist that the Smoky Mountains were noted for. The heavy mist left the trees and surrounding thick undergrowth soaked with dew. Two droplets of moisture from the tree that towered above him landed on his right cheek and slowly trailed down the side of his neck past the collar of his plaid shirt.

Shaking his head, he tried to regain full mental faculties but a strange feeling; a feeling of being slightly out of kilter lingered in the recesses of his brain. As he watched a gray hawk glide effortlessly to a large branch of a tall pine, he drew in a deep breath while trying to erase the cobwebs from his thinking process. The familiar aroma of mountain ferns mingled with the smell of moss-covered rocks seemed to be reversing his unsteadiness. He took another deep breath, and listened to the pleasant mountain sound of the birds: chickadees, Wood Warblers, wrens and cowbirds creating a natural symphony, a nearby woodpecker keeping perfect beat with the music of the forest.

Blinking his eyes twice he began to take in the surroundings. Aside from the dense trees and underbrush, he noticed a well-traveled trail ten yards off to the left flanked by a steep wall of weeds and rocks that disappeared behind the tree line. A squirrel suddenly appeared at the edge of the trail, looked in his direction, then scampered off into a clump of tall grass. He tried to step forward but was restricted from doing so. It was the oddest feeling. Looking down he noticed that he was secured to a tree by means of gray duct tape, not only around his chest and upper arms, but also his knees and ankles. It was all starting to come back to him now.

He recalled how he had been walking out of his cabin just after the Late Night News in order to bring in more wood for the fireplace. He had heard a noise like someone stepping on a twig behind him but before he could turn to see what had caused the sound, someone grabbed him from behind placing a rag over his nose and mouth. He had struggled but the combination of the strength of his assailant and the fumes from the rag rendered him unconscious. That was the last thing he remembered *and now* he was tied to a tree. *Where* and *why,* he had no idea.

Wiggling back and fourth he tried his best to loosen the tape, but whoever had secured him to the tree had taken great care to ensure that he would not escape. The tape was wrapped so tightly around his torso that the more he struggled, the more difficult it became to breath. During his powerless attempt to get free he noticed he had no feeling in either of his hands. Maybe the circulation to his hands had been cut off by the tape, restricting the flow of blood. *Strange,* he thought. His arms had feeling, but not his hands.

Following the trail with his eyes he noticed a glimpse of civilization twenty-five yards away where there was a small standard Smoky Mountains trail sign that read THUNDERHEAD TRAIL. Despite his strange predicament, he managed a lame smile as he knew exactly where he was. Over the past thirty years he had traveled every trail there was in the Smokies a number of times. Thunderhead was not only utilized for hikers but horseback riding as well; a 13.9 mile trip that was considered one of the more strenuous hikes in the Smoky Mountains. The highest elevation on the hike reached over 5500 feet. Being a man of the mountains he could tell by the shaded sunlight that it was around seven thirty in the morning. He also knew the first riders would leave the Anthony Creek Trailhead which was located at the edge of the Cades Cove Picnic Area about ten o'clock which meant they would make Spence Field by eleven. Spence was about two hundred yards from where he was currently bound to the tree. The first group of riders would pass by in about three and a half hours. All he had to do was remain patient and when they passed he could give a shout out and then he would be rescued.

His head was starting to clear and he tried to relax. His cabin was located eight and a half miles above the town of Townsend, just a half mile from Cades Cove. After he had been abducted he figured he had for some reason been tied to a tree that was approximately nine miles from his cabin. But *why* and *who?*

Then, it came to him. Today was April 1, April Fool's Day.

Now it all made sense. The group of old farts he met with every Monday, Wednesday and Friday morning at The Parkway Grocery in Townsend for coffee and small talk had no doubt played a joke on him. He was always messing with his four friends: Charley, Zeb, Luke and Buddie, for as long as they had been meeting. Every year on April Fool's Day he had pulled a prank on his old pals. Like three years ago when he came running into the store stating someone had just run into Buddie's new truck. Buddie went flying out the front door cursing up a storm only to find his new Ford truck unscathed. They all had a good laugh that day at Buddie's expense.

Or last year, when a week prior to April 1, he had informed the group he had won a hundred thousand dollars playing the lottery over in Gatlinburg and the following Monday he was going to take them all to dinner at the Old Mill, one of the most popular places to eat in the area. They were to meet in Townsend and then drive down to Pigeon Forge to celebrate his new found fortune. Climbing into Luke's old Cadillac, the four drove into town where he had told the group dinner was on him. The sky was the limit. When the check finally arrived after they had all stuffed themselves, he stood, waved the bill in the air and shouted, "April Fools," explaining that he didn't have a cent on him. It was the best April Fool's prank he had ever pulled on the boys. He had completely fooled all of them. They took it well, but vowed they would get even with him.

He had to admit they had indeed gotten even with him for not only last year's prank but for every trick he had ever played on them. To think they had actually kidnapped him, possibly drugged him and left him tied to a tree. This was definitely over the top. He laughed to himself. He was sure they were nearby busting at the seams and that at any moment they would step out from behind the tree line as they all yelled, "April Fools!"

Not able to contain himself any longer he looked to the right, then the left as he yelled, "Okay fellas, ya got me. Ya got me good. Ya kin come out now!"

There was instant silence, his loud voice startling the birds. He waited for a few moments then yelled again, but with less enthusiasm, "All right guys...fun's over. I git it!" The ominous silence that followed caused him to break out in a sweat. Maybe his pals hadn't played a joke on him. Maybe this was real!

Just then a figure stepped out from behind a tall pin oak. It was a man; a tall man just over six-foot in height, thin lips, eyes that appeared as slits in an unfamiliar face beneath a black slouch hat. His body was covered in a dingy, faded brown trench coat, his feet in muddy, worn work boots. In his right hand he carried a black gym bag.

He peered at the figure, trying to see if the man was one of his old pals in disguise, but after a few seconds he realized he was facing a man he had never met before.

Suddenly the man smiled which seemed out of context for his rough appearance. He spoke softly, "Good morning, Asa…how are you feeling?"

Thinking that maybe, just maybe his buddies had hired this strange man and that he was part of the joke Asa decided to play along. "Well, not too good. Think I was drugged."

The man stepped closer, placed the bag on the ground then smiled again. "How perceptive…you *were* drugged."

Since the stranger was smiling, Asa knew he was part of the prank. He was obviously trying hard to keep a straight face but was losing it. Asa's four friends were probably back behind the trees trying their best to contain their laughter. Asa grinned, shouting toward the trees, "Okay guys…ya kin come on out. Yer friend here done a great job." Looking at the man, Asa remarked, "This is the best April Fool's joke ever. You fellas really had me goin'."

The man looked back at the trees then to Asa, commenting in a serious manner, "This is no joke my friend." Stepping closer, now eye to eye with Asa, he continued, "This is April 1, April Fool's day. Your friends, whoever they may be, are not back there in the woods and what's about to happen to you is no joke. The only fool around here…is you."

Looking directly into the man's eyes, Asa suddenly felt a sense of fear invade his body from head to toe. The stranger, whoever he was, was playing his part to the hilt and if this was indeed a practical joke staged by his pals the whole thing had gone far enough. "All right, mister, this has gone too far. I've learned my lesson. I'll never play a joke on anyone again…ever. I promise! Now please…cut me loose…please!"

The man nodded his head in an affirmative fashion, smiled, leaned over and unzipped the bag. When he stood back up he held a large pocket knife in his hand, which he proceeded to open as he displayed the knife to Asa. A broad smile came to Asa's face. He realized the joke was coming to an end. He was now going to be freed and he, his pals, *and the man* would all have a good laugh. But then the man leaned over once again and extracted something else from the bag; a roll of duct tape. Asa watched silently. The man brought the tape up to his mouth, where with the use of his teeth, he gripped the edge of the loose end and pulled the roll forward, stopping when a six-inch section appeared, at which point the man cut it. He then stuck the knife into the trunk of a nearby tree and hung the roll on the knife. Asa was once again confused. He looked toward the tree line for his friends, then back to the man who was again smiling. He was about to say something when the man placed his index finger across his lips indicating that Asa should be silent, then placed the tape across Asa's mouth and smoothed it to ensure a tight fit. Asa's objection sounded like nothing more than muffled, indescribable words.

The man removed the knife and tape from the tree and placed them back in the bag. "I realize that taping your mouth may seem a bit uncomfortable but it's necessary. We wouldn't want anyone who just happens to be out walking in the woods this morning to hear you screaming...now would we?"

The man then pulled a pair of old brown gloves from his coat pocket, and after wiggling his fingers into them, leaned over and removed some sort of a tool from the bag that he held up in front of Asa's face. As Asa stared at the heavy-duty lopping shears he once again began to object, the only sound coming from his taped mouth was senseless mumbling. "Now, now," said the stranger. "You need to calm down so I can explain what is going to happen. I want to make sure you understand." Examining the shears, he explained, "I've had this tool for years. I originally purchased it to cut unwanted branches down from the trees in my backyard. It really does work quite well: a fifteen inch, heavy-duty wooden handles with plastic grips, four inch blades that can snap anything from a small twig up to a sizable branch." Reaching up he placed the shears around a two-inch, low hanging branch and with both hands squeezed the handles, the sharp blade snapping the branch off instantly. The sharp snap sent a shiver through Asa's body. "Everyone should own one of these," said the man. "You see it can be used for many other things...like locks. Just last week I went out to my storage shed and wouldn't you know it, I had lost the key. Then, I thought about my lopping shears. They did the trick. Cut right through that metal lock like a hot knife through butter. Cutting through skin and bone should be a piece of cake." Reaching out he took Asa's left hand and balanced it on his raised knee, placing the shears around Asa's pinky finger. Asa's eyes grew wide with fear. He tried to pull his arm back, but the duct tape restricted his movement. The man gripped his arm tightly and then lopped off the little finger. Following a spurt of blood the finger fell to the ground as Asa let out a scream that sounded like the lowing of cattle. As the stranger reached for his right hand Asa resisted as best he could. The man, growing impatient with Asa's feeble struggling brought the lopping shears down across Asa's right knee. The instant pain in his leg captured Asa's attention for the next second at which point the man calmly grabbed his right hand and repeated the lopping shear process, Asa's right pinky falling to the ground.

The man leaned the now bloody shears up against the trunk of a nearby tree then placed his hands on his hips, admiring his handy work. Asa's muffled screaming and weak attempts to loosen himself from his restraints caused the man to smile. He sat on a tree stump, removed a pipe from his trench coat pocket and pointed the pipe at Asa. "The more you thrash around the worse it's going to get. The faster your heart beats the more blood you'll lose. If you will try to remain calm the loss of blood will not be so rapid. You might want to cup your hands to slow down the process of bleeding out." Looking down at his slightly blood smattered trench coat, he remarked, "Good thing I wore this old coat. I knew this was going to be messy work."

Asa stared at his hands, his two blood-stained little fingers lying on the ground at his feet, blood slowly dripping from where his fingers moments earlier had been attached. He couldn't believe what had just happened. His heart was racing and it felt like the life-giving muscle would pop right through his heaving chest. Placing his head back against the tree he closed his eyes and tried to scream but it was to no avail. Taking the stranger's advice he slowly cupped his hands. The bleeding didn't seem to slow, but rather than dripping directly down to the ground the blood momentarily delayed its flow where the fingers had been severed. Within seconds it ran across his hands forming a small ever-growing pool of blood in his palms, then dripped in between his fingers and onto the ground.

Getting up, the man walked over to the tree and wiped Asa's forehead with a white handkerchief that he had taken from his trench coat. "There, there now, you're really sweating. Try and relax. The pain you are feeling is nothing more than mental. If you'll calm down I'll tell you why all of this is happening."

Walking back to the stump the man sat down and removed a pouch of tobacco from his coat. "Earlier when I asked you how you were feeling you said you thought you had been drugged. You were drugged, and I might add at the moment, I'm rather proud of myself. When I initially decided to embark on this venture I had no idea where to get chloroform and Novocainee. Being quite uneducated when it comes to drugs, be they legal or illegal, I dropped by the local drugstore and asked the pharmacist if these drugs were still available. The pharmacist explained to me that first of all, these two drugs are actually not utilized much anymore. They had been replaced with newer drugs and secondly, even if they were available, I would not be able to purchase them unless I had a specialized license. The government closely monitors the sale of these drugs."

Opening the tobacco pouch he removed a small portion of the leafy substance and then proceeded to tap it down into the bowl of the pipe by using his thumb. Closing the pouch, the man continued his explanation, "The internet can be and often is a wonderful thing. Did you know you can purchase just about anything over the net, legal or illegal? The other unique thing about the internet is you can learn how to make just about anything." Pointing the pipe at Asa he went on, "The point is, I did find an outlet to purchase chloroform but it was quite expensive. However, while I was looking for a place to buy the drug up pops this article with instructions on how to make your own. It was easy. You see, what you do is go to a hardware store and purchase a bottle of acetone. When you mix acetone with baking powder, the acetone becomes reactive. When you boil it down at 70 degrees Celsius, and you collect the drain-off, what you have is a type of chloroform. I tried a small pinch on myself and nearly passed out. When I grabbed you back at your cabin, the rag I soaked with the homemade solution did the trick. Later on I gave you another dose and well, you know what happened after you came out of your temporary stupor, and here we are."

Placing the pouch on the edge of the stump, the man removed a lighter from his coat pocket and proceeded to light the pipe, puffing on the stem until a small cloud of smoke rose from the bowl and wafted off into the morning air. "I hope I'm not boring you with all of this but I want you to know the great effort I have gone to."

Asa's breathing was slowly returning to normal and surprisingly the man was correct. Now that he was beginning to relax, there didn't seem to be any pain, but the sense of fear remained as he looked down at his blood-splattered boots and the ever-growing puddles of blood from his severed fingers. Walking back a few yards, the man looked up and down the trail, his back to Asa. It was at that moment Asa realized he had to try to somehow escape.

The man turned and walked back to the stump, bumping his head on a low hanging branch. Pushing the branch away from his face, he hesitated, took three puffs on the pipe then remarked in a satisfied manner, "Nothing like a good pipe...I say. I always smoke Peach Brandy. I just love the aroma that this particular brand of tobacco gives off." Stepping close to the tree he held the pipe beneath Asa's nose. "Now tell me doesn't that smell great?"

Asa looked away from the man. His mind was on other things. Things like the realization that this was not a practical joke and that he was at the mercy of this man and that he might eventually be killed. The man picked up on Asa's disinterest in the smell of pipe tobacco, walked back to the stump, and started to talk again, "Now let me explain to you about this Novocaine business. I was able to purchase this nerve-numbing drug over the internet from a source that, let's just say, is not your everyday store you would find in most communities. Novocaine is really quite an amazing drug. Now I don't want to go all scientific on you but I think it's important that you know how the drug works."

The man sat back down on the stump. "When an individual is injected with a numbing drug like Novocaine a number of things begin to happen in their body which causes impulses that arrive in the injected area to be stalled, thus preventing the pain from reaching the brain...hence...no pain! So, you see when your fingers are being lopped off there is no physical pain...only mental pain, the imagination of what it must feel like."

Getting up he walked back to Asa. "It really is quite amazing to think that you can actually see your fingers being cut off, see the blood and all the while experience no pain...well, at least until the drug wears off." Looking at his watch he announced, "And that should be in about forty minutes." He took another puff on the pipe then stepped close to the tree, picking up the shears. "Now that you understand how all this works, let's try this again." Asa's muffled screams were not a distraction to the man as he forced the lower part of his arms down, then calmly and methodically lopped off two more fingers. Asa watched in utter horror as both of his ring fingers fell to the ground. Staring at his dismembered fingers he noticed ants and assorted insects gathering at his feet for the blood feast. Asa stopped screaming. His eyes were watering, he was sweating profusely, and his breathing was labored. He then felt the warmth in his pants as he slowly urinated himself, his urine slowly trickling down his legs and into his boots.

The man leaned the shears against the trunk of the tree then noticed the wet stain in the crotch area of Asa's pants. "I must say...you're not doing a very good job of controlling yourself." Shaking his head in disgust he then discovered that his pipe had gone out. "Damn it...I can never seem to keep this thing lit for more than a couple of minutes." Relighting the pipe, the man stepped close to Asa and said, "Aside from pissing yourself, you seem to be doing better than with the first cuts. It's rather amazing what the human body can condition itself to."

Seated on the stump once again, the man picked up the tobacco pouch and placed it in the gym bag, then leaned back and stretched his neck muscles as he looked up through the towering trees at the sky above. "I didn't get much sleep last night what with kidnapping you and then carting you through the woods, but I should get a good nights' rest tonight." Looking at his watch the man stated, "It's almost eight o'clock. That Novocaine will start to wear off soon. I'll be long gone by then so we need to move this one-sided conversation along. You're probably wondering who I am. It's not important that you know my name. What is important is that I know who you are: Asa Pittman...sixty-four years old...divorced...you live north of Townsend in a remote mountain cabin...you make your living by making moonshine and selling animal pelts." Standing, the man went into a deep knee bend then walked back out to the trail and looked both ways before continuing, "I've been watching you for the past year and I am of the opinion that you are not what one would consider a good man." Walking back toward the tree the man asked, "Asa...do you read the Bible much?"

Asa didn't respond with any type of nod so the man just shrugged and remarked, "Well, it doesn't make any difference if you do or not. In the first book of the Old Testament, Genesis, it is written that God created the world in six days and then rested on the seventh. On the fourth day he created all of the animals and then *on the sixth day* he created man. Kind of makes you wonder why He waited until the end to bring man onto the scene. I am of the opinion that He created the animals first because He has great love for His creatures and after observing you for the past few months it is obvious to me that you view animals as simply a means to make money. You hold no respect for our animal friends who, as I have already mentioned, were here before we were created. Actually, to tell you the truth, I don't think you have respect for much of anyone. Just last week I was watching you one morning when you were leaving The Parkway Grocery in Townsend after having breakfast with your so-called friends. One of them said something to you at which point you made an obscene gesture by using both of your middle fingers. I hate people who express themselves in that manner. As a matter of fact, we need to take care of that little situation right now."

Asa knew what was coming. The man approached the tree and picked up the shears. He struggled to keep his hands from being grabbed. The man, who up to this point seemed to be patient, slapped Asa across the face and ordered him, "Stop resisting me or I'll put an end to your miserable life right now…understand?"

Asa lowered both of his hands. The man demanded, "Offer your right hand to me."

Asa remained still, his hands frozen at his sides.

The man made a fist and punched Asa, breaking his nose, blood splattering across his right cheek and down his shirt. The man repeated himself, "Offer me your hand…now!"

Asa still did not respond.

The man placed the shears between Asa's legs and calmly stated, "It's either your fingers or something else if you get my meaning."

Asa slowly raised his right hand. The man smiled as he cut the middle finger off and watched it drop to the ground. Asa felt like he was going to pass out; a welcome reprieve to the torture he was receiving. "That's enough for now," said the man. He leaned the shears up against the side of the tree. Asa had been holding his breath preparing himself for the shock of the next finger cutting, but it looked at least for the moment the torture was going to stop. For how long, he wasn't sure. He forced a long, deep breath through his broken nose trying to compose himself. Suddenly the man hesitated, turned, walked back and picked up the shears. "Come to think of it there isn't any sense in leaving you lopsided. Let's even things up a bit." Asa was not prepared for the next swift attack as the man grabbed his arm and severed his other middle finger. The spurting blood from the cut caused the finger to adhere to the blades on the shears. The man reached down and removed the bloody finger and held it up in front of Asa, commenting, "Guess you won't be giving anyone the finger anymore." He tossed the finger to the ground and turned to walk back to the stump when Asa started to get sick as his body convulsed. The first flood of vomit raced up his throat but was road blocked by the duct tape. It backed up and went down Asa's throat causing him to gag. The man had prepared for the possibility of just this thing happening. He savagely ripped the tape from Asa's mouth, then punched him in the stomach which caused Asa to spew a large amount of brownish vomit down the front of his shirt and onto the ground, covering two of his severed fingers. The man inspected his trench coat, the front of the old coat soaked with vomit. "Well, that was uncalled for. I thought I could get through this without getting too messy but it looks like I was wrong."

Walking to the bag the man removed a bottle of water, unscrewed the top and took a long drink. Approaching Asa he held out the bottle. "Care for a drink?"

Now that Asa's mouth was no longer taped he stammered, "Yes...yes...I would."

Asa leaned his head back. The man placed the bottle to his lips, the water partially washing away the aftertaste of vomit. Coughing, Asa almost threw up again, his chest heaving in and out a number of times.

Pulling the bottle back, the man ordered gently, "Now, now...not too much." Using the handkerchief he cleaned away the vomit and moisture from around Asa's chin, then started to reapply the duct tape over Asa's mouth.

Asa, even though breathing heavy managed to get the words out, "Please mister...I have...no idea...who ya are...or why yer doin' this. I've had 'nough. Let me go...please!"

The man immediately adhered the tape to Asa's mouth. "I've already explained to you that you don't need to know who I am. Now, on the other hand, I am perfectly willing to clue you in on why this is happening." Walking a few feet toward the trail, the man tried to clean the front of his coat with the hanky. "Like I said I have been watching you for about a year. It's a known fact around these parts that you are no friend to the wildlife in the area and that you have been trapping for years: deer, bear, coyotes…whatever happens to fall prey to your illegal activities. I imagine you fashion yourself a hunter, and let me add I have no objection to hunting. I have never had a desire to hunt myself but I do know the game commission has a responsibility to control the animal population. It's hard for someone like me, an animal lover, to view hunting as a sport." Turning around and walking toward Asa, the man became louder, his demeanor changing. "I know the law! It's people like you that give hunters a bad name. You hunt out of season. The law says you are allowed one bear each year and yet you kill three or four a year. You kill deer, strip them of their antlers and leave them to rot out in the woods. I also know there is a no kill limit on coyotes, but it's the way you kill them that upsets me. It's a known fact if one gets caught in one of your traps and if they live you beat them to death with a club. I know you skin these animals, sometimes before they are completely dead, and sell the pelts for profit." The man stood directly in front of Asa, his attitude had changed once again, but this time to anger, his face twisted in disgust. With his face just inches from Asa's, he yelled, "In short…you make me sick!"

Looking around, the man picked up the branch that he had cut with the shears. "I can't believe you would beat an animal to death…that you wouldn't have the decency to put them out of their misery with a quick bullet." Turning from Asa he was now talking to himself, "You beat all those coyotes to death…you beat them!"

Before Asa realized what was happening the man turned and brought the branch down over Asa's head three times, yelling at him, "You beat them…you beat them…how does it feel?" Turning, he pitched the branch into the tall weeds a few yards away.

Between the shock of having six of his fingers cut off, being beaten over the head and the loss of blood he had experienced Asa started to pass out, but was prevented from doing so. The man slapped him hard across the face, speaking sternly, "Don't you pass out on me yet! We're not quite finished."

The man grabbed his left hand. Placing the bloody shear blades around the left index finger, the man looked directly into Asa's eyes. He spoke angrily, squeezing the blades together. "This is for all the times you sat on the front porch of your cabin and shot crows, rabbits and squirrels just for the fun of it!" The severed index finger fell to the ground, then the man moved to the left thumb as he continued with his tirade, "This is for all the times you shot deer, stripped them of their antlers and then left them to rot in the forest." The crunching of the thumb bone caused Asa to attempt to scream louder than he had before as the man grabbed his right hand and lopped off the index finger. "This is for all of the bears you illegally shot out of season, and last but not least," he placed the shears around the right hand thumb, "this is for all the coyotes you beat to death while they laid helpless in one of your traps." The final cut was made, the thumb joining the bloody collection of body parts at Asa's feet.

Without the slightest hint of remorse, the man returned to where the bag was laying, wiped off the shears then placed them inside. After zipping up the bag, he went about the process of trying to clean the front of his trench coat. He looked back at Asa. "If I can't get these stains out I guess I'll have to ditch this coat. What a shame...I've had it for years." Sitting down on the stump, he removed the tobacco pouch from the bag and placed two pinches into the pipe, then proceeded to light it. Following two puffs he took a deep breath enjoying the wonderful aroma. "Nothing like a fine smoke after a good day's work."

Asa was breathing so hard it was all he could do to keep from passing out. The man stood and picked up the bag, then stepped closer to Asa. "My work is done for the day except for an explanation. You certainly deserve to know what will happen over the next hour or so." Pointing the pipe at the severed fingers, he continued, "The drug will start to wear off in about ten minutes at which point the pain will no longer be blocked from your brain. The pain you will experience will be nothing short of unbearable. It will start slow and steadily increase to the point where you might just pass out. If you get lucky, you might throw up again which could result in drowning in your own vomit. If you do manage to remain conscious, well, eventually you'll bleed out...and die. If you make it that far you won't be alone. You'll have plenty of friends come to pay a visit. The smell of blood does funny things to wildlife. There are bears, insects, crows and let's not forget our friends...the coyotes." With that the man turned and walked toward the tree line, but then stopped as if he remembered something. Placing the bag on the ground, he removed a small flask from his coat pocket. Holding it up so Asa could see it, he unscrewed the top, then in a toasting fashion he took a long swallow. "When I was up at your place waiting for you to get home last night I discovered some of your homemade brew. Have to admit, you make some good hooch! Have a good day." The man then picked up the bag, took another drink, turned and disappeared into the dense forest.

Asa, now alone, following the worst hour of his life, looked up through the tall trees at the sky. The morning mist had drifted off, the sun shining brightly. He drew in a deep shot of air. Despite the horror of the morning the forest had returned to a setting of peacefulness. The birds chirped, whistled and sang their individual music from every tree. In the middle of nature's beauty he was an entity that was out of sync. Looking down over his body, tears streamed down his cheeks. He stared at his blood and vomit soaked shirt, his blood-soaked boots and his eight fingers and two thumbs which were rapidly being attacked by insects. Blood ran down the side of his head from the beating he had suffered. He then stared at his two hands that were now bloody stumps. He watched as blood, slowly, drip by drip vacated his body and fell to the ground. A sudden, sharp first shot of pain raced up his arm as the drug was starting to wear off. The pain was beginning and he knew it would only get worse. He wished he could close his eyes and die, yet his body fought death with every labored breath he took.

He wasn't sure how much time had passed. His body was experiencing a series of moments where he would drift off only to be snapped back to consciousness by a new, more intense wave of pain. The bleeding from his head wound had stopped, the dry blood now crusted to the side of his face. Looking down at his feet he noticed the hundreds, if not thousands of insects that were not only congregating in and around his blood but had started to climb up his legs and were now crawling over what was left of his blood soaked hands. A crow flew down from a nearby tree and started to peck at one of the fingers. The large black bird was instantly joined by two others. Asa tried to move his feet to ward them off but he had no strength to do so. A muffled grunt signaled the birds he was still alive. They flew off and landed high up on a tree a few yards away. He drifted off again.

He was startled back to consciousness by a movement somewhere behind the trees. He squinted his eyes trying to focus on what was causing the noise. Then, he saw what it was. A gray and black colored coyote carefully slinked out from behind the tree line. It sat and raised its nose at the smell of the blood. Another coyote, totally gray, joined the first but remained standing. Three more appeared. Not as bold as the first two, they stood back further in the trees. The first coyote carefully approached, but was scared off by Asa's weak grunting. Asa knew how coyotes operated. They always hunted in packs. They were extremely timid and the slightest human noise would cause them to cower. Asa grunted again and the pack bolted back to the safety of the trees, only to appear a few minutes later, this time venturing closer. Another grunt from Asa only sent them to the edge of the trees. Coyotes were intelligent and would eventually figure out he could only make noise, that this human could not harm them. Despite Asa's grunting one of the gaunt animals crept close enough to grab a finger which it devoured instantly.

All of the fingers had been eaten by the pack except for two that were the closest to Asa. His grunts now were no more than a barely audible hum. He continued to ward off the pack by moving his arms or his head slightly letting the pack know their prey was still alive. The coyotes sat in a small semi-circle just a few feet away, a crow landed on his shoulder, another on one of his boots. The end was coming; it was just a matter of time. The coyotes were patient. They would wait.

CHAPTER TWO

DOUG ELAND TURNED OFF the air-conditioner in his car and rolled down the windows. He was only seven miles from Townsend, Tennessee and wanted to get his first whiff of pure mountain air. He took in a deep breath and exhaled. *Yep, there it was.* The smell of pine and honeysuckle that always reminded him of his many trips to the mountains.

His Mercedes hugged the narrow two-lane road, taking each curve and dip on Highway 321 with ease. It was almost eight-fifteen and he was hungry. Turning onto the Lamar Alexander Parkway he slowed down and pulled into the parking lot of Lily's Cafe.

Once out of the car, Doug stretched his arms over his head and headed toward the restaurant. He opened the door and smiled. A blast of good ol' mountain music blared from a radio tucked in the corner. He parked himself at a table and leaned forward to retrieve a menu. The strong smell of tobacco clung to the clothes of the man sitting at the table next to him. He was dipping a glazed donut in a cup of black coffee. He licked the liquid off the donut then took a huge bite. Wiping his mouth with the back of his hand, he looked over and said, "Whar ya from?"

"Louisville," Doug answered, scanning the menu for a hearty breakfast order.

"Ya goin' huntin'?" the man asked. "Ya got on them cam-e-flage pants that 'posed ta make the critters not know'd yer a fella." Leaning back he let out a loud laugh, spraying coffee and pieces of donut on the table.

"I hunt with a camera," Doug mumbled, not really wanting to carry on a conversation with the man.

The waitress came over with her pad and pencil and nodded to Doug. "What can I get you?"

Interrupting the waitress the man said, "Whatcha gonna do, hit them critters with yer camera? Ya'd be better off with a gun." Doug knew what was coming this time as he moved to the side as another spray of donut crumbles hit the table.

"I don't kill animals!" said Doug sharply. "I take their pictures. Now if you'll excuse me. I'd like to order my breakfast."

Pointing the half-eaten donut at Doug, the man continued, "Name's Darrel Hobbins. Lived heah all mah life. Ya best git yerself a gun ta take with ya. Don't do no good ta wander 'round them thar hills by yerself with no weapon. You ferners come up heah takin' pitchers of them purty mountains and trees. Well, thar's a lot goes on up thar ya don't know nothin' 'bout. Ain't all purty. Ya take some pitchers of some of them things and mebbe you'll win an a-ward."

Past being annoyed, Doug turned to the man. "Look, I've been coming up here every year since I was nine. That makes twenty-four years and I'm still around." He turned around on his chair hoping to end the conversation.

"Suit yerself," Darrel smirked, dumping a toothpick out of a small jar on the table. "Jest thought I'd warn ya." He stuck the toothpick between the gap where one of his front teeth should have been and left just as the waitress placed two plates of steaming food in front of Doug: country ham, eggs, biscuits and gravy and of course, a bowl of grits, which he pushed to the side. A stack of three slices of toast and hot coffee finished off his order. It was the same breakfast he had eaten since the first time his father brought him to Cades Cove. He smiled to himself, remembering his father betting him he couldn't clean his plate. Doug ate every bite and asked for seconds on the biscuits. Today he ate alone. His father had died the previous winter and now it was just Doug and his camera in the woods.

Fifteen minutes later he put a ten dollar bill on the table, nodded to the waitress and left. It was almost nine o'clock. He had to make sure he was on the mountain and at the Cades Cove Riding Stable by ten. That would give him about four hours to ride up the trail and take pictures. He had to make sure he was back on the horse and heading down the trail by three o'clock. His father had always told him to make sure he allowed himself plenty of time and to never get caught in the woods after dark.

An hour later he arrived at the stable. He recognized two of the men who were working the horses and as usual they were aware he would be riding up the trail alone. Doug was one of few people who were given that honor. Most tourists were required to go with a guide and stay together.

After a few minutes of pleasantries followed by condolences on the death of Doug's father, a brown mare was saddled and ready to go. Retrieving his backpack from the car, Doug locked the doors and mounted his horse. Just like every year he was given last minute instructions, after which he turned the horse toward the trail.

Stopping at the ranger station, Doug once again carried on a brief conversation with the two uniformed park rangers. "Anything new guys?" he asked, signing the log sheet.

The younger of the two, a man named Alan Shields answered, "Naw, not much, it's too early in the year. Same old crap: nuts leaving their campfires burning, people trashing up the woods and those bastard poachers who come up here to kill anything that moves."

Doug shook his head. "Well, I promise not to do any of that. See you in about eight hours."

He loved to ride up to the loop and breathe in the tranquility of this beautiful place. He loved the sound of pinecones crunching under the weight of the horse, the occasional rustle in the undergrowth lining the trail and the call of the birds from their woodland habitat. God had done Himself proud when He created this part of the country.

Six miles up Thunderhead Trail, Doug reined the horse off the trail and onto a small patch of open grass. The trees had been cut low to allow riders to have someplace to tie their horses while they hiked. A wooden rail attached to a watering trough was all that marred this pristine spot. Leaving the lead long enough so the horse could graze, he patted her mane and started into the woods. Narrow footprints were carved into the wilderness by thousands of hiking boots that had tramped into the dense forest in search of some new adventure. A few hundred feet into the thicket, Doug stopped and sat on a log. He pulled his camera from his backpack and took it out of the leather case. After checking the lens and the battery pack he slung it over his shoulder and continued on.

Each step he took was a warning to some woodland critter that a human was present in their territory. Hoping to catch a glimpse of local wildlife before they were once again hidden, he positioned his camera, ready to click off a few shots at anything coming into view. A covey of buttonquail scurried across the forest floor, their images caught on film. A few minutes later he stared into the faces of two female deer. His camera captured the large brown eyes and their ears standing at attention.

A faint sound interrupted his concentration. Low growls, an occasional yip and the squeal of something injured. He knew that sound. He remembered the times sitting around the campfire with his father listening to the night sounds of animals feeding, especially the coyotes, who were quite vocal. His father told him that coyotes prefer to hunt under the cover of darkness, but the idea of a free meal would bring them out of their dens anytime of the day. The scent of a dead deer or some other large animal had brought the pack to this site. Moving closer, hoping to get a clear shot of the feeding frenzy, he inched within twenty feet of the sounds. Pulling back a clump of vines growing up the side of a hickory tree, he could see the coyotes. Doug adjusted the lens for close-up shots and then put the camera to his eye. Just as he started shooting something caught his attention. *What was it that the coyotes were eating?* He panned across the ground, picking up views of coyotes pulling on pieces of plaid material. There was a boot laying a short distance away and a bloody bone protruding through a patch of denim. *My God, are they feasting on a human?*

Standing up, Doug began to yell and hurl anything he could find on the ground at the pack of coyotes. It only took a few seconds for the timid animals to run to safety and out of view. Doug waited a few minutes to make sure there were not any other predators around. A bear or a cougar wouldn't give up so easily. Moving forward he slowly approached where the coyotes had been. He wiped at his forehead. It was only sixty degrees but he was sweating profusely.

Mounds of insects clamored out of every open orifice, carrying away bits of flesh and bone as they skittered through the pools of black blood surrounding the corpse. Doug pulled the front of his shirt over his nose and swung at the air trying to chase away some of the insects. Trying to remain calm he slowly began to snap off pictures. He wasn't sure why he was doing it; maybe this was what the old man back at the restaurant had been talking about.

Long strips of duct tape, the sticky side of a snare for all the insects who dared to cross it, lay on the front of the body and across the face. Doug carefully moved in for some close-ups. It was a man's body he was looking at. Snapping off a few more pictures he backed away. Turning from the grizzly scene he bent over a decaying log and gave up his breakfast. He heaved until there was nothing left in his stomach. His throat hurt from gagging.

Once he was able to stand he ran back to the clearing. Stumbling over tree roots and rocks he finally made it to his horse. Mounting the mare, Doug dug his heels into her sides trying to make her go faster, but it was useless. After years of riding the familiar trails the horse had become conditioned to go a certain speed and nothing or no one could change her mind.

Arriving at the ranger station, Doug quickly dismounted and ran inside the eight by eight shed. "Ya gotta call the police…there's a dead body up on Thunderhead." The older man, named Jack, who Doug had known for years, was sitting at a cluttered desk. "Jack…Jack, you gotta call someone! There's a body laying up near the clearing, it's a mess!"

"Whoa, hold on, Doug," said Jack. "Take a breath and start over."

For the next few minutes Doug repeated his story, but added more details.

"Before we call anybody," said Jack, "let's ride up there and check it out. The National Park Service is directly responsible for anything that happens within the bounds of the park." Placing his hand on the top of his holstered revolver he took a deep breath as if to reassure himself that he was prepared for whatever was up there on the trail. "I'll get the ATV, you can leave the horse here." Turning to Alan he ordered, "I'll take the short-wave. You stay put. When I find out something I'll call."

Seconds later as the ATV bumped up the trail, Doug told Jack the story again: "Yeah, I had just gotten up there and I was looking forward to having a good day and damn…not ten minutes later I come across the body." Holding up his camera he pointed out, "I got pictures Jack, a bunch of pictures. I figured that after I left those coyotes would return and help themselves to whatever was left so the pictures I took might help. I did the right thing…didn't I?"

Guiding the ATV around a bend in the trail, Jack answered Doug's question as best he could, "I guess so…I don't know. Right now I'm just interested in getting up there." Hitting a straight stretch he gunned the motor, the ATV picking up speed. "I haven't had anyone reported missing in the area. In fact my log sheet was clear last night."

Ten minutes later Doug yelled, "Over there! Pull in that clearing. The body is a couple of hundred yards back in the woods."

Leery of going back into the woods again Doug stepped aside letting Jack take the lead. There was complete silence as they made their way through the thick underbrush. When Jack pushed back the vines of the hickory tree, he let out a low whistle. "Damn, you were right. It sure is a body. Looks like the predators really worked it over." Pulling his radio out of its holder he pushed a button.

"Ranger Station…this is Alan."

Placing the radio near his mouth Jack spoke calmly, "Alan, it's me. Call the chief of police over in Townsend and tell him to get up here right away. We're about six miles up Thunderhead, just past Spence Field. I'll be coming down to get him in about twenty minutes."

Clicking the radio off, Jack looked at Doug and then down at the body. It was a horrible scene, but something magnetic held them captive and wouldn't let them turn away. It was as if they were kids at their first horror movie hunkered down in their seats, their hands covering their eyes, spreading their fingers apart just enough to see what was going on.

Doug broke the eerie silence. "Looks like more of the body is missing since I was here before." Pointing at a set of footprints pressed into the blood, he remarked, "Looks like a big animal."

"Cougar prints," said Jack professionally. "They like to tear off a part of their prey and carry it off somewhere to eat it." Sitting on a stump, Jack shook his head. "Man, this is the first thing like this to happen up here in years. Fact is, I can't remember anything like this ever happening." Removing a pack of cigarettes from his shirt pocket he lit up then stood. "Listen, I'm going to head back down to the station and wait for the Townsend Police. You coming along or are you going to wait here?"

"Well, if you think it's safe I'd rather stay here. If we both leave the body is going to be easy pickin's again. If there is any evidence of what happened here I'm sure the authorities wouldn't want it disturbed."

Turning, Jack spoke with confidence, "You'd be a fool to stay up here alone. No, I think you better come back with me."

"Townsend Police Department, Chief Axel Brody speaking."

"This is Alan Shields at the Smoky Mountains Ranger Station Number 29. We need you up here right away. A body has been found up on Thunderhead Trail."

"For sure," said Brody. "You got a body out there?"

Alan, slightly irritated at the chief's doubt, sarcastically confirmed, "For sure. There's a body up there."

Brody reached over and grabbed his Stetson off the doorknob. "I'm on my way." Walking quickly down the hallway he stuck his head in a small office and ordered, "Come on, Wonder Boy. We gotta check out a body up on Thunderhead Trail."

Officer Grant Denlinger jumped up from his desk without saying a word and followed Brody out the front door to a bright red pickup truck parked in front of the station. Jumping into the passenger seat Grant held on tight. He was familiar with the drill. Once inside the truck Brody would put on his mirrored sunglasses, switch on the siren and overhead blue flashing lights and speed out of the lot onto the street. Heads turned as they sped through town. This was Brody's favorite part of the job and Grant's least.

Reaching the edge of town where Route 73 intersected with the parkway, Brody made a left hand turn and started up Laurel Creek Road as Grant asked, "You got any particulars?"

Giving Grant a stern look Brody answered, "Yeah, I got particulars. I got a dead body up in the mountains. That's pretty particular don't you think?"

Rolling his eyes, Grant looked out the passenger side window as Brody switched on the two-way radio. "Butch...Brody here. Me and Grant are on our way up to Thunderhead. Looks like there's a dead body up there. Get back to the station and keep an eye on things. We could be right busy later this evenin'."

A voice on the other end responded, "Got it, boss."

After twenty minutes of Brody pushing the truck to its limits on the twisting uphill road, they finally pulled into the ranger station. The truck no sooner came to a stop when Brody stepped on the path in his silver-tipped alligator skin boots; a one of a kind pair he had bought in Las Vegas three years past. He put his thumbs in his belt and tried to pull up his pants but it was to no avail as they refused to budge over his protruding stomach. Approaching Jack, who had been standing outside of the station waiting for their arrival, Brody demanded, "Gimme the details!" Grant climbed out of the truck and leaned against the door. He knew this was Brody's show.

Jack offered his hand to Brody. "Nice to see you, Axel. Been awhile. Wish it could be under more pleasant circumstances." As they shook hands Jack turned and introduced Doug. "This is Doug Eland. He found the body a couple of hours back."

Brody ignored the introduction as he held up his hand, "Hold on just a minute here. What were you doin' up on Thunderhead, Mr. Eland?"

"I was taking pictures," said Doug. "I'm a photojournalist. I take pictures of wildlife all over the United States. I took pictures of the body. I thought they may be helpful…"

Cutting Doug's explanation short, Brody spoke sternly, "Look, Mr. Eland, I didn't ask for your life history. Let's get to the meat of the matter. So you found the body and then you came back down here and reported it?"

Doug, a little frustrated at the way he was being treated answered, "Yes!"

"See anybody else up there?"

"No."

Grant stepped forward. "Don't you think we should go check it out, Chief?"

"I'll handle this, Denlinger. You just listen and learn." Turning to Jack he asked, "How we gettin' up there?"

Jack pointed with his thumb. "We'll use the ATV."

Brody gave Grant a dirty look as he ordered, "All right, let's get movin'."

As they started to walk toward the ATV, Doug followed, "What about me?"

Brody gave him a sour look. "I think it'd be best if you stay here."

"Well, if you wouldn't mind I'd like to tag along. Maybe take some more pictures. A camera might come in real handy."

"I think it's a good idea," said Grant.

Blowing both of them off with a wave of his hand, Brody rudely stated, "Suit yourself."

The four men climbed onto the ATV, which was not an easy task for Brody, the all terrain vehicle leaning to the left from his excess weight.

Following the same trail Doug had taken earlier in the morning, twenty-five minutes later they pulled over in the clearing. They got out and started back through the woods, Jack leading the way, Doug checking his camera to make sure he had enough film. Arriving at the crime scene, somehow it didn't seem so frightening to Doug as the first time he had been here. It seemed more interesting. Standing next to Grant he just shook his head. "That's one hell of a way to die. Gives me the chills."

Grant didn't say anything. He simply nodded. He was too intent on the scene to make conversation. He noticed the way the jaw was slightly open as if it wanted to scream. The side of the skull that still had some remaining flesh and bits of hair attached to it was missing an ear. The hands seemed strange to him. All of the fingers were missing and yet the hands were pretty much in tact. *Wouldn't an animal pull the whole hand off?* he thought. There were still small pieces of gray duct tape hanging on the tree. *If the victim had been secured to a tree did someone cut him down or did the animals pull him down?* He took out his pad and pen and began to take notes.

Chief Brody stood directly over the body. "Well, ain't this just somethin'." Picking up a stick he poked it into the stomach area of the body.

Stepping forward, Grant spoke firmly, but carefully, "I don't think you should do that. You're stepping in the blood and moving the evidence around. We need to cordon off the crime scene and wait for the coroner to get here."

"Oh, hell yes," objected Brody. "Get me a roll of yella tape. I'll just put it around the whole damn forest. Look Denlinger, this ain't some fancy classroom back in Connecticut or wherever the hell it was you studied law. This is real. Your booklearnin' won't do you no good out here. I've been the Chief of Police in Townsend for the past seventeen years so give me some credit." Pointing the stick at the ground he continued, "Look at them prints around here. Animal tracks are everywhere. Most of the evidence is long gone. Now here's what we're gonna do…"

"Hold on," interrupted Jack. "Axel, you seem to be forgetting something." Gesturing at the surrounding trees, he explained, "This is a National Park we're in…federal land. My authority takes precedence over the Townsend Police up here and it will continue to be that way until the county coroner arrives and claims the body. Here's the way it's gonna go. Once we get the body moved we'll look around and see if we can find any evidence." Walking in the direction of the ATV he spoke directly to Chief Brody, "You might want to leave your man up here while you and I head on back to the ranger station and get the coroner on the horn."

Axel, not happy about being put in his place, looked at his watch. "The coroner has to come all the way from Maryville. He might not make it up here until late afternoon...early evenin'. We better get movin'."

"I'll stay with Grant," said Doug.

Without looking back Brody answered like he didn't care, "Don't pay me no never mind."

Walking out to the trail Grant sat on the trunk of a fallen tree. Doug joined him as he extended his hand, "I'm Doug Eland. We were never properly introduced."

Grant shook his hand. "Yeah I guess we never were. Name's Grant...Grant Denlinger. So you have pictures of this mess?"

"Yes, I do. Something told me they might be important."

"They are important. Listen, I was wondering if you could do me a favor. I'd like to see those when you get them developed."

"No problem...well, there might be a problem. Don't you think Chief Brody will want to see them first?"

"Of course he will. What I'm talking about is a set of my own. In case you haven't noticed Brody is like the proverbial bull in a china shop. Did you see the way he was tramping all over the area? Besides that, if there is any evidence on those pictures Brody will never pick up on it. A professional needs to have a gander at those pictures."

Doug swatted at a passing insect. "And you're a professional?"

"Not yet," said Grant. "I've got one more year of schooling to go before I receive my associate degree in crime scene investigation. But even so, with just three years of study beneath my belt I'm more qualified than Brody."

"So that's why you were busy taking notes. You were actually investigating the crime scene."

"Well, you never know...I mean at this point it's just wishful thinking, but maybe I'll be assigned to the case." Grant laughed. "Who am I kidding? Chief Brody will want this one for himself and that's if he can get past the National Park authorities."

Doug kicked at a rock next to the trail. "Doesn't seem like you two get along all that well."

"You've got that right," said Grant. "He's an ass!"

"Then why do you work for him?"

"Long story, but I'll give you the short version. I grew up on the outskirts of Townsend. My family owned a small paint and hardware store in town. We made just about enough to keep our heads above water. When I graduated from high school I was working there full time and hating every minute of it, hoping that I could somehow get the hell out of Townsend. Don't get me wrong, Townsend is a nice place to live, but I had been here for eighteen years. I needed a change. There was a whole world out there beyond the mountains."

Standing up, Grant continued, "My Pop had a heart attack five years ago and died. It was quite a shock. Anyway, he had been saving some money on the side over the years that my mom was not aware of. When she found out about the money, she told me to take it and go to school…to make something of myself. I did just that. I went to a school up in Connecticut to study law enforcement…mainly crime scene investigation. It was something I had always been interested in. Three years into my studies my mom falls off of a ladder at the store and breaks her back. She winds up paralyzed from the waist down. She decided to move in with my grandfather who owns a small farm over near Maryville. He's in pretty good shape for his age, but probably not good enough to care for my mother. I had no choice but to drop out of school and move back to Townsend. I couldn't keep the store. The hours were too long and we weren't making that much money anyway. We sold the place.

"I got bored just sitting around the house. My mom knew I was going stir crazy. She insisted that I get some sort of a job. She and Dalton, that's my grandfather, said they would be fine. Little did I know that she and my grandfather were in cahoots. The next thing I know Dalton is telling me there's an opening with the Townsend Police for an officer. Dalton goes on to tell me that he made a few calls and if I was interested the city council was willing to give me an interview. I knew it was a done deal. You see, my grandfather was the former police chief in Townsend and still swings some weight around town. I go for the interview…two days later, I'm on the force."

"Sounds to me like you fell right into a great job," said Doug.

"Yeah, I fell into it all right," remarked Grant. "I fell into a pile of crap. Chief Brody turned out to be a real S.O.B. He calls me Wonder Boy and I know it's just because he's jealous of my knowledge of the law. I can't even make a simple suggestion without him getting all bent out of shape. Eventually, I'll move on, but for now I'm just kind of stuck here. Between Brody and Butch, I feel like I'm working with dumb and dumber."

Doug, with a look of confusion asked, "Who's Butch?"

"Butch Miller. He's the other officer in Townsend. I went to high school with him. He was always in trouble. If it wasn't speeding through town, it was drinking. If it wasn't punching somebody in the face, it was stealing hubcaps. I could go on and on. But to tell you the truth he's just not worth it."

"How did this Butch person…this model citizen, get to be an officer?"

"He and Brody are cousins. According to my grandfather Butch had turned over a new leaf…saw the light so to speak. But even though, he's still a piece of work. He thinks he's a tin God. He'd give his own mother a speeding ticket. He comes and goes as he pleases. If it weren't for Brody being the chief he'd be fired in a New York minute." Walking toward the corpse, Grant laughed. "He would have crapped his pants if he'd come up here today. He hates the sight of blood."

Joining Grant, Doug cracked his knuckles then began to check his camera. "I wish you luck. I couldn't work with jerks like that." Looking in the direction that Jack and Brody had taken, Doug scanned the surrounding forest. "I sure wish they would get back here."

It took nearly three hours for the coroner to make it to the ranger station. Jack had already hitched a utility wagon to the rear of the ATV for the body. The coroner arrived in a tan van, the lettering on the door boldly announced: ***BLOUNT COUNTY CORONER.*** Climbing out of the van, he stepped into blue, one-piece coveralls then entered the station carrying a large standard black body bag and his medical kit. Nodding at Chief Brody, there was no smile on his face as he said, "You ready…let's go!" Jeff Bookman was a no-nonsense individual. He liked to get to a scene before he started making small talk. The three men climbed in the ATV, Jack behind the wheel as they headed up the trail.

Fastening the top button of his coveralls, Jeff was the first to speak, "So, give me the details. How long has the body been up there? Who found it?"

Brody turned to Jack and spoke sarcastically, "You were the first one on the scene. It's federal land. You tell 'em."

"Things are still kind of sketchy," remarked Jack. "We're not sure, but we think it's been up there at least since last night. A fella who was up there taking wildlife pictures found the body. Nothing's been touched." Jack gave Brody a strange look as if to say, 'I just covered your ass!'

At three-fifteen they pulled into the clearing. Jeff, who for at least the moment had control of what would happen, ordered, "Now look, I don't want anyone touching anything. Understood? Not a leaf, rock, twig...nothing! When we get in there you just need to stand back and let me do my job." Sitting down on the edge of the ATV he placed a pair of light blue, heavy-duty plastic disposable shoe covers over top of his shoes. Picking up his medical bag, he looked at Brody. "Lead the way."

Doug was the first to notice the threesome as they emerged from the trees. Tapping Grant on his shoulder he said, "The calvary has arrived!"

Jeff didn't acknowledge Doug or Grant but immediately walked to the body. Opening his kit he removed a pair of rubber gloves and forced them onto his hands snapping them to ensure a good fit. Scanning the area he commented in a professional tone of voice, "Nasty business. We'll determine the cause of death later. Right now all I want to do is bag up as much potential evidence as possible. First, I'm going to need some help getting the body in the bag." Looking at Grant and Doug, he suggested, "You two will do just fine. Get in my bag over there and put on some shoe covers and gloves then we'll get started."

Picking up the remains of the body was not an easy task. Most of the middle section had been eaten away and the neck was dangling by just a few strands of muscle. Each time they tried to pick up the body hundreds of insects would crawl up their arms. After a few futile attempts, Jeff laid the unzipped bag on the ground right next to the body and soon the bag was filled with a pile of skin, bones, and entrails that at one time had been a human being.

Brody and Jack helped Doug and Grant lift the bag as they prepared to carry the body back to the ATV. Grant, realizing that Brody for the moment was playing second fiddle to the county coroner, spoke up, "Excuse me, Mr. Bookman, but do you think I could stay with you while you investigate the scene? You see, the thing is I've spent three years at school studying crime scene investigation. I've only got one more year to go. I'm far from even being close to your league but this is right up my alley. I'm sure I can learn something."

Despite the horrid surroundings, Jeff smiled as he asked, "You're Dalton Denlinger's grandson...right?"

"Yes, I am. Do you know my grandfather?"

Giving Brody an unsavory look, Jeff answered, "You bet I do. He's a good man. Best police chief we ever had over here in Townsend. Be glad to have some assistance. Not too many people appreciate what we do." Grant looked at Brody who at the moment had anything but a smile on his face.

Ignoring Brody, Jeff motioned for Grant to step closer. "Now, let's have a look around and see what we can find." Looking up through the trees, he commented, "It's going to be dark in a few hours and it's supposed to rain tonight. It's clouding up already. No thanks to Mother Nature the rain will wash away most of the evidence so we better get cracking. Now, just take your time and keep an eye out for anything that looks out of place." Smiling at Grant he stated, "This experience will be far better than any classroom you've ever sat in."

The ground surrounding where the body had been was soaked with blood. There were numerous fragments of small bones, pieces of flesh and bloody material from the victim's clothing, all of which Jeff was picking up and putting in small bags which he marked with a pen.

"Hey Jeff, look at this," said Grant as he pointed at a tangle of duct tape covered with bugs and blood. "Looks like two fingers stuck to the tape. I can't believe the local critters didn't take them. I guess they couldn't get them loose from the tape and gave up." He carefully picked up the edge of the tape and held it in the air. "God, these look like they were cut right off."

Holding them closer for the coroner's inspection, Jeff agreed, "You're right, Grant, look at the cuts. There are no jagged edges from teeth or claw marks. These were definitely cut off with some sort of instrument."

Dropping the tape and the fingers in a plastic bag, Grant noticed something else a few feet to the right of where the body had laid. Walking closer he bent down and picked up what appeared to be a long section of leather with a blood-stained buckle. "Looks like some sort of a belt," said Grant. Flipping the backside of the buckle over, he saw a set of initials: *A.P.*

"My God, I know who this man is...or was!   It's ol' Asa Pittman!"

Jeff flashed Grant a strange look then asked, "How would you know that the initials A.P. stand for this Asa Pittman?"

Grant, rather amazed at the identity of the body himself, explained, "Just the other day, I think it was three days ago, I stopped by The Parkway Grocery in Townsend to have a cup of coffee.   On Monday, Wednesday and Friday mornings just like clockwork, Asa and four of his pals, some of the other old cronies from the area met for coffee. Well, they were in there sitting at their regular table, which is in the front corner. Asa as usual was being loud, bragging about this belt and buckle he had got over in Cherokee. He said it was genuine leather with an honest to God silver buckle. He said he traded some coyote skins to a fella over there for the belt *and* buckle, which he went ahead and personalized for Asa with his initials: *A.P.* His pals got to kidding him saying that it looked like plated silver, not genuine. With that Asa takes off the belt and removes the buckle and hands it around the table for inspection. They even called me over and handed it to me and asked my opinion. Three days ago I held this buckle in my hand. That bag of bones and flesh that they hauled out of here is none other than Asa Pittman.

CHAPTER THREE

STARING OUT THE WINDOW of his small eight by ten crammed office, Grant noticed a flash of lightning off to the north. The round clock on the wall just above a row of file cabinets displayed the time at 1:17 a.m. Sitting back in his swivel chair he stretched and thought about what a long day it had been. After heading back down to the ranger station, they had loaded the body into the coroner's van. Jack reminded both Brody and the coroner that since the body had been found on federal land the park service held jurisdiction and to expect the FBI to send agents into the area to spearhead the investigation. Jack also informed them since the death had taken place in the state of Tennessee the state police would also have to be notified. Following their lecture about the pecking order of the law, he and Brody headed back down to Townsend, Brody giving him a piece of his mind scolding Grant for getting out of line not only at the ranger station but up at the crime scene. He was nothing but a "wet behind the ears" college boy who didn't know his ass from a hole in the ground. He didn't appreciate being made to look stupid in front of the county coroner and the park service.

They no sooner arrived back at the office when the phone started ringing. Apparently some tourists that had been waiting at the stable for the next scheduled ride were upset when they were told that the park was being closed down for at least two days because there had been a horrible murder up on Thunderhead. The word had slipped out. Phone calls were made. The news spread across the area not only in Sevierville, Pigeon Forge and Gatlinburg but to the north up in Knoxville. Reporters from local newspapers, radio and television stations were calling Townsend seeking information on the murder. The Townsend Police received the dreaded call from the FBI, as they had been contacted by the park police. Just like Jack had said, the murder had been on federal land so the FBI was having two agents drive down from Knoxville the next day to get all of the known details.

The hallway light went out as Axel stuck his head in the office, "Denlinger, ya need ta git on home. Tomorrow's gonna be hectic. Hell, we're gonna have reporters in here from Sevierville, Gatlinburg, Maryville…shoot, I bet we have radio, newspaper and T.V. stations from as far out as Knoxville. The damn FBI's even gonna be here tomorrow. You'd think Asa Pittman was the President of the United States. Ain't been anythin' like this around here in, well I can't remember when. They'll all have questions…we won't have no answers. Like my wife, Marsha always says: 'Wherever there is a carcass…that's where the vultures will gather.' Ya need to get out of here and grab a few hours." Looking at the clock he frowned, "We gotta be back in here at seven."

Grant stood up, hit the wall switch and followed Chief Brody down the hall and out the front door, another band of lightning racing across the sky. Brody locked the door, turned and walked toward his pickup truck, "See ya in a few, Denlinger."

Grant looked toward the sky, the first raindrops starting to fall. "Good night, Chief."

He climbed in his four-wheel drive Jeep and took a deep breath. The skies suddenly opened up, large rain drops pelting the windshield. After turning the ignition key, he flipped the wipers on HIGH, the rubber blades pushing the excess rain from the windshield. Turning on the headlights he backed out, drove to the exit of the small parking lot, made a left on Tiger Street, a right onto Mountain Road, a right onto Route 73, finally turning onto the Lamar Alexander Parkway. Heading up the parkway Grant noticed that there wasn't one single car on the road, not one house with any lights on. He smiled to himself thinking about how it was after one o'clock in the morning. Who in their right mind would be up at this hour? His stomach let out a deep growl, signaling the need for nourishment. He hadn't had anything to eat all day, except for two stale donuts and a cup of yesterday's coffee when he had first reported for work. That was eighteen hours ago. What with the murder and everything he hadn't even given food a thought. The bright lights of Parkway Grocery pierced the dark rainy night. Pulling off into the paved lot, he decided on a cup of coffee and one of their hotdogs.

Parking the Jeep, he got out and quickly ran to the front door. George Nieber, one of two locals who worked the nightshift looked up from a book he was reading. "Well, I'll be, if it isn't one of Townsend's finest, Grant Denlinger. What are you doing out on a night like this?"

"Just on my way home," answered Grant. "Haven't had a bite all day. Thought I'd grab a hotdog and a cuppa."

"You couldn't have timed it any better...just put on a fresh pot. Got two dogs left in the warmer. Probably been in there for a few hours. Tell ya what. If you take both of 'em you can have 'em for free. Nobody's gonna be in 'til later on in the morning. I'll just wind up throwing 'em out."

"Sounds like a deal," said Grant. He opened the case, removed two buns and inserted the two shriveled dogs into them, then slathered ketchup, mustard and onions on both.

"The word's already getting out about the murder up at Thunderhead," said George. "Some fella named Doug was in here a few hours back. Said he was the one who discovered ol' Asa. He said it was horrible. Worst thing he'd ever seen in his life. Said Chief Brody told him he had to stay around town for a couple of days until they get this mess straightened out. Said Brody was going to confiscate his camera. Got himself a room over at the Econo Lodge. Buelah Kimms was in here, getting her a Coke just like she does every evening when this Doug fella was telling me about the murder. She knows everybody from here to Pigeon Forge. I'd lay odds she's still on the phone calling everyone from here to Timbuktu."

Grant laid the two hotdogs on the counter then poured himself a cup of coffee, adding cream and sugar. From the back stock area the other night employee, Meg Phifster, walked up behind the counter. "Evenin', Grant. You're up late."

Taking a huge bite out of the first hotdog, Grant nodded, "Grabbing some chow before I head up the road."

"So, tell me...was it really Asa Pittman they found out there in the woods?"

"That's the way it's looking."

Stocking three cartons of cigarettes up into an overhead display rack, Meg remarked sarcastically, "Don't bother me none. Townsend can get along just fine without the likes of Pittman around."

Finishing off the hotdog in two more bites, Grant gave Meg a strange look. "Not one of your favorite citizens I take it?"

Turning back to face Grant, Meg held up her index finger to make a point, "Let me tell you something. Asa Pittman was a mean ol' bastard. Couple of years back me and my husband and our two daughters were over at the county fair. We had our dog with us. We had her on a leash. She was just a small terrier...wouldn't hurt anybody. Maxie, that was her name, was always friendly. She had a tendency to jump up on people. It was never a big deal to folks. I mean hell, she only weighed twelve pounds. Well, to make a long story short, Asa was walking along with those jerks he hangs with when Maxie jumps up on his leg. It happened so quick. He shook the dog off his leg and yelled at my youngest daughter who was holding the leash. 'Get that damned dog away from me!' Maxie didn't understand and jumped up again. Asa kicked that little dog so hard she flew five yards and bounced off the side of a trailer. Broke one of her legs right in two. My husband was so livid that he lunged at Asa but was held back by some people in the crowd. The police showed up and the whole thing eventually was ruled an unfortunate accident. Asa Pittman injured our pet and got off Scott-free. He refused to pay the vet bill. Our two daughters were devastated. Poor Maxie limped the rest of her life." Throwing the empty cartons in the trash, Meg further explained, "Then last year, we were at the mall when who do we run into...Asa Pittman. My husband, Earl, said he felt like walking over there and wringing his neck but I told him to just let it be. Asa notices us, stops and says, 'Well, if it ain't the Phifsters.' Looking at our two daughters he smiles and says real cocky like, 'I see you folks didn't bring your stupid little mutt with you!' This time there was no holding Earl back. Before I realized what was happening Earl slams Pittman into a trash container and down they go, ass over tea kettle. Earl got a couple of good licks in before security broke it up. Asa wanted to file charges but the local authorities knew what a butt hole he was and said that the whole matter would be dropped. My husband is not what you would call a violent man. He doesn't even own a gun, but on many an occasion when we have seen Pittman around town Earl always says if he had a gun he'd put a bullet right through his head. So, as far as Asa Pittman's death is concerned...I say he had it coming."

George and Grant remained quiet after she finished her story. It turned into a moment of awkwardness for everyone. Meg, pulling a pack of cigarettes from her apron, stuck one in her mouth. "Think I'll go out back and have a smoke."

As she walked through the backdoor George rolled his eyes, holding up the coffee pot. "Ready for another shot?"

Grant held out his cup. "Warm 'er up."

Still on the subject of Asa Pittman's death, George inquired, "That Doug fella said it was a mess up there on Thunderhead. Was it really that bad? Do you have any clues who may have murdered Asa? You got any leads? What happens next?"

Walking to the front window, Grant looked out at the pouring rain. An older, white van pulled in under the canopy that covered the gas pumps. The driver climbed out of the van and inserted a credit card into the appropriate slot then began to fill the tank. Grant answered all of George's questions with a single statement, "George, we really don't have that much information yet and even if we did you know I can't go around talking about a case like this. Everything we have will no doubt be in tomorrow's paper, besides that the FBI more than likely will take over the case."

Realizing Grant didn't want to discuss the Pittman murder George changed the subject. "Heard Dana Beth Pearl is back in town. Weren't you two sweet on one another back a few years?"

Grant, not ready to have a conversation about this subject either finished up the second hotdog and took another swig of coffee and walked back toward the counter. "Yeah, we dated in high school and up through my second year at college, but then things just sort of tapered off. You know how that goes."

"Yeah, I guess," said George. "Ya know she's been seeing Butch Miller."

Grant, refilling his coffee looked at George but made no comment.

"Well, I was just thinking with you and Butch both being officers here in town it's got to be a little uncomfortable."

Reaching for his wallet, Grant pulled out a one dollar bill. "Me and Butch get along just fine. How much I owe you for the coffee?"

"Seventy-five cents."

Folding the bill in half Grant tossed it on the counter. "Keep it. Listen, have a nice night and try to stay dry. I've got to get on up the road."

Grant walked out the door, George's voice trailing behind him, "Night, Grant."

Sitting in his Jeep he finished the last of his coffee. Through the pouring rain, he watched as the driver of the van was getting gas. The man opened the backdoor of the van, removed a bundle of some sort and pitched it into the trash. The man hesitated after closing the rear door of the van while he puffed on a pipe, then walked around to the driver's side and climbed in.

Grant followed the van out of the parking lot and noticed a tattered blue bumper sticker on the rear of the van that read: **WILL BRAKE FOR ANIMALS.** He followed the van down the parkway, the driver traveling at just twenty miles per hour due to the blinding rain. Just before the red light at the intersection of Route 321, the driver pulled over to the side of the road, the driving rain making it difficult to see where he was going. Grant, stopping at the light, looked over at the man who was nothing more than an opaque figure. A small light flashed as the man relit his pipe. The light changed and Grant slowly pulled out, thinking that you just don't see many people smoking a pipe anymore.

The rain started to let up and was now a steady drizzle, Grant guided the Jeep up the road toward Maryville where his grandfather's farm was located six miles from Townsend. It was strange how one moment you could be thinking about something— then the next how the mind could completely change to something else. He had been consumed the entire day with the horrible death of Asa Pittman, the man's body mutilated beyond description and yet all of a sudden his thoughts turned to Dana Beth. George was right—she was back in town but no doubt just for a few days. In two months she would be graduating from college.

He thought back six years ago when they had first met in their junior year of high school. They had become friends while working on the school newspaper, one thing led to another and soon they were dating. They quickly became 'an item', a couple that held a strong relationship that eventually down the road would result in marriage. Two years later during the summer before they were both off to college they made the possibility of marriage a reality as Grant asked Dana Beth to marry him. She accepted his proposal and the ring, but with a condition. It was a condition Grant could not only live with, but that he agreed with wholeheartedly. They would wait until they both graduated from college, which was four years down the road. Their parents agreed with their four-year plan of saving some money and completing their education before walking down the aisle, especially Dana Beth's father who was a professor at

The University of Tennessee in Knoxville.

That fall Dana Beth went off to Tennessee Tech in Cookeville where she would pursue a degree in nursing while Grant was off to the Manchester Community College in Manchester, Connecticut to study law enforcement and graduate with an associate degree in Crime Scene Investigation. There was the usual negative talk around town that their relationship could not survive the distance they were placing between themselves. They were merely high school sweethearts, had never been away from home and had never dated anyone else. Once they got out into the world and met other people the relationship would die on the vine.

For the first two years he and Dana Beth had defied the odds, writing each other every week, returning to Townsend when they could to spend a day or two together, and of course the summer months. On one occasion Dana Beth had even driven all the way up to Connecticut to spend a weekend with him.

But then, when his third year of school kicked off, a series of unforeseen events turned his world upside down. The previous summer Dana Beth started to drop hints that maybe they should just go ahead and tie the knot, rather than waiting until they graduated. She wanted to start a family—and soon. Grant pointed out that his last two years of school were going to be the most difficult. He was going to have his nose stuck in books constantly. It was critical that he focus on his studies. If they got married, well, it would be a distraction he just didn't need. What if she got pregnant, then there were other things: finding a place to live, bills to pay, furniture to buy, insurance, and on and on. He felt they should wait. Dana Beth wouldn't budge. She still wanted to be a nurse, but she also wanted to be a wife and mother. Following months of discussions which eventually turned into arguments, early that fall she mailed him his ring and said if she was considered a distraction—then it was over! He wrote to her and apologized but the damage had been done. He had lost her.

Just when he thought things couldn't get any worse, three weeks following the breakup his grandmother died of a heart attack. Dalton, his grandfather, was no longer interested in living alone on the small farm that had been in their family for years. Grant's mother, Greta, decided to move from Townsend onto the farm with Dalton; the nasty fall she had taken at the hardware store led to some complications that left her wheelchair bound. Dalton who was in his mid-sixties was in no condition to care for his daughter all by himself. Much to the objection of both his mother and Dalton, Grant made the decision to drop out of school and return to Tennessee to help Dalton care for his mother. He reassured them that he had already checked it out, and his professors said he could complete the rest of his schooling on line. With three years of school under his belt he returned to Townsend and moved to the farm to live with his mother and grandfather.

His daydreaming combined with the steady rain caused him to miss the turnoff to the farm. Turning around at the next farm he drove the half mile back up the road and turned down his grandfather's lane. Pulling in front of the two story farmhouse, he noticed that the kitchen light was on. That was odd, he thought. His mother and especially his grandfather were always in bed by no later than ten. He looked at the dashboard clock: 2:11 a.m. Maybe they had left the light on for him. In the pouring again he ran to the safety of the front porch. Stopping to remove his jacket, he looked in the front window where he saw Dalton sitting at the kitchen table nursing a cup of coffee and reading a day-old newspaper.

Opening the door, Grant hung his hat and coat on the wooden rack just inside a small foyer then stepped inside the country kitchen surprising Dalton who turned from the antique table. "Dalton, what are you doing up so late?"

"Me and your mother decided to sit up and wait for you to get in, but it just got too late for her." Looking at the clock over the stove, Dalton explained, "She headed on up, I guess it was around midnight. We heard about the murder of Asa Pittman. She was worried about you. I told her to go on up...I'd wait for you."

Looking at the stove, Grant asked, "That coffee fresh?"

"Yep, just made it about an hour ago, it's my second pot of the night."

Grabbing a ceramic cup from the cupboard Grant poured himself a cup. "How did you find out about Asa Pittman already?"

Dalton stood and walked to the kitchen counter. "I was in town earlier at the post office about eight o'clock. The news was already out...you hungry?" Holding up a fresh baked apple pie he smiled. "Greta baked this for supper. There's four slices left. I'm having a slice...you in?"

"Actually," said Grant, "I am. Cut me one."

Leaning against the counter Grant sipped at his coffee, watching Dalton cut into the pie. "I assume you already had a slice at supper?"

Dalton laughed. "Now what do you think? Have you ever known me to turn down pie?"

Sitting at the table Grant agreed, "Can't argue with you on that. You're usually the first in line. So this will be your second piece of the day?"

Dalton turned and looked over the top of his glasses. "I suppose the next thing you'll be saying is I need to watch the sweets...that I need to watch my sugar level..."

Grant interrupted him, "I'm just saying two pieces of pie in the same day might be overdoing that's all."

Dalton slid a plate with a giant slice across the table as Grant sat with fork in hand ready to dive into his own piece. "For a college boy, you ain't too bright," Dalton joked. "I had a slice at eight-thirty last night and now I'm having a slice at two in the morning...different day."

Grant stood and walked to the refrigerator. "If I'm going to have pie then I'm going all the way." Turning he displayed a can of whipped cream.

Placing a generous portion of cream on his pie, he looked at the rain beating against the kitchen window. "Boy it's really coming down out there." Stabbing a bite of pie, he picked up on their previous conversation. "So you were saying you were at the post office and heard about Asa Pittman."

"That's right," said Dalton, his mouth full of pie. "And as far as I'm concerned the world just got a little better."

"That's not a very nice thing to say."

"Well, Asa Pittman wasn't a very nice man. Believe me...he won't be all that much missed or mourned over." Taking another bite of pie, he corrected himself, "Let me take that back. I forgot about those clowns he hung out with at the Parkway Grocery. I'm sure they'll miss Pittman."

"Why so bitter?"

Pointing his fork at Grant, Dalton stated very profoundly, "Don't forget...I was the chief of police in Townsend for almost twenty years. I had my share of run-ins with ol' Asa Pittman, besides that I went to school with him in Maryville. When I was growing up the Pittmans lived down the street from us. He had an older brother,

Merle. The two of them were like a nightmare in our neighborhood, always stealing stuff, skipping school, and beating up on younger kids. But…Asa was the worst of the two. I remember one time when I was walking home from school; guess I was about ten or so. I come up on Asa sitting next to the sidewalk with a lighter. He was burning something. I got closer and I noticed that he's burning ants. I thought it was kind of odd so I asked him why he was doing that. He stood up, got right in my face and told me he could because *he* had the power. Confused, I said, 'What power?' He informed me that he has the power over all insects, fish, animals…anything that is not human. I remember the look in his eyes. Well, from then on I always thought he had bats in his belfry.

"He and his brother were always in trouble; like the time they were stealing pears from a tree in Mr. Fauhauber's backyard. He had this dog we were all afraid of. If we even went near his fence this dog, if I remember correctly it was a Collie, would always bark and raise a fuss. Well, that particular day the Pittman boys climbed over the fence and there wasn't a peep from the dog. Later that day Mr. Fauhauber found his dog dead in the corner of the yard by the fence. The dog had been poisoned with a slice of tainted bologna. Everyone in town knew the Pittman boys killed that dog but nobody had any proof. The next day at school Asa was laughing and joking about how the Fauhauber's dog wouldn't be bothering him or his brother anymore. In short, Asa was a basket case growing up. His father was in and out of the county jail, could never hold a job and his mother…well she just couldn't handle Asa and his brother."

Finishing up his pie, Grant laid his fork down. "You said earlier when you were chief you had your share of run-ins with Asa Pittman?"

"Lots of times. You probably don't remember this…you were probably about nine or ten. I got a call from a man who lived about a quarter mile from Asa's place. This man complained and said Asa had shot their family dog. It was a Irish Setter that had a habit of getting out of their yard and wandering off. A few weeks before the shooting the man had driven down to the station and complained that Asa had threatened if the dog ever stepped on his property again, he'd shoot him. Well, being the police chief I had to drive on up to Asa's place and check things out. You just happened to be with me that day.

"So when we get up to Asa's place there he sits on the front porch, his shotgun laying across his legs. I knew right then I made a mistake taking you along. I shoulda known better. I'm no more than out of the car when Asa stands up and levels that gun at me and tells me I'm trespassing. I told him the law had every right to be on his property. Well, he came down off the porch and said he'd listen to what I had to say. I asked him if he had shot the Irish Setter and he said, 'Hell yeah, that dog was trespassin' and I had the right ta shoot 'im.' The long and short of it is that in his own demented mind…he was right. It was the law. He had a right to protect his property. There wasn't much I could do except to tell him that he was a mean ol' fart and there wasn't any reason to shoot a harmless dog. I went to visit that family and told them he was within the limits of the law. I'll never forget how their little girl cried. But that's just the way Asa Pittman was. Just like there was no logical reason for him to burn ants or poison Fauhauber's dog…there was no reason for him to shoot that setter."

"Come to think of it," said Grant. "I do remember going up there with you. Yeah, I remember it real well."

Getting up to rinse off his plate, Dalton went on to elaborate, "I have no doubt there are a great number of folks around here that would just as soon piss on his grave. If I went to his place once I must've been up there a hundred times. I got reports all the time about how he was hunting out of season, or bagging more than the state limit. It was reported that he set illegal traps not to mention skinning deer, and leaving them to rot in the forest. I could go on and on, but like I said we're all better off now that he's no longer amongst the living."

Grant joined Dalton at the sink. "So you never arrested him for any of the things that you mentioned?"

"Locked him up plenty of times, but his brother Merle, who actually turned out to be quite successful, was a lawyer over in Gatlinburg…still is today. We just couldn't seem to get him on a serious enough charge to stick. Merle was always getting him off the hook. Merle was and still today is very connected here in Blount County. He swings a lot of weight." Turning to face Grant, Dalton pointed out, "But none of that makes any difference now. Asa's dead and there's nothing Merle or anyone else can do to change that."

Sitting back down at the kitchen table, Dalton sipped at his coffee. "So tell me, Grant, I take it you were up on Thunderhead at the scene of the crime. Was it really as bad as folks are saying?"

"Worse," replied Grant. "There wasn't much left of Asa. It appeared the coyotes got to him…maybe a cougar."

"Do you think he was alive when they got to him?"

"No, I think he was already dead when they started in on him. We should know more tomorrow after we talk with the coroner." Grant stood, "I've got to get to bed. It's almost three in the morning. I've got to be back at the office by seven. I have a feeling the next few days are going to be nuts."

Hesitating at the kitchen door Grant thought for a moment then asked, "Gramps…you were the chief for…what was it…twenty years? I'm sure you've had your share of things you'd rather forget…but I've got to tell you that being up there on Thunderhead and seeing what was done to Asa Pittman, I don't think I'll ever forget it. It was absolutely horrible. I've learned a lot about Pittman today and it sounds to me like he had a lot of enemies. But what kind of a person would do that to another human being?"

"I can't tell you that, Grant," said Dalton, "but I can tell you this. Sooner or later it'll all come out and we'll all know who did it and why they did it. It'll just take some time. Remember, if police work was that easy, well then everybody would be on the force. Now get on up to bed. I'll see you tomorrow night sometime."

Climbing the stairs to his bedroom Grant debated whether he should take a shower or not. At the top of the stairs he decided to wait until morning. He was just too tired at the moment. Draping his uniform over a chair in the corner he looked out the window at the pouring rain, a flash of lightning lit up the distant sky. Staring off into the distance he thought about the location out there on Thunderhead Trail where Asa Pittman had been murdered. Right now at this very moment Mother Nature was washing away any clues they may have overlooked. Sitting on the edge of the bed he wondered about the person who had murdered Asa. What kind of a person could possibly sleep after committing such a heinous crime?

He opened his Bible and silently started to read, a habit he had gotten into when he was just a youngster. His mother was a very strong Christian and had taught him the value of reading the Good Book on a daily basis. He never missed. It was the only thing in his life that he could say he was persistent about. After just two pages, his eyes became heavy. Closing the Bible he lay back on the bed and stared at the rain beating against the bedroom window. How on earth could he be a Christian and a police officer at the same time? Dalton had told him when he first headed off to school that in the future as a law enforcement officer he would eventually run into some pretty horrible things and that his faith in God would be tested. Rolling over onto his side he thought that today, up there on Thunderhead Trail—he had been tested. *God...give me strength,* he thought.

CHAPTER FOUR

GRANT TURNED OVER and looked at the clock—five-forty five. Sitting up in bed he yawned as he thought, *Might as well get up.* He had set the alarm for six. Fifteen more minutes wasn't going to help him get over the restless night. He sat on the edge of the bed and stretched. The daily routine of a shave, shower and a good cup of coffee would help him get started. He padded down the hall in bare feet, the hum of the television coming from the living room downstairs let him know his grandfather was already up.

Staring bleary-eyed in the bathroom mirror, he applied a long swath of shaving cream to his chin. Before he could apply a second handful he heard Dalton calling for him. Because of his mother's condition he had accustomed himself to react quickly whenever anyone called out. Wiping his face on a towel he walked back down the hallway and descended the stairs.

The six o'clock news from Station 8 had just come on. "Grant, come here...come on in here. Will you look at what WVLT out of Knoxville is reporting?" Scooting forward on the couch Dalton pointed at the image of Asa Pittman. It was a mug shot taken from an old file that displayed Asa as an unshaven, rough looking sort of character, the scowl on his face sending out a message of 'Don't mess with me.' The newsman was reading from copy: "*A Mr. Asa Pittman of Townsend Tennessee has been found dead on Thunderhead Trial in the Great Smoky Mountains State Park late yesterday mornin.*" The announcer continued giving out additional information that Grant already knew.

"Crap!" said Grant in an irritated voice, wiping the remainder of the shaving cream from his face. "How in God's green earth did they find out about this already?"

Dalton, sipping at his morning coffee sat back on the couch. "Hell, Grant, you know news travels faster that Kudzu in these parts."

Heading back up the stairs, Grant shouted, "I gotta go. I'll call you later."

Dressed and out of the house in ten minutes, Grant wasted little time as he exceeded the speed limit on the way into Townsend, thinking about what a horrible day it was going to be. Brody, whose temperament to begin with wasn't exactly the most pleasant, would be off the chart. Once the news media started to descend on Axel Brody's little empire he would be impossible to deal with.

Grant was no sooner passed the Route 321 intersection when he discovered that it was not going to be a typical morning in Townsend. Normally the traffic flow on the Alexander Parkway was minimal, but come the first of June, at times it was bumper to bumper, tourists coming from every part of the country to take in some leisure time in the mountains just relaxing or fishing in one of the local streams. Many would stop at The Outfitter's for fishing line, hooks, styrofoam coolers and a can of red wigglers. Their next stop was often the Parkway Grocery to pick up anything they may have forgotten, others stopping at The Hearth and Kettle, Victoria Station, Sister Cats Café, or one of the other restaurants in town before heading up to Cades Cove or the entrance to The Great Smoky Mountains National Park.

Today was April 2, still the off-season, yet it seemed like mid-June as Grant had to park three blocks from the police station. Vans and cars of all shapes and sizes were parked on both sides of the street, many double parked. Heavy pieces of camera equipment were set on tripods, a jumble of wires crisscrossing the sidewalks and streets, groups of people stood in small groups smoking, drinking coffee and chatting.

Reaching under the seat of the Jeep, Grant pulled out a plastic bag from the Valley Market. He removed his hat and badge, unbuckled his holster and placed them in the bag, then incognito, started up the street. Many people who appeared to be news reporters were talking on cell phones, others roaming through the crowd picking out locals they could interview. It seemed like everyone in the county was in town today. Passing through the throng of people Grant could hear bits and pieces of varied conversations:

"What was the victim's name?"

"They said he was murdered."

"Did he live around here?"

Walking as fast as he could down Tiger Street, Grant kept his head down to keep from being noticed. Finally arriving at the police station parking lot he was no more than twenty feet from the door when he heard his name mentioned, "There's Grant. He's one of our police officers. I bet he could answer some of your questions." Before he could turn to see who it was he was mobbed by a small group of reporters firing questions at him:

"Do you have any suspects?"

"Do you think Mr. Pittman was killed on the trail?"

"How did he die?"

A man stuck a microphone in his face as a cameraman pushed his way to the front of the crowd. Grant just kept shaking his head and finally edged close enough to the front door and yelled, "Axel, it's me Grant, let me in!"

Brody opened the door just wide enough for Grant to squeeze through and then slammed it shut behind him. "Damn vultures," growled Brody, "They done been here since five o'clock this mornin'. Where you've been Denlinger? I told you to be here by six. Butch got here on time. Obviously he cares more about this case than you do."

Grant looked at Butch who was sitting at a desk, his feet propped up as he read the morning paper. Grant was accustomed to getting snide remarks from Brody that he normally just blew off, which is exactly how he would handle the chief this morning. "You said seven, Chief, but it doesn't matter. I had one heck of a time getting through that crowd. What's going on? How did they find out about the Pittman murder?"

"Damned if I know," said Brody, "but I heard one of the reporters say that the TV Station in Gatlinburg got a call late last night from somebody who told them we had a murder over here. I don't have any idea who that could have been. Hell, it goes way beyond Gatlinburg. We've got reporters out there from Nashville, Knoxville and who knows where else. Damn idiots are talkin' with the locals...who, by the way, don't know squat about this case. Before you know it they'll probably be tellin' them we have Bigfoot roamin' around in the hills..."

The office secretary interrupted Brody, "Chief, excuse me, but the coroner just called from Maryville. Said he's running late. He got a call from the FBI. Apparently two agents are driving down from Knoxville. According to the coroner they are going to meet him in Maryville. They want to take a look at the body. He said he'll try to get over here as soon as he can but it could be awhile." Turning to walk back into the office she snapped her fingers, "Oh I forgot to tell you. The state police will be dropping by later this morning."

Brody exploded, kicking over a trashcan that was setting next to a desk. "Great...just great! We got a three ring circus out there and now I've got to be the damn ring master. Hell, I don't know what to tell those people." Grabbing his Stetson, he yelled, "Butch! Get your ass up. We've got to go out there and talk with these news people." Looking at both Grant and Butch, he emphasized, "It's your job to keep them from swarmin' all over me when I get out there."

Butch, without a word, got up slowly and followed Brody to the door where they stood facing each other. "All right, let's get this over with," ordered Brody, edging his way out the door in front of the crowd. The reporters, cameramen and others standing around pushed toward the open door.

Brody held up his hands indicating that they needed to stop. "Now look! You need to move back and give me some breathin' room and I'll tell you what we have so far. Otherwise...I'm goin' back inside." Six microphones were placed in front of him. Grabbing the closest he shouted, "If I could have everyone's attention." Following a few seconds when the crowd started to settle down, he began, "Name's Chief Axel Brody. Been chief here in Townsend for seventeen years. We received a call around one o'clock yesterday afternoon from the Park Ranger Station up near Cades Cove. A body had been reported found. I can't get into any specific details at the moment, but it appears that there was foul play involved..."

A reporter near the back shouted, "We heard the victim was murdered...any truth to that?"

Another reporter spoke up loudly, "They claim the victim is a man by the name of Asa Pittman...a local resident. Is Mr. Pittman from Townsend?"

Brody placed the microphone close to his mouth, answering, "Things are still kind of sketchy and as soon as we hear somethin' from the county coroner we'll be able to determine the cause of death. Right now all we know is that the victim's name is Asa Pittman and he did live in the immediate area. Based on what we have gathered so far it has been determined that Mr. Pittman was murdered sometime on April 1, and that the killer is still out there."

Questions were being shouted from every corner of the crowd. Brody pointed to an attractive young female reporter standing near the front. Stepping even closer, she asked, "Yes, Chief Brody, can you tell us anything at all about Mr. Pittman other than his illegal poaching activities that he was arrested for several times?"

Brody cleared his throat, then answered, "Aside from a few disorderly conduct and minor assault charges and a couple of speedin' tickets...no."

"Anything recently?"

"No...nothin' in the past couple of years."

After answering a few other questions Brody ended the interview by telling the crowd that was all he had for the moment. Walking back toward the main doors he smiled. He had gotten what he wanted: his face on television.

Back in his office the chief pitched his hat on the desk and sat down. Grant walked to the water cooler for a drink but Brody stopped him. "Don't get too comfortable, Denlinger. Tell you what. You need to hightail it up to Asa's place before those media vultures and the FBI get up there. I don't reckon they could find the place without a map or a guide, however we can't take a chance on them gettin' up there and tramplin' all over the place, destroyin' any evidence. Anyways, you need to check it out and see if you can stumble across anythin' that might help us clear up this mess." Opening his desk drawer, he continued, "Here, let me draw you a map so you know how to get there..."

Interrupting Brody, Grant removed a small paper cup from the water dispenser. "That won't be necessary, Axel. I already know where Pittman's place is."

Brody surprised, responded, "You do? How's that?"

Grant downed the cup of water then answered, "I've been up there with my grandfather. It was a long time ago when I was just a kid, but I remember the way. The problem as I see it is not getting up there but getting up there undetected by the hoard of news hounds hanging around in our parking lot." Snapping his fingers he reached for an old plaid shirt and tan fishing hat a local drunk had left on the coat rack at some point in the past. It had been hanging there for quite some time. Hitting the hat on the back of a chair, puffs of dust fluttered into the air. He pulled the hat down over his eyes, slipped into the shirt and picked up the bag that contained his holstered gun. "This should get me out the backdoor. I'll see what I can find up there. I better get going." Hesitating, Grant addressed the chief, "Uh…don't I need a warrant…a search warrant?"

Brody gave Grant an odd look as he answered, "I'll handle that end…you just get movin'."

Grant objected, "But how can I go on the property without a warrant?"

Brody, becoming impatient stood. "The Feds will get up there sooner or later. They can get a warrant if they choose to do so."

Grant was about to say something else but Brody stopped him. "Besides that, the owner of the property, the sole occupant is dead. We don't need a warrant. We have probable cause. Now, move your ass!"

After walking back to his vehicle, Grant managed to slip out of town unnoticed. Heading up Laurel Creek Road for three miles, he made a right on another paved road that was four miles of uphill twists and turns. Coming to an old fence that had a hubcap hanging on a post, he turned left onto a narrow dirt, weed infested path that was just wide enough for one vehicle. Low hanging trees and brush hugged the road from every angle. After carefully driving for a quarter mile Grant came to a rusted, iron cattle gate with a lopsided, sloppily painted **KEEP OUT** sign hanging on it. Getting out of the Jeep, he pushed the gate open. The road ahead seemed to be swallowed by dense trees and underbrush. Getting back in he drove fifty yards then made his way around a curve, where another thirty yards away lurked Asa Pittman's property.

Even though it had been twelve years since he had been here the place looked the same. The cabin was a jumble of mismatched and weathered gray boards, the paint peeling in many sections, torn screens hung from boarded up windows, while others stood wide open. The cabin was topped off with a patched tin roof. The grass and weeds on either side of the cabin stood knee high, the front yard which was dirt was muddy due to the recent rain, a number of chickens and goats roamed around looking for something to eat. Off to the left and behind the cabin there was an old barn. Seven rusted out cars practically covered with tall weeds and vines surrounded it. It was the perfect setting for a B-Grade horror film.

Grant, sitting back in the seat recalled the first time he had been to the old barn. It was when his grandfather was still Chief of Police in Townsend. He didn't remember much about the past visit, except that Asa and his grandfather had shared some heated words. He recalled how when they had pulled up in front of the cabin, Asa had been setting on his porch, his shotgun across his legs. While his grandfather and Asa were arguing, Grant, curious as ever slipped out of the car and went around to the barn. He thought he had witnessed a mother cat and four kittens run beneath the barn door. Opening the large wooden door he looked inside. What he saw was far better than kittens.

In the corner of the barn stood a three piece contraption of some sort. A large copper tank with a gooseneck pipe affair that attached with a second smaller copper tank, out of which there were a number of clear tubes and copper tubing, some of which were connected to a third tank where there was a bucket and a spout. Approaching the strange looking object Grant wondered what on earth he was looking at. Then he noticed a number of slanted wooden shelves that contained rows of jugs and bottles filled with what appeared to be water. Then it hit him! He was looking at a genuine moonshine still. He had seen similar ones on television. Realizing that he needed to get back to the car before his grandfather was ready to leave he scurried back out the barn door. The next day at school he told Willie, his best friend about the still. They discussed the still for the next two days and then decided that on Saturday they would go up to Asa's farm and steal a jar of shine.

Come Saturday they got up early and started on their journey. By the time they arrived at the gate to Asa's farm they were tuckered out from pedaling their bikes but the thought of getting a jar of real moonshine outweighed their fatigue. Resting for fifteen minutes, they hid their bikes in the underbrush then ducked under the old gate and cut through the woods coming out on the backside of the barn. Hiding behind a large boulder they looked across the short open distance to the barn. There was no one in sight. Stooping down they ran across to the eerie barn and peered in an open window. It was all clear. Grant hoisted himself through the window, dashed across the dirt floor, picked up a quart jar and was back out the window in less than a minute. It had been so easy.

The two boys laughed and snickered all the way to Townsend. Stopping about a mile from home they sat on a large flat stone next to the Little River and sampled their first taste of white lightning.

Grant remembered how it burned like hell as it trickled down his throat, he and Willie trying to be braver than the other, handing the jar back and fourth taking small sips. It had taken two days for Grant to recover, his mother convinced it was a bout with the flu that had been going around. Willie had only missed one day of school, therefore claiming he had won the drinking contest.

Looking out the side window of the Jeep, Grant thought about his days as a young boy growing up in and around Townsend. Those were the best days of his life. Days when he and Willie felt like they were immortal, like nothing could hurt them. Despite their unnoticed hangover from the previous week they decided to return to Asa's place the next Saturday and steal a second jar. Their plan was to drink just a little and hide the rest for later.

When they arrived at Asa's his truck was parked near the back of the house. They waited for a while then decided to at least have a look and see if the barn was empty. Just a few feet from the window they heard a noise coming from inside the barn. Ducking down they scrambled up next to the old building. Peering through separated boards they could see Asa standing over an old door that had been placed over the top of two sawhorses. He was cutting something up. The two boys watched, their eyes got bigger as they discovered that Asa was in the process of skinning a fox. He was methodically inserting a sharp knife just below the surface of the skin and pulling it back with his other hand. Two more foxes lay dead on the barn floor. Willie suddenly put his hand over his mouth and ran across the clearing to the safety of the woods. Grant remembered how Willie had been upset, saying Asa had no right to do that. Grant recalled how, at the time, he too had a sick feeling in the pit of his stomach at the sight. That day on the way home, they agreed they would never hunt for animals, and they never did. It was the last time either boy had gone up to the Pittman farm.

Realizing he had been daydreaming, Grant stepped out of the Jeep, snapped on a pair of plastic gloves and started walking toward the cabin, looking from side to side. The place was just as creepy as when he had been here years ago. Stepping up onto the porch he sidestepped a number of loose boards. He pushed on the door. It was locked. Walking the length of the porch he came to an open window, the dirty curtains blowing from a slight mountain breeze. Crawling through the opening, he stood and took in the surroundings. It was dark inside the cabin, just enough light filtering through an open window, which allowed Grant to make it to the living room without falling over the jumble of furniture that was scattered around. Pulling back the curtain from another window he looked around the room and noticed three couches, each one in worse shape than the other, six chairs and two tables. One chair, positioned in front of a small television, was covered with a lime green afghan. Except for the room being on the junky side nothing seemed particularly odd about this part of the house.

Walking down a gloomy hallway, he stopped to look into a bathroom, which was encased with grime and rust. Nothing here either, just a misshapen bar of soap, a razor and a can of shaving cream on the grimy sink. An old soiled towel was draped over the back of the toilet.

He carefully opened the door to the bedroom. The smell of sweat and musty clothes almost caused him to gag. There were stacks of old magazines surrounding the rumpled bed: *Guns and Ammo; Today's Hunter; Hunting for Profit;* and others. A small rickety table next to the bed held some loose change, several keys and a book of matches. Removing a plastic bag from his pocket he carefully scooped up the keys and matches and placed them in the bag. He opened every drawer in the dresser, but nothing caught his attention.

The kitchen was next. It was filthy. The counters were cluttered with jars containing rice, salt, flour and other staples. Dishes were stacked haphazardly on the open shelves above a food-stained, stainless steel sink. The worn red and white linoleum had a yellow tinge to it. Grant opened the refrigerator; eggs, butter, a package of bologna and a bottle of ketchup. That was it.

Closing the refrigerator door, Grant sat down at the kitchen table. This was his first real crime scene investigation being on his own. Well, it really wasn't the scene of the crime but there might be something in or around the house that might render some sort of a clue. What was he missing? There had to be something. He thought about what his instructors at school had taught him: Use all of your senses when searching for clues. Don't depend on just your eyes to reveal what is right in front of you, listen, smell, feel, touch. Drumming his fingers on the table, he felt something grainy. He rubbed his palm across the surface then picked up what looked like coffee grounds or something similar. He put his hand to his nose. The substance had a sweet aroma, nothing he was familiar with. He took a plastic bag from his pocket and brushed the particles into it.

Back out on the porch, Grant took a deep breath of fresh air as he surveyed the area. There wasn't any sense in looking for tire tracks. Last night's rain, the chickens and goats would have altered them. Heading toward the barn he had an eerie feeling that someone was watching him. It was probably just his imagination.

Opening the large wooden barn doors the smell coming from the inside was so strong it stung his eyes. There were piles of animal skins tied together with twine, others laid on the dirt floor, while some were tacked to boards for drying. A tin barrel full of animal skulls and bones was loosely covered by a faded bloodstained tarp. It seemed like there were flies in every corner of the barn. The two side walls were covered with rusty hooks that held traps of all kinds. Most were the clench leg type with sharp barbs on each cuff. There was an array of different sizes of cage traps strewn across the floor near the back of the barn. In the corner stood the same old still that Grant remembered. *Man, that Asa was a piece of work*, thought Grant.

Something drifted in front of his eyes. He looked up and saw bits of hay falling through the cracks of the loft floor. Grant steadied himself and moved his hand to his holster and slowly unsnapped the leather strap. Carefully, he walked out from under the loft, turned and pointed his revolver up toward the area where the hay had fallen. "Don't move," he ordered. "I have you covered. Stay where you are." There was complete silence. He sidled around the wall and stood at the bottom of the loft ladder. "I'm coming up. If you have a weapon you better drop it now!"

With his revolver positioned to fire he placed his foot on the first rung. Eight steps up he carefully raised his head just long enough to see three chickens pecking at the hay. He let out a long sigh, turned around and went back down.

The streets were still filled with reporters and people interested in the day old murder when Grant arrived back at the station. Once again he had to force his way through the mingling crowd. He shut the station door almost catching someone's hand holding a microphone.

Walking down the hallway past his office he heard a voice, "Hello, Grant." He turned to see Dana Beth sitting in his office.

Taken by complete surprise, Grant struggled for the right words.

"Uh…Hi, Dana Beth. It's good…to see you. I heard you were back in town."

She nodded. "Yes, I've been back about two weeks. I'm working at the hospital in Maryville. I have to go back to school next week to complete my final two months…then it's graduation."

"Congratulations," said Grant as he tried not to act that surprised at seeing her again. "That's good. I'm glad you're getting your degree." There was a brief moment of silence as he thought, *All right…what do I say now?* He was running out of small talk. He knew that he would run into her sooner or later, *but why today…of all days! She looks good. Shorter hair…just as pretty as ever.* Without thinking he blurted out, "I hear you're dating Butch Miller now. He talks about you all the time. Doesn't make things easy for me…with the way we broke up and all. I can't believe it, Dana Beth. Why him? When we were in high school you couldn't stand to get within ten feet of him. He was the biggest jerk in our class."

Defensively, she answered, "He's not like that anymore. He's changed, Grant."

Walking into his office Grant threw his hands in the air. "Oh you poor little blind girl. I work with him everyday. He's still a jerk! Even a bigger jerk than he used to be. Is this your way of getting even with me for not marrying you? If it is…give yourself a break and find someone else. Someone decent!"

Just then, Butch stormed into the room, "I heard every damn thing you said about me, Denlinger. Who in the hell do you think you are, Mr. almost college man? You think I'm a jerk…well prove it!" Stepping closer, Butch, using both of his hands shoved him on the chest sending Grant backward, knocking over a chair and scattering papers across the room. Grant caught himself from falling to the floor, grabbing the edge of his desk. Before Butch could react Grant recovered, swinging his right arm out catching Butch on his right jaw with his fist knocking him out into the hallway and up against the bathroom door.

Brody, in the bathroom yelled through the door, "What the hell's goin' on out there?"

Butch lunged back at Grant and they both slammed into the wall as Brody, zipping up his pants, came out of the bathroom. Butch had Grant by his shirt collar while Grant stepped hard on Butch's foot, at the same time pushing him into Brody, who was yelling, "Got dammit…cut it out!" Brody managed to grab both Grant and

Butch by their shirts as he separated them banging each up against the wall. "I can't believe this! I got an unsolved murder, a street full of out of towners, people breathin' down my neck for answers and I ain't got time to baby sit you two snot-nosed dumb asses fightin' over a woman!" Turning to Dana Beth he ordered her, "Dana Beth...you go on and git." Putting his finger directly in Grant's face, he shouted, "I oughta fire your ass right now, Denlinger. If I thought I wouldn't have to deal with your grandfather, you'd better believe it...you'd be gone!" Regaining his composure Brody took a deep breath and backed away. "Grant, you go on and try to get the coroner on the phone and find out when he's gonna get his ass over here and give us somethin' to go on."

"No, you do it!" Grant yelled back. "You want to fire me then go ahead. No, on second thought...I quit!" Ripping his badge off of his shirt he tossed it up against the wall.

"Well, it's about time," remarked Butch sarcastically.

Brody turned and shoved Butch roughly as he commanded him, "And you...get back in the office now! You and I are goin' to have a little chat." Turning back to Grant, the chief confirmed, "Nobody's quittin' today and I ain't firin' you. Now...get out of here and go cool your heels." Grant shot Dana Beth a hard look, then headed for the door.

Outside the door he was met by a throng of reporters. "Get out of my way," he yelled, as he shoved his way through the crowd. Once out of the crowd he looked back. *Great...they probably got all that on film. Dalton's just gonna love that.*

Back inside the Jeep, Grant rolled down the windows and slowly pulled out onto the street. Two blocks later he pulled over into the lot of the Parkway Grocery got out and left the motor running. Normally, he didn't drink all that much, but his run in with Miller motivated him to head directly for the cold case area where he picked up a six-pack of beer. Grant noticed a few people in the store, nodded at them but remained silent, paid for his beer and left.

Walking across the lot he heard someone holler his name. "Grant!"

Clenching his fist, he was in no mood to talk with anyone at the moment. Turning he recognized Doug Eland.

Jogging across the lot, Doug with a smile on his face, commented, "Grant, I'm glad I caught up with you. I was just on my way down to Gatlinburg. I need to get some pictures for a client." Sticking his hands in his front pockets he went on, "I have to make this trip pay for itself even though it wasn't exactly what I would call a vacation. Chief Brody said I could leave town for a few days but that I'd have to return to talk with the Feds at some point. I'll be glad when this is all over. By the way, I've got those pictures you wanted. I have your set in my car. Hold on a minute."

In less than a minute Doug trotted to his car and back, an envelope in his hand. Handing it to Grant, Doug remarked, "I hope these will come in handy."

Looking at the envelope, Grant asked, "How did you manage to get these? I thought Brody confiscated your camera?"

"If there is one thing I've learned about your chief it's that what he's says he's going to do is quite different than what he actually does. When we all got back to the police station he was so flustered he forgot about what he had told me. I got a room over at the Econo Lodge. I always bring my equipment with me to make sure I get good shots. I just put the scanner card in my computer and ran off a couple of sets. Then I put the card back in the camera and dropped it off at Brody's office. He'll never know the difference."

Reaching out Grant shook Doug's hand. "Thanks, Doug, I appreciate this. Be careful. Don't run into any dead bodies." He grinned. "I gotta run before this beer gets warm."

CHAPTER FIVE

THREE WEEKS FOLLOWING Asa Pittman's death, the county coroner's final report concluded that Mr. Pittman had been the victim of a homicide. His nose had been broken, there were lacerations on the side of his head from being struck by a wooden object, possibly a branch or small log, and his fingers had been severed from his hands by some sort of sharp instrument. Traces of a numbing drug such as Xylocain or Novocaine were present in the body along with a minimal amount of a substance similar to chloroform. Evidence of animals clawing or chewing at various body parts was also found. The coroner deduced that more than likely the body had already bled out before the animals came onto the scene.

The report was not only sent to Chief Brody, but also to the Blount County Sheriff based out of Maryville. The FBI and the state police received a copy, the state police bowing to the Feds stating that they wanted to be kept abreast on how the investigation was going. Two Federal agents, Ralph Gephart and Harold Green spent the better part of April conducting an investigation of their own. They questioned Doug Eland who had been summoned back to Townsend. They also interviewed a number of the local residents who had known Asa. From these interviews they established a number of suspects which led to absolutely nothing. They were just people Asa had pissed off over the years. People like Earl Phifster who had made it known that if he had a gun he'd shoot Asa Pittman, or some of the local animal activists that said Asa should be shot. Even though these and many others in and around Townsend felt the same way about Asa Pittman, they were just normal folks who didn't think about what they said. When approached by the agents they were amazed that they were considered suspects. Sure, they didn't like Pittman, but killing the man, well that was something they could never actually do. Apparently, there was someone who not only disliked Asa but had taken matters into their own hands; a murderer who was still on the loose.

The FBI along with the cooperation of the Townsend Police searched Asa's farm and the area around Thunderhead Trail extracting bag after bag of what they thought might pan out to be eventual evidence. At the beginning of May a report was issued stating the investigation was ongoing and the Asa Pittman case would be classified as an unsolved murder.

When the articles about Asa's death shifted from front page news to the back section of the paper and then eventually disappeared, Chief Brody and everyone else in town breathed a sigh of relief. Townsend was teetering on the edge of tourist season and Blount County surely didn't need an unsolved murder mucking up the works.

As the weeks passed most of the locals who knew Asa had come to their own conclusions why he was murdered. The list of people who admitted that they disliked him grew longer by the day. Asa Pittman's murder was the topic of conversation at many of the restaurants and gas stations in town. The four men who had met with Asa regularly at the Parkway Grocery claimed he had never been an individual they were fond of but rather that he was a unique person. He could tell a great story and was always willing to buy the first round of coffee in the mornings, not to mention the fact that he supplied them all with a jar of homemade brew from time to time. The flipside of the coin was they were not going to miss his yearly April Fool's pranks which at times had been not only insensitive but cruel. Then there was his constant bragging they would no longer have to sit and listen to.

Even though the murder was six weeks in the past, a dark cloud of wonder seemed to hang over Townsend. The way Asa had died was still a mystery and no one wanted to believe he had still been alive when his fingers had been cut off. It was a haunting thought to imagine there was someone right there in the vicinity that could be that sadistic.

As the days drifted by folks who still talked about the recent murder referred to the victim as poor ol' Asa. Grant, himself wondered how something so terrible could have happened and yet with each day that passed it seemed to be talked about less and less. From all outward appearances life in Townsend seemed to be returning to normal. Storekeepers still swept the sidewalks in front of their shops, mothers still took their children to the park and the restaurants were filled with customers dining and laughing as if nothing had happened.

Grant pulled up in front of the police station, took his last swallow of coffee, stuffed the styrofoam cup down into a trash bag that he kept on the front seat, got out and walked to the door. He was no sooner in the door when Brody passed him in the hallway. "Denlinger …meetin' in two minutes…my office."

Walking into his office Grant removed his coat and hung it on the doorknob as he thought, *Tomorrow is Saturday…and I'm off.*

Strolling down the hall he entered Brody's office where Butch was already seated drinking a cup of coffee. Grant took a seat on the opposite side of the room. Brody was going through a pile of papers stacked on the corner of his desk.

Brody, frustrated because he couldn't seem to find what he was looking for finally looked up and addressed his two officers, "Now listen up. The Feds and the Staties are finally out of our hair. They pulled out yesterday. Things are startin' to calm down around town and I want to keep it that way. From now on they'll be at least one or two of us patrollin' at all times. We ain't gonna sit on our asses and wait for the phone to bring us trouble. I want the people of Townsend to know that we're takin' care of them. Make yourself visible. Talk to people, smile and don't answer any dumb questions without thinkin' about it first. Any questions about the murder investigation should be answered briefly and with the least amount of information you can give. Try to reassure the people in town and especially the tourists that whoever did this is no doubt miles away." Hesitating, Brody stared at both Grant and Butch. "You get my drift?"

Grant sat silently, nodded and thought at the same time, *How could we not get his drift? Just like everything else in this department, Brody will sweep it under the carpet and hope that it goes away.*

Butch answered, "Yes, sir."

Brody gave Grant a stern look and remarked, "Did that nod of your head mean 'Yes' or 'Go to Hell?'"

Grant answered immediately, in a sarcastic military fashion, "Yes sir…I understand…sir!"

Brody responded with a look that said, 'Don't be a smart ass.' Looking at his watch the chief continued, "The park service has sent four more rangers up to Cades Cove. They want to make sure the folks comin' in know this is a safe place to be and, once again, we'd like to keep it that way." Brody stood and removed a cigar from his shirt pocket. "Now…go find somethin' to do!"

It was only nine o'clock in the morning and Grant had patrolled each and every street in Townsend twice. If he wouldn't have known there had been a horrific murder back in April, he wouldn't have been able to tell from the way the residents of town were acting. As he cruised through the surrounding neighborhoods and small subdivisions people went about mowing their yards or watering flowers. There were a few joggers out and about town, people walking their dogs, Harvey Fields, the local mailman on his familiar route, people going about their everyday lives. Out on the parkway, the main drag of town, the population of Townsend had already started to increase with tourists starting to arrive on a daily basis.

Grant decided to pull over in his favorite spot beneath a large shade tree at the local municipal park next to the Little River, which ran through town. Watching two mothers and their small children in the play area and a man throwing a frisbee for his dog, Grant sat back in the seat and thought about the past few weeks. He had already decided that no matter what happened back at the station, he wasn't going to let Asa's murder just fade away without at least trying his best to solve the case. He knew he was a far cry from a profiler but he had decided to keep a record of all of the information he could garner about Asa Pittman and anybody who knew the man. Somewhere in the jumble of words written in his blue, spiral binder there might just be a clue to the murder. He poured over the photographs that Doug had given him, time after time, but the ghastly pictures of the Thunderhead crime scene did not reveal anything new. If anything they were a vivid reminder of how horrible it had been that day.

He had a lot of time to think over the past weeks. He had thought about the murder, his mother and grandfather and also about Dana Beth. It had been a shock to see her sitting in his office. He hadn't seen her since before she had sent him the letter breaking off their relationship. Up until that morning in the office he hadn't seen her in almost two years. During that time he had thought of her often and seeing her again reminded him of the first time he laid eyes on her in high school. He had the same feeling in his office that morning as the first time he met her. He still had feelings for Dana Beth.

Turning the ignition key of the cruiser, he pulled out of the park and headed down the parkway, noticing he was getting low on gas. Pulling into Frank's Market, he stopped next to the pumps. Getting out, he reached in his pocket for one of two City of Townsend credit cards that he carried. Just before inserting the card into the scanner on the front of the pump he was interrupted by a familiar voice, "Good morning, Grant." Turning he saw Professor Pearl, Dana Beth's father standing on the other side of the pump, placing the nozzle into the gas tank of his red Fiat. Grant hadn't seen Mr. Pearl since last summer and hadn't talked with him since before the breakup. He looked the same: tall, slender, graying hair that was always cut in a conservative style, clean shaven, always dressed impeccably.

"Good morning Professor," said Grant. "What brings you into town this morning?"

"Just filling up the tank before I head up to Knoxville."

Grant smiled, trying to make the best of what he considered to be an awkward moment. He searched for the right words. "Guess you'll be looking forward to the summer, what with school being out soon?"

Professor Pearl in his soft spoken, gentle voice, answered, "Yes, I am looking forward to this summer. The Mrs. and I will be heading down to Gulf Shores for two weeks of leisure on the beach. She'll lounge in her beach chair from sunup until sundown reading one book after another while I'll log many a mile strolling up and down the beach." Changing the subject, the professor inquired, "How is your mother doing, Grant? I heard she moved out with your grandfather on his farm."

"She's doing fine. We had to sell the hardware store. It was just too much for her and she can't get around the way she used to. Dalton is as ornery as ever. He keeps busy with his garden. Mows his six acres of grass. He still sits on the Townsend City Counsel. I don't think he'll ever slow down."

Checking the rotating numbers on the pump, Professor Pearl cleared his throat then asked, "How is your schooling going? I heard that you had to drop out due to your mother's unfortunate fall. I hope you haven't given up on getting your degree."

"I'm completing my final year on line. With any luck I should finish up sometime next summer. My job on the Townsend Police keeps me pretty busy so I don't get to study much."

The tank of the Fiat full, the pump automatically shut off. The professor placed the nozzle back onto the pump holder, then pushed the receipt button. "And how is your position with the local police going?"

"It's all right," answered Grant. "It's only temporary. After I get my degree I'd like to get a job in law enforcement in a larger town: Maryville, Gatlinburg or maybe even Knoxville."

The gas transaction complete, Professor Pearl reached out and shook Grant's hand. "Don't be a stranger. Drop by sometime and pay me and the wife a visit. I know she would love to see you."

"I might just do that," replied Grant.

Filling up his tank Grant thought about how strange it was to run into Dana Beth's father when he had moments earlier been thinking about how he still had feelings for her. He had always liked Professor Pearl and had been looking forward to him being his future father-in-law, but the way things were going it looked like Butch Miller had the upper hand.

Once in the cruiser Grant thought about how Professor Pearl had stayed away from mentioning anything about Dana Beth or Butch. He had been sensitive to Grant's feelings and for that he respected the man.

Turning onto the parkway he drove for not even a quarter mile where he turned into the Parkway Grocery. It was almost ten o'clock and he was hungry since he had skipped breakfast. Maybe he'd grab a soda and a sandwich. Walking through the doors he went to the cooler and selected a Mountain Dew, then a ham and cheese sandwich from the deli display. He paid for his purchase and walked down the narrow aisle near the front window where there were three tables and sets of chairs for locals to relax and read the morning paper, enjoy a drink or sandwich. Taking a large gulp of his soda he heard familiar voices, then thought, *Of course...it's Friday.*

As usual there at the last table next to the window sat Zeb, Charley, Luke and Buddie. Buddie, the first to see Grant pulled a chair out from the table with his foot and slid it across the floor. "Come on over here Grant and take a load off."

As Grant seated himself, Charley commented, "It's a hot one

today."

"That's 'cause it's almost summer, dumb ass," said Luke. "It's always hot this time of year."

Grant grinned. *Same ol' group. Always at each other.*

Before anyone else had an opportunity to say anything, a loud honking noise caught their attention. All the men including Grant rubbernecked out the front window. A black sports car was so close to the car in front of it that their bumpers were almost touching. "Damn, would you look at that?" exclaimed Zeb. "Looks like Mildred Henks is trying to push that car down the street. I reckon it wasn't moving fast enough for her." Just then the driver in front of the black sports car stuck his hand out the window and made an obscene gesture, which was reciprocated by another round of horn honking from Mildred.

Charley let out a snorting laugh. "That Mildred...she sure is a pip!" Pointing his coffee cup at Grant he went on, "Ya know ol' Asa was sweet on her. I remember one day, guess it was about a year back or so, she was in here buying a pack of smokes. She had on a bright red suit and that white scarf she always has draped around her neck. Ol' Asa, he was just staring at her and licking his lips. Then, with that weird look he always got on his face he says, 'Now that's somebody whose bed I wouldn't mind parking my shoes under.' Course, we all laughed, and he got right up and went over there and said hello to Mildred. Well, she looked at him like she was just sprayed by a skunk, turned around and left him standing there."

"Boy, we really gave him a hard time over that one," said Zeb. "He was boiling and told us all to go to hell. Yep, poor ol' Asa."

Charley slammed his cup down on the table, "Oh, poor ol' Asa my ass! He's gone and before you know it something else will happen that will turn this town upside down. That's just the way life is."

"Well, what got your goat?" snarled Luke. "Don't need to spill coffee everywhere."

Charley's outburst seemed to quell the spirited conversation. Grant stood up and tipped his hat. "I gotta run. See you boys later."

Once back out in the car he jotted down some notes in his blue binder then headed back out on patrol.

By the middle of June, Townsend was once again alive with the sights and sounds of summer. The tourist season was in full swing.

Chief Brody and Butch were running from one call to another, breaking up fights, taking complaints from campers who had articles stolen from their vehicles and catching underage drinkers tipping over trashcans. Grant was left to man the station most of the time which was a Godsend. He didn't have to deal with Brody or Butch. Sitting at the light at the intersection of Route 321 he watched a stream of tourists enter town: cars piled high with camping equipment, some pulling small boats, trail bikes and ATV's bungeed onto trailers, large recreational vehicles hugging the white line on the street and the occasional group of riders on horseback. Townsend was alive with people from all over the country. Summer had descended on the Great Smoky Mountains and the murder of Asa Pittman would soon be forgotten.

CHAPTER SIX

MILDRED HENKS FASHIONED HERSELF an attractive woman. Standing at just a tad over six foot, her slender, almost underweight figure was always adorned in designer dresses and business suits, her longer than normal feet always displayed in spiked boots, normally black. She had a tendency to wear an overabundance of makeup and gaudy jewelry that did absolutely nothing to enhance her short, dyed red hair. She had a habit of frequenting the local tanning salon to the point where her skin had taken on somewhat of a bronze, leathery appearance.

The word around Townsend and Maryville was that she had gone through three husbands, all of whom had left her. Apparently no man could stand to live with her. She was widely known in and around Blount County as a career woman: a fifty-six year old questionable diva who drove back and forth through the surrounding counties in her jet-black Thunderbird convertible. She had been employed by the Tri-County Real Estate Company for eighteen years and held the distinction of being their best sales person—year in, year out. Her trademark in the local real estate market was that she always sported a long white silk scarf.

She was quite involved, especially in the Maryville area. She was a member of a fiction book club, an active member of the Blount County Gardeners and was president of Women in Business, a local women's organization. Many of the local women, especially other career woman were pushing her to run for public office. She knew everyone who held any importance, was very well connected with business owners and was known as a tough woman, a woman who wouldn't take any crap from anyone. She had the perfect personality to become a politician.

It was late Friday morning, Mildred looking forward to a long, relaxing weekend. It was June, not a great month for selling real estate in the Smoky Mountains Region. The month was practically over and the tote board in Tri-County's office displayed a big fat zero next to her name. She had experienced bad months in the past but this was the worst in some time. She was taking a few days off in order to regroup. She had slept in, something she normally did not do, fixed herself a breakfast of eggs Benedict, a peach yogurt and to top things off, a Bloody Mary in a tall glass. Later on in the afternoon she was planning on driving over to the Laurel Hills Country Club in Townsend to lounge leisurely by the pool and hobnob with some of Blount County's wealthier residents.

Dressed in bright pink, skintight pants, a pale pink cashmere sweater, and white, fur-lined heeled slippers she lit up a cigarette and walked from the kitchen to her spacious living room. Picking up a multiple listing guide, which she intended to take with her to the pool, she was interrupted by the ringing of the phone on the round Italian marble table next to the couch.

Picking up the receiver she answered, "Hello."

The man's voice on the other end of the line responded, "Good morning...is this the Henks' residence?"

"Yes it is. Who may I ask is calling?"

"My name is Owen Webb. I'm calling for a Mildred Henks. I'm new in the area and I'm looking for a three-bedroom log home. An acquaintance of mine told me that she is the best real estate agent in the Smoky Mountains Region."

Mildred smiled, taking a long drag on her cigarette. "You're speaking to Mildred *and* you have called the right person. It just so happens at the current time I have two log homes listed. Only one of them is a three bedroom. Are you set on three bedrooms or could you live with two?"

"Depending on where the home is," said Owen, "and how it is set up I might be able to get by with two bedrooms. I'm single. I need a master bedroom, then an extra for guests. The third bedroom is going to be utilized for office space. If there is enough room someplace else in the home I suppose I could get by with two."

"What price range are we looking at?"

"Price is not an issue with me. If I find what I want, I'll write a check. I'm rather picky about the home where I live. That's why I wanted to contact a no nonsense agent. According to my friend...that's you."

Always interested in referrals, Mildred inquired, "What is your friend's name? I never forget a past client."

"Carlos Mendoza is his name," answered Owen.

Mildred, looking toward the ceiling made a confused face, commenting, "I don't recall ever selling a home to a Mendoza family."

Owen corrected her, "You didn't sell the home to Carlos. A few years ago one of his friends was a client of yours. I can't remember the name, but Carlos told me that she was very happy with the job you did for her. Besides that I've seen your FOR SALE signs in a number of front yards. Listen, do you think we could connect today? I'm really itching to get settled in."

"Well, I wasn't planning on working this weekend. I was just going to drive over to the country club and spend the afternoon, but a good agent, as they say, is always on duty. What would be convenient for you?"

"I'd hate to ruin your weekend, but I really want to get moving on this. Would it be possible for us to meet today?"

Before Mildred could respond, Owen explained, "I thought that maybe we could knock out two birds with one stone. I also heard from time to time you have Fox Terrier pups for sale. I had a Fox Terrier when I was a young boy growing up. He was a great pet. I've always wanted to get another one but with my moving around, I just thought it wouldn't be fair to the dog. Now that I'm ready to settle down I think I'd like to get one." There was silence on the line for a moment then Owen asked, "Would you happen to have any available pups at this time?"

Mildred walked to her couch and sat. Flicking the ashes from her cigarette into a black onyx ashtray, she answered, "It must be your lucky day. I just got a new litter eight weeks ago. I've got four males and two females. What did you have in mind?"

"I'm looking for a male."

Mildred perked up at the prospect of selling a pup, especially to a potential real estate client who said he was ready to write a check if she could find him the right house. Apparently money was not a problem for Owen Webb. "Mr. Webb...my Terriers are the best in the state and because of that they are not cheap. I normally sell them for $800.00, however if we can come to an agreement on a property I might be able to work out a deal...a win-win situation for both of us."

"Sounds good," said Owen. "How about if we hook up later? Maybe I could drop by your home and see the pups. I'm really anxious to get one."

"Yes, I think we can get together today. Where would you be coming from?"

"Gatlinburg...I'm currently staying over in Gatlinburg."

"All right...what say we meet at my home in about two hours. Would that suit you?"

"Yes it would. Now how do I get to your place?"

Mildred thought for a brief moment then gave directions. "Take Route 73 out of Gatlinburg until you come to Townsend where you'll take a right onto The Lamar Alexander Parkway, go through town and continue going toward Maryville. About five miles on the right you'll see a road called Cold Spring. Take a right and go for about a half-mile until you get to Old Chillhowee Road. Go right and about a quarter of a mile down you'll see my place. You can't miss it. It's kind of out of the way. It was a big white house with four pillars in front and a large stone three-tier fountain in the center of a circular drive. If you get lost you have my number."

"I think I'll be able to locate you. Thank you for taking the time to see me today. I'm sure there are other things you'd much rather be doing."

"It's my pleasure, Mr. Webb. I'm looking forward to meeting you. See you when you get here."

"I'm heading out the door when I hang up. See ya in a few."

Hanging up the phone Mildred stubbed out her smoke, sat back on the couch and smiled, then stood, realizing she needed to get moving. Aside from fixing her hair and making herself a little more presentable, she had to go out back and get the pups, clean them up and get the kitchen blocked off where she would place them. Maybe if she had some time left before Mr. Webb arrived she'd make some iced tea. Between the possible sale of one of the pups and a log home this could turn out to be a very profitable weekend. She wondered who it was that told him about her dogs. It really didn't matter—a sale was a sale.

Walking through a back porch area, she grabbed a long white smock and a pair of rubber boots. She kicked off her slippers and donned the boots and the coat. Proceeding across her large backyard down a cobblestone pathway flanked by short dwarf pines she entered a secluded wooded area then a barn that had seen its better days. Once inside the old building she wrinkled her nose at the smell of old urine and waste matter as she placed a protective mask over her mouth and nose and slipped on a pair of plastic gloves. A number of dogs in wire cages began to bark when she walked toward the rear of the barn. "Shut the hell up!" The dogs went quiet. They knew of the violence they would suffer for not obeying.

In a corner stall she approached a wire cage on the ground where six small pups cuddled up next to each other. She kicked a half empty water bowl out of the way, bent down and opened the cage door. Picking up the pups roughly, she examined each one, tossing the females to the side like they were worthless. One of the four males had a severe rash on its stomach. Pushing him to the side, she commented, "Well, you're not worth a crap." She took the remaining three males and walked back to the front of the barn where she placed them in a round metal tub. Next she dumped a bucket of cold water over the pups and then lathered them up with some household soap. Minutes later after rubbing the soapy solution over the pups she dried them off with a hair dryer that was hanging next to the barn door. Placing them inside a cage, she returned to the house and placed the three pups on the kitchen floor, which was barricaded by a one by six that she leaned across the doorway. She placed a nice comfortable rug, dish of cold water and some dog toys on the floor for looks then went to the large downstairs bath where she ran a brush through her hair and spritzed a shot of her favorite perfume lightly across her body. Looking at the walnut grandfather clock next to the fireplace she thought that she had time to whip up some iced tea.

She scurried around the house, sipping on her tea, picking up magazines, emptying ashtrays, straightening pictures and picking up a pair of shoes and a coffee cup. Finished, she gave her massive living room the once over. The white couch and matching white and beige chairs sat on either side of a large, stone fireplace, her wall of walnut bookshelves tastefully decorated with wood carvings and crystal statues gave the room a stately appearance. Two large banana plants in oversized, white oval planters flanked the front door. A number of framed paintings accented the sage green walls while the plush off-white carpet gave the room a cozy feeling. She placed a pitcher of iced tea and an additional glass on her glass-topped wooden legged table then inspected the room one last time. Satisfied, she spoke to herself and looked in a large floor-length mirror, "Mirror, mirror on the wall, who is the fairest and I might add best female real estate agent of all?" Curtsying, she remarked in a cocky fashion, "Of course…me!"

Her self admiration was interrupted by deep sounding chimes that signaled someone was at the front door. Looking out of the glassed-in side door panel she saw a man holding a briefcase. He stood, casually looking down at her assortment of pansies and begonias that surrounded a number of stone gnomes along the front of the house. Poofing her hair one last time she opened the door, and turned on the charm, displaying her expensive dental work as she smiled. "You must be Owen Webb?"

The man returned a soft smile. "I am…and you must be Mildred."

Opening the door widely so that he could enter she didn't see a vehicle of any sort in the driveway. "I hope you didn't walk all this way," she remarked, nodding toward the empty drive.

"Oh, my car," said Owen. "I just pulled around to that gravel section at the side of your house. If it's a problem I can go move it."

Shutting the door, Mildred waved her hand indicating that it was of no importance. "Not a problem. Please come in."

In the next few seconds she watched him walk into the living room. She not only surmised that he had sounded like a wealthy man due to their previous phone conversation, but now seeing him in person she thought that he looked very successful: tall, slim, but with a body frame that seemed to be well-toned. He appeared to be about her age give or take a few years, salt and pepper medium-length hair, nice facial features, and reading glasses that hung around his neck by a gold chain. His attire was casual but shouted of good taste: white trousers, fashionable leather belt, pin-striped gray and a white starched shirt beneath a turquoise light weight sweater. What impressed her the most was his shoes. She had learned early on that you could determine in most cases how successful an individual was by the condition of their shoes. In this case, the expensive looking cordovan loafers and brown argyle socks that encased his feet definitely gave the impression of success.

Turning in a complete circle, Owen spoke, "My compliments to you. Your home is absolutely gorgeous Mildred. I love your fireplace and your choice of colors. It's easy to see that you have very good taste."

Mildred smiled, gesturing toward the couch. "Why thank you, Mr. Webb. Please have a seat."

Seating himself, Owen laid the briefcase next to the couch. "Please...call me Owen."

"Picking up the pitcher of tea, Mildred offered, "How about some iced tea?"

"Love some," he answered.

Pouring Owen a glass she handed him the tea then walked to a chair opposite the couch and seated herself. "You look so familiar to me, Owen. You said that you were staying in Gatlinburg?"

"A lot of people tell me that I seem familiar to them. Just one of those faces I guess. And yes, I'm currently in Gatlinburg. It's only temporary until I can find the house I want."

"Did you just relocate in the area?"

Owen was about to answer her question when he looked in the direction of the kitchen, hearing the sharp, short yip of a pup. "Is that a pup I hear?"

"Yes it is. I've got them penned in the kitchen."

Standing, Owen held out his hands. "Could I take a look at them now?"

Mildred answered, "Of course. Just follow me."

Owen glanced toward the downstairs bath as he trailed behind her.

The pups were busy playing on the tiled floor, one chasing another; the third occupied his time by chewing on a small dog toy. The sight of the three pups brought a wide grin to Owen's face. "How cute!" Motioning toward the kitchen he asked, "May I?"

Mildred, still holding her tea answered, "Enjoy yourself."

Kicking off his loafers, Owen stepped over the low barricade and sat crossed legged on the floor, the pups instantly congregating at his feet. Picking one up, Owen brought it to his face and examined the belly of the pup then looked into the adorable face. One of the pups was nibbling at his socked feet, the third trying to crawl onto his leg. Owen placed the pup he was holding down onto the floor and picked the one up that was now on his leg. Inspecting the pup he looked up at Mildred, asking, "They seem to be having trouble walking. Their feet appear to be splayed. Is this normal for young pups?"

"It is quite normal," answered Mildred. "They are a little unsteady on their feet for the first two months or so. At about nine to ten weeks they seem to get their bearings."

Putting down the pup and picking up the third, Owen smiled. "I have no doubt that I'll be leaving with a pup today…that is if they're ready? I mean if I could get one today I'll write you a check."

"You've just purchased a new puppy," said Mildred. "Is there a particular one you'd like?"

Putting the pup on the floor, Owen stood. "It's really hard to make a choice. Why don't we return to the living room where you can tell me about the two log homes that you have. I'll choose one of the pups before I leave today."

Mildred took a drink of tea and smiled, realizing that everything seemed to be going her way this morning. As she walked back toward the living room, Owen slipped back into his shoes. Sitting on the couch, Mildred poured herself a second glass of tea while Owen walked over and bent down to open his briefcase. "I've got all of my credit and banking information with me."

Picking up her MLS listing Mildred responded, "We won't need any of that until after you decide on a house." The end of the couch prevented Mildred from observing Owen open his briefcase and slip on a pair of plastic gloves, then quickly soak a rag with the homemade chloroform. He walked nonchalantly around to the back of the couch and came up behind her.

"Let's see…the three bedroom is toward the middle of the listings. Right here…" Mildred's voice trailed off. She struggled slightly, but between Owen's arm across her chest and the drug-soaked rag she quickly succumbed to the chloroform. Her eyes rolled back in her head and she slowly drifted away.

Owen allowed Mildred to slump sideways on the couch, then looked at his watch. He had plenty of time but he had a lot he needed to accomplish before the drug wore off. Walking calmly to his briefcase he removed a roll of duct tape and a pocketknife. He cut a short section off and placed it firmly across her mouth then went about the process of binding both her legs and hands with longer strips. Satisfied with how everything seemed to be going, he put the knife in his pants pocket and the tape back into the case, then grabbed Mildred by her short hair and pulled her off the couch, her legs banging down onto the floor one of her white slippers jarred from her foot. Dragging her across the floor he opened a closet, stuffed her inside, then closed the door.

He went to the kitchen and checked on the pups. They would be all right for the moment. He walked back into the living room, picked up his case and went to the front door. Opening it slowly he made sure no one was around then walked around the side of the house to his van. He crawled inside and quickly changed from his casual business clothes to a pair of jeans, flannel shirt, heavy-duty white socks and work boots. With his black gym bag in hand, he headed for the back of the house.

Owen, reclining on the couch, was enjoying a good smoke with his pipe when he heard a thumping noise coming from the closet. *Finally, she's conscious,* he thought. He walked to the closet, opened the door and dragged Mildred out into the middle of the living room by her feet, her other slipper coming off of her foot. She looked up at Owen. Her eyes surprisingly were not filled with fear, but anger. She thrashed from side to side trying to yell, but the tape across her mouth prevented her from doing so. Grabbing her by the hair he pulled her to her feet and shoved her back into a chair. She tried to get up but it was impossible. She jerked violently from side to side. *Enough of this crap!* thought Owen. He ripped the duct tape from her face, grabbed her sweater and pulled her forward, slapping her three times then pushed her back down placing his hand around her throat. His face just inches from hers, he emphasized very clearly and precisely, "Mildred...if you don't settle down now... and I mean now...right now, I'll kill you right where you sit." The combination of the slapping and his stern tone of voice caused her to stare back at Owen, tears starting to stream down her face. "That's better now," said Owen. He let her drop back against the chair.

Back to the couch, Owen took a drink of his tea and sat down facing her. "I know you have questions...so ask. Asking and talking in a normal tone of voice is permitted, but there can be no screaming. If you scream it will only lead to me hurting you very badly, and we don't want that...right?" He took another drink then waited for her to speak.

Out of breath from struggling, Mildred spoke slowly, "Why are you...doing this?"

"Let's not put the cart before the horse. I think that first of all you should know who I am...or maybe a better way to put it is who I'm not. My name is not Owen Webb. That's just a name I thought up, however ,for communication purposes you can still refer to me as Owen. I'm not from Gatlinburg, not in search of a log home, nor do I need a puppy." Crossing his legs, Owen continued, "Now let's talk about who you are: Mildred Henks, successful real estate agent, tops in the state, well connected in Blount County, a potential political candidate, a very talented individual, a person who can not only deal with the little guy but who also runs with the big dogs. An impressive portfolio to say the least, however, like most folks, you have a dirty little secret that most people are not aware of. It's all connected to those cute pups out there in the kitchen. Despite the fact that there are legitimate breeders in the state…you're not one of them. You have been operating a puppy mill for years in that old barn you have out back."

Getting up and walking to the fireplace Owen placed his foot on a hassock that was setting in front of a chair. "I've seen programs on television and I've looked up puppy mills on the internet. The information I saw and learned about brought tears to my eyes. Dogs, both male and female kept captive in cages for years, never getting any exercise, never getting any fresh air, eating old dog food and never having fresh water to drink. They eat, sleep, crap, piss, breed and oftentimes die in a cage. And from the puppies that are produced, if they do not meet certain standards then they are destroyed, usually drowned or suffocated. I've been out to your barn. Your facility, if you want to call it that is deplorable. It's filthy, unhealthy and it stinks. There are many forms of inhumanity that one might consider low, but to treat animals in the fashion that you have ranks right at the bottom…"

Owen's description of Mildred's dreadful care for her dogs was interrupted by a bark that came from one of two downstairs bedrooms. Mildred, noticing the bark looked toward the room as Owen explained, "The beginning of the rescue of dogs from your grasp has already begun. I took the liberty of bringing all of the dogs into the house. The three adult males are in what I believe looks like your spare bedroom and the females, which I counted nine, are in your master bedroom. It appears that a couple of the females are pregnant. I also found three pups in the barn that I placed in the kitchen with the others."

He walked back to the couch and picked up his glass of tea. "How rude of me. Here I am going on and on when I told you if you had any questions to ask." Motioning toward Mildred, he offered, "Please, ask me anything you would like to know."

Mildred thought for a moment then in a soft voice asked, "What do you want from me? If it's money I can pay you a substantial amount."

Owen smiled. "I don't want any of your money."

"Then what do you want? Do you want the dogs? Take all of them."

"I want you to pay for what you have done to these dogs. The form of payment will not be in money. Your payment will be in the form of labor and I think we need to get started because you have a lot of work to do today." Walking over to her he attempted to retape Mildred's mouth but she wildly moved her head from side to side. He slapped her violently and warned her once again, "Settle down or I'll end your life!"

After the tape was placed over Mildred's mouth, Owen sat her up straight in the chair. Taking a long deep breath he stood back and looked at her then turned and walked toward the kitchen. "All right then…let's get to work."

The pups had curled up on the rug and gone to sleep. He grabbed a fifty pound unopened bag of dog food that he had located in the barn. Walking to the middle of the living room floor, with the use of his pocketknife he sliced open the bag and scattered the dry food across the rug, from one end of the room to the other. Throwing the empty bag in the corner, he went to an expensive looking walnut hutch on the opposite side of the room and opened the heavy wooden doors. Taking out a stack of what appeared to be expensive china plates, he dropped them on the floor. The dishes shattered, broken pieces scattering across the floor. Looking back at Mildred he shot her an *Oh well* glance, then shrugging his shoulders he remarked, "Sorry!" Tears were running down both of Mildred's cheeks. It appeared that Owen was going to destroy her home and everything in it.

Next, Owen removed a stack of china bowls, walked to the other side of the room and placed them in a neat row. Walking past Mildred, Owen winked at her and commented, "Interesting…isn't it?" Returning from the kitchen with a plastic bucket of cold water he filled the bowls then tossed the bucket in the same direction as the empty dog food bag. Making another trip to the kitchen he located a broom and a large dustpan in a utility closet then returned to where he had dropped the plates. Sweeping up the broken pieces he commented, "We can't have any of the dogs cutting their feet now can we?" Mildred's face was twisted in confusion. She had no idea what he was referring to.

He opened the master bedroom door and ushered out the nine females. He then opened the spare room door and let out the three males. The dogs were filthy from years of being harbored in the barn, their fur was matted, their toenails far beyond the point where they needed trimming. When the dogs slowly entered the living room, they seemed timid since they were not used to their new surroundings, but then two of the females discovered the dog food on the floor. After sniffing at the food they began to eat vigorously, the remaining ten dogs joining in on the feast.

Smiling, Owen walked to the couch and seated himself, facing Mildred. Removing his pipe from his gym bag he opened his tobacco pouch and went through the process of filling and lighting the pipe. Sitting back, he blew a long stream of smoke toward the ceiling and relaxed. He looked at Mildred. "You were in the closet when I first brought the dogs in. They seemed hesitant, almost skittish about being inside the house. I guess they're not used to the better things in life. Things like fresh food and water, nice soft carpet to walk on or a bed to lay in. I suppose it may be hard for them to adapt to the luxury of your home compared to the squalor you have forced them to experience for years." Looking back at the dogs that were busy eating and drinking, he commented. "Actually they seem to be adapting quite well...wouldn't you say?"

One of the dogs threw up on the carpet after eating too much. One of the females walked to the edge of the fireplace and crapped on the carpet, a male raised his leg and whizzed on the edge of a chair. Owen took another puff of his pipe and remarked, "Good dog!" Getting up, he said, "I need to check on the pups." On the way to the kitchen he stopped and looked down at Mildred. "Ya know if we had the time...which we don't, but if we did have the time, eventually your beautiful home could wind up being just as filthy as your barn." Laughing he walked to the kitchen.

Returning to the living room, Owen clasped his hands together and looked at the dogs scattered around the room. Some were still eating, others lying comfortably on the carpet. "Well, now let's see. Everyone seems to have had enough to eat and drink. Everyone seems to be comfortable, so I say...let's move on to the next thing, which is baths." Walking to the center of the room holding out his hands he explained, "I'm sure from the looks of your dogs that they have not, or may never have experienced the feeling of being clean. So...it's bath time! We don't have enough time for them to be groomed but I'd say if we…sorry, I mean *you* spend let's say about ten minutes per dog that means you'll be spending the next two hours bathing all of the dogs. The pups don't look all that bad but when you finish up with the others if we have the time I'll probably have you give them a quick bath also." Reaching into his gym bag he extracted three large bottles. "I took the liberty of dropping by the local pet store and I purchased some dog shampoo. I knew chances of finding anything like that around here would be remote to say the least." Snapping his fingers, Owen reminded himself, "That's right…we need something to put the dogs in so they can be washed." Opening a door that led to a back porch, Owen picked up two large stainless steel tubs that he sat in the middle of the dining room floor. "At first I was going to have you use your tub, but after thinking about it I thought it would be best if you bathed them out here."

He cut the tape from her ankles and wrists and helped Mildred to her feet and explained, "Now, here are the ground rules. I have hooked a hose up to your sink in the bathroom. I have also rounded up every towel I could locate in the house. Your job is to walk into the bathroom, turn on the water…we'll say lukewarm, then carry the end of the hose out here where you'll fill up both tubs, dumping in a small amount of shampoo in one. When the tubs are about three quarters of the way full, you'll go back and turn the water off, then I'll bring you the first dog which you will hand wash. Ten minutes later, after rinsing the dog in the other tub and drying the dog, we will dump the washing tub and repeat the process with each dog until the job is completed." Looking toward the ceiling thinking if he had overlooked anything he added, "One last thing. The tape will remain on your mouth the entire time." Clapping his hands once then rubbing them together, he ordered, "Let's get started." He then guided Mildred to the bathroom.

When both tubs were filled he forced her to her knees and brought the first dog to the washing tub. "Put him in," he instructed, "and be careful."

Mildred hoisted the first filthy dog into the tub and then began to rub her hands over the matted hair, the soapy water splashing out over the sides of the tub onto her hardwood flooring. Sitting on the couch Owen watched as he poured himself another glass of tea then lit his pipe.

When the ten minute mark arrived he ordered Mildred to remove the dog, rinse him and dry him off. When she hoisted the dog from the tub the dirty water ran down over the front of her pink outfit. After drying the dog from a stack of towels that Owen had placed in the corner of the room, he ordered her to let the dog go. The dog obviously feeling better now that he was relatively clean ran off into the living room and lay on the carpet rolling back and fourth. Owen smiled. "One down eleven to go." Getting up he started to drag the tub across the floor. "Don't get any ideas about running out the front door. You'll never make it!" When he got the tub to the doorway for the master bedroom he tipped the tub over, the filthy water ran into the room. Tears filled Mildred's eyes as she watched.

He returned the tub to the dining room and spoke sternly, but calmly, "Well, what are you doing on your knees? You know the drill. Get the hose, fill the tub, bathe another dog. Now move it!"

An hour and a half later Owen returned from dumping the ninth tub of dirty water into the master bedroom only to find Mildred curled up in a fetal position on the floor. She was soaked, mascara ran down the sides of her face, her bright red lipstick had been smudged, parts of her hair were wet and sticking out. She had given up.

Placing the tub on the floor in front of her, Owen looked at her with disgust. "You can't quit now. You've got three more dogs to go."

Mildred in defiance, shook her head back and forth slowly indicating. 'No more!'

"I don't have time for this," said Owen. Grabbing her by her right foot he started dragging her toward the bathroom, her screams muffled by the tape on her mouth. "Looks like I'm going to have to be a little more persuasive." Throwing her roughly to the tiled bathroom floor he grabbed her by the hair and forced her head down into the toilet bowl then flushed. Seconds later he jerked her head back up. She gagged and snorted, small bubbles forming in her nose. Forcing her head down again he hit the flush lever and repeated the process.

Dragging her back to the dining room he threw her down on the floor and calmly said, "And now I believe we can get started again." He placed his hands on his hips and stood over her, gently patting her on the shoulder. "I'll give you a moment so you can catch your breath...but then we must resume." Looking at his watch, he commented, "We're getting a little bit behind schedule."

After a few seconds, Mildred got to her feet and walked to the bath where she grabbed the hose. There was no fight left in her. All she could do now was to obey and hope that she would somehow survive. Falling onto her knees she began to fill the tub.

Thirty-five minutes later the last dog after being dried ran into the living room. Mildred lay on the floor exhausted. "Very good," approved Owen. Helping her to her feet he guided her to a chair. Positioning her, he once again secured her ankles and wrists with duct tape. "It's almost time for us to leave," he pointed out, placing a rag soaked with the homemade chloroform over her nose. Mildred's head slowly dropped forward then she slumped back on the chair.

Putting a fresh pair of plastic gloves over his hands, Owen went to the back porch where he brought a dog cage into the house and sat it in the middle of the kitchen floor. Placing a soft blanket inside the cage he carefully scooped up the pups and deposited them in the cage. He watched as they snuggled together. He smiled. Their lives were about to get a lot better. Setting the cage near the back porch door he walked back into the living room and checked on the other dogs. Two were eating, one was drinking, the others were lounging around on the carpet. They too had begun the journey toward a better way of life.

Making sure that the front door was unlocked he turned the kitchen light on, grabbed his gym bag and pipe, and set them next to the cage that the pups were in and then stepped out onto the porch and brought in yet another larger cage that he had taken earlier from the barn. Next he dragged the unconscious Mildred across the floor where he proceeded to stuff her inside the cage. It was a tight fit and he had to pull her back out in order to position her the way he wanted. Once she was in position he taped her hands and bare feet to the cage so that her fingers and toes were sticking out between the wires of the cage. He then went to the refrigerator and opened the freezer where he found a frozen steak, some hot dogs and some ground beef which he put in the front of the cage along with a small stack of Mildred's business cards.

Outside, he walked to the van and checked to make sure no one was around then returned to the porch where he picked up his bag and the cage with the pups and carried them to the van. Then he returned and dragged the cage containing Mildred around the side of the house to the van and placed all three in the back.Going back inside, he walked the living and dining rooms and the kitchen making sure everything was left just like he wanted it to be. Satisfied, he walked back to the living room, petting each dog. "Well, boys and girls, within a few weeks you should all have new homes."

Making sure the backdoor was unlocked, he walked out to the van, started it and backed out to the front of the house where he turned around and drove down the long driveway, thinking to himself: *An eye for an eye and a tooth for a tooth!*

CHAPTER SEVEN

KENNY JACKS STOOD in front of the shift board posted on the station wall. He rubbed his eyes and yawned. It had been a long night and he was ready to sign out and call it a day. Coming up behind Kenny, Brody ordered, "Move!" Kenny quickly stepped to the side so that Brody could pass. Brody dropped an old canvas bag on the floor and went over to the coffee pot.

After almost a month ón the Townsend Police force, Kenny still wasn't used to the way Brody talked to him. When he was in Maryville everything ran much smoother and Sheriff Grimes had respect for his officers. Kenny realized that if he had just seven more months' time in on the Maryville force, he wouldn't be the one putting up with Chief Brody. He was the rookie and he was the one who had been temporarily transferred to Townsend for the summer. With an unsolved murder on the books the Sheriff's Department of Blount County decided that Townsend needed an additional officer to keep the place running smoothly and make everyone in town feel a little safer.

Grant, seated in the corner, tied his shoes. Butch, on the other side of the room, was holding a cup of coffee. Brody put his cup on his desk and threw his Stetson at the hook on the wall. The hat landed on the edge of the hook, rocked back and forth and settled in for the day. "Now listen, and listen good!" he barked, "I haven't had any time off in thirty days and I'm goin' fishin'. Against my better judgment I'm goin' to leave you three bozos to run this place for a few hours." Looking around the room, he asked sarcastically, "Do ya think you can handle it?"

No one responded. When Brody was in one of his moods everyone realized that normal communication was out the window. Picking up his coffee and taking a drink, Brody commented, "Good. Jacks, you get out of here and get some rest so you can be ready for tonight. Butch, I want you to stay here at the station. Denlinger…you're on patrol. Any questions?"

There was a moment of silence then Brody remarked, "Good, I didn't think so. I'll be leavin' in a few minutes. I'll have my cell phone with me and my radio will be on the whole time I'm gone." Standing, he ordered, "You don't call me unless it's a got damn emergency. You call me to ask some piddly ass question and I'll kick your butt when I get back. Understand?"

No one responded. Brody shook his head in approval, then picked up the canvas bag and strode toward the bathroom. "I need some time off and by God, I'm gonna get it." He disappeared into the small bathroom, Grant, Butch and Kenny just looking at one another, well aware that if anything was said Brody could still hear them. Brody reappeared a few minutes later wearing baggy green pants, a white tee shirt and a baseball cap with a Caterpillar emblem advertised just above the bill. "See ya'll later," he snapped as he opened the door, slammed it shut and headed for his truck.

Butch, who was normally in Brody's pocket, stuck his middle finger in the air and smartly remarked, "Hope you fall in and drown you fat bastard!"

"What's got you going?" asked Grant. "I thought you an ol' Axel were good buddies."

"Hell no!" said Butch, pitching the rest of his coffee in a nearby trashcan. "I cuddle up to him here at the office, but I'm sick of him coming by my house in the evening and drinking all my beer and rattling off his line of crap. Me and Dana Beth can't even spend an evening alone without his fat ass sitting on my porch."

Grant, remembering weeks ago, the fiasco between he and Butch over Dana Beth felt like responding but didn't want to start his day off with sore knuckles from punching Butch in the mouth. Taking a deep breath he calmed his emotions then said, "I'm gonna hit the john, then I'm outta here."

Minutes later Grant came out of the bathroom, a broad grin plastered across his face. "Look what I found on the back of the toilet." Holding up Brody's cell phone he elaborated, "Wonder how long it'll be before he discovers it's missing?" Setting Brody's cell on the desk, he turned to Kenny, "If you're ready to go I'll give you a lift over to the motel."

Kenny, getting up from his chair yawned and stretched his hands over his head. "Yep, I'm ready."

Climbing into the patrol car, Grant asked, "What on earth made you decide to stay here at a motel when you could just drive home every night?"

Kenny, rolling down the passenger side window laughed. "I'm still living with my folks and at the moment I don't have a girlfriend, so there really isn't a reason for me to drive back to Maryville every night. Besides that, it was Sheriff Grimes' idea that I stay here. The county is paying for the room. Grimes said if I got tired of staying over I could drive back and forth if I wanted to. For now, I think I'll just stay put."

Laughing, Grant pulled out of the parking lot. "Wonder how long it will be before the chief realizes he doesn't have his phone with him? I've heard about his so-called fishing adventures. It's more about drinking than it is fishing. I bet he's got a twelve pack with him. Hell, he's probably sucked down at least two already."

Turning onto Chestnut Hill Road, Grant slowed down to allow two women walking dogs to cross the street. Watching the women and the dogs cross the intersection, Kenny remarked, "Ya know it's strange. We've had at least six or seven calls that I know of in the past few weeks about neighborhood dogs missing. The last lady that called said she and her neighbor were talking and thought that someone was stealing dogs in the Townsend area..."

Before Kenny could finish up what he was saying the radio crackled with static. Leaning over Grant removed the radio from its holder and flipped the ON switch. "Officer Denlinger."

"Grant, it's Butch. Just got a call from the Laurel Hills Country Club. They want somebody up there right away. Manager seemed pretty upset. He said it was an emergency."

"On my way," answered Grant. Returning the radio to the dashboard he looked across the seat at Kenny. "Wanna ride along or do you want me to drop you off? I mean this won't take long. Someone probably left without paying a tab or maybe some local kids are up there vandalizing the golf course again."

"No problem," said Kenny. "I can ride along." He slid down in the seat and closed his eyes. "Wake me when it's all over."

Turning on the siren Grant headed for Laurel Valley Road. Once out of the city limits he floored the patrol car. He remembered how, when he was much younger, his grandparents had been members of the club. From time to time they used to take him there for lunch. There were white tablecloths on every table and fancy looking chairs with ornate arms, huge chandeliers hung from the ceiling and the waiters always wore tuxedos. He told Dalton that someday he wanted to be rich enough to be a member at the club. That was years ago. He sure wasn't going to get rich working as an officer of the law.

Five minutes later he turned onto Country Club Drive, drove the short distance to the main entrance where he saw Dave Browning, manager of the club and Bob Pierce, the local golf pro standing on the elaborate steps. Pulling up to the front of the circled drive Grant stopped the car and climbed out. "Hey Dave…what's up?"

Dave bounded down the steps quickly. "You're not going to believe this one. Follow me…I've got a very upset golfer in my office."

Following Dave back up the steps, Grant shook Bob's hand. "What's going on Bob?"

Entering the building the trio started down the carpeted hall, Bob pointing toward the office at the end of the hallway. "I better let the golfer tell you the story. I may leave some of the details out." Dave opened the office door. There were two valets standing by a man seated next to a desk.

Grant immediately recognized the man. It was Clark Deering, the owner of a restaurant in Townsend. He was part of a foursome that played the course every Saturday. Clark's hands were shaking while he wiped the perspiration from his forehead. One of the valets handed him a glass of water.

"Mr. Deering. What's going on?" asked Grant.

Taking a sip of water Clark started his story, "I got here early this morning. The others weren't here yet so I decided to go up and chip some balls on the ninth green. That way I could watch for them when they came in. I was doing okay, but then I started hitting one ball after another into the woods behind the green. After a while I went into the woods to retrieve any balls I could find. They were Titleist, good balls and I didn't want to lose them all. Well, I'm walking along swinging my club back and forth in the tall grass at the edge of the woods when I hit what I thought was a ball. It landed right on the edge of the green. When I bent down to pick it up I couldn't believe my eyes. It was a toe…a toe with bright red polish on the nail. At first I thought it was one of those fake plastic toes you can buy at the novelty store. I thought maybe somebody was just playing a trick by putting it near the golf course where it would be found. But when I started to pick it up I noticed there were bugs crawling on it and I could also see the crusted blood. Man, was I shocked!" Clark shook his head, squinting his eyes, still not believing what had happened. "I've never seen anything like it. I just kept thinking there's a person out there that's either dead or hurt really bad."

Grant was taken completely off-guard. He had expected a drunken guest or maybe someone trying to slip out without paying their bill. He hadn't, in his wildest imagination been expecting something like this. Looking at Dave, he asked, "Where's the toe? Did anyone pick it up or is it still out there?"

Dave picked up a plastic bag from the corner of the desk. "Got it right here, Grant. I didn't touch it. I picked it up with the bag."

Taking the bag from Dave, Grant examined it as best he could. It definitely was a toe. There was a small collection of insects inside the bag crawling over the flesh. "Good, Dave. You did the right thing. Now, will someone show me where it was found?"

Clark stood, took another drink of water and announced, "I think I'll be all right now. Come on…I'll show you."

Walking out a side door of the office, Dave, Bob, Clark and Grant started across a grassy area that led to the ninth green. Clark, walking just in front of Grant, turned and asked, "What do you suppose happened? Do you think it was a bear attack? I remember one time, I guess it was about two years ago, when we had our cart parked on the path over on the main fairway. We happened to look over and there bigger than life is a big ol' black bear trying to get our sandwiches out of our cooler. We kept our distance but started to yell and wave our hands. He took off running into the woods after a few seconds."

"It's hard to say at this point," said Grant. "Until we get in there and check things out…well, we just won't know." Walking across the manicured grass of the ninth hole, Grant experienced an uneasy feeling that was beginning to creep into his mind: *I sure hope this isn't what I'm thinking. Not again!*

At the edge of the green, Grant stopped and began to take control of the situation. "Here's what I want you to do, Bob. I want you to clear the golf course right away. Get some of your employees to go out on the course and tell all of the golfers that they have to come back in. If they give you any crap tell them there has been a serious accident and the police are here. Dave, I want you to go into the clubhouse and make sure the guests stay inside. The last thing we need is a bunch of gawkers getting in the way."

"But what am I going to tell the guests?" asked Dave. "They'll want to know what's going on."

Grant thought for a moment then responded, "Just say we think there is a bear in the area and we can't take a chance on anyone getting injured. Whatever you do, do not, and I repeat, do not tell them about the toe." Dave and Bob turned and started for the clubhouse as Grant spoke to Clark, "Look, you just stay put for a moment. I need to go back to my car and get a few things I might need. Be right back."

"Well don't take too long," said Clark. "Hell, there might just be a damn bear out here!"

Back at the patrol car Grant shook Kenny's shoulder. "Hey, wake up! I think I'm gonna need your help."

Kenny sat up, for a moment not remembering where he was. "Oh...sure. I must've really dozed off. What's going on?"

He watched Grant open the glove box and removed a couple of small plastic bags and two sets of plastic gloves. Then he reached up and unlatched the rifle from its holder behind the seat. Taking the safety off Grant checked to make sure the gun was loaded.

Kenny was definitely awake now. "Hey...this looks serious!" He quickly exited the car and joined Grant.

Grant took a deep breath, then ordered, "Come on...follow me." They trotted across the grass back to the green where Clark was still waiting. Clark had a strange look on his face when he saw the rifle.

Grant walked past Clark but then stopped as he said, "All right Mr. Deering, lead the way."

Reluctantly taking the lead Clark walked across the green and then into the weeds at the edge of the woods, pointing at a row of Azalea bushes. "It was right over there."

Seeming to be a little unsteady on his feet Grant took his arm. "Are you sure you're okay, Mr. Deering?"

"Yes...I think so. I'm just a tad bit shaken from this ordeal." He walked closer to the Azaleas that were in full bloom, their red and orange colors a sharp contrast to the deep green grass that separated the woods from the ninth green. "There...it was right there," he blurted out, pointing to a small clearing just behind a shrub.

Looking down at the shrub, Grant spoke without looking at Clark, "Thanks, Mr. Deering. You can go back to the clubhouse and don't mention anything about this."

Clark didn't need any prodding. He turned and immediately started across the green.

Grant stepped into the tall weeds. "Kenny, we're going to have a look around. We need to stay close together especially after we get in behind the tree line."

Kenny not too sure of what was going on, asked, "And what is it exactly that we are looking for?"

Grant answered then stepped deeper into the weeds, "Well, I'm not sure. One of the golfers found a human toe out here. It had red nail polish and blood on it. Probably belonged to a woman."

Kenny stopped walking, then repeated, "A human toe!   No body...just a toe?"

"That's right," said Grant. "Now let's see if we can find any other body parts or maybe even a body."

"Wait a minute. Shouldn't we call for backup? I mean if there's a body out here."

"We don't know that for sure. There might be nothing more to report. Come on."

Stepping between two bushes Grant kept his eyes on the ground. Kenny followed all the while looking from the right to the left. A few yards into a thicket they came to a dirt hiking path. There was nothing that seemed unusual or out of place. No sign of blood on the leaves or low shrubs, no area of the forest floor that seemed to be disturbed. Slowly they started down the path searching both sides for something out of the ordinary.

Grant suddenly stopped, turning in a complete circle. "Okay...come on now. There must be something around here we're missing. A toe just doesn't up and walk onto a golf course." Ready to give up, he suggested, "Maybe we should go back and call the station." Starting up the path again he looked off into the nearby trees. "Aw, what the hell. A few more minutes won't make a big difference."

A few yards further up the path Grant saw something that was rectangular laying just on the edge of the path. It was light brown and stuck out like a sore thumb. Slowly he bent down and picked the article up. "Look at this, Kenny. It's a business card. Silently he read the card, then read it out loud:

MILDRED HENKS
REALTOR
Specializing in vacation
homes for those who wish
to be pampered

Flipping the card over, he read the other side:

MILDRED HENKS
REALTOR
1-645-555-9000
593 Old Chilhowee Rd.
Townsend, Tennessee

Mildred Henks...Mildred Henks, he thought. Where had he heard that name before? It seemed like it had been recently. Then he remembered that day weeks ago when he had been at the Parkway Grocery and had run into Asa's pals. It was her horn honking that had gotten their attention and eventually led to a conversation about how Asa had been sweet on her but that she didn't want anything to do with him. What in the hell was one of her cards doing out here in the woods? Sticking it in his pocket he thought that someone had just dropped it accidentally.

Kenny drifted off the path a few feet into the woods thinking that he saw something. "Oh my God...I think I just might have found what we're looking for."

Joining Kenny, Grant stared at a wire animal cage that was lying in plain site next to a tree. A pool of dark blood surrounded the cage. There was something in the cage but they couldn't tell what it was. Walking closer they tried to make sense of what the object was. An army of insects was feasting on whatever it was. Grant gently kicked the side of the cage many of the insects scrambled for safety. Leaning closer they noticed strands of what appeared to be red hair and pieces of torn flesh protruding through the small wire squares of the cage. The ground surrounding the cage was covered with chards of soft tissue and bones along with sections of torn material that looked like pink satin. Kenny, just about to puke backed away, commenting in a disgusting voice, "At first I thought it was an animal carcass...but it's a human being."

Not paying attention to what Kenny was saying Grant bent over and looked inside the cage. "Look at that. It looks like the remains of one of those packages of ground beef that you get at the market...and that's not all. Look there in the corner of the cage. It looks like hotdogs that have been chewed on."

Kenny, having regained his composure, leaned closer for a better look. "Yeah, and look at that large bone next to the ground beef package."

Standing up Grant looked around the area. The ground in places was covered with muddy or blood soaked business cards. Carefully he picked one up. It was identical to the card he had found back on the path. Then he noticed something that was definitely out of place in the woods: Hanging on the tree was an unsullied white, silk scarf with the initials *MH* embroidered on the end. Grant looked down at the card in his hand then back to the scarf and then finally back to the body in the cage. It didn't take any great feat of detective work to figure that the body in the cage was more than likely that of Mildred Henks.

Kenny let out a low whistle. "This is bizarre. Somebody stuffed a person in that cage and left them out here. Look here," he said pointing at her hands. "Her fingers have been cut off...or chewed off." Snapping his fingers as if he had a revelation Kenny suddenly perked up. "Hey wait a sec. That other guy that was murdered...Asa Pittman. Weren't his fingers cut off?"

Grant, who was standing at the back of the cage, noticed the bloody stumps that at one time had been feet. "Yeah...you're right. Pittman did have his fingers cut off. I was at the crime scene and saw his hands up close. They were definitely cut off by some sort of a tool. If the same person committed both murders they've changed up their methods a little bit. In this case the toes were cut off also."

Walking around to the front of the cage Grant looked into the face of Mildred Henks. Her mouth was covered with duct tape and her eyes were wide open like she wanted to scream and scream and scream. "I've seen enough," said Grant. "We need to get some help up here."

Kenny just kept staring at the cage. "Whew! Whoever did this was one crazy son of a bitch. They must have really hated this lady."

Retracing their steps they finally made it back to the ninth green where Dave and Bob were waiting at the edge of the woods. When Grant and Kenny stepped out of the trees, Bob spoke, "We're working on getting the course cleared. Most of the golfers are being cooperative but a few of them are really pissed."

Dave waited until Bob was finished talking, then spoke, "We told the members and guests to stay in the clubhouse until further notice." Looking past Grant and Kenny into the woods, Dave commented, "We were worried about you two. Did you find anything?"

Putting the rifle over his shoulder, Grant answered, "Yeah we did. There's a body back there on the trail. It's pretty bad." Glancing toward the clubhouse and the throng of people looking in their direction, Grant suggested, "Kenny, why don't you, Dave and Bob hang out here and make sure nobody gets back in there. I need to make some calls. I'll be back in a few."

All eyes from the clubhouse were on Grant as he walked across the grass to the patrol car where he reached in the window for the radio. Placing the rifle on the seat he spoke into the transmitter, "Butch...come in. It's me,Grant. Is Brody back yet?"

A response came back instantly, "Nope, haven't seen him," said Butch. "Are you still up at the country club?"

"Yeah, and we've got quite a mess up here."

"What's going on?"

"I'll tell you what's going on! There's a dead body up here in the woods just off the ninth hole and I need some help."

There was silence on the other end of the radio but Butch finally asked, "Do you need me to drive up there?"

"No, but you do need to see if you can find Brody. I can't wait around until his sorry ass decides to show up. I've got to make a decision on what needs to be done out here."

"Well, you do whatever you think is right but," said Butch, "just remember, you better be ready for the wrath of Brody when he finds out you did something without his permission. This is his town, his territory, and we all know he doesn't like anyone making decisions without his blessing."

"The hell with Brody," said Grant. "I can't wait on him. Look, if he calls in or shows up at the station tell him to get up here...pronto!" Hanging the radio back up, he fastened the rifle back on the rack. Grabbing a roll of yellow crime scene tape from under the seat, he started back toward the green. Tossing the tape to Kenny he ordered, "You need to cordon off the green and also the path back there in the woods. Once you get the path taped off stay back there in case anybody comes down the trail. Tell them it's closed and that they need to get out of the area. No explanation, just tell them they have to leave. Anybody gives you any grief give me a yell." Turning to Dave and Bob he continued to give instructions, "I need you two to stay here on the course and keep people away. I've got another call to make."

Back at the car again he picked up his cell phone that was laying on the dash and dialed the number he desired. Following two rings a pleasant female voice answered, "Blount County Sheriff's Office. Can I help you?"

"Yes, this is Officer Grant Denlinger of the Townsend Police Department. I am at the Laurel Hills Country Club and we have a body up here. It looks like a definite homicide. I'm going to need the sheriff, a couple of men and the coroner up here."

The dispatcher seemed a little confused. "Officer Denlinger. Where is the chief of your department?"

Frustrated, Grant responded, "Look I don't know where he is. Sorry, but he's out of contact. He took the day off. I don't have time to play twenty questions, so just get this message to the sheriff."

There was a slight hesitation on the other end of the line then a response, "Hmm, okay. We're on our way!"

Throwing his cell phone on the seat, Grant knew the next few hours were going to be chaotic. He had a lot on his mind and the last thing he needed was to overstep his authority and put his whole department in jeopardy. He hated to do it, but he had to soft pedal Brody's abrupt disappearance. Leaning up against the car he hoped Brody would call before the Blount County Sheriff arrived.

Looking out across the vast golf course the last few golfers were walking toward the clubhouse. Soon they would no doubt join the crowd of people who had gathered at the outdoor swimming pool as they stared across the grass at the ninth green. Looking at his watch he knew it'd be a good fifteen to twenty minutes before reinforcements arrived.

Walking back to the green he asked Dave, "I don't suppose you have any drinks in the clubhouse you could bring out?"

"We sure do," said Dave. "I'll get some. What'll it be...beer, wine, whiskey?"

"Well, you fellas can drink whatever you want but me and Kenny are on duty so we'll have to settle for water or soda. Tell you what. Surprise us."

Dave trotted off across the green as he hollered back, "Be back in a jif."

As tense as things seemed to be Grant managed a smile. "I need you to stay here, Bob and keep watch for the county sheriff. I'm going to check on Kenny and see if he needs a hand."

After talking with Kenny for ten minutes Grant walked back out to the green when three Blount County Police vehicles followed by the coroner's van pulled in. Grant signaled them to drive across the grass.

Bert Grimes, the county sheriff, who Grant had met before on a couple of occasions climbed out of the first car before it even came to a complete halt. Walking across the green he approached Grant. "Whatcha got, Denlinger?"

Pointing in the direction of the woods, Grant explained, "We've got a woman's body stuffed inside some sort of animal cage back in there next to a hiking trail. I think her name is Mildred Henks. She's from out on Old Chilhowee Road somewhere." Then he remembered. Reaching in his pocket he removed the card. "We found a number of her business cards scattered around."

Grimes gave Grant a sideways look and asked, "You sure about all of this."

"Yeah, I'm pretty sure and when you get back in there you'll see what I mean."

Jeff Bookman, the coroner, overheard the very end of the conversation. Stepping forward, he shook Grant's hand. "Good to see you again, Grant. You're becoming an old hand at this. Lead the way."

Bert called his three men over to where he was standing. "One of you needs to station yourself over there by the pool. Don't answer any questions and keep those people away from this area. I see some folks starting to gather down in the parking lot. Keep an eye on them. You other two men need to remain here around the green."

Just then Dave returned with a bucket filled with ice and sodas. "Afternoon, Sheriff Grimes. Just thought you boys would like something cold to drink." Grimes made a face that indicated 'No thanks.'

Grimes turned to walk away and Dave tried his best to defend his position and to make sure he had done everything right up to this point. "Sheriff, I had the golf pro clear the course and we have tried to keep our guests confined to the swimming pool area."

"That's good," said Grimes, walking into the woods.

Seconds later, he found himself on the trail, yellow tape wrapped around several trees and across the path. Nodding his approval he asked, "Who put the tape up?"

Grant stepped close to Grimes. "That would be Kenny Jacks." Pointing to Kenny who was standing guard near the body, Grant explained, "He's actually one of your men on loan to us for the summer."

Grimes remained quiet while he walked around the area assessing the crime scene. Satisfied, he turned to Bookman. "It's all yours, Jeff." Looking at Grant, he asked, "Where's Chief Brody?"

Grant, taken off guard couldn't think of anything to say except, "I don't know, Sir."

Grimes put his hands on his hips and looked off into the deep woods, then commented, "When you boys get finished in here give me a holler. I'm gonna try to get hold of Brody."

Jeff, already gloved up, motioned to Grant, "Come on, I need some help. If this sort of thing keeps up, why you'll be an expert before you know it."

Jeff stood over the cage and looked at the body. "Same M.O. as the Pittman murder. All the fingers cut off." Looking at the back of the cage he went on, "Only difference is…well, got the toes this time also." Surveying the inside of the cage Bookman explained "Looks like the local critters tried to get at that meat in the cage." Leaning over he smelled the arm that was hanging out the front of the cage. Gently running his finger down the bare skin he remarked, "Her arm feels greasy and it smells like someone smeared raw ground beef on her arm." Pointing at a ripped styrofoam package he indicated, "The rest of the ground beef was pitched in the back of the cage along with some hotdogs, and that bone next to her body, that is not from a human. It's from a t-bone steak. Whoever did this wanted to attract animals." Standing he pointed back down at the body. "There's lots of bite marks on the body…maybe raccoons or possums. See all those long scratches on her sides and back?"

Leaning up against a tree he scanned the ground. "There are a lot of animal tracks around here. Raccoon tracks for sure. Probably mice or rats, maybe fox or coyotes. Depending on how long the body has been out here she could have had quite a few furry visitors." Holding up a finger to make a point he suggested, "Now this is just speculation on my part, but the killer may have just figured that if he was lucky the combination of the smell of the blood and the raw meat might just attract a bear." Nodding at the surrounding woods he gave his further opinion, "Even though this area would be considered on the remote side, still, with all the activity at the golf course which is only, what twenty, thirty yards away most bears would tend to shy away. This is just too close to civilization. However, if the body was here long enough a bear might be bold enough to attempt a careful examination of the smells and would be quite capable of prying the cage open and getting to the body, especially the meat."

Looking around at the surrounding trees, Bookman went on, "I'll tell you what, Grant, I've been doing this kind of work for quite some time. We don't get that many murders in these parts, but these last two, Asa Pittman and it looks like Mildred Henks are by far the weirdest. We may not know tomorrow or maybe even for a few days but right now it's looking like we've got a real psychopath on our hands." Looking back at what was left of the body he walked toward the trail. "Let's see what else we can find around here."

A crowd had formed on the balcony of the clubhouse and in and around the swimming pool area. Occasionally someone would yell out a question directed at the officer who had been stationed near the clubhouse. The officer wasn't giving them much in the way of information and the crowd was becoming more insistent as they shouted at the officer. Finally, Bert had enough. Walking over to his car he retrieved a bullhorn from the backseat. Standing in the middle of the grassy area in front of the green he raised the horn which he very rarely used to his mouth and ordered, "Now listen up folks. I know you all have questions but right now we don't have any answers. What I need is your cooperation. I want everyone to remain in the clubhouse unless you're leaving for the day. But if you stay you must not enter the golf course."

A low grumble went up from the crowd, one man shouting back, "This is private property. We pay dues!"

Bert was getting irritated but his anger was not reflected by the tone of his voice. "You'll have more than dues to pay if I catch anybody out on the course before it reopens."

Walking back into the woods he removed his sunglasses and remarked to Grant and Jeff, "This is one hell of a mess. I can't imagine what tomorrow is going to be like when the news gets hold of this."

Grant didn't say anything but in his own mind he knew that if tomorrow was anything like the aftermath of Asa Pittman's murder the town was going to be in chaos.

Picking up his black medical case, Jeff commented, "Well, we've got a lot of work to do, Grant. We need to go over this area with a fine toothcomb. We have to make sure we don't miss anything."

Grant noticed Kenny who had remained silent for the past few minutes. Despite the horrific scene and the intense conversation, Kenny looked like he was asleep on his feet. Approaching Kenny, Grant asked, "You gonna be all right?"

"Yeah, I'll be fine…just a little tired."

"Why don't you go back out and check with the sheriff," suggested Grant, "and see if there's anything he needs done. If not, then maybe you can catch a ride back to town with one of the other officers. You need to get some rest. Tomorrow will be a day when there won't be much."

Nodding, Kenny walked back to the path and disappeared in the woods.

His attention once again focused on the crime scene, Grant joined Jeff at the tree where he was bagging up the scarf. "All right, what do you need me to do?" asked Grant.

"For starters," said Jeff, "You can start to bag those business cards while I gather some hair and skin samples."

Grant picked up the first of many cards. "Do you think Mildred was already dead when she was brought up here?"

"I doubt it," remarked Jeff. "Whoever killed her wouldn't have cut off her toes and fingers until they got here. Otherwise, it would have been a bloody mess. There would be blood in the killer's vehicle and traces of blood on the trail where the victim had been dragged in. No, I think that deed was done right here. Let's pray that she was drugged…possibly like Pittman, before the killer left her. One thing for sure. The killer wanted her to be found for some reason." Jeff pointed at the small ruts in the ground leading from the trail, then at the marks on the path. "The cage had to be dragged from that direction. The closest place to park around here aside from the country club would be over at Laurel Lake which isn't that far from here…maybe a couple of hundred yards. Why don't you follow those marks up the trail while I finish up here."

Grant nodded and started up the trail. Going around a slight curve in the path he tried to imagine the scene that took place hours earlier. The perpetrator had to be someone with a decent amount of strength to get the cage out of the vehicle and then drag it down the path.

Before he knew it the trail ended at a small paved parking lot next to the edge of a small inlet that was part of Laurel Lake. He had been to this location many years ago when he had been in the Boy Scouts. Laurel Lake was a popular spot for hiking and fishing. The marks made on the dirt path where the cage had been dragged ended at the lot. This is where the vehicle had been parked. He stood there looking out across the water wondering what the killer was doing at that very moment. As he or she sitting at home watching television or maybe enjoying lunch somewhere, or perhaps one of the crowd standing back at the country club? Maybe they were planning who their next victim was going to be.

Returning to the crime scene Grant told Jeff that he had located the area where the vehicle may have been parked.

"I think I've got just about everything I need," said Jeff. "Let's walk over to the parking area by the lake and take a look around."

Walking up the path toward the lake, Jeff explained, "These outdoor murders are hell to investigate. You're never the first one on the scene. A lot of varmints and insects always arrive before we do. It's strange we didn't locate any more fingers or toes. They were probably carried off into the woods somewhere where they made a great snack. Later on today I'll get some boys to comb the surrounding area to see if we can find any. It'll be like searching for a needle in a haystack. If and when we do find them there may be nothing left but bone."

Arriving at the lake, Jeff looked out across the beautiful body of water and commented, "This is such a beautiful place. It's hard to imagine the pain Mildred Henks had to go through out here." Placing his arm around Grant he continued, "I have a feeling this might just be the beginning. I know this hasn't been easy...especially for you. I mean you've been at both crime scenes. From what I've been able to tell you're a pretty good officer. I'm sure you'll do everything you can to find out who did this."

Grant looked at the peaceful lake and thought to himself, *Two murders in less than three months. Asa Pittman and Mildred Henks.*

Is there a connection between the two? Then he remembered what Asa's friends had shared with him that time at the Parkway Grocery: *Asa had been sweet on Mildred.*

CHAPTER EIGHT

GRANT, STANDING ON THE EDGE of the country club's paved parking lot stared out across the expansive golf course, the lush fairways of the first and second holes appearing as long, giant green snakes. The remainder of the course was hidden from his view except for a small section of the third and tenth holes that peeked out from behind a tree line separating the rest of the course. The popular golf course, a Mecca for golfers from across the country in the Great Smoky Mountains area was normally packed with avid golfers this time of year. It was a unique course to say the least. A great place to play golf; a course that seemingly had been dropped in the middle of wooded hills and mountains, the seclusion and peacefulness of The Great Smokies makes a golfing experience that would not soon be forgotten.

In the distance to the east the low Foothills of Eastern Tennessee jutted just above the trees. Glancing back down at the empty golf course, it reminded him of a picture postcard vacation setting with various shades of green from the meadow and the surrounding forest, the curving gray pathways that weaved in and out of tall clumps of trees. The course, normally buzzing with foursomes carrying golf bags, some less physical golfers riding golf carts, was barren of habitation at the moment. The valley before him was the perfect example of what Blount County was more commonly referred to: The Peaceful Side of the Smokies.

Turning he faced the pristine clubhouse with its beige siding and green roof. A long row of green golf carts adorned with white lettering: *Laurel Hills Country Club and Golf Course* lined the back of the building. The swimming pool and outdoor dining area was packed with golfers, vacationers and club members, congregated in groups, smoking or sipping on their favorite beverages. They were all facing west, many pointing in the direction of the ninth green some fifty yards away where the Blount County Coroner's van and three police cruisers had been parked. Bright yellow crime scene tape encircled the area. The coroner instructed three officers of the Maryville Police to load the remains of Mildred Henks in the back of the van. A few miles to the west stood the Great Smoky Mountains. *What a peaceful backdrop* thought Grant. *Not today.* The spectacular view was marred by the heinous murder of yet a second victim in less than three months.

The van pulled out followed by one of the cruisers. Grant decided to try and locate Chief Brody once again. Reaching in the open window of his cruiser he unhooked the radio from its holder. "Marge...this is Grant."

The Townsend Police Department's secretary answered immediately, "Brody is still not her,e Grant. I've tried to call him at home, on his radio...nothing!"

Grant, frustrated, tried to remain calm. "Where in the blazes is he?"

Marge responded, trying her best to answer, "You know it's his day off Grant. He normally goes fishing somewhere."

"Maybe so," said Grant, "but still he should at least have his cell phone on him in case of an emergency...and we do have an emergency on our hands...another murder!"

"There's nothing I can do Grant...I'm so sorry."

"It's not your fault Marge, listen, where is Butch right now?"

"He left here about an hour ago. Said he was gonna try to find Axel."

"I can't believe this. We've had a second murder and our police chief doesn't even know about it." Taking a deep breath Grant looked out across the golf course. "Marge...if and when you get hold of Brody have him give me a call."

"Will do, Grant."

Hanging the radio back up, he turned, coming face to face with Bert Grimes. Bert as always was dressed in a khaki brown county sheriff's uniform. His black shoes were shined to military standards. Lighting a cigarette Bert smiled, then asked, "Did you manage to raise Brody yet?"

Embarrassed that the county sheriff from Maryville had to respond to a murder in the Townsend area because the local police chief could not be located, Grant answered, "Not yet. I just called the office. They still don't know where he is. Miller just left the office to see if he could locate him."

Looking back toward the ninth green, Bert took a drag on his smoke. "I'm going to leave two of my officers here to keep an eye on the crime scene. I gave the state police a call. They'll be sending over a crime scene investigator."

Grant, wanting to get off the subject of his absent chief asked, "I guess the Feds will be dropping by also?"

"Not on this one," said Bert. "From what we've been able to deduce so far it appears Henks was found on land that is not part of the National Park Service; however with there being some similarities to the Pittman murder there may be an inquiry from them." Looking toward the throng of people at the clubhouse, Bert commented, "Two murders in less than what...three months? This could wreak havoc with the local tourist business." Turning back to Grant, he continued, "The coroner said you were present at the Pittman crime scene and you were quite helpful."

Grant, never one to blow his own horn, humbly answered, "Well, yes...I was there. I really don't know how much help I was."

Walking toward the front of the cruiser Bert looked out across the golf course. "Give yourself some credit, son. I know that you're about to get your degree in crime scene investigation. Ran into your grandfather last week over in Maryville. Told me all about it. Your grandfather and I go way back. He's a good man." Looking back at Grant he remarked, "He said you're pretty sharp. I guess the apple doesn't fall far from the tree." Finished smoking, he flicked the unfinished cigarette down onto the pavement and ground it out with his shoe. "I'm heading over to Mildred Henks' place to have a look see. Thought you might want to tag along. I could use your help."

"Chief Brody won't like it. He thinks I'm a know it all."

Bert smiled. "I'm sure you don't know it all, but I'm pretty confident when it comes to investigating a crime scene that you know more than Brody. Besides that...he's not here...you are!" Turning, he walked across the grass to where his cruiser was parked. "Meet me at the Henks' place in say...forty-five minutes. That should give me enough time to get over to see the judge in Maryville and pick up a search warrant."

Grant shook his head as he laughed.

Bert stopped and asked, "I say something funny?"

"No," said Grant. "It's just that when Brody originally sent me up to Asa Pittman's place, when I asked him about getting a warrant he blew it off saying the Feds could handle that if they chose to do so. Brody claimed since Asa was dead and that we had probable cause a warrant wasn't necessary. Now, you and I both know that is not the case. It really doesn't make any difference if the sole owner of the home is dead or if we have probable cause. If and when we catch the person or persons who have committed these two murders, any evidence we have collected without a warrant could get tossed out and a good lawyer could get them off."

Bert, impressed, shook his head in agreement. "Your grandfather was right. You're one sharp fella. If you ever get tired of working for Axel...give me a jingle. I'm sure I could find a spot for you in Maryville. Think about it. See ya in forty-five."

Watching Bert walk across the grass to his car, Grant reached into his pocket and removed one of the business cards that were found at the crime scene. They had found over fifty of the cards. The fact that he had taken one would go unnoticed. The card was simplistic.

TRI STATE REALTORS
MILDRED HENKS
Member
MILLION DOLLAR CLUB

The opposite side of the card also included her E-Mail address and her home phone number and address. Climbing in his car Grant drove across the lot and made a right turn onto Country Club Drive. It was only a twenty minute drive to Old Chilhowee Road where Mildred's home was located. It had been a long morning. He hadn't eaten breakfast. He was famished. He had some time to kill before meeting Bert at the Henks' residence. He'd stop in town and grab a quick bite before heading out.

Turning onto Laurel Valley Road he thought about what Bert said about how a second murder would affect the tourist business that was so prevalent in and around the Townsend area. Eight to ten million people from all over the country visited the Great Smoky Mountains each year. For the most part the majority of those who came to the mountains seemed to gravitate toward Pigeon Forge and Gatlinburg; the nucleus of the Great Smoky Mountains. From late April up through mid-November Townsend got its fair share of the tourist business. Townsend was one of the three main entrances to the Great Smoky Mountains National Park, the other two being in Gatlinburg and then over in Cherokee. Townsend, aside from holding a population of less than three hundred residents was like a magnet for attracting tourists. Everyone who came to the Smokies eventually took a trip up to Cades Cove, located just eight miles beyond Townsend. Townsend had a lot to offer vacationers: numerous campgrounds, secluded cabin rentals, hiking, fishing, horseback riding, gift shops, restaurants and of course golf, which, at least for the moment, had turned out to be a nightmare for the golfer who had discovered Mildred's toe. Turning onto Old Tuckaleechee Road Grant thought to himself that the Peaceful Side of the Smokies was not living up to its name.

Grabbing a soda, bag of chips and a banana at Frank's Market, he was surprised that aside from a few folks saying hello to him no one had mentioned or asked anything about the recent murder. Apparently the bad news had not reached town so far. Getting back into the cruiser he knew it was only temporary. When the news of the murder hit, it would spread like a grass fire on a windy day and there would be no way to control what people said or what they thought.

On the outskirts of town he tried to relax, thinking maybe he should try and contact Chief Brody again. Taking a bite out of the banana he thought better of it. Once Brody found out he was on his way to or at the Henks' place without his permission he would be impossible to deal with. Despite the fact he had the blessing of the county sheriff, Brody would be steaming. The more he thought about it the less he seemed to care. After all, Grimes had all but offered him a position in Maryville. If Brody pushed him too hard he just might take Bert up on his offer. To think he wouldn't have to deal with Brody, not to mention Butch Miller was a pleasant thought.

He thought back to the ninth green at the country club where they had found Mildred Henks and the clues that were left behind announcing very clearly and quite loudly that the same individual had killed Asa and Mildred. To think anything different was the wisdom of a fool. Both victims had their fingers cut off by some sort of tool. Mildred had her toes cut off as well. Both victims, according to the coroner, had most likely bled out before the arrival of animals that, just by natural instinct, had their turn at the bodies. Duct tape had been utilized at both sites. Both bodies had been positioned in somewhat remote areas but still in a location where they would be discovered. The killer wanted them to be found, but why? Between the two scenes it seemed to Grant that there was a more definite sense of urgency that Mildred be identified. Why was a number of her business cards left where they could be found? And then there was her monogrammed white scarf she always wore hanging in plain site in a tree. How about the traces of meat that the coroner said appeared to have been rubbed over Mildred's bare hands, feet and arms? It was almost like the killer had invited the local wildlife to become involved in the attack on her body. Looking up, he saw the road sign for Cold Spring Road. Making a right he drove on through the peaceful Tennessee countryside.

He'd never been on Old Chilhowee Road before. As a young boy he had gone with his grandfather out Cold Spring Road a number of times to a farm where they had picked strawberries. They had to drive right by Old Chilhowee. He had never been down the road before but he knew where it was; just a couple of miles up the road. It seemed peaceful and serene as he drove past a number of farms and country homes. Life was different out in the country away from businesses, traffic lights and especially all of the tourists. Going around a sweeping curve in the road he passed a herd of grazing cows. A large flock of birds descended into a grove of trees.

The sign for Old Chilhowee Road popped up on the right. Pulling over to the side of the road he removed Mildred Henks' business card from his shirt pocket. He looked for the address at the bottom of the card: 593 Old Chilhowee Road. Starting up the road he passed the first house, the mail box displaying: The Jeffries 143 Old Chilhowee Road. A few hundred yards later the next mailbox read: Reeds 298 Old Chilhowee. He thought about how strange it was in the country compared to a town or a city when it came to addresses. In town the street addresses were numerical, one number following the next. But on a country road it seemed like a lot of numbers got skipped for some reason. Going up a slight hill he passed 427 Old Chilhowee, then around another corner he saw the yard sign beneath the mailbox. **MILDRED HENKS TRI STATE REALTORS.**

Turning right onto the gravel driveway, the driver of a car coming in the opposite direction honked and waved. *Probably a neighbor,* thought Grant, returning the greeting with a wave of his hand. If the news about Mildred's murder hadn't reached Townsend then the chances of folks out in the country knowing of it were nil.

Driving up the driveway he wondered what the neighbor could be thinking what with a Townsend police cruiser paying a visit to the Henks' residence.

The Henks' place sat back from Chilhowee Road by a good seventy yards fronted by a well-manicured yard. A white fence bordered the attractive property; the front yard alone looked to be close to two acres. There was a small pond on the left, flanked by three tall oak trees. Next to the pond there was a set of white wrought iron chairs and a table. Three ducks floated peacefully on the calm water. The drive circled around a huge three-tier concrete fountain in front of the large, white, two story brick home. Four large gleaming white colonnades and black window shutters accentuated the beautiful home. Mildred's black Thunderbird was parked off to the side in a small parking area. Parking on the side of the house where the driveway wrapped around to the back, Grant got out and stretched. Grabbing his blue spiral notebook, a pair of plastic gloves and some small evidence bags he started for the front of the house when a call came in over his radio. "Denlinger…this is Brody! Denlinger…come in…dammit! Denlinger…you out there?"

Grant reluctantly picked up the radio. "Grant here."

"Denlinger. Where in the hell are you? We got another murder dumped in our laps. It's Mildred Henks."

Grant rolled his eyes. "First of all I'm over at the Henks' place, and secondly I already know that there's been a second murder. Apparently just about everyone knows about the murder…except you. Where have you been? I've been trying to get you all morning."

"Don't get smart with me, boy," snapped Brody. "Doesn't make any difference where I've been. What in the hell are *you* doin' over at the Henks' place?"

Just then, Grant looking down the driveway noticed Bert turn onto the property. "Look I gotta go," said Grant. "The county sheriff just pulled in. He asked me to come over here and help him. Over and out."

Brody's voice trailed off, "Denlinger…talk to me…you can't…" Grant replaced the radio back in its holder and smiled to himself.

Sheriff Grimes parked his cruiser behind Grant's. Getting out he heard Brody's voice as another call could be heard coming though the open window of Grant's cruiser. "Denlinger, pick up the damn radio. You're gonna talk with me before you do anythin' over there at the Henks' place. Denlinger…damn it…pick up the radio!"

Walking to Grant's cruiser, Bert smiled. "Brody giving you a hard time?" Reaching in Bert picked up the radio. "For crying out loud, Axel…calm down. This is Sheriff Grimes. I asked your man to meet me over here at Henks. I need him to help me look around. Now, if you want to join us…fine."

"Look, Bert, I just don't want Wonder Boy to mess anythin' up. I swear…sometimes I think he thinks he's in the movies. Just keep an eye on him. I'm on my way."

Placing the radio back in its holder, Bert gave Grant a sideways look. "Ya know…you really need to consider the offer we talked about earlier."

"I am," said Grant. "I'm going to give it some serious consideration."

Looking at the house, Bert pulled out his revolver and checked the cylinder. "Full load. You ready."

Grant placed the notebook in the back of his belt then reached for his holstered gun. "Right behind ya."

Walking across the gravel drive, Bert commented, "I was in this house…about three, four years back. Mildred had just come off of her second divorce. If I remember correctly it was a fourth of July shindig. Everybody that was anybody in the county was invited: doctors, lawyers, real estate people, business owners, public officials, you name it…they were there. Her home was spectacular, and I'm sure it still is. She had exquisite taste…the best of everything." Pointing at the Thunderbird, he explained, "Like that car…she buys a new one every year."

Stepping up onto a small alcove, Bert peered in one of the glass side panels. Suddenly from the other side of the door came the sounds of five consecutive barks. "That's unusual…sounds like dogs inside the house. Mildred would never have allowed that." Suddenly Sheriff Grimes pulled back from the panel as he raised his revolver. "I saw movement in there. Couldn't tell who or what it was…but it was something." Reaching for the doorknob he slowly turned it and gently pushed. "Door's unlocked…ready?"

Grant, holding his gun tightly whispered, "Yeah."

Opening the door a few inches Grimes yelled his warning, "This is the Blount County Sheriff's office. We're coming in!"

Turning back to Grant, Grimes whispered, "When we get in there I'll go to the left…you the right."

Grant, taking a deep breath answered softly, "Got it."

Shoving the door open Bert moved to the left and leveled his gun back and fourth across the expansive living room, Grant lunged to the right holding his gun with both hands. The twelve dogs scattered around the living room, stared back at the two armed men. Both men stood in silence for a moment then Bert lowered his gun, shrugged at Grant, then spoke, "I think you can put your gun down. They look harmless to me. I'm going to check upstairs. You go through the rooms down here."

Five minutes later, Bert came back down the stairs. Grant was standing next to the fireplace petting two of the dogs. Smiling, he said, "Made some friends."

Walking around the living room and the dining area, Bert shook his head in disbelief. "This doesn't add up. All these dogs inside the house, dog food spread all over the carpet, fine china utilized for water bowls, a hose hooked up to the bathroom vanity, a pile of vomit, places where dogs have crapped and pissed. I guarantee you this is not the way Mildred Henks kept her house. When I was at the party I told you about she told me she had a cleaning lady come in every Wednesday. She couldn't stand a dirty house."

Grant, who had by now slipped on a pair of plastic gloves, offered a pair to Bert which he took as he holstered his weapon. Stepping over the one by six section of wood leaning across the doorway to the kitchen Bert glanced at the tiled floor, "Looks like there were some dogs kept here in the kitchen: water dish, dog toys; probably a pup or puppies from the looks of the low barricade. Something this low wouldn't keep older dogs from jumping over." Opening the refrigerator, then a cabinet door, Bert asked Grant, "You find anything interesting or odd?"

Grant, now on one knee had attracted three more curious dogs that came and sat or stood by his side. "Yeah, I did. The carpet in the master bedroom is soaked clean through and the hutch door is standing wide open. It looks like there are some small pieces of broken china along the baseboard." Walking to the empty dog food bag, he carefully picked it up and examined it. "Whoever scattered the food across the carpet wasn't very neat. They slit the back of the bag open rather than cutting it across the top like most people would do." Folding the bag in half he laid it on the couch along with his notebook. "We'll need to take this along as possible evidence."

Grimes added, "Mildred was definitely here." He pointed at her two white, heeled slippers that were lying in different areas. Going down on his haunches he touched the rim of the metal tub that was in the middle of the dining room. Then, picking up a bottle of unopened dog shampoo he frowned as if he were confused. "Dog shampoo, metal tubs, a pile of dirty towels, a hose running from here back to the bathroom. It appears that Mildred, or someone gave a dog or a number of dogs a bath right in the middle of the house. Now, that's strange. Even folks that don't keep all that clean of a house would not bathe their dog in their dining room." Picking up two empty bottles of shampoo, he remarked, "The bathroom tub...yeah, but not out here. Something really strange went on in this house."

Grant, pushing a curtain to the side looked out the back window. "Did you find anything upstairs?"

"No. Everything on the second floor is neat as a pin. Whatever went on in this house was confined to the downstairs."

Joining Bert in the dining room, Grant noticed some scratches on the hardwood flooring. Bending down he ran his fingers across the marred flooring. "These scratches look recent. It looks like something about two foot wide and quite heavy was dragged across the floor." He pointed to where the carpet and the wood flooring met. "The marks stop here at the edge of the carpet."

Walking across the carpet to the backdoor, Grant opened it and stepped out onto the back porch. "The marks begin again on the porch and stop at the back steps."

Bert walked out onto the porch and removed a cigarette from his coat pocket. "And we know what made those marks."

Grant gave Bert a look. "We do?"

"Think about it," said Bert, lighting his smoke.

Suddenly it hit Grant and he realized what Bert was talking about. "The cage that Mildred was stuffed in. It could be a dog cage. I bet if we were to measure it, it'll be the same size across as these marks! That means the murderer was here in the house. Henks was abducted right in her own home." Waking down the steps he motioned at marks that were made on the steps where the object had been dragged over each step allowing the wood to be slightly marred. "She was dragged in the cage across the floor inside the house, across the carpet and down these steps." Looking down at the gravel drive, with his boot he pointed. The marks left behind from the cage continued along the side of the house. Following the lines in the gravel Bert followed Grant around to the side of the house where the marks stopped dead. "The marks stop here," said Grant. "Mildred was probably loaded up in some sort of vehicle then at some point hauled up to the lake."

Bending down, Bert said, "Sounds about right." He looked closely at the surrounding gravel in the driveway and took a drag on his cigarette. "Loose gravel like this doesn't leave much in the way of tire tracks. Maybe when the state boys get up here later today they might be able to lift some but I doubt it."

"What about all those dogs inside?" asked Grant. "What do we do about them?"

"That's the least of our problems, but I do need to get that handled right now."

Walking toward the front of the house Bert ordered Grant, "Check around out back and see what you can come up with. I'm going to call the animal care shelter and get them over here to collect these dogs."

Grant with a look of concern on his face, asked, "They won't kill them will they?"

"No...I doubt very seriously if they'll kill 'em."

Grant turned and headed for the back of the house thinking about what Grimes had said: 'I doubt very seriously if they'll kill 'em.' Being an animal lover he would have rather heard the sheriff say, 'They definitely won't kill 'em.'

Going back to the steps, he closely examined the marks that had been made on the porch. Then he remembered that he had left his notebook on the couch. As he entered the house three of the dogs welcomed him back inside. Sitting on the edge of the couch he opened his notebook and removed a pen and jotted down a few things that he thought were important.

Finished, he put the notebook back down on the table and noticed something—something that was familiar. On the table there was a small area where there was a tiny portion of what appeared to be the same substance he had found at Asa's place. Picking up a few small granules he put them to his nose. It had the same sweet aroma he had discovered at Asa's. Removing a bag from his coat pocket, he carefully swept the particles into the bag thinking to himself that his discovery of the strange substance at both Asa's and now the Henks' place only bolstered what he and everyone was starting to believe: that both murders had been committed by the same person.

He placed the bag back in his coat pocket when the front door flew open, the dogs startled, started barking. Marching across the room, Brody was livid. "Denlinger…what in the hell are you doin' in here? Grimes told me you were out back. You just can't seem to follow direction…can you?"

Grant realized that the presence of Axel Brody in the house had suddenly ruined his day. Not that it had been all that great to begin with. The site of Mildred Henks' bloody body stuffed in a cage was not the best way to start the day off but now having to deal with Brody was like going to the dentist office and having a root canal procedure without any anesthesia, then having the dentist say, 'Let's do this all over again!'

Grant held up his notebook tried to explain, "I was just taking a few notes that I thought were important."

Brody was right in his face. "Is that right! Who in the hell do you think you are, Sherlock Holmes?"

Most of the dogs cowered in the corner of the room at the loud sharp tone of Brody's caustic voice, three of them continuing to bark. Brody turned to the dogs and yelled, "Shut up!"

Grant had enough. "Look there's no reason to yell at them. They've gone through enough today. Why don't you just head on back to your fishing hole…oh, and don't forget. Make sure you take your cell phone along. God forbid that you might get an important call…like a second murder!"

Brody was just inches from Grant's face. He pointed his chubby index finger at him. "Listen, boy…you don't question me…on nothin'…understand? I'm the chief…you're the officer. You work for me. I don't work for you and I don't answer to you!"

"Speaking of answering to people. Why don't you try answering your phone? Ya know something, Brody, dealing with you is like looking at a clock with one hand. It just doesn't make any sense."

Brody, out of breath placed his hands on his paunchy hips, took a deep shot of air and tried to calm himself. "If it wasn't for your grandfather I'd…"

Sheriff Grimes' voice interrupted the heated discussion, "Boys…boys, I can hear you clear out in the driveway." Stepping between the two, he continued, "Look we've got a murder…a second murder, possibly by the same individual. Rather than arguing and fussing amongst ourselves, I think we should focus our efforts on collecting any evidence that we can."

Grant, thankful for the intervention of Sheriff Grimes headed, for the backdoor. "I'm on it."

Grimes, following Grant motioned to Brody. "We've already checked out the house. We were about to look out back. You coming or not?"

Brody remained silent and started for the back porch.

Joining Grant who was standing in the middle of the backyard, Axel and Bert looked at the surrounding woods that bordered the property. Bert was the first to speak. "Axel, why don't you take a look in the garage and then the tool shed. Grant, you need to walk the edge of the property over there on the east. I'll start on the other side. Anybody finds anything interesting…give out a shout."

Grant answered, "Yes,sir," as he headed for the far edge of the property. Brody just stood there and without a word glared at Grant, but when Bert walked off, he then headed for the garage.

Standing at the edge of the property, Grant looked off into the woods just on the other side of an old barbed wire fence. It looked like it was impassable: the forest crammed with tall pine trees, thick shrubs, jaggers, poison ivy, and trees that had fallen sometime in the past. It was one of those places people would not normally go; a place where the local wildlife could live in peace without the intervention of humans.

Walking slowly down the fence line, he concentrated trying to erase Brody's tirade from his mind. The barbed wire fence was old and rusty, bent in places but uncut. In some places the vegetation had grown so thick that the fence was completely covered. The grass up to the fence had recently been cut. There was a small garden area that had been tilled but nothing planted, at least that he could see. Then he saw the side of a vine covered barn twenty yards down the fence line.

Looking across the vast yard, he saw Bert Grimes on the other side walking toward the barn. Grant looked back toward the house but Brody was nowhere in sight. By the time he got to the front of the barn Grimes was already there waiting for him. The barn appeared to be ancient: two stories high, boarded up loft door, the old weathered boards cracked and peeling. Large tree limbs hung over both sides of the old building, vines and weeds practically hiding the barn from sight.

Bert removed his revolver from his holster, and remarked, "This could be interesting. Smell that odor?"

Grant drew in a short whiff of air then wrinkled his nose. "Smells like urine."

"That's exactly what it is, and if my guess is right what we'll find inside the barn will not be pleasant." Pointing his gun, Grimes ordered, "Open the door...I'll go in first...you follow."

Grant nodded and reached for the two by four held by rusted, heavy duty brackets securing the large double doors. Sliding the section of wood to the right he pushed on the door. When it opened the stench emanating from inside hit Grant and Bert like a ton of bricks, both men backing away as they tried to shield their faces. Grant, leaning against the front of the barn gagged, then mumbled, "God...what is...that smell?"

Removing a hanky from his pocket Bert placed it over his mouth. "I'm going in."

Grant watched Bert disappear into the darkness of the barn. After a few seconds, the interior of the barn was illuminated. Grimes had located a pull string that allowed the light from a one hundred watt bulb to penetrate the darkness. Signaling for Grant to enter, he spoke, "I want you to see this."

Replacing his revolver back in its holster, Grant placed his hand over his mouth and nose and entered. The smell of urine penetrated his nose and stung his eyes. He squinted to see what was in the barn. The roof of the barn was covered with cobwebs that over the years had formed a network of lace. Three birds flew through one of four openings where the roof had deteriorated. Three quarters of the barn was filled with rusty, old farm implements, rusted tools hung on the walls, along with some old license plates. Grant stared in disbelief at a long row of old dog cages setting on the dirt floor. Walking up to the cages he saw bowls of moldy dog food and dirty water. There were piles of fly-infested dog crap in every cage. In the corner there were three, fifty pound bags of dog food. Two rats ran from the bottom of a bag that was chewed open at the bottom. Seeing enough Grant retreated to the outside where he took a long deep breath of fresh air.

Bert turned out the light and joined Grant, leaving the barn doors open. Wiping his eyes with the hanky he commented, "That place needs to be aired out before anybody goes back in there."

Grant noticed Brody and a younger woman walking side by side, approaching the barn. Placing his arm around Grant, Bert introduced him to the woman. "Grant, this is Hazel Finley. She's the manager of the Humane Society of Blount County." Lighting up his third cigarette since he had arrived at Henks, he politely asked, "So what's the verdict, Hazel?"

Placing her gloved hands inside of a white smock she walked toward the open barn doors. "I brought two vans and three employees with me. They just loaded up the last of the dogs. They are undernourished and in desperate need of grooming, although it appears that someone recently tried to bathe them. A couple of the animals have infected eyes and ears. Two of the females are pregnant. When we get them back to the clinic we'll know more. We'll give them all a physical and get them cleaned up. From what I've seen I'd say they'll probably all survive." Looking inside the barn she remarked, "I thought so...a puppy mill. God, this kind of stuff really pisses me off. This is Mildred Henks' place...isn't it?"

Bert puffing on his cigarette answered, "That's right."

Walking back to join the group, Hazel commented, "I find it hard to believe she would be involved in something like this...but if she is...well, then I say she should be taken out and shot."

No one said a word in response to what she had said. Noticing that everyone seemed a little uncomfortable, she inquired, "I say something wrong?"

"Look," said Bert. "You're going to find out about it sooner or later. Mildred Henks was found earlier this morning murdered. Now whether or not she was involved in this puppy mill business remains to be seen."

"Not as far as I'm concerned," said Hazel. "I've never liked the woman. There was always just something about her. She's been selling terriers for years. No one ever questioned her activities because of who she was, but behind the scenes she was running an illegal business." Turning, she went on, "Well, I've got to get back to Maryville and get to work on the dogs. Far as Mildred Henks is concerned, I don't know how she was killed...but she no doubt got everything she deserved." Snapping her fingers she turned back around. "Now it makes sense! Last evening someone dumped six Fox Terrier pups in a cage off at the clinic. Bet ya anything they came from right here on this property. I gotta get moving. I'll keep you posted, sheriff."

"I'm outta here, too," said Brody. "I'm heading back to Townsend." Giving Bert a hard stare, he suggested, "When you're finished up with *my man,* if you would be so kind to send him back to Townsend. We've got a lot to prepare for. When the news of this murder gets out, it'll be twice as bad as the Pittman murder." Turning, he walked away.

Bert, blowing off Brody's sarcastic remark looked back at the barn then up toward the house. "Well, Grant, I think that about wraps things up for the moment. By the way, regardless of what Axel says…I want you to know you were a big help out here today. I guess you better get on back to Townsend. Brody's right on one account. It's gonna get nuts around here. You boys are gonna have your hands full. I'm gonna hang around here until a couple of my officers arrive to keep an eye on the place. Thanks again for all your help. I'll see you tomorrow sometime."

Grant started toward the house and gestured, "No problem, Sheriff."

Walking across the grass, Grant stopped at the gravel driveway and stared down at the marks that just might have been made by the cage Mildred had been stuffed into and dragged out of the house. Going around the side of the house he wondered if she had been alive while in the cage or if she had already been killed. Climbing into his cruiser, he started the engine and stared at the mountains in the distance. He really didn't relish the thought of returning to Townsend and listening to Brody chew his ass. He was of the opinion that somebody needed to chew on Brody's backside a little bit. Pulling out of the driveway he realized he had to go back to town. He was part of the Townsend Police force, and they were going to need everyone to get involved to prepare for the media onslaught that would settle in on them the next morning. A second murder had been committed in less than three months and by tomorrow everyone from here to Knoxville and probably beyond would know about it and the three ring circus would begin again.

CHAPTER NINE

GRANT TURNED OFF THE MOTOR and sat back in the seat, staring at the police station. He wanted to make sure he had his thoughts together before going inside and facing Brody. He had decided that he wasn't going to take any more of his crap. Brody would rant and rave, but he wasn't going to let it get to him. He would do his job, he would do what was required of him, but he wasn't going to allow himself to be verbally abused.

Both Brody and Butch were on the phone when he walked in the station. Grant ambled over to the desk and sat down. Brody slammed down the phone at the same time giving Grant a nasty look. "Well, look what the cat dragged in. I was wonderin' when you were goin' to grace us with your presence." Leaning back in his swivel chair he pointed a fat finger at Grant. "I'm gonna tell you this just one more time, Wonder Boy. I'm the chief of police...not you!" Leaning forward toward the desk, he emphasized, "Get my drift?"

Grant looked at Butch who was seated in the corner out of Brody's vision. It was all Grant could do to contain himself from laughing as Butch mimicked the chief, holding up his hands and moving his head back and forth signifying a talking puppet.

Blowing off the fact that he was nowhere to be found earlier in the day, Brody shrugged in a smart fashion, "So I made a mistake by forgettin' my damn cell phone. That has nothin' to do with the fact that *you* didn't have the sense to send someone up to the lake to get me. Instead you make me look like a fool."

Grant couldn't help himself. "Send them where? You never informed us where you were going. You said you were going fishing...and that's all. Butch was assigned to the station and Kenny went with me. Who was I going to send out looking for you?"

Brody didn't have much of a defense for what Grant had said so he changed the subject. "Where is Jacks anyway? Why isn't he here?"

"He worked almost eighteen straight hours," said Grant. "He'll be in tonight."

The phone rang. Frustrated, Brody picked it up. "Chief Brody…Townsend Police."

There was silence then Brody snapped again, "I understand. We're doin' everythin' we can, but right now we have no answers." There was another moment of silence then Brody's voice got louder. "I can't come over to your house right now. I'm in a meetin'." Slamming down the phone he clenched his fist. He looked like he was going to lose it. "Dammit! Right in the middle of this mess and I have to deal with another missin' dog." Placing his hands over his head he took a deep breath and asked no one in particular, "Where in the hell is Marge? I ain't gonna answer this friggin' phone all afternoon."

Butch, who seemed to be enjoying Brody's meltdown spoke up, "She went to get something to eat."

Another call came in and Brody almost ripped the phone from the desk. "Brody, Police Department!" The call was short, the look on Brody's face indicating that he was getting more riled as the seconds passed. Slamming the phone down again, he shook his head in disgust. "Well, we're piss out of luck now! That was Dave, the manager up at the country club. Somebody from Knoxville has already been over there to interview him. I was hopin' the Henks' murder wouldn't break until tomorrow, but it looks like it's goin' to be on the six o'clock news."

Pushing himself away from the desk, Brody stood and looked out the small window at the back of the office. "Dammit!" Composing himself he turned back facing Grant and Butch. "We all need to be in here early tomorrow mornin', I'd say…let's make it five. It's gonna be a zoo tomorrow. The Pittman murder is still fresh on the public's mind and now we have a second murder. From what I've heard so far it looks like the same nut that did in Asa took out Mildred Henks. We're gonna have a lot of questions thrown at us and we're not gonna have a lot of answers."

Grant cracked his knuckles then stood. "I'm staying in town tonight. No sense in going home and then having to deal with what went on last time. I'll stay here until Kenny gets in, which should be in about two hours. I'll just crash in his room over at the motel, try to grab a few hours sleep and a shower then I'll be in at five like we agreed."

"Sounds good," said Brody. "When we get in here tomorrow mornin' we need a plan. Here's what we'll do. We'll have a quick meetin'…say from five to maybe five-thirty and then we'll come up with a plan of action. You boys need to be thinkin' about that."

Grant objected, "Plan…what plan? Just tell them the truth! The news people will already have all the gory details by the time they're parked on our front porch. Depending on who they talked with, they might know more than we do. So, just tell them the truth. We've had two murders, more than likely committed by the same person. We have no clues that amount to anything and we're continuing to work on both cases."

"Bullshit!" said Brody. "That'll make us look like a bunch of dumb-ass hicks that don't know what we're doin'."

Speak for yourself, Grant said under his breath.

"I'm outta here," said Butch, heading for the door. "I'm going back out on patrol for a couple of hours then I'm heading home. See you guys in the morning."

Brody, following Butch held up his cell phone, his next comment directed at Grant. "Keep in touch with me. I'm goin' to check on a few things. I'll make some calls and try to get a grasp on how bad it's goin' to get tomorrow with those media clowns comin' in here."

Grant walked to the front door and watched Brody walk to his truck. He no sooner closed the door when the phone rang. The call and the next seven calls which came one after another were all in regard to the recent murder.

Minutes later, Marge walked in the door carrying a large picnic basket and a cooler. Grant, puzzled, asked, "Planning on staying awhile are you?"

Walking to the refrigerator in the supply room she answered, "Tomorrow we're all going to be here for a long time. I got with my neighbor and we whipped up a batch of fried chicken, some deviled eggs, baked beans and some coleslaw." Loading up the fridge with food she remarked, "I also made up a few gallons of iced tea. If we're going to be here all day we might as well have some good food to eat."

Lifting the three, one gallon jugs of tea out of the cooler, Grant patted Marge on the shoulder, "You're a peach…ya know it!"

The phone rang again. Marge went to her desk. "I'll get that."

Walking back into Brody's office Grant decided to call home. Dalton answered on the second ring, "Denlinger residence."

"Hey, Dalton…it's me Grant. I'm staying in town tonight. Just didn't want you and mom to worry."

"What's going on? Are you all right?"

"I'm fine," answered Grant. "There's been another murder. Someone killed Mildred Henks and left her body on the Laurel Lake Trail that skirts the country club golf course. Her fingers and toes were cut off. Right now it looks like whoever killed Asa Pittman has struck again. I think we've got a real crazy on our hands."

"Lordy," exclaimed Dalton. "Mildred Henks! Never cared much for her. She always struck me as a mean ol' witch, but why would anyone want to kill her?"

"I don't have an answer for that and to be honest with you, I don't have answers for anything that's been going on lately. Listen, I gotta go. It's nuts here at the station. The murder will be on the six o'clock news tonight. I'm not sure which station. Hell, they'll probably all have it on. I better run. I've got a call coming in. I'll see you and mom sometime tomorrow, probably tomorrow night."

The next two hours passed quickly. The phone calls kept pouring in, one after another. All calls were screened by Marge and when she explained that the chief was out and not expected back until the next morning most of the callers were upset and said they would call back then. The few callers who demanded to speak with the officer on duty were patched through to Grant. He was polite with each caller and told them to watch the six o'clock news for further information. This seemed to satisfy the callers who thanked him and hung up.

At five-fifty five, Marge turned on the small fifteen inch television in the corner of Brody's office. At exactly six o'clock, the ever-punctual Kenny walked through the door. Poking his head in Brody's office he asked, "What's up gang?"

Eating a deviled egg and holding up a glass of iced tea, Marge motioned to him. "Just in time. Our murder is supposed to be on the news. We haven't found which station yet. Pull up a seat."

"You're kidding me," said Kenny, plopping down in a chair, his eyes glued to the small black and white screen.

"Ah, here it is," said Grant, placing the remote down on Brody's desk.

An attractive young woman smiled and glanced at the monitor

then looked at the viewing audience. *"Good evening. This is Wendy Peters of WTNZ Fox 32 News. Our top story of the day is that a second body has been found near the sleepy-eyed community of Townsend. Stay tuned for further information following a rundown on the weather with John Preston."*

The weatherman with his straight white teeth and pressed suit began the standard format of forecasting the local weather: *"Thank you, Wendy. Looking at the map our forecast..."*

Kenny, not the least bit interested in the weather turned to Grant. "How in the world did the news get hold of the murder already?"

Grant, finishing up his tea explained, "We got a call from Dave up at the country club. Apparently some news station from up in Knoxville got a call, drove down and they interviewed him. Someone, maybe one of the guests called Knoxville and hungry for a story the station showed up."

Marge, jumping in on the conversation asked, "I wonder if Sheriff Grimes knows about this?" Just then the phone rang. Marge answered, "Townsend Police Department." For the next thirty seconds she nodded her head a few times answering, "Yes, sir," or "No, sir." At one point her answer was, "He's not here, sir."

Hanging up the phone she had a weird look on her face. "Speak of the devil. That was Grimes. He's pissed! He's watching the news just like us, only it was a complete surprise to him. He never got a call from the country club, the station, from Brody, nobody. The last thing he said was that he was calling Brody at home."

"The shit's really gonna hit the fan," said Kenny. "Sheriff Grimes is one of the most patient men I've ever met, but when he gets pissed you don't want to be anywhere near him."

Grant, with a smile on his face added, "Boy if I could only be a fly on the wall at Brody's when he gets that call."

Everyone laughed. Kenny pointed at the television. "Looks like they're back on."

Wendy smiled into the camera. *"And now for tonight's top news story. A body was found in the Lake Laurel area in Townsend near the Laurel Hills Country Club. Dave Johnson, manager of the club, and a number of guests who were interviewed said they thought foul play was involved. The body at this time is being said to be that of Mildred Henks from Blount County."* To the surprise of Grant, Kenny and Marge the screen suddenly switched to an actual short film of officers carrying the cage containing Mildred's body across the green and then loading it into the coroner's van. All the while Wendy continued with the report, *"This is the second murder in the Townsend area in the past three months. Last April the body of Asa Pittman was found up on Thunderhead Trail in the Great Smokey Mountains National Park. Further updates will follow at eleven."*

Grant grabbed the remote and switched to one channel after another. "How in the world did they get that film footage?"

Kenny offered an explanation, "Somebody, maybe one of the guests who was watching from the clubhouse had a camera. It looks like they took a telephoto shot during the time we were there."

Grant continued to scan the channels but there was no additional news of the Henks' murder. "I guess ol' Fox 32 News lucked out on this one."

Marge, who got up to answer the phone said, "Not for long. It'll be on every channel of tonight's late night news." Picking up the phone she politely spoke, "Townsend Police." After a few seconds of silence she spoke again, "Yes, a body has been found up near the golf course...No, we're not sure it's a murder... No, we don't know if the same person committed the crime...Thank you...we should know more later on in the day." Hanging up the phone she looked at Grant, "The flood gates have been opened."

Grant got out of the chair. "I'm getting out of here before Brody calls in. He's going to be steamed after Grimes gets done with him. I'm going to grab a bite then hit the hay. See you guys in the morning."

Looking at Kenny, Marge said, "I'm going to stay for maybe an hour but then I've got to go home and get some rest. Brody will want us all in here tomorrow."

Grant was no sooner out the door when he noticed a bright yellow van with **WBIR CHANNEL 10** in bold red lettering plastered across its side pull into the lot. Walking to his Jeep, he thought, *The first of many.* Fumbling for his keys he dropped them to the ground. Bending over to pick them up he was startled by a voice, "Excuse me, sir!"

Looking up he saw a young man running in his direction, a clipboard in his hand. Grant unlocked the Jeep but it was too late. The young man was at his side within seconds. "Excuse me, sir. I'm Brent Hennerman of WBIR News." Looking Grant up and down, he politely asked, "Are you with the Townsend Police?"

Grant looked at the reporter in amazement, then sarcastically answered, "No, I'm not on the force. The reason why I'm wearing a Townsend Police uniform and the reason why I'm sporting this Townsend Police badge is because I'm just a local citizen who was dissatisfied with the way the police operate so I decided to get me a uniform and a badge and come on down here to the station and show them how it's done."

"Really?" said the young man.

Grant climbed into the Jeep and turned the ignition key. Rolling down the window he backed out, addressing the reporter, "Where do they get you people?"

Pulling out of the lot, Grant realized that he had been rude to the reporter. After all, the young man was just trying to do his job; trying to get a leg up on the competition of other stations. He was just trying to get the story, but still the way they went about doing things always rubbed him the wrong way. Turning out of the lot he thought that maybe he'd drive over to Lily's Café and get a good meal but then decided against it since by now, the news of the Henks' murder would be all over town. He didn't feel like answering a ton of questions while he was trying to eat. Then it hit him. A pizza! He'd go to the motel, call in an order and have it delivered.

An hour and a half later following a refreshing shower, he stared at the two pieces of crust in the pizza box. He was stuffed. He looked at his watch. It was just after nine o'clock. Going out onto the balcony he had a perfect view of cars being driven back and forth on the parkway. Pulling up one of two cheap plastic chairs he sat down propping his bare feet on the other chair. For some reason his mind drifted away from the horrible events of the day. He thought about Dana Beth. Ever since running into her at the station and the confrontation with Butch she had been on his mind quite often. He wondered how his life might have been different if he would have decided to marry her. He would probably still be living on the farm with his mother and Dalton, he'd no doubt still be an officer with the Townsend Police and still struggling to get his degree. He would also still have Dana Beth, the love of his life. He was beginning to realize that without her he was nothing more than a twenty-three year old with a big hole in his life that could only be filled by her. If he would have only agreed to marry her when she wanted she wouldn't be with Butch Miller. The very thought of

Butch kissing her, touching her, really pissed him off. He had no one to blame but himself. He was the one who had let her go. He had been so intent on getting his degree. Now he didn't have either, Dana Beth or his degree.

The streetlights were just beginning to flicker on, the very edge of darkness starting to settle in over the town. He sat for the next twenty minutes watching the traffic. Standing, he stretched, noticing a black van pass by, the white lettering on its side advertising: *WATE CHANNEL 6.* Going inside to turn in for the night he thought to himself that he didn't agree with Brody on most things but the chief was right about one thing. When the media received the word that Asa had been murdered Brody had said, 'Wherever there is a carcass it is there that the vultures will gather.' Here it was not even three months later and the vultures were circling over Townsend once again.

Crawling beneath the sheets, Grant looked at the clock; 10:27 p.m. He closed his eyes and fell asleep quickly. When the alarm pierced the darkness of the room at 4:00 a.m. Grant found himself in the exact same position as when he had pulled the sheets up over his exhausted body. He hadn't tossed, turned or moved a muscle. Sitting on the side of the bed, surprisingly he felt refreshed. He had only gotten five and a half hours of rest. Rubbing his hands over his face and through his hair he thought about what Dalton was always saying when it came to sleep: 'A man doesn't need more than five to six hours of rest. The secret to a good night's rest is to fall asleep quickly, stay asleep and wake up alert.' He turned on a small table lamp, dropped to the floor and knocked out fifty sit ups and twenty-five pushups. Following a quick ice cold shower, he was dressed and out the door before 4:30. Climbing into his Jeep he noticed another media van. It had parked right next to him. The local newspapers were not about to be outdone by the television networks, the lettering on the passenger side door read: **The Mountain Press-Sevierville Tennessee.**

He skipped breakfast and besides that he didn't have enough time if he was going to be at work by five. Ten minutes later he pulled into the police station parking lot. For so early in the morning it was buzzing with activity. It reminded him of the old car show that Townsend held each spring in a large field just on the outskirts of town. Van after van was lined up around the perimeter of the lot: Television stations WBIR, WVLT and WTNZ from Knoxville were lined up next to WMYU, a radio station also from Knoxville. Two newspaper vans representing the Smoky Mountains News and the Sevier County News sat at the end of the lot next to WIVK and WIMZ radio vans. There were a number of 10' x 10' Easy Up tents scattered around the grass at the edge of the lot. Technicians were running wires from vans to a number of microphone stands that had been set up next to the station. Cameramen were busy adjusting cameras and setting up tripods. Reporters sat in folding chairs and talked on cell phones and sipped on cups of coffee, while others were giving instructions to their crews. A young lady with a carrier of cups of coffee walked by Grant as he was getting out of his Jeep. Unexpectedly, she offered him a cup. "Good morning, Officer. Would you care for some coffee?"

Surprised, Grant took a cup. "Yes I think I would, thank you." Starting for the door he thought that the day was getting off to a good start.

He entered the building and walked down the hall only to come face-to-face with Brody who was sitting on a fold out cot in the corner of his office. The chief's eyes were red and he was chewing gum. His hair was sticking out in every direction. His uniform shirt was wrinkled and he looked like he had been on an all night drunk. Grant, making light of things said enthusiastically, "Good morning Chief!"

Brody looked up and with a scowl on his face answered, "What's good about it?"

Walking back to the supply room Grant found Marge busy at the small counter and Kenny was removing a gallon of orange juice from the fridge. Noticing Grant, Marge held up a large spoon, "Morning, Grant, brought us in some biscuits and gravy."

Kenny poured himself a cup of juice and motioned toward Grant, "Come on, get over here and get in on this."

Grant grabbed a paper plate. "What's the deal with the Chief? He's just as negative at five in the morning as he is at five at night."

Marge, plopping two biscuits and then some gravy on Grant's plate offered an explanation, "I came in early at three o'clock. I decided to get this place straightened around before the media onslaught. Kenny was nowhere to be found. Turned out he was out back having a smoke. I heard this coughing coming from Brody's office. I went to investigate and who do I find? The chief all piled up in that old cot we keep in the closet. I just left him be. He looked plumb tuckered out. He just woke up about ten minutes ago. He called me back there and told me to tell you guys that the meeting for five o'clock is still on."

Butch came out of the bathroom and nodded toward Brody's office. "The ol' bear up yet?"

Brody strolled into the room, rubbing his hand over his five o'clock shadow. "Bet your ass, I'm up. I need you three yahoos in my office right now so we can get this meetin' out of the way."

Brody turned and walked back down the hall. Marge rolled her eyes and handed Kenny a stack of messages that had been left for the chief. "Here, give these to grumpy when you get back there."

Grant led the way down the hall, Kenny taking a bite of his breakfast, Butch looking in a mirror making sure his uniform looked good. He knew he would no doubt be on camera today. He wanted to look sharp. By the time the three reached the office Brody had folded up the cot and was putting it back in the closet. Plopping down in his chair he looked over his three officers who had seated themselves. Rubbing his eyes he started the conversation. "Got a call last night from Sheriff Grimes who was pissed to say the least. I don't know why that stupid ass Dave from the country club didn't think to call Grimes also. Looks like the media zoo has already started out there in the lot and to tell you the truth, I could give a damn! After being raked over the coals last night by Grimes I can only tell you this. We, the Townsend Police will only have a bit part in what takes place out in front of the station later on this afternoon."

Brody sat back in his chair. "There is a scheduled press conference for two o'clock today. That's what…nine hours from now? Our job will be to keep the media sharks at bay. The media people will be pissed. They're not just gonna sit around and twiddle their thumbs all day. They want the story…the complete story, so they can get it on the six o'clock news. The newspapers will especially be pressin' us for information. They have a cut off time, at which point they have to go to press. The radio and television stations on the other hand have an advantage since they can wait until the last moment to televise or broadcast the news. So, here it is. Nobody…I mean nobody, from the media gets in here. Now, Grimes told me that we have to go out and tell the media at nine o'clock about the scheduled press conference at two. The media is not goin' to be happy and they'll try to grill us for information which I am told we can not discuss until the press conference. I'll be doin' the talkin' and you three will keep the crowd under control. Grimes told me he was sendin' eight additional officers over here from Maryville, not only for crowd control but to direct traffic. The last thing he said was if anybody gets out of line regardless of who they are, they are to be arrested. We cannot allow the media to control how things go around here. That is our job."

Butch crushed his empty coffee cup and tossed it in a trashcan. "That's crap! I mean hell, the damn murder was in our jurisdiction and you mean to tell me we have to play second fiddle to Grimes and his crew?"

"Look," said Brody, "I don't like this any more than you but that's the way things have panned out. We not only have to take a backseat to Grimes, but the county coroner, FBI, state police and the park service and probably anybody else that shows up. The only input that we're likely to have will come from Mayor Flemming who I have been informed is comin'."

Suddenly, Kenny remembered the small stack of messages from the previous evening Marge had given him. "Oh, by the way, Chief, Marge told me to give these to you."

Standing, Brody took the slips of paper and tossed them on his desk, some falling to the floor. "We've got bigger fish to fry right now. Kenny, I want you to man the phones with Marge. Butch, you and Grant are goin' to be out front. Split up and make sure you're visible. When you two get out there you'll be wearin' a red target on your back. They'll be on you like a monkey on a cupcake. You'll have to walk a fine line. You might be filmed when asked questions. Don't be rude, although I know it will be hard because they'll be pressin' you. That's the reason I'm not goin' out there. I don't have the patience to deal with those buzzards. If someone says the wrong thing to me the way I'm feelin' right now, why I just might pop them square in the mouth. Our department doesn't need that kind of publicity. Hell, I'm already on Grimes' shit list for not callin' him yesterday about the interview up at the country club, plus he's pissed at me for not havin' my cell with me yesterday. So, I'm stayin' inside until nine o'clock when we have to go out there and face those creeps." Hesitating he looked at Grant, Butch and Kenny. "Any questions?"

No one answered.

"Good," said Brody "Now get out of my office. I need to shave, get spruced up and put on a clean shirt. Be back in here at eight-thirty sharp so we can go over how we want to deal with these people."

It was only a matter of a few seconds after they stepped out into the lot that they were noticed, Grant going to the left, Butch to the right. Grant hadn't even walked twenty yards when a young woman carrying a clipboard approached him. "Excuse me, Sir." Looking at the badge on his uniform she politely asked, "May I ask you some questions?"

"Certainly," said Grant.

Removing a pen from behind her ear, she smiled and pleasantly asked, "What is your name, officer?"

Grant tapped the metal nametag just beneath his badge with his finger.

Looking closely at the tag she introduced herself. "Officer Denlinger, my name is Steffanie Ray. I'm with WIMZ Radio out of Knoxville. What can you tell me about the murder?"

Grant noticed two more media vans pulling into the lot. "Nothing more than what was on the news last evening. A body was found up at Laurel Lake near the golf course."

"We have had reports that the body was identified as a Mildred Henks. Is that correct?"

"That is only speculation at this point. We have to wait until we hear the coroner's report which will be here at the station at two o'clock this afternoon at the press conference."

"We are being led to believe that she was murdered?"

"That very well may be, but once again until the coroner gives us a complete report we can't say."

"Officer Denlinger, were you at the crime scene at the golf course?"

"Yes, I was."

"Can you describe for me what you saw?"

"At this time...no. Everything that went on up there or was seen will be revealed at the press conference this afternoon." Breaking the conversation off, Grant excused himself, "Now if you will please excuse me I have to patrol the lot. Good day." He no sooner walked away when he was approached by another female reporter trailed by a cameraman. It took almost a half an hour for Grant and Butch to circle the small lot. They no sooner finished talking with one when another would approach. Seven o'clock came around and those who approached them for interviews became less and less. The word had gotten out that even though they were officers they couldn't offer much more information than what was already known. By eight o'clock the ever growing crowd of reporters and interested citizens understood that at nine o'clock Chief Brody would be coming out to talk with them.

Glancing at his watch, Grant walked over to Butch, "It's just about eight-thirty. Let's go back in and report to Brody how things are going out here."

Brody looked like a new man: fresh shirt, clean shaven, hair combed. When his three officers entered his office he was just finishing mopping up some leftover gravy with a small morsel of biscuit. Throwing the empty plate in the trash, he stretched and then said, "In about twenty minutes or so we'll head out front to talk with the media." Looking at Butch and Grant he asked, "What's it like out there?"

Butch was the first to answer, "I thought that it was crazy last time with the Pittman murder. There isn't a radio, television or newspaper station in the area that is not out there. I was asked everything from if we have a serial killer on our hands to if we have any suspects to is there a connection between the two murders."

"Yeah," added Grant. "They've been talking with a lot of people in town; people who don't know much about the Pittman case or about the Henks' murder and yet everything that they hear is misconstrued as the gospel. They soak up everything they hear like a sponge."

Brody shook his head in agreement then asked, "Where do they have us set up?"

"Right outside the door and to the left," said Grant. "They have a number of microphones, cameras and what not set up for whenever we go out there."

"Change of plans," said Brody. "We're gonna go out at 8:45. Maybe if we go out before they expect us, then we just might be able to avoid a lot of questions, ya know before they get on line."

"I don't know about that," said Butch. "When we came in they were already jockeying for position. They do this sort of thing for a living. They're not going to miss a beat."

Brody stood, "All right...in five minutes we go. I'll do the talkin'...you three keep the wolves back from the door."

At 8:45 on the nose Brody pushed open the door and stepped out, Grant, Butch and Kenny following. Someone in the crowd yelled, "There they are!"

Before Brody was even near one of the nine microphones that had been set in place, people were yelling questions:

"Chief Brody...do we have a serial killer on our hands?"

"When do we get the results of the coroner's report?"

"Has the victim been identified?"

"Who found the victim?"

Brody held up his hand for silence but it was to no avail as questions continued to be fired at him:

"Do you have any leads?"

"What can we tell our viewers?"

"Is the FBI involved in this case also?"

Brody finally grabbed a mic and shouted, "Settle down folks...settle down!"

The crowd began to quiet down when someone from the back yelled out, "We've been here since early this morning. We need some answers!"

Chief Brody nodded at Butch, Grant and Kenny who stepped forward toward the crowd. "Here's the way it's gonna go," stated Brody. "We are not answerin' any questions at this time." There was a low grumbling and some cursing. Brody hesitated, then began again, "I know you've all been here for awhile, but you are just goin' to have to remain patient. The county sheriff has informed us there will be a press conference held right here at two o'clock this afternoon." Looking at his watch, he verified, "That's just about five hours from now. At that time you will hear from not only the county coroner, but the county sheriff, the state police, the FBI, the park service and the Mayor of Townsend. There will be plenty of time for questions after they have told you what we know. Now, if I were you I'd go have breakfast or lunch or whatever and get ready for the press conference at two. Thank you."

Stepping away from the mic, people still continued to shout questions:

"Is the murder tied in with the one back in April?"

"Do the missing dogs in the area have anything to do with the murders?"

Once everyone was back inside the station, Kenny shut the door and leaned up against it, folding his arms across his chest. "God, this is just like the Alamo. A few of us...a lot of them. It's like the Mexican Army is just on the other side of these walls. It wouldn't surprise me if they didn't start shelling us with cannons and scaling the walls with ladders."

Everyone had a good laugh. Brody walked toward the refrigerator in the supply room. "I'm gonna eat lunch now. The rest of you can do what you want, just don't bother me. In the next hour or so we're gonna be gettin' a lot of visitors. Better relax while ya can. When two o'clock rolls around we're all gonna be like a one legged man in an ass kickin' contest." Opening the fridge he stuffed a deviled egg in his mouth and grabbed a chicken leg.

In the next two hours everyone started to show up. Mayor Flemming was the first, then Jake from the park service. At twelve noon the eight officers from Maryville showed up and after reporting to Brody were dispatched out into the lot and up onto the parkway to direct traffic and control the crowd. At ten after one the Feds and the state police walked in the backdoor. Finally at 1:50 Sheriff Grimes and Jeff Bookman showed up. Following a brief meeting in Brody's crammed office they were ready to face the media or whoever else was waiting outside.

At two o'clock, Mayor Flemming led the small entourage out the door and to the microphones. Grant stood off to the side with Kenny and Butch. It was the strangest sight. The mayor, Brody, Sheriff Grimes, the county coroner, two state police, two FBI agents and Jake from the park service lined up facing a crowd of over two hundred people: newspaper, radio and television reporters, local business people and interested citizens.

The mayor got things rolling, thanking everyone for coming then introduced Sheriff Grimes who stepped up to a mic, cleared his throat then began, "Yesterday morning at approximately eleven we received a call from the Laurel Hills Country Club in regards to a golfer finding a severed human toe near the ninth green. Officers from Townsend were dispatched and a body was discovered back in the woods along a hiking trail near Laurel Lake. The body has been identified as Mildred Henks of Blount County. From clues found at the crime scene we have deduced that Mrs. Henks was definitely murdered and that she could have been murdered by the same person or persons who murdered Asa Pittman last April." Grimes continued on for another five minutes describing the crime scene and what clues were found and that if anyone had any information no matter how insignificant it may seem to please contact the Townsend Police Department. Finished, he turned the microphone over to the coroner.

Of all the people there, Jeff Bookman was the one they were waiting to hear from. Jeff looked out across the crowd, then spoke, "There is no doubt that after an extensive review of the body it is that of Mildred Henks. Mrs. Henks was murdered. We have still not determined if she was killed up at the lake or at her home. The cause of death has been recorded as a probable loss of blood. The victim's fingers and toes were amputated by the same type of tool that was used in the Pittman murder. So, therefore we have established that there is a pretty good chance both murders were conducted by the same person or persons. There were also traces of the same chemicals used during the first murder along with claw and teeth marks where some of the local wildlife tried to get at the body." Following a few more minutes of medical jargon and details, Bookman turned the meeting over to the state police who said a few words about their involvement. The Feds and the park service also spoke briefly and then the question and answer period began which lasted for just under an hour and only came to an end when Mayor Flemming called the press conference closed, stating that the local chamber would be conducting a meeting in the next few days to ensure the safety of the citizens and residents of Townsend.

It was just after midnight when Grant stood in the now empty parking lot of the station. Brody, Butch and Marge had called it a day, Kenny was working the night shift. Looking out across the lot the scene reminded Grant of the county fair and what it always looked like after a long day of activity: cups, paper plates, cigarette butts, assorted paper blowing this way and that. Someone had even left a folding chair behind. Climbing into his Jeep Grant checked his cell phone to see if anyone had tried to call him. A strange number, one that he did not recognize popped up on the light blue screen. It was too late to call the number but then he thought, *What the hell*. It was a long distance number and he couldn't imagine who had called him. The phone rang seven times and just when he was about to end the call a voice answered, "Doug Eland."

CHAPTER TEN

THE CITY OF TOWNSEND normally held its monthly Chamber of Commerce meeting on the third Tuesday of every month, but at times was changed due to unforeseen situations. The murder of Mildred Henks coupled with the prior murder of Asa Pittman went far beyond an unforeseen situation. Two murders in less than three months had upset the Townsend apple cart. Following a great number of phone calls and letters from not only local business owners but concerned citizens as well, the mayor, Andrew Flemming called for an emergency chamber meeting on Thursday, July 1.

Ten days had passed since the discovery of Henks' body up at the Laurel Valley Golf Course. July fourth was just three days off, an extremely busy time for Townsend's economy, tourists flooding into the tiny community and surrounding area. The mid summer season was just around the corner.

Grant parked his Jeep in the already crammed parking lot. He had never attended a chamber meeting before. There had never been a reason. He had never given it much thought. Townsend had five elected commissioners, one of which was the mayor. Grant felt the Townsend Chamber had always done a great job in running the city. Besides that, Dalton, his grandfather, was in his third year of a four year term as Police Commissioner. In the past few years anything that was not confidential and discussed by the chamber, usually Dalton had shared it with Grant. Brody informed Grant that he had been contacted by the mayor's office and he, Butch and Grant were to attend the meeting.

Opening his blue binder, Grant went over the notes he had made in regard to both the Pittman and Henks' murders. Coming to the notes he made about the substance he had found at both homes he knew that soon he was going to have to share that bit of information with Brody. He had shown the substance to Dalton who said he thought it was tobacco. At the bottom of the last page he had jotted down Doug Eland's home phone number. He had an interesting talk with Doug the night following the press conference about the Henks' case. Doug said he had received a call from a friend of his from over in Cherokee about the second murder. His friend was saying that they had a serial killer in the area. Following a ten minute conversation about both the Pitman case and the recent murder, Doug told Grant he was planning on making a fall trip down to Townsend. Maybe they could get together and grab some lunch. Grant closed the binder and thought about Doug. He seemed like a nice man. He was looking forward to when he came down again.

Grant walked across the lot and looked at his watch: 6:58. The meeting was set to kick off at 7:00 p.m. In the very first parking slot he saw Brody's truck. Brody was no doubt inside probably wondering where in the hell Grant was. Looking around at the variety of vehicles in the lot Grant realized that every level of authority in the county was going to be present: park service, state police, Blount County Sheriff and of course the Townsend Police.

Arriving at the front door he ran into two of Townsend's prominent businessmen: Franklin Barrett and Bobby Kerr. Barrett was a self-made millionaire, a man who owned two riding stables, a campground and a restaurant in town, a hotel, along with a number of log cabins that he rented out. Kerr owned a gift shop and also had some rental properties.

"Evening," said Barrett.

Grant responded and tipped his hat, "Evening."

Kerr reached out and shook Grant's hand. "Looks like everybody's here tonight."

Grant shook his head in an affirmative manner and opened the door for the two men. Katherine Beckley, who was the mayor's secretary, sat at a small desk just inside the door, greeting everyone who entered. Brody was stationed by the door, giving all who entered the once over. Brody for a change seemed rather polite. He motioned for Grant to join him. "Grant, your job tonight is to remain by the door and make sure no media people get in. This is a closed meetin' for city officials and local business people only. Katherine has a list of those invited. If they're not on the list, then they don't get in…especially the media. I just sent Butch out the back to patrol the lot. Anyone gives you any crap…come get me. Understand?"

Grant leaned up against the wall. "Got it, Chief."

From where Grant was standing he could see the large meeting room. Folding chairs had been arranged in five rows of ten evenly spaced chairs. An eight foot card table had been set up to the left where there were assorted sodas, coffee, bottles of cold water, cups and a tub of ice. Glancing around the room he noticed a lot of people he knew: Sheriff Grimes; Jack from the National Park Service; Nelson Mofit, the Planning Commissioner for the city; Joe Wheeler, principal of the local elementary school; Perry Shoemaker, who owned a bait and tackle store.

The door opened as Pete Muir, the city's Maintenance Commissioner entered, followed by Nancy Kruzinski, a representative from the Tourist Information Bureau. Grant nodded at them as they passed and melted into the crowd of people who were mostly standing around in small groups.

Grant walked to the table where Katherine was sitting and remarked, "Guess the whole town is up in arms."

Katherine rolled her eyes and answered, "That's an understatement if I've ever heard one."

Mayor Flemming moved to a small podium that had been placed in front of the chairs and got the group's attention with his loud voice. "Could everyone please be seated so we can get started?"

A few people immediately took a seat, but most just continued to talk. The mayor reiterated calmly, "Everyone...please take a seat."

He waited patiently while everyone located a seat and looked out across the group, nodding his approval at their cooperation. Within a minute there was silence except for the sound of a scooting chair or a cough. The mayor adjusted the height of the microphone, cleared his throat then began, "First of all I would like to thank all of you for attending tonight's meeting." Scanning the group before him, he continued, "I think we can skip any introductions. I'm positive that everyone knows each other." Removing a sheet of paper from his suit coat pocket he unfolded it and smoothed it out on top of the podium. He hesitated then began once again, "Townsend is a destination city for many tourists who come to the Great Smoky Mountains. They come to our community to enjoy the natural beauty and grandeur of the mountains, wildlife, streams and forests. We have the privilege of being one of three main entrances to the Great Smoky Mountains National Park. The other two entrances in Gatlinburg and Cherokee have become heavily commercialized with entertainment, shows and various other tourist attractions. Here in

Townsend we offer tourists a restful, peaceful time away from the day-to-day hustle and bustle of life and over the years we have come to be known as the Peaceful Side of the Smokies. However, that being said, our peaceful city, not to mention Blount County, has recently been thrown for a loop. We have experienced two brutal murders in the last three months." Stopping for a moment, he took a swig of water from a glass that was on the podium.

"To say we have been flooded with letters and phone calls, well, let's just say there is great concern amongst our citizens and business owners." Glancing down at his notes, he went on, "The citizens of our community are concerned for their safety while business owners, many of which are here tonight, not only share the safety issue but also hold a great concern about how these recent tragedies will affect business." Gesturing toward the commissioners who were seated in four chairs off to the side of the podium, Flemming stated, "To get things started I feel we should hear from our commissioners first so we can be updated on where we stand and what's being done. Please reserve any questions until all of the commissioners have spoken. When they are finished we'll conduct a question and answer period. Thank you."

Dalton, the oldest of the commissioners, was the first to stand and approach the podium. Looking out over the group he nodded at many people he considered friends. Folding his hands on the podium he began, "Being the Police Commissioner here in Townsend has always been a pretty uneventful position. It is merely a political position, a liaison between the chief of police and the mayor's office. The day in, day out activities are handled by Chief Brody. To be honest, we just don't have a lot of problems here. Last week I had a meeting with Chief Brody and the County Sheriff, Bert Grimes. I can assure you after listening to what has been accomplished thus far that everything is being done to make our citizens and those coming here for vacation feel safe." Looking at Brody who was seated on the end of the first row, Dalton complimented him, "My hat is off to Chief Brody. As many of you are aware in the past I was the local chief of police for a number of years but in all those years I never had to experience or handle anything remotely equal to what Chief Brody has been dealing with the past three months."

Pointing at Bert Grimes, he added, "Sheriff Grimes has assigned an officer from the county sheriff's office to temporary duty here in

Townsend. This will allow our two officers to spend more time patrolling our neighborhoods and streets. In addition, the county sheriff's office will also be patrolling the Townsend area at intervals throughout the day. I'm sure their presence will be greatly appreciated by all and we thank them for their assistance." Nodding toward Jack he smiled, "The National Park Service has assigned four more park rangers to the Cades Cove area...have I got that right, Jack?"

Jack stood, answering the question, "Yes, that's right and we are prepared to have more rangers on site if needed. We want to make absolutely sure visitors to the park feel safe."

"The last thing I want to inform you about," added Dalton, nodding at two state troopers who were seated in the back row, "is that we have set up a hotline with the state police so if anyone notices anything out of the ordinary, there is someone they can call. Thank you."

Dalton returned to his seat and Meg Tyler stepped to the microphone. "As Commissioner of Recreation I have been working very closely with the Tourist Bureau the past few weeks." Holding her hands out toward the group, she explained, "I don't wish to be morbid but it's the only way to get my point across. Following the first murder there was no drop in tourism and we actually only had two inquiries about the murder in the area and that was over a ten week period." Holding up her finger, she emphasized, "Now, since the second murder which was about a week and a half back we have had five inquires from visitors. So, the level of concern about the safety of Townsend is still not a pressing issue but concern is rising. I feel the best way to handle the situation we are faced with is to go on with business as usual. We cannot live in or create an environment of fear. We are going to have our traditional Fourth of July fireworks just like always. We may have more officers present during the festivities but we are not going to cancel activities that folks look forward to. We are now in the planning stages of having a city wide picnic for the local residents in order to display our confidence in the safety of our city." Looking at Nancy, she asked, "Nancy, is there anything the Tourist Bureau would like to add?"

Nancy, sitting in the second row stood, then spoke, "I'd just like to add that it is extremely important for our community to remain upbeat despite the recent problems we have had. We get visitors from all over the United States and even other countries. Most of them will come here to spend a day or maybe a few days with us. It is my opinion that perception is everything. If the citizens and business owners of Townsend go around town with long faces all the while talking about the horrible murders we have had here recently, then we are shooting ourselves in the foot. I say, let's be upbeat and not make things worse than what they are."

Meg thanked Nancy then returned to her seat. Nelson Mofit stepped to the podium. "Good evening. As Planning Commissioner of Townsend it is the job of our committee to keep this valley as it is known, The Peaceful Side of the Smokies. At times, this has not been an easy thing to accomplish. We have always strived to retain the *charm* that our city is famous for. I too, do not wish to seem morbid *but* the two recent murders in our area are not what one would call charming. The Planning Commission has had little to do with the investigation but we stand ready to help our city to get through these times. Thank you."

Pete Muir, the Maintenance Commissioner got up to walk to the podium. Franklin Barrett who was seated in the first row stood, turned and addressed the group, "Enough of this crap about what we are doing to make people feel safe or what events we are planning on doing like a damn picnic to bring folks together. What I want to know, and if you'll be honest with yourselves, what we all want to know is what..." Turning he pointed at Brody. "...Chief Brody is doing to solve these murders. The killer is still out there. Hell, he or she or whoever it is might live right here in Townsend!"

Brody stood as the mayor banged a gavel on the podium at the same time speaking loudly, "Franklin, please take your seat. We have one more commissioner that has to speak before we start the question and answer portion of the meeting."

Pete stopped halfway to the podium and just stood there, staring at Barrett who at the moment was not going to take his seat. Barrett complimented Pete, "Look I've known Pete Muir for years. A finer man we could not ask to be one of the city's commissioners, but what on earth is the Maintenance Commissioner going to tell us that is going to help solve these murders? Are we going to be told our streets are going to be kept clean and well lit? What does any of that stuff and a number of other issues that have been brought up tonight have to do with catching whoever killed two of our local residents?"

The mayor backed away from the podium when Pete approached but Brody quickly moved to the microphone. "Barrett, why don't you just sit down and listen."

Mayor Flemming, getting more upset by the moment, raised his voice, suggesting, "Why don't both of you sit down so that we can continue."

From the back of the room, Pete Rankin, a local business owner stood, throwing in his two cents. "Franklin is right. Enough of this beating around the bush. Let's get to the meat of the matter. I want to know what is being done to catch whoever it is that murdered Asa Pittman and Mildred Henks!"

Cal Trosi, another business owner stood, addressing Rankin, "So you're assuming that the same person committed both murders?"

Franklin jumped in on what was rapidly becoming a heated conversation. "Of course it was the same person. Both of the victims had their fingers cut off and poor Mildred...her toes as well!"

Brody yelled loudly, his voice cutting through the crowd like a knife, "Everybody...sit down!"

Pete and Cal took their seats, but Barrett remained standing. "Look, Brody, I don't work for you, so where do you get off bossing me around?"

Nan Phillips who owned a florist shop stood. "Yeah, Franklin is right, Brody. We don't work for you...you work for us and we deserve some answers...like where in the hell were you when Mildred Henks was discovered? We pay you to be on top of things that go on in this town and when something like a second murder in less than three months occurs we expect you to be on the job." Turning around she addressed the entire group, "Now far be it from me to begrudge a man from having a day off but when you're the police chief you're on duty pretty much twenty-four hours a day, seven days a week."

Three more people stood and expressed their opinions loudly, Barrett was pointing at Brody who was shouting back at him, two of the commissioners stood and mingled with the crowd trying to restore some semblance of order to the meeting. Grant, amazed at how quickly things had gotten out of control, stood at the back of the room, looking at Brody, then to the crowd and finally at Dalton who was calmly seated, crossing his arms. Mayor Flemming threw his arms up into the air realizing that at the moment gaining any control of the meeting seemed impossible. Katherine, who was by now standing herself looked at Grant. "Maybe you should get Butch in here?"

"I think you're right," said Grant. "Looks like Brody is outnumbered."

Stepping out the door Grant closed it behind him, the peacefulness of the parking lot a reprieve from the arguments inside the chamber building. Butch just happened to be walking toward the door when he noticed Grant. Watching Grant lean up against the side of the building to take a deep breath, Butch asked, "What's the matter...you look frazzled?"

Grant shook his head and explained, "It's a nightmare in there. Everyone's arguing and pointing fingers. The mayor has lost control of the meeting. Everyone is ganging up on the Chief. I thought it'd be best if I came out and got you. People are getting pretty hot under the collar...especially Barrett."

Butch reached for the door handle, remarking snidely, "Barrett's a dipshit. Just because he's got a ton of money he thinks he rules the roost around here. He needs a good swift kick in the ass!"

Butch and Grant were no sooner back inside when Pastor Mark Dearman of the Bethel Baptist Church and Pastor Raymond T. Smith of the Tuckaleechee United Methodist Church had stepped up to the podium and had begun to regain order. As everyone was returning to their seats Pastor Dearman leaned toward the microphone speaking in the strong, deep voice that he was known for. "If everyone would please be seated we can continue with the meeting."

Mayor Flemming took a seat with the rest of the commissioners crossing his legs and adjusting his tie. Brody returned to his seat but then decided to join Grant and Butch at the back of the room. Rolling his eyes he leaned toward his two officers and whispered, "Bunch of idiots!"

When everyone was finally seated Pastor Dearman turned to the mayor and gestured that he should return to the podium. Flemming, still a bit flustered, motioned to the pastor. "No you go right ahead. I think that right now we could all use a little of God's intervention." His comment seemed to ease the tension that had filled the room. A number of people laughed.

Pastor Dearman looked out across the group then in a calm soothing manner he began, "I believe I received the same letter in regard to tonight's meeting like the rest of you. The topic that was going to be discussed was what our Chamber of Commerce and we the citizens and business owners are doing to ensure that those who live in Townsend and the surrounding area are safe. We also have a concern about all of the tourists that will be visiting our city and how safe they will be." Looking from the left of the group to the right, he went on, "Now I don't think pointing fingers at Chief Brody is going to solve anything. We need to give our police, not to mention the park service, state police and the county police our support."

Stepping back, Mark offered the floor to Pastor Smith. Pastor Smith was a tall man so he unhooked the microphone from its holder and held it to his lips. "I concur with Pastor Dearman. All of this bickering will get us nowhere. Ya know, the Bible tells us in Proverbs 24:10, 'If you falter in times of trouble, then how small is your strength?' The outburst that we experienced a few minutes ago is a perfect example of faltering during a time of trouble. We have had two horrible murders in our community; something that has not happened in well, I can't even remember the last time something like this happened here in Townsend. So, I think it's safe to say that we are experiencing a time of trouble. Let me ask you this. Where is our strength tonight? Did we display strength when we stood and yelled at one another?" He hesitated and looked over the group who was silent like they were in church on a Sunday morning. "Now, are we going to agree on everything...certainly not! Do we have to respect each other? Definitely! And, therein lies our strength." With that he turned to the commissioners and gestured to Pete Muir. "I believe that moments ago you were about to address the group."

Both pastors took their seats when Pete walked to the mic. Smiling he laughed then spoke, "It's funny. Usually when I get home after one of these meetings my wife has a tendency to ask me how things went. I always answer, 'same ol', same ol'. Won't she be surprised tonight when I tell her that we had a knock down, drag out." After giving a quick boxer pose, there was more laughter while he began his portion of the meeting, "As Commissioner of Maintenance..."

Brody, Grant and Dalton, except for the mayor and his secretary were the last to leave the chamber building. Butch had been sent back outside to keep an eye on the parking lot. Mayor Flemming locking the door turned to Brody and apologized, "Axel, I'm sorry that a number of our local business owners came down on you tonight. I can assure you that was not the reason for our meeting."

"It's all right." said Brody. "These are difficult times. I can understand that folks are gettin' a little antsy. We're doing everythin' we can to clear this up, but at the moment we just don't have much to go on. It's not like we can just sit down and read the tea leaves and presto...the case is solved."

The mayor shook Brody's hand then responded, "I know in time we'll get this cleared up. All I ask in the meantime is that you keep me posted on any progress."

After the mayor and his secretary walked across the lot to their cars Brody turned to Grant, "You're off tomorrow, right?"

"Yep, that's right," answered Grant. "Do you need me to come in?"

"No...you enjoy the day. God knows recently we haven't had that many off." Brody started for his truck and finished the short conversation. "See ya Saturday mornin'. Take it easy, Dalton."

Dalton punched Grant lightly on his arm. "I've been to a lot of chamber meetings over the years. Most of the time it's just business like always...run of the mill stuff...but tonight, well, folks seemed a little out of joint. Can't say I blame them. These two murders are things you read about in the paper or see on television. It always happens somewhere else and we become callous and conditioned to tragedy...but then when it hits close to home...it's like a wake up call, that when it comes right down to it Townsend is just as vulnerable as anyplace else. It's just a little hard for people to believe this sort of thing could happen here." Realizing that he was rambling on, Dalton placed his arm around Grant's shoulder. "Listen, how about a slice of pie and a cup of coffee over at the café. It's on me."

Grant smiled. "You're on. Meet ya there in a few."

Grant walked to his Jeep and noticed Butch and Dana Beth standing next to her car. She looked in his direction and smiled. Butch immediately kissed her on the lips then turned and smirked at Grant as if to say, 'She's my woman!'

CHAPTER ELEVEN

GRANT BUTTONED HIS YELLOW polo shirt and tucked it into his favorite pair of jeans. He ran a brush through his hair and then stuck his wallet into his back pocket. Grabbing his keys off the nightstand he spun them around his finger and bounded down the stairs.

His mother was seated comfortably on the couch in the living room. She put the quilt pattern she had been going over down on the coffee table and commented, "Well, son, don't you look nice this morning."

Dalton, sitting in his old recliner looked up from the morning paper. "Hey, no uniform. That's a switch."

Grant smiled and headed for the kitchen as he answered back over his shoulder, "Finally, a day off." Pouring himself a cup of coffee he returned to the living room where he leaned up against a large bookcase. "Listen, I'm heading over to Gatlinburg. Got a few errands to run. Anybody need anything?"

"Don't think so," answered Dalton. "But, thanks for asking."

"How about you, Mom? Any requests?"

Picking up her knitting needle and a ball of green yarn she replied, "Not a thing, son. Drive safe and have yourself a nice day."

Outside on the front porch he took a deep knee bend and drew in a shot of morning mountain air. He had three specific things he needed to get done but he was in no hurry. Climbing into the Jeep he decided to put the top down. Turning on the radio he hit the scan button until it stopped on a country and western station where Rascal Flatts was belting out a song. Turning out of the driveway he hummed along with the tune coming from the rear speakers. Finally in fourth gear the Jeep cruised along at sixty miles an hour down the road that led to Townsend. A Charlie Daniels tune came on the radio. He turned the volume up while singing along, the wind blowing through his hair. He was in a good mood, and the day was just beginning.

Once he arrived in Townsend the traffic slowed down considerably. Tourists seemed to be everywhere. Both gas stations he passed were lined with cars, the parking lots of the local restaurants were jammed, people were out walking, some jogging. Turning left on Wears Valley Road he opened the glove compartment, removed a pack of gum unwrapped a stick and stuck it in his mouth.

Ten minutes later, he had to slow down on the outskirts of Hatchertown for a group of cyclists who hugged the right side of the road. Once he was clear of the line of riders, he glanced in the rearview mirror. He couldn't help but notice the wallet size photograph of Dana Beth that he had attached to the sun visor when she had given it to him years ago following their senior year in high school. He glanced up at her picture once again, smiled, but then suddenly frowned. He thought about the fact that she was with Butch Miller. It was hard to think of her and not Butch. *Crap!* he thought. He had been in such a good mood and not even ten miles down the road he was allowing his imagination to prevent him from having a nice day.

Spitting his gum out the window, he remembered how his mother had told him to have a nice day. It occurred to him just because someone told you to have a nice day that did not ensure your day would be filled with happiness and bliss. There was any number of things out there waiting everyday to derail people from having a nice day. Problems—problems that had no conscience. Problems had absolutely no concern over screwing up a good day. Problems were not patient either. They didn't line up behind a problem that was already in your life and wait for it to be solved. They just kept piling up. He realized there was little one could do to eliminate problems from popping up in life except to deal with them.

Slowing down for a groundhog that scampered across the road, Grant thought about the past couple of years and how problems seemed to pile up in his life. There was the death of his father, then his mother's fall at the hardware store which had been life changing for her. Then there was the fallout with Dana Beth, his dropping out of school, the murders of Asa Pittman and Mildred Henks and the worst problem of all; Butch Miller was dating Dana Beth. Taking her picture down from the visor, he opened the console and placed it inside. He had to get her off his mind.

Before he knew it, he was at the red light at the intersection where Wears Valley Road butted into the main drag that ran through the heart of Pigeon Forge and eventually to Gatlinburg. Making a right hand turn the going was slow. Traffic was backed up, people pulling in and out of restaurants, hotels, gift shops and novelty stores. Pigeon Forge always reminded him of a miniature Las Vegas with all its activity and signs, attractive, colorful signs advertising where to eat, what to do, where to go: Dollywood, Dixie Stampede, Burger King, The Pancake House, Comedy Barn, Go Cart Racing, Nantahala River Rafting and on and on.

Thirty minutes later, which should have only been a five minute drive he broke away from the hustle and bustle of Pigeon Forge, the road now surrounded by the tall green forest. It was only a six mile journey before he reached the outskirts of Gatlinburg and more signs: Gatlinburg Skylift, Castle Tours, Miniature Golf, Hollywood Wax Museum, The Smoky Mountains Winery and a variety of other tourist attractions.

Another ten minute drive through the maze of shops and stores he finally arrived at his destination, Buzzy's Auto Repair. Pulling into the lot he put the top up and locked the Jeep. Walking into the garage he walked past two cars up on lifts. Buzzy, an old friend of his was standing next to the open hood of a late model Chevy as Grant approached, waving. "Yo, Buzzy!"

Buzzy, who was baldheaded, sported a full beard and had a smile that was second to none. Wiping his hands on his already grease stained coveralls, he saluted Grant. "Good to see you, Deputy Dawg! How goes things over in Townsend?" Wiping his hands on a clean red shop towel he reached for Grant's hand. Over the blaring noise of air guns and motors Buzzy motioned toward the front lot, "Let's step outside."

Stopping at a bright red coke machine up against the side of the building, Buzzy reached into his pocket for some change and asked, "Soda?"

"No thanks," answered Grant.

After making his selection, Buzzy retrieved the soda, turned to Grant and inquired, "Anything new on the murders?"

"Nothing yet," replied Grant. "It's gonna be a tough nut to crack." Wanting to change the subject Grant asked, "How are things going here?"

"Not bad. Thinking about expanding, maybe over in your neck of the woods…probably Maryville. Right now most of my business comes from Sevierville, Pigeon Forge or right here in Gatlinburg."

"Sounds good. Then when I need some work done on my Jeep I just drive up the road a piece."

Looking over at Grant's Jeep, Buzzy commented, "Saw your name on the work list for today. What did ya bring her in for?"

"Just standard stuff. Ya know, oil change, check the filter, and oh yeah, I want to get my tires rotated. Been hitting a lot of bumps lately. I've been putting a lot of wear on the front tires."

"Shouldn't be a problem." Looking at the cars parked in the lot he had to work on, Buzzy estimated, "Probably have her finished up in around two hours. We're really busy today. You gonna wait?"

"Actually, I've got a couple of errands I need to get out of the way up the street. Listen, thanks for squeezing me in. I appreciate it."

Turning to walk off the lot, Buzzy stopped Grant. "I did want to ask you something."

"Two ears…no waiting," said Grant

Taking a drink of soda Buzzy asked, "You having any problems over your way with missing dogs?"

Grant surprised, answered, "Yeah, we are. What made you ask?"

"Somebody stole my two beagles. They reached right over the fence and took them out of the yard."

"You saw this take place?"

"No, my neighbor did. He just happened to be down cleaning out his basement when he looks out his basement window and sees this guy grabbing the dogs."

"Could your neighbor describe the man?"

"No, it was one of those small basement windows: dusty, covered with cobwebs. It happened so quick."

"Did you report it to the police?"

"Sure I did, but without any way to ID the thief, there really was nothing they could do. They did tell me that for the past couple of weeks there have been a number of dogs reported missing."

"That's strange," said Grant. "The same thing has been happening in and around Townsend. We're kind of in the same boat over there too. We don't have anything to go on. I'm sorry that your dogs are gone."

Taking another drink, Buzzy remarked, "Damn they were really good hunters. Keep an eye out for them, will you?"

"Sure, listen, I'll be back in about two hours."

Walking up the street Grant thought it was strange that the same thing involving missing dogs was happening in Gatlinburg also. A block down from Buzzy's Grant looked in the display window of the Smokezy Tobacco and Pipe Store. The window was tastefully decorated with various pipes and types of tobacco, boxes of imported cigars and cigarettes. Entering the store a bell over top of the door jangled. A voice from the back of the store rang out, "Be right with you!"

Grant walked over to the counter taking in the familiar aroma of new cut wood and pine resin. The back wall displayed a kaleidoscope of brightly colored tobacco tins while the glass case beneath the counter exhibited cigars wrapped in gold or silver bands and custom wood pipe holders.

An elderly gentleman came through the half door from the backroom and politely asked, "What can I do for you, young fella?"

Grant reached into his pocket. "I have a question for you." Opening his wallet he removed a small folded plastic bag and laid it on the counter. "I know this isn't much to go on but I was wondering if you could identify this? I think it's some sort of tobacco. I'm not sure."

The man picked up the bag opened the top and bent down, placing his nose close to the opening. After taking a few short whiffs he straightened up. "This is an easy one. Peach Brandy. It's a course-leaf tobacco, comes in a tin. I carry a few different brands." Turning he pointed at the selection of tins on the wall. "Let's see...I have Cornell, Diehl and Danske Club. I also have a brand called Uhle, but I'm out of that right now." Handing the bag back to Grant, the man asked, "You a pipe smoker?"

"No, sir," said Grant. "I was just wondering if this type of tobacco is hard to find or if it's only sold in certain stores?"

"No, not really. It's pretty common, but most people don't like the taste that much. It's rather strong, but it has a great aroma. I'd say I sell most of it to older men who know what it's like to enjoy a good pipe."

"So you sell a lot of it then?"

"Enough to keep it in stock, but it's pretty easy to find."

Grant folded the bag and placed it back in his wallet, smiled, then explained, "You must think I'm a strange one standing here asking you all of these questions?"

"Not at all," laughed the man. "We get all kinds of questions in here."

"The truth is," said Grant. "I'm a police officer from over in Townsend. I'm trying to identify this type of tobacco so I thought I'd come to an expert."

The man proudly smiled. "Well, that'd be me."

Grant leaned on the counter and asked his next question, "I don't suppose you keep records of who buys what around here."

"Afraid not. Aside from my local customers we get people from all over the country coming in here on a daily basis. I specialize in a lot of imported tobacco products so I sell a lot over my website. I ship stuff all over the country."

"Are there any locals who buy it on a regular basis?"

The man thought for a moment then answered, "Not anyone I can think of. Sorry."

"That's all right. I appreciate your help."

Grant turned to leave when the man asked, "How are those horrible murders over in Townsend coming?"

Grant, walking toward the door answered with a wave of his hand, "They're coming!"

Standing in front of the store, Grant realized it was time for him to turn in the tobacco sample as evidence since he had discovered it at both crime scenes. He wanted to hand it over to Sheriff Grimes but he knew from past experience that Brody would go through the roof. He'd make sure Brody got the sample soon.

His next stop was two blocks away. It had grown cloudy in the past half hour and rain was starting to spit tiny droplets. Good thing he had put the top up on the Jeep. The Candle Cottage was one of his mother's favorite stores. She loved candles, especially Yankee Candles. He had decided to surprise her with one. The store was filled with customers, mostly women. He made his way to the Yankee Candle display at the rear of the store. Unlike the tobacco shop, an array of aromas that he was familiar with filled the air: Baked Apple, Summer Meadow, Ocean Breeze.

Opening a number of glass jars and sniffing the various scents he was startled by a soft voice, "Good morning, Grant."

Turning around, Grant found himself face-to-face with none other than Dana Beth. He was so shocked to see her, especially in Gatlinburg that he was at a loss for words. She looked great: yellow and white flowered summer dress, fashionable sandals, her short blond hair tucked behind her ears. "Good morning, Dana Beth," he stammered awkwardly. "What are you doing over here in Gatlinburg this morning?"

Looking past him at the candle display, she answered, "The same thing you are I guess. My mother's birthday is coming up in a week and I thought I'd get her some nice doilies for her hutch."

Grant, feeling a little more comfortable nodded toward the candles. "Well, you know how my mom loves candles. I thought I'd surprise her and pick one up."

Moving past Grant, Dana Beth picked up a jar, opened the top and took a deep sniff. "I think you should get her the vanilla. Remember that one year at Christmas when I got her a vanilla candle? She really seemed to like it. She told me that vanilla was her favorite."

"I do remember that."

"Seems like a no brainer to me," remarked Dana Beth.

Picking up the jar from the shelf Grant looked at his feet trying to find the right words. Turning back to her he asked, "So are you still at the hospital?"

Smiling pleasantly, she replied, "Yes, but today is my day off."

"Me too," said Grant. Struggling for the next thing he should say, he became flustered and blurted out, "Well, I guess I better pay for this. It was good to see you again."

"You too, Grant."

Brushing past her he walked to the sales counter feeling like such a fool. This was the girl that he had planned on marrying at one time and he couldn't even think of anything to say to her. *What an idiot!* he thought to himself while he waited to pay for the candle. Handing his debit card to the clerk, he casually turned around to see if she had left. There she was still browsing in one of the aisles. She looked up and caught him staring. She smiled at him as he quickly turned around while the clerk handed his card back and placed the candle in a bag. *God, she must think I'm stupid!* he thought. *Oh, what the hell. It's now or never. I've already made a fool of myself.* Walking over to her, he felt like a little kid asking a girl to dance for the first time. "Look, my Jeep is just up the street getting a once over. I've got about an hour before she'll be finished up. I was wondering if you would like to go next door and grab a coffee or something?" He took a deep breath waiting for her refusal.

Looking directly into his eyes, she pursed her lips then answered, "Yes, I think I would like that."

Grant was beside himself. "All right, well...let's go!"

As they headed for the door the clerk hollered out to Grant, "Sir, you forgot your candle."

Two buildings down, The Mountain Edge Grill was hopping with the early lunch crowd. Stepping inside the door, Grant and Dana Beth were greeted by the hostess and then led to a corner table next to the front window. She placed two menus on the table and told them that their waitress would be right with them.

Grant fiddled with the saltshaker and looked out the window wondering how to start the lunch conversation. Nothing was coming to his mind. He was rescued from the moment of silence by the waitress who had a heavy Irish accent, "Afternoon. Wha' could I be gettin' fer ya then?"

Fumbling with the menu, Grant made a rapid decision. "I'll have a cup of coffee...make that decaf and I guess a slice of peach pie."

Turning to Dana Beth, the waitress poised her pen over top of her pad and waited patiently. Dana Beth scanned the menu, tapping her teeth with her index finger. "Ah...let's see. I'll go with a glass of milk and a piece of the apple pie."

"Right back then," said the waitress. She scurried across the restaurant disappearing into the kitchen. Looking across the table Grant's eyes met Dana Beth's. They stared at each other for a brief second when Dana Beth broke the silence. "You seem nervous Grant. Maybe this wasn't such a good idea."

Folding his hands in front of him, Grant answered, "I just don't want to say the wrong thing."

"The wrong thing," Dana Beth repeated. "Now how could you possibly say the wrong thing to me?"

Glancing out the window and then back to her, Grant shook his head and explained, "Look, I seem to have a habit of screwing things up...like that day when I saw you at the police station. I said some things I shouldn't have...about you and Butch. Well, we know how that all turned out. If I would have just kept my mouth shut. I'm sorry it happened. I don't know what got into me."

Reaching across the table, she gently touched his right hand. "You don't have anything to be sorry for. It was my fault. I went there to see Butch and to be honest I was hoping I'd get a chance to see you. It was stupid of me. I don't know what I expected to happen. We hadn't seen each other for almost two years. I should have known it would be awkward. I should be the one who is apologizing…not you."

Just then the waitress arrived with their drinks and pie. Setting them down on the table, she asked, "Would ya be needin' anythin' else then?"

"No, I don't think so," said Grant.

The waitress no sooner left the table when Dana Beth picked up where she had left off. "I was the one who broke it off with you. We had an agreement about when we would get married and I decided to change things and when you wouldn't see things my way, well, I just got so upset."

Grant couldn't believe how quickly the conversation was moving and the direction that it was heading. "True, you did break it off, but still it's my fault that even happened. I was so focused on my schooling and look what's happened now. Because I was so bullheaded I let you slip right through my fingers and besides that, I still don't have my degree…*or you.*"

Dana Beth picked up her fork and stabbed a bite of pie. "I was just getting so tired of our long distance relationship, I thought if I gave you an ultimatum you would see things my way. When I broke up with you and sent your ring back my parents were so upset with me." Swallowing the bite of pie Dana Beth took a drink of milk, pointing her fork at Grant's pie. "Are you going to eat that or just let it set?"

Pushing the pie to the side, Grant leaned forward, "When I woke up this morning if someone would have told me you and I were going to have this conversation today I would have told them they were nuts but since we've opened this can of worms I just have to ask…and please, don't get mad. What about Butch? I wish I could say I'm sorry for punching him, but I'm not."

"Grant, listen to me. Butch Miller is nothing more than an experiment that, for lack of a better phrase…backfired! When I came home for the summer I thought maybe you would come and see me and when you didn't I did a stupid thing. I wanted to make you jealous and it just didn't work out the way I thought it would." Waving her fork in the air she went on, "Butch tells everyone we're a couple and nothing could be further from the truth. We just don't connect. I know he would like our relationship to be more than what it is, but he just isn't my type."

Grant fingered the rim of his coffee cup. "So, you're telling me you're not in love with him...and you're not..."

Dana Beth put up her hand. "I know what you're going to say and the answer is no. We are not having an intimate relationship. It's getting tough to keep it that way...and he just keeps getting more and more aggressive. I've told him I think we should see other people and he gets so upset. I'm going to break it off with him...completely."

The words coming out of her mouth were like sweet music to his ears. He wasn't quite sure what to say. His lack of a response caused Dana Beth to ask, "So what do you think about this?"

Grant cleared his throat. "I'm glad you're breaking up with Butch and I won't interfere. When you're ready to call it quits with him, I'll be there for you. I guess I've always been there for you. Just this morning on the way over here I was looking at the photograph you gave me back in high school. Over the past year or so I've thought about you more times than I can remember. Every time I look at that picture of you it makes me mad that you're seeing Butch. This morning I took your photo down and put it in my console. I just couldn't stand to think about you with him."

Sitting back in her chair, Dana Beth took a deep breath. "This is the first time I've felt good about anything in quite some time. I'm really glad we talked."

"Me too!" said Grant. "So how is your job over at the hospital going?"

For the next thirty minutes they talked about old times, laughing at silly things they had done and said in the past. Grant's coffee had grown cold in the cup, Dana Beth's milk had gotten warm. Taking his last bite of pie Grant looked at his watch. "I better get going. My Jeep is probably done by now." Dana Beth nodded as they both stood up. She waited by the front door while he paid their bill. Walking out into the warm sunshine Grant touched her arm. "I want to tell you that I really enjoyed the time we spent together today."

Before she could respond her cell phone rang. Digging it out of her purse, she flipped it open and answered, "Hello." After listening for a few seconds she spoke into her phone, "Okay, I'll be home real soon." Placing the phone back in her purse, she said, "That was mom. She needs me to pick up some things at the grocery before I head home." Raising her hand she placed it on the front of his shirt.

"I really need to go. Take care of yourself, Grant." Placing his fingers around her hand he gently squeezed it.

She turned and walked up the street. "If you need anything, just give me a call," yelled Grant."

She gave him a thumbs up and continued up the street.

After picking up the Jeep he drove back to Townsend and stopped at Arby's to pick up a late lunch for Dalton and his mother. Pulling up to the drive through window a white van pulled out. He noticed the sticker on the back. **WILL BRAKE FOR ANIMALS.** He'd seen that very same van somewhere before. He recalled the bumper sticker. Then he remembered. The night after Asa Pittman's murder, at the Parkway Grocery, that van had been parked out by the gas pumps. Probably just a local.

On the short drive home, Grant thought about how the day had gone. He had set out to accomplish three things: get the Jeep serviced, get the tobacco identified and purchase a candle for his mother. He had not only accomplished the things he wanted to get done but had added a fourth dimension to the day. He had cleared the air with Dana Beth. He felt like he had gotten his foot back in the door.

Pulling up in the driveway of Dalton's farm he smiled to himself, opened the console and placed Dana Beth's picture back where it belonged. He wasn't going to give up on his chances with her.

CHAPTER TWELVE

JUST LIKE CLOCKWORK, the dog days of summer settled in like a heavy shroud across the Smoky Mountains. The sweltering heat and high humidity signaled the middle of summer. Grant pulled his Jeep into the Parkway Grocery, turned off the ignition and wiped his brow. Looking at the clock on the dashboard, he noted the time at 6:32 a.m. Not even seven o'clock in the morning and the temperature was already in the mid-eighties. It was only mid-July. The sultry heat and the stagnant air of late summer had arrived earlier than usual.

Getting out of the Jeep, he looked in the direction of the mountains, the low mist practically blocking them from view. The morning mist that covered the mountains normally burnt off around eight or nine o'clock, but during the dog days of summer the picturesque fog seemed to hang around until noon, sometimes even later. Glancing at an outdoor thermometer hanging next to the store entrance Grant shook his head, noticing the red mercury marker right on the eighty-five degree mark. Just as he was about to enter, Jake Peabody, the owner of a local nursery located on the outskirts of town was coming out. Almost bumping into Grant, he juggled a large soda he was carrying. "Mornin', Grant." Holding up his drink, he took a large sip. "Way too hot for coffee today. They say it's gonna hit ninety-seven…heat index over a hundred."

Tipping his hat to Jake, Grant responded, "Stay coo,l Jake."

Inside the store the cool air conditioning was like a slap in the face. Putting the hat back on his head Grant stopped just inside the door and took a deep breath. The store was packed with customers, many purchasing bags of ice and coolers, sodas and bottled water.

Grant really didn't care how hot it was. He still needed his morning coffee, *a cup of ambition,* as Dalton always called the first cup of the day. Walking to the back of the store where the three tall, chrome coffee dispensers were located he grabbed a styrofoam cup, dumped in a package of sweetener then inserted the cup beneath the dispenser marked Robust Dark Brew, and hit the button. The dark liquid quickly filled the cup. Reaching for a stir stick, he noticed a middle-aged man taking a drink from a bottle of soda while he inspected the donut selection. When the man turned to face him Grant noticed the black bold lettering on the front of a gray tee shirt:

TOWNSEND
THE PEACEFUL SIDE
OF THE SMOKIES
NOT!

Staring at the shirt, Grant was speechless. At first the man didn't seem to notice, but following the prolonged attention focused on him, he looked behind him, then to the right and then the left. The man, feeling just a bit uncomfortable, despite the fact that Grant was wearing his uniform turned and began to walk away but was stopped by Grant. "Excuse me, Sir?"

The man slowly turned around and politely asked, "Are you speaking to me?"

"Yes, I am," said Grant. "That tee shirt you have on. If I could ask? Where did you get it?"

The man seemed relieved. "Over in Pigeon Forge. We're taking the tour."

Grant, confused, slowly stirred his coffee. "What tour?"

Just then the man's wife came around the corner carrying a bottle of sun tan lotion. The man pointing at the gray tee-shirt she was wearing said, "That tour."

Grant was absolutely flabbergasted as he read what was professionally stenciled on her shirt:

I SURVIVED THE
PITTMAN-HENKS
MURDER TOUR

Setting down his coffee, Grant pointed at both shirts. "So you're telling me you purchased those shirts over in Pigeon Forge and you're taking some sort of tour?"

"That's right," said the man. Staring at Grant for a moment he looked at his wife then back to Grant. "It says on your uniform Townsend Police. I can tell from the look on your face that you don't seem pleased. Have we done something wrong, officer?"

Grant smiled. "No…and if I gave you that impression…I'm sorry. It's just that we've had two murders here in town recently and they are actually still under investigation. The people here in town are still kind of on edge and I'm afraid if they were to see you wearing those shirts…well, it just wouldn't go over very well." Stepping closer to the couple, Grant asked, "When are you supposed to take *this tour?"*

The man, still thinking they had done something wrong, stumbled for words, trying his best to answer, "Look…we really don't want to upset anyone. We're just on vacation. This is the first vacation we've had in years. We paid good money for the tour. The man in Pigeon Forge said…"

The man's wife stepped forward and interrupted her husband, "For God's sake, Harry, just answer the officer's question. He didn't ask for a rundown of your life." Extending her hand toward Grant, she introduced herself, "My name is Stella Barman. This is my husband, Harry. We're from New York, live just outside of the city. We decided to visit the Smokies. We have friends that came down here a few years ago and they couldn't stop talking about how lovely it is in these parts, so this year we decided to make the trip. We were going to stay in Pigeon Forge but when we stopped at this kiosk advertising tours for over here in Townsend we got a great deal, not only on a cabin, but some great tours. We got the package deal. Our first tour starts this morning at nine o'clock. We're riding up some trail to see where…what was the man's name? Oh yes, now I remember Asa Pittman. We're going to see where he was murdered. Then, later on this afternoon after lunch we're riding up to the Pittman Farm to see where the man lived."

Harry jumped in on the conversation, "Then tomorrow, we take a tour bus over to the Henks' place to see where some woman was murdered. We thought about taking the Pittman-Henks ghost tour at night, but we're not really into all that spooky stuff."

Stella picked up where Harry left off, "And we got a great price on a cabin to boot."

Grant was stunned at what he was hearing. His lack of response to what he had been told caused Stella to reach into her pocketbook. "Actually, I still have the brochure we received at the kiosk over in Pigeon Forge." Handing a bright yellow 3 x 8 inch card to Grant she smiled. Grant looked at the card and couldn't believe what he was reading:

**Barrett-Pittman Tours
In
Townsend, Tennessee**

**Home of the Famous
Pittman-Henks
Murders**

**Guided Van Tours
Horseback Riding**

**Special Rates On
Cabin Rentals
And Hotel Rooms**

Stella informed Grant, "If you'll flip the card over on the back they have all the information on the different tours."

Flipping the card over, Grant read silently:

Barrett-Pittman Tours

**Thunderhead Trail
Murder Scene $49.00**

**Asa Pittman Farm Tour
$49.00**

**Laurel Lake Murder Tour
$49.00**

**Mildred Henks Home Tour
$59.00**

**Pittman-Henks
Ghosts Tours
$69.00**

Grant flipped the card back over, looked at the older couple then asked, "And how many people are going on these tours today?"

The wife answered, "We were told there were nine couples so far. We met one of the other couples. Real nice folks...I think they said they were from Wisconsin."

Grant took a swig of his coffee then asked, "I don't suppose I could keep this card...could I?"

"Sure, why not," said Harry. "I guess we don't need it anymore."

"And how about those tee-shirts," said Grant. "Would you be willing to sell those to me?"

Stella spoke up, "Well, we really didn't have to purchase these. They came with the package. But I do remember seeing a sign that advertised them at $9.95 each if we just wanted a shirt."

"Tell ya what," said Grant. "I'll give you twenty dollars each for the shirts. That's forty dollars for both. Deal?"

"Deal," said Harry. "We've got some extra clothes out in our car. Come on, Stella, we'll change out of these in the restroom."

Five minutes later, Harry and Stella Barman were forty dollars richer, and Grant had some very interesting items to show Brody.

Pulling out onto the street Grant couldn't fathom the idea that someone had come up with a way to make money off of the Pittman and Henks' murders. This was the first he had heard about *the tours.* Was this something the chamber could have approved and he just wasn't made aware of it? He couldn't swallow that. The chamber would never allow the town's name to be smeared and besides, how could anyone go on Asa's farm or Mildred's place without permission? The whole thing just didn't add up. Stopping for a red light he noticed two people crossing the street, both wearing the Pittman-Henks Murder Tour tee-shirts. According to the Barmans there were eight other couples scattered around town that were going on the tour. The light changed and he drove through the intersection.

Pulling into the station lot, Grant grabbed the card and the two shirts, climbed out of the Jeep and started for the entrance. He was about to enter when Butch came out. Before Butch could even say a word, Grant spoke, "Might want to go back in. I've got something that's gonna send Brody right through the roof."

Following Grant down the hall, Butch responded, "What the hell's going on?"

Brody was on the phone as Grant and Butch entered the crammed office. Brody, the phone to his ear didn't look happy.

After shaking his head in wonder, he spoke to whoever was on the other end. "Look, Mrs. Birch, I understand you're upset but at this point we just don't know why this is happenin'. We're continuin' to look into the matter. If we…"

Brody slammed down the phone knocking over a half full cup of coffee. "Can you believe it? Mrs. Birch, one of our elementary school teachers just hung up on me! That's the ninth call we've had in the past few months about dogs disappearin' in Townsend." Grabbing a roll of paper towels from on top of a filing cabinet, Brody began to sop up the spilled coffee. "What are we? The SPCA for cryin' out loud!"

Just then Marge stuck her head in the doorway, "Chief, excuse me but we just got a call from the Little River Campgrounds. Somebody's car was broken into and don't forget about those drunk college kids over at the park."

Slumping in his chair, Brody tossed the soggy paper towel into the trash and looked toward the ceiling, "God…why me? What in the hell is wrong with people around here?" Seeing Grant and Butch standing off to the side of the doorway, Brody frowned. "What do you two idiots want?"

Grant walked over to Brody's desk and laid the two shirts on the desk smoothing them out so they could be read, then he placed the yellow card between them. At first Brody wasn't all that interested but then he read the message on the shirts. "What the hell is this…some sort of joke?"

Grant sat down opposite Brody and explained, "I was over at the gas station earlier this morning when I ran into a couple of tourists from New York." Pointing at the shirts he continued, "They were wearing those shirts. I couldn't believe it. When I asked them where they got them they said over in Pigeon Forge at a kiosk. They went on to tell me they received the shirts as part of a package deal for some sort of a tour. They said they even got a great deal on a cabin here in Townsend. They also told me there were eight other couples taking the tour which starts this morning at nine o'clock. A riding tour up to Thunderhead Trail to see where Asa Pittman was murdered."

Brody held up his hand for Grant to stop. "Whoa, whoa, whoa. Are you shittin' me?"

Grant nodded toward the card. "It's all on that card there, Chief."

Picking up the card Brody silently read both sides of the card then sat back, exclaiming in a whisper, "Well, I'll be dipped in shit if this doesn't take the cake. Someone has figured out a way to make money off of two horrible murders. I thought the media people were bad, but whoever started this business…well, they need to be stopped."

Standing, he tapped the card in his hand then asked, "You said the tour up to Thunderhead starts at nine?"

Grant shrugged. "That's what the couple said."

Grabbing his hat, Brody ordered, "Here's what we're gonna do. There are only four stables in town near enough to take a ride up Thunderhead: Cades Cove Stables on Route 73 and out on Campground Drive. Then there's Davy Crockett and Mountain View Stables. We're gonna stop this nonsense. We'll split up. I'll take the Cades Cove Stables on Route 73. We'll skip the stables on Campground Drive. They are run by the National and State Park Service. I doubt very seriously if they would permit this sort of thing without checkin' with us first. Butch, I want you to head on over to Davy Crockett Stables and Grant, you take Mountain View." Heading for the door Brody looked at this watch. "It's not quite seven thirty. We might just have time to stop this nonsense before it gets started."

Out in the parking lot, Brody gave his final instructions. "All right, whoever stumbles onto the stable where this tour is goin' to take place needs to call the other two so we can converge."

Marge came running out the door as Brody was getting in his truck. "Chief, chief…what about the car break in at the campgrounds and then there are those rowdy kids at the park?"

Starting the truck, Brody yelled back, "Call the campgrounds and tell them we'll be sendin' someone up there shortly. As far as the damn kids go, well, they'll be long gone by the time we show up." Backing out of his parking spot, he jammed the shifter into first gear and sped out of the lot his tires squealing on the hot pavement. Turning onto Tiger Drive he hit the overhead lights and the siren. Butch followed suit, trailing Brody out of the lot. Grant shook his head and backed out slowly, thinking that Brody really was an idiot. Stopping a group of people from riding up into the woods was hardly a reason for all the fanfare of flashing lights and loud sirens.

It was only a ten minute drive up to the Mountain View Stables which were located just off Route 73. Grant hoped Mountain View was not the culprit of this tour business because he knew he was going to have to disappoint a lot of tourists. Pulling off the highway and traveling down a short dirt road he passed a sign that read: ***Mountain View Riding Stables***.

Pulling into the dirt parking lot, he took in the surroundings before getting out. There were three buildings, all rustic. An office and two large barns. A group of six people, all sporting the gray controversial tee-shirts were gathered on the porch of the office, many seated in old rocking chairs. On the side of the first barn there was a long hitching post where there were twelve horses lined up. Two young girls were in the process of watering and brushing down the animals while two men and another girl were busy straightening out saddles, harnesses and reins. Standing next to the cruiser, Grant frowned. It looked like he had drawn the short straw. The Mountain View Stables was where the tours were going to take place. Reaching into the cruiser he unhooked the radio and placed it to his lips, "Brody, Butch...come in. I've hit pay dirt over here at the Mountain View. This is definitely where the tour is. There are a number of people over here with the tee-shirts on."

Brody answered, "On my way. Whatever you do, Grant do not...I repeat, do not let that tour go off. I should be there in about five minutes."

"Right behind you chief," Butch responded.

Grant looked at his watch: 7:45. An hour and fifteen minutes before the scheduled tour. He decided to wait for Brody and Butch. He'd let the chief do the talking. There was plenty of time to shut down the tour. Relaxing by his cruiser, a number of tourists noticed him standing next to a split rail fence.

Two men walked out of the office onto the porch. He noticed the man on the left. It was Franklin Barrett, the businessman who had caused the ruckus at the chamber meeting. Dressed in a fashionable cowboy shirt, jeans and custom stitched boots he placed his arm around the other man who Grant did not recognize. The man was adorned in a three-piece suit and expensive looking shoes. In his hand he carried a leather briefcase. Noticing Grant across the dirt and straw covered parking lot, Barrett said something to the other man then they approached. Grant lowered his head and spoke to himself in a low voice, "Come on Brody...get here! I don't want to have to deal with this all by myself."

Barrett was just in front of the other man as he addressed Grant, "Grant Denlinger…what brings you out this way." Reaching out, he offered his hand. "The last time I saw you was at that rousing chamber meeting we had. How's your grandfather?"

Grant, sidestepping the first question of why he was there, answered the last question instead. "Dalton is just fine."

Turning to the other man Barrett started the introductions, "Merle Pittman, this is Grant Denlinger." Grant shook Merle's hand while Barrett went on, "Merle is Asa's brother. He's an attorney. Works out of Gatlinburg." Addressing Merle, Barrett continued, "Grant is one of our two officers here in Townsend. His grandfather, Dalton was the sheriff a few years back and now sits on the city council as our current Police Commissioner."

Barrett went back to his original question. "So, why are we blessed with the presence of the Townsend Police today?"

Grant nodded toward the front porch. "It seems there are some folks, some of who are sitting on the porch over there that are wearing tee-shirts that could be considered offensive to some of the local residents. I met a couple this morning and they told me all about the tours being offered. Chief Brody is on his way to shut it down."

Barrett crossed his arms. "Grant, you seem like a sharp young man. Do you think for one moment I'm going to let a buffoon like Brody interfere with my business? Brody doesn't know his ass from a hole in the ground. He isn't going to shut this tour down or anything I choose to do…because I haven't done anything wrong. I haven't broken the law." Motioning toward the porch and the surrounding acreage, he strongly stated, "This is all legal…a legitimate business. Brody will wind up looking more of a fool than he already is…if that's possible."

Just then the sound of Brody's speeding truck with flashing blue lights and siren blaring could be heard. The truck turned up the dirt road and came to a sliding halt, a trail of dust slowly engulfing the area. Merle, waving dust away from his face looked at Grant. "I'm going to have your boss's ass for this."

Brody climbed out of his truck and marched over to where Grant, Barrett and Merle stood. Removing his hat from his large head, he tried to clear the dusty air from his face as he approached. "Should have known it'd be you, Barrett. For a wealthy man you sure are one stupid son of a bitch!"

Merle doing his best to clean the front of his suit off from the dust stepped forward. "Franklin, let me handle the chief here. You see Axel and I are old adversaries. We've been at each other for years. We've fought many battles all of which happen to be over my brother, Asa. Now, I'll admit my brother was no walk in the park but regardless, I think it's safe to say I kept my brother out of jail and out of trouble. I can't remember every time I went up against ol' Brody here, but I can tell you this, I always walked away the winner. He never got anything to stick when it came to my brother. In short, Brody's side of the scorecard reads, zero, nada, zilch…a big fat goose egg!"

Just then Butch sped into the lot causing another explosion of dust. Barrett, looking at the arriving cruiser remarked smartly, "I see the rest of your clan is here." Turning to Merle, Barrett explained, "That'd be Brody's cousin. Another stupid ass. I guess it just runs in the family."

Brody moved forward until he was directly in Barrett's face. "You better watch yourself boy!"

"Really," said Barrett calmly. "You going to arrest me for using foul language?"

Butch joined the group, looked at the porch then to Grant.

Placing his briefcase on the hood of Grant's cruiser, Merle, holding out his hands spoke, "Your man here," as he pointed at Grant, "says you intend to shut down our tour *and* that the tee-shirts advertising our new business may be considered offensive to some of the locals."

"That's right," snarled Brody. Pointing at the porch he ordered, "Those people *are not* goin' to wear *those* shirts…" Stepping closer to Barrett, Brody got louder. "And that tour up to Thunderhead to see where Asa Pittman was murdered or anywhere around here that interferes with our investigation *is not* goin' to happen in this town!"

Barrett was about to say something but Merle held up his hand. "Franklin, let me deal with this no nothing man of the law." Opening the briefcase he spoke professionally, "It's time for Mr. Brody here to get schooled on the law. First of all, Chief, this facility, that which is called The Mountain View Riding Stables, is not only owned by one Mr. Franklin Barrett but is a bona fide business, registered with Blount County and with the State of Tennessee. He is licensed to conduct horseback riding in all of Blount County and on private land with the permission of owners.

Mr. Barrett has a Federal ID Number and is a member in good standing with the local Better Business Bureau."

Removing a document from the case, he further explained, "Second, this document that I hold in my hand states that as of last month according to my brother, Asa Pittman's will, I am the sole beneficiary of everything he owned...which includes his farm. I own the Pittman farm and since Mr. Franklin and I are business partners, that business being named Barrett-Pittman Tours, he has every right to guide tours to said farm."

Folding the paper he placed it back in the case and removed another document, "This document is proof that Mildred Henks was in fact just about bankrupt. Following her death, it was discovered that unfortunately she never took the time to prepare a will so her property and everything on the land she owned was to be auctioned off. Mr. Barrett contacted the company who was to handle the auction and wrote them a check for the entire property. So, Mr. Barrett now owns the Henks' place and it is his prerogative to do with it as he pleases. He and I together have decided that The Henks' place would be a great tourist attraction...hence we can if we choose to do so, which we have, conduct tours there as well." Waving the form back and forth slightly, he looked directly at Brody. "I could go on and on but with your limited knowledge of the law you would no doubt get more confused than what you already are."

Barrett spoke up, "What Mr. Pittman is saying is you don't have a leg to stand on and further more, if your poor judgment in coming here today or any day in the future in any way interferes with any of my customers canceling a tour I will have your butt in court faster than you can imagine."

Merle closed his briefcase and turned to walk away. "Well, Franklin, what say we get this tour underway?"

Brody stood silent. He had been leveled; beaten at his own game of intimidation. Turning he faced Grant and Butch. Butch laughed silently trying to cover his mouth. "What the hell's so funny, Miller?"

Butch looked at Grant then shook his head. "You just got your ass kicked, Axel!"

Brody walked to his truck and remarked curtly, "Don't worry about my ass, Butch, you just get yours over to the campground and check on that car break in. Move it!" Pointing at Grant he ordered,

"And you…get over to the park and see if those kids are still raisin' hell."

Grant stood by his cruiser, watching Brody and Butch drive out of the parking lot, a trail of dust forming behind them. As Grant was getting in his cruiser Barrett approached. "Hold on a minute, Grant."

Grant, sitting in the seat left the door open. Leaning over and looking in Barrett smiled. "When Dalton was chief things were handled much smoother. He never seemed to get upset like Brody. Let me ask you something. Why do you hang around here…I mean on the police force? It's got to be a nightmare working with Brody and his nutcase cousin. You could do much better elsewhere. Look, I've got connections…I know a lot of people. One of my golfing buddies is the chief of police over in Sevierville. I'm sure I could get you on over there."

"No thanks," said Grant. "At least not right now. I'd really like to stick around until we get these murders solved." Grant closed the door but then asked, "Mr. Barrett, I do have one thing I would like to ask you?"

"Go ahead." said Barrett.

"Mr. Pittman and you seem to have your ducks in a row on this Pittman-Henks Murder Tour business. Maybe it is all legal, but that still doesn't make it right. What do you think a lot of folks in and around town will think about you?"

"Grant, I'm a businessman. I don't care what the locals think about me. I didn't become wealthy because of the people who live here. They don't come here to my stables for horseback riding, they don't stay at my campground, they don't stay at my hotel or rent cabins from me. But the tourists do. I am concerned over those who come here, not those who live here." Standing back from the cruiser, he pointed out. "If you will take the time to think about these tours, well, in time you'll see that it is for the best. Sure, there may be a few folks who get their necks bent out of joint over those tee-shirts, but I guarantee you, as the season rolls on and even into next year these tours will attract more tourists which equates to more business for the riding stables, motels, restaurants, cabin rentals, campgrounds, gas stations…you name it. Although the murders of Asa Pittman and Mildred Henks were horrible, we just have to make the best of things."

Grant turned the ignition key and nodded at Barrett who waved as he pulled out of the lot. Driving up Route 73 Grant thought about what Barrett had said about getting him on over at Sevierville. Maybe people were trying to tell him something. Sheriff Grimes had all but offered him a job in Maryville. Turning onto the parkway, he put the thoughts of going to another police force in the area out of his mind. He wasn't going to jump ship just yet. He had the strangest feeling the person who murdered Asa Pittman and Mildred Henks might just strike again.

CHAPTER THIRTEEN

THE WEATHER HAD TURNED unseasonably cool as the end of August rolled around. The daytime temperatures were hovering in the mid-seventies and the evenings becoming jacket weather. Tinges of color were beginning to show on the tips of the leaves, the last of the summer flowers bent their heads, the first day of autumn just three weeks away and another round of tourists would soon descend on the Smokies.

During the fall season retired couples and free spirits who loved the crisp autumn air and the vibrant color of the trees would flood into Townsend. They came in hiking boots with backpacks and tents and set up camp in the wooded areas of the campgrounds. They rode mountain bikes up and down the narrow trails and hummed along in ATV's. Some rented small cottages or cabins and sat on their balconies in the evening in rocking chairs and hot tubs as they drank alcoholic beverages and gazed out across the vast mountains escaping to a way of life so different than what they were accustomed to.

There were also the nature lovers who came equipped with cameras and tripods who waited patiently for hours just to get a good photograph of a bear. The tourists would eventually go home from the Smokies with apple pies, paintings, homemade quilts and bags of rocks their children had collected. To the tourists The Great Smoky Mountains represented the best vacation a person could ever experience. Despite the fact there had been two horrific murders in the Townsend area in the past five months, the tourists still came.

To the people of Townsend who depended on the tourist trade for much of their livelihood, they were glad people continued to come to their town for a visit, be it a day or a week. Franklin Barrett had been right on the money with his prediction that the Pittman-Henks Murder Tours would be a hit and create additional income for everyone across the board. Initially some of the locals put up a fuss over the tee-shirts, but as days and weeks went by more and more tourists showed up sporting the controversial shirts and taking the tours. The riding stables were overflowing with business as well as the campgrounds, hotels, restaurants, gas stations, gift shops and seemingly every type of business in town. The most popular tours that were offered were the horseback rides up to Asa's farm which was a spooky place to begin with and the bus ride out to The Henks' place. The ghost tours were especially popular. The tours became so successful that eventually a kiosk was set up at the Mountain View Stables. Many businesses in town were now selling the popular tee-shirts. Merle Pittman and Franklin Barrett had added another notch in their belt of successful ventures.

It was Friday morning in the drizzling rain when Axel Brody roared into the police station parking lot. Getting out of his truck, he slammed the door and trounced across the lot. Flinging open the door,he stormed down the hallway and yelled, "Got dammit! Here we go again. Somebody is tryin' their best to set off another A-Bomb in my town. First thing you know, I'm goin' to have people walkin' around in tee-shirts with pictures of dogs on the front."

Stomping into his office he pointed at Grant, Butch and Kenny, then continued in a loud fashion, "I've got two more missin' dogs and I'm damn sure it ain't the coyotes who are takin' 'em. I bet you a dime to a dollar we got ourselves a dog fightin' ring around these parts somewhere. This missin' dog business is gettin' out of hand. The thought of another media frenzy around here this year is all we need!"

Plopping down in his chair, he pounded his fist on top of the desk. "We've got to find out who's stealin' these dogs." He looked at Grant and Kenny who were both sitting in front of the computer in the office, then at Butch who was reading the morning paper. Brody firmly stated, "You three hotshots need to get out there and put your noses to the ground. I want you to look down every mole hole and every abandoned farm buildin' in the area. We have to solve this mess quick before the media realizes what's goin' on."

Butch objected, laying down the paper. "Aw, come on, Axel. Somebody is just trying to start some crap. If there is a dog ring around here, don't you think somebody would know about it?"

Brody exploded, "Exactly...dumb ass! And it's your job to find out who it is. Now, I want this over with...like now!" Calming down, Brody started to give specific orders. "Kenny, you take the list of missin' dog owners and go talk to them again. Maybe someone will remember somethin' they forgot to mention. Butch, you get on the horn and call Maryville and find out how many missin' dog reports they have received."

Grant raised his hand and stood up. "Before you tell me what to do, I think I have an idea." Turning off the computer, he swerved around Brody. "I'll be back in an hour." He was down the hallway and out the door before anyone could react.

Brody, surprised at the brashness of Grant simply stared at the chair where Grant had been sitting. Butch stood up, slamming the paper down on the desk. "Axel, are you going to let him get away with that? If we can all do just want we want around here, well, then we sure don't need you sitting behind that desk."

"Sit down," ordered Brody. "I'm givin' Denlinger a pass on this one. I think he has a leg up on us all on this missin' dog business. He came to me two weeks ago and said he thought there was a dog fightin' ring somewhere in the area. I was so busy goin' over the two file cabinet drawers we have on the murders that I just blew him off. We're still gettin' tips on the murders and we have to check every one out. So far nothin' has come to the surface and the murders have suddenly taken a backseat to these missin' dogs. This dog business has moved to the front burner."

Grant turned onto the Lamar Parkway and drove the short distance to the Parkway Grocery. It was Friday and Grant knew Asa's old pals would be at their corner window table just like always. Parking in the lot, Grant entered the building, threw a dollar bill on the counter and headed for the coffee near the back. Pouring himself a cup he walked to the front of the store and ambled up to the old cronies. "Hey fellas, what's going on?"

Zeb looked up and grinned. "New day...same ol' crap! How 'bout you, Grant?"

Gesturing with his coffee, Grant answered, "Holding my own. Mind if I sit with you guys?"

"Sure," said Buddie, scooting his chair closer to the window.

"We got a murderer yet?" asked Luke.

Grant sat. "Nope, still working on it. Say, listen, I guess you all heard about the mystery surrounding all the missing dogs in town. You fellas have any ideas?"

"Hell fire...there ain't no mystery to it," exclaimed Charley. "Dog fighters pay good money for neighborhood dogs. Those people are some nasty sons a bitches. They steal those dogs for training their fighting dogs. The ones doing the stealing might be a gang from out of town. The dog fighting organizers move around a lot and set up a ring whenever they can get away with it. I've never been to a dogfight but I hear they pull down a lot of cash."

Grant sipped at his coffee. "I figure if anybody in town knew of anything it would be you guys. Not much goes on around these parts that you fellas are not up on."

Zeb tapped his fingers on the table. "I'll tell you what. One of those sons a bitches touches one of my dogs, I'll blow a hole in his damn head."

Buddie whispered, leaning in closer. "There a reward for information, Grant?"

"No," said Grant as he stood. "However, how's this for starters?" Reaching into his wallet he took out a ten dollar bill and tossed it on the table. "I'll buy the next round of java. If you guys come up with something we can use, I'll find a couple of bucks for you. How's that sound?"

"Sounds good to me." said Zeb. "Of course, I'd tell ya for free just to catch those bastards."

"Gotta run," said Grant. "I'm counting on you guys." Walking out of the building Grant took the last swig of his coffee and pitched the empty cup in a large trashcan, thinking to himself, *If anybody can find out what's going on...those four could.*

Back in the cruiser, a call came in over the radio. It was Marge. "Grant, Brody wants you back here. Butch had to leave. Said he had some personal business to attend to...whatever that means. We just got a call about some kids letting a whole sack of frogs loose over at the IGA store."

"On my way," chuckled Grant, the picture of Brody running around trying to catch frogs made him laugh.

During the next week with patrols being stepped up, the incidents of missing dogs all but disappeared, only one dog reported missing. The owner had left his gate open and was not sure if the dog ran away or was stolen. The dog's name was added to the list with the rest of the missing pets.

Friday night, September 3, Grant signed out and headed for his Jeep. He had Saturday off and was looking forward to some downtime. Butch had been bragging all day about how he was picking up Dana Beth at the bus station in Gatlinburg at three o'clock and he couldn't wait to see her. It was just that kind of talk that was enough to get Grant riled up. It had been nearly six weeks since he had met Dana Beth at the candle shop over in Gatlinburg, when she had confided in him saying she was going to break it off with Miller.

Driving down the parkway, he thought that should have been more than enough time for her to end the relationship. *Well, maybe not,* he thought. Butch had said she had gone to the shore with her parents for two weeks of vacation and then there was a month-long nursing course she had to attend over in Nashville. Butch himself had commented about how he hadn't seen her in the last six weeks, so maybe she didn't have the time to give him the bad news. Looking out at the distant mountains Grant remembered what he had told her: *He would not interfere.*

When he pulled into the driveway of Dalton's farm, he was surprised to see his mother and grandfather sitting on the front porch. Had they eaten dinner without him? Stepping out of the Jeep he noticed someone else sitting with them. He walked across the yard and up the wooden steps. A large grin crossed his face when he saw Dana Beth seated on the porch swing, her legs tucked up beneath her. "Hey, Dana Beth...what a surprise." Upon closer inspection, the smile faded from his face. Her eyes were swollen and red. She held a wadded up Kleenex in her hand. He could tell she had been crying. Quickly, he asked, "What's wrong?"

Dalton stood up. "I'm going to take mom in the house so you two can talk." Placing his hand on Dana Beth's shoulder he gently suggested, "Now you be sure and tell Grant everything...okay?"

Dana Beth dabbed at her nose and slowly nodded.

The screen door on the front porch no sooner slammed shut when Grant asked, "What is it? Is there something wrong at home...with your parents?"

Sitting up straight on the swing, Dana Beth finally spoke, "No, they're fine. It's just that..." She stopped and tears began to roll down her face. "I shouldn't have come here. I called and you weren't home. Your grandfather came and got me. I guess he could tell how upset I was. I didn't want to stay at home by myself and I wasn't really sure where to go...so, here I am."

Grant sat next to her on the swing. "Dang, Dana Beth, tell me what's wrong."

Composing herself, she turned facing Grant. "Well, Butch insisted on picking me up at the bus station. I told him it wasn't necessary but he just kept insisting. When I got off the bus he was standing there waiting for me. He took my suitcase and put it in the back of his car and opened the passenger door for me. It had been almost six weeks since I had seen him, so it was the first opportunity I had to break up with him. I had been practicing on the bus all the way down from Nashville how I was going to break the news to him. I knew he wouldn't accept what I had to say very well, so I waited until we were almost in Townsend. I told him I didn't think our relationship was working out and that we should start seeing other people." Wiping her eyes once again, she went on, "He became livid. He started beating on the steering wheel and telling me there was no way he was going to let me go. I tried to reason with him, but he wasn't having any of it. He just kept getting madder and madder. It got to the point where there was nothing I could say. I just sat there the rest of the way home. Butch was ranting and raving about this and that. When we got to my house, I started to get out but he pulled me next to him and tried to kiss me. I pushed him away, but he grabbed my face and started pawing at me. He grabbed my arm so tight that it bruised."

Looking at the dark blue bruise on her arm Grant clenched his fists. "That bastard...I'm gonna..."

Placing her hand on his leg, Dana Beth spoke softly, "Please, Grant, let me finish." Wiping her face again, she picked up where she left off. "I don't know where I got the strength but I pushed him away and jumped out of the car. I opened the backdoor and grabbed my suitcase. By that time he was out of his side of the car and right next to me. He put his arm around my shoulder and told me he was willing to forget everything I had said and he would be back later to take me to dinner. He let go of me and I ran into the house, leaving my suitcase on the ground. Thank God, my mother had gone up to Knoxville to spend the weekend with my dad. He had some work to do and couldn't get home. If my parents would have seen what Butch had done to me, who knows what they would have done."

Managing a slight smile, Dana Beth tried to fix her hair. "I must look a mess. I was so scared. I locked the front door and looked out the window to make sure he was gone before I went out to get my suitcase. A few minutes later I went back out and picked it up. I noticed something laying on the ground. It must have been on the backseat and when I pulled out the suitcase it came with it."

Reaching next to her at the end of the swing she picked up a blue dog collar. "This is what I found."

Grant took the collar from her and examined it closely. Looking at a metal disc just beneath the rabies tag, Grant read the name: "Prince." Holding up the collar he examined it again then looked at Dana Beth. "Butch doesn't own a dog...does he?"

Dana Beth shrugged. "Well, if he does...he never mentioned anything about it to me."

Setting the collar down on the swing, Grant looked out across the yard. "We might just be on to something here." Looking back at Dana Beth, he asked, "Did Butch ever mention to you or say anything about the missing dogs we've had around here recently?"

"No...he didn't." Putting her hand to her lips she thought, then stated, "Well there was one time, I think it was back in June when I happened to ask him what was going on with the missing dogs. He gave me a strange look and told me to make sure our dog was never let out without supervision. I thought it was rather strange, because the next thing he said didn't make any sense. It didn't have anything to do with what we were talking about. He said he had a side job and he was making a lot of money. I asked him what it was and he just laughed."

Grant picked up the collar again. "I'm getting the strangest feeling about this. Listen, I've got to make a call." Handing her the collar he pulled his cell out of his pants pocket and hit speed dial. Within four seconds he was speaking, "Marge...this is Grant. Do me a quick favor. Give me the names of the missing dogs we've got so far."

As usual, Marge never questioned any of the officers. She fumbled around on her desk until she located the list. "I've got it right here: We've got a Brownie, Major, Prince..."

Grant stopped her, "Prince...did you say Prince?"

"Yup, Prince."

"Large or small dog?"

"Says here on the report...medium sized...Collie Shepherd mix."

"Thanks, Marge...you're still a peach!"

Closing his cell, he stared down at the blue, frayed collar as he ran his hand over the tags. "I have a strange feeling this belongs to one of the missing dogs."

Dana Beth seemed confused, "What are you saying, Grant?"

"Nothing could be more clear to me. I think Butch Miller has been stealing or at least is part of the reason we're missing those dogs."

She drew in her breath. "Oh, God. Why would he do such a horrible thing?"

"Why, I'll tell you why! He's a lowlife bastard. I'm going to make sure he never touches you again or takes another dog."

Touching his arm, she pleaded, "No, Grant, not tonight. Please don't do anything rash. Don't get yourself in trouble."

The screen opened and Dalton walked out onto the porch. "Why don't you two come inside. Greta's just put a fresh pot of coffee on. I think we have pie."

The four of them sat around the kitchen table eating the last of a chocolate meringue pie. When they finished off the coffee, Grant suggested a second pot. Grant's mother was a compassionate woman and was quite concerned about Dana Beth and told her no woman should ever be manhandled or laid a hand on.

Dalton shared her concern but was more on the stern side. Dumping some creamer into his third cup, he asked, "Young lady, how is it that you have been seeing Butch Miller all summer? Has he ever displayed signs of violence before?"

"Up until this afternoon he was always nice to me," said Dana Beth. "I told him from the start I wasn't interested in a long term relationship." She shot a glance in Grant's direction. "He said okay, but whenever I tried to break things off he just wouldn't hear of it. I thought eventually he'd take the hint and back off. Looking back now I can see, well, just after Asa Pittman was murdered he started to act different. From there on I always felt uneasy around him."

"Did he ever hit you before?" asked Grant.

"No, this was the first time he ever showed any aggression." Looking around the table she asked, "What am I going to do?"

Dalton cleared his throat. "It's really out of your hands now, Dana Beth. As the Police Commissioner I have to tell you this is a matter that, first of all, Chief Brody has to deal with. As small as our police force is there is still a chain of command. If Butch Miller is involved in these dog kidnappings, he needs to be arrested and put behind bars. If it turns out there is any truth to any of this then he needs to be looking out from the opposite side of a jail cell. Now, there is one thing you can do. You can press charges against him for aggravated assault. But to be honest with you from the looks of that bruise he'll probably get off with a slap on the hand. If something like that went to court, why it wouldn't even be considered a misdemeanor. Now, if we can get him on stealing dogs for the purpose of dog fighting then that ties him right in with, excuse my French…those bastards. Dog fighting is a felony and means if convicted an individual can not only be fined but can receive jail time. I think that is the direction we should take. But, there is a problem. You see, these type of people are always dodging the law. If we try to expose them before we locate where they are conducting these fights they'll simply close up shop and move elsewhere. They need to be caught red handed…in the act."

The conversation was interrupted when Grant's cell phone rang. "Excuse me," he said as he walked into the living room answering the call, "Hello."

"Grant…it's me Charley. I'm over here in Sevierville and I got a lead on you know what. It's at J.J.'s Junk Emporium out on Route 66. The owner has a big metal abandoned building out there behind the junkyard and they're holding you know what every Friday and Saturday night. They start about one o'clock in the morning. Should be on for tonight."

"You're kidding me," said Grant. "I've got to get the state police out there tonight."

"Not that easy," said Charley. "They got a twelve foot fence topped with barbed wire surrounding the place and three of the meanest guard dogs you ever seen roaming around in there. There's a cut through on the side, but once the police are spotted coming down that road the whole bunch of 'em will scatter like cockroaches when the lights come on."

Grant thought for moment, then said, "Maybe the police could go in on foot, ya know, mingle with the crowd and then once they have the place surrounded they could nail them all."

"You just don't waltz into one of these affairs," responded Charley. "I know this because Asa told us a few years back he had been invited to a dogfight. You have to be invited. They check you at the gate. If you're not with someone they know…you don't get in. Here's what I'm gonna do. I'll make some anonymous calls: the state police, Sevierville Police, Burt Grimes over in Maryville.

They can handle it as they see fit."

"I'll just stay out of it tonight," said Grant, "but tomorrow I'm going to have to say something to Brody."

"Just promise me you won't mention me or the other guys. Brody never cared for any of us."

"I won't...and thanks Charley. I owe ya. I knew if anybody could find out anything it'd be you guys."

"Don't mention it. Hell, if I was twenty years younger I'd go over there and shoot the whole damn bunch myself. I gotta make a call. See ya around."

Walking back to the kitchen Grant clapped his hands once and smiled. "That was an interesting call I just had. I've been asking some people around town about the missing dogs and I just received some information. Someone found out where the dog fighting ring is located. He's calling the state police right now. Maybe, they'll get lucky and Butch will be there tonight."

"Where is it?" asked Dalton.

"I'd better not tell you, Dalton. I'm not supposed to know about this. Besides, depending on how things go tonight, it'll probably all be in the morning paper."

Greta, getting uncomfortable with the way the conversation was going spoke up, "Enough of this dog fighting business. It's too depressing. Let's move on to the problem at hand." Gesturing at Dana Beth she explained, "Dana Beth is staying the night. She can sleep in your room and you can bunk in with Dalton. I don't want her at home alone tonight. She's going to call her parents and tell them she is spending the night with a friend."

"My room!" exclaimed Grant. "You better give me some time to clean it up."

Thirty minutes later Grant came down the steps entered the kitchen, bowed and announced to Dana Beth, "Your suite is ready Madam. Fresh sheets, warm quilt...the room is spotless."

Everyone laughed then Dana Beth folding her hands spoke graciously, "I want to thank you for helping me. If it's all right I think I'd like to go on up to bed."

At the bottom of the stairs Grant placed his arm around her. "Don't worry. Everything is going to work out. I promise you. Butch Miller will never bother you again. I guarantee it."

The next morning Grant was up and on the way to work before anyone at the farm was awake. When he got to the station he found Brody already parked in behind his cluttered desk, a mug of coffee in his hands. Grant, taking a seat asked, "Where is everybody?"

Motioning with his cup at the front door, Brody coughed then answered, "Jacks just left, Marge called in sick, and Butch should be in soon. Got an interestin' call from Grimes last night. Said he got an anonymous call about a dog fightin' ring over in Sevierville. Since it wasn't his jurisdiction he called the police over there who informed him they had received a call and they and the state police were in the process of organizin' a raid. Said it was at J.J.'s Junk Emporium. I asked if he needed us to tag along and he said since it was in the next county they needed to handle it. Before he hung up he did tell me he was confident the missin' dogs were being stolen by the ring. Last night for the first time in quite awhile I got a good night's rest. I laid my head on my pillow and thought finally we're gettin' somewhere around here. In the past months we've had two unsolved murders and a passel of missin' dogs and it seemed like we were gettin' nowhere. Three problems with no answers. Last night I told my wife that it looks like at least one of them was goin' to be solved. Well, this mornin', I'm havin' breakfast and Grimes gives me another call. Said by the time the boys in Sevierville hit the junkyard they'd already cleared out."

"So they didn't catch anybody or find any dogs?" asked Grant.

"Nope, just an empty building. There were a few empty dog cages and some beer bottles layin' around but that was all. I guess they'll question the owner but without any real solid proof he'll get off."

"That's a shame," remarked Grant. "We were so close."

"Well, not all is lost. We threw a scare into 'em. They're long gone and won't be back until things cool down which could be for quite some time. I'm just as disappointed as the next guy we didn't nail 'em but at least the missin' dog dilemma has been solved. Now we can get back to workin' on these damn murders."

"Speaking of the murders," said Grant. "I've got a couple of things I need to share with you. Ya know that notebook I'm always writing in? Well, I've stumbled on two things you need to know about." Opening his wallet, Grant placed the small bag containing the tobacco sample on the desk. "I found traces of tobacco at both Asa Pittman's farm and the Henks' place. I'm sorry I didn't tell you about it before but until just recently I didn't even know it was tobacco. I took the sample to a smoke shop and had it identified. It's peach brandy...a pipe tobacco. It's a pretty popular brand."

Brody's reaction to what Grant said was the opposite of what he expected. Brody was always giving him a hard time over his stupid blue notebook and Grant had been sure when he revealed the tobacco sample to him he would go off for not bringing it to him sooner. Brody calmly reached across the desk and picked up the bag and looked closely at it. "You say this is tobacco?"

"Yeah, that's what I was told."

"Did Asa smoke a pipe?"

"I don't think so. I mean we didn't find any evidence that he did when we went over his place. We never found any pipe or tobacco tins. There wasn't even an ashtray in his place. I don't think he smoked at all."

"Where did you find this tobacco at Asa's?"

"It was on his kitchen table."

Looking at the bag again, Brody took another sip of coffee. "You say you also found the same thing at Mildred Henks?"

"That's right...found it on one of her end tables."

"We know Mildred smoked cigarettes. She always struck me as an odd ball but I doubt very seriously if she smoked a pipe."

Pointing at the bag in Brody's hand, Grant gave his opinion, "Since I found the tobacco at both locations I figure our killer smokes a pipe which rules out about ninety-nine percent of women. Our killer is probably a man and if he does in fact smoke a pipe that narrows the field down quite a bit. You see very few men today smoking a pipe."

Laying the bag on the desk, Brody inquired, "You said there were a couple of things you wanted to share with me. The tobacco makes one. What else you got?"

"Right after Asa was killed," said Grant, "I talked with his four coffee drinking buddies down at the Parkway Grocery. They told me Asa was sweet on Mildred but that she didn't want anything to do with him. It just seems strange they both wind up being murdered."

Pointing his cup at Grant, Brody elaborated, "I think I see where you're goin' with this. Asa and Mildred might have had an affair and someone, maybe that was also interested in Mildred, decided to snuff them both out. And, this person which is probably a man smokes a pipe."

"It's a long shot," said Grant, "but what else do we have to go on?"

Brody opened his desk drawer and placed the bag of tobacco inside then closed it. Grant, a little confused over how smoothly the conversation was going leaned toward the desk, asking, "You okay this morning, Chief? I mean, are you feeling okay?"

Brody shrugged, "Feelin' great. Why do you ask?"

"It just seems like you're being extra nice this morning. I thought you'd rip my head off for not turning in that tobacco earlier."

Brody smiled. "I'm in a good mood this mornin'. Looks like we've got this missin' dog mess cleared up. But don't go gettin' used to it. The day is young." Getting up he refilled his cup, turned and looked at Grant. "I guess it's no secret you and I don't see eye to eye on most things, but I've gotta say I think someday you're gonna make a fine chief of police somewhere."

Grant was flabbergasted. "Thanks chief, that's means a lot to me."

Just then, Butch walked into the office, plopped down in a chair and remained silent. Brody looked at Grant then back to Butch. "What the hell's wrong with you, Miller? Grant and I were just sittin' here talkin' about what a good mood I was in, then you come stumblin' in here like it's the end of the world."

Butch looked back at Brody and waved his hand. "It's nothing!"

Grant positioned himself in his chair, then straightened up preparing himself for the attack. "Butch had a rough night, Chief. Isn't that right, Butch?"

Butch, giving Grant a hard look, responded, "What are you talking about?"

"Well, my friend. Your bad mood stems from three different things. First of all: Dana Beth broke it off with you yesterday after you picked her up at the bus station. Word is you didn't take the news very well, actually I hear you got quite upset and roughed her up a bit. Gave her a bruised arm…"

Brody interrupted, "Hold on right there, Denlinger. I recall the last time you two got into it over Dana Beth Pearl. It was like World War Three out there in the hall. If I've told you once I've told you a thousand times, leave your personal business at home. We've got enough problems around here."

Grant turned, addressing Brody, "So you're saying it's okay for an officer of the law to go around beating on people?"

Before Brody could respond, Butch spoke, "Look Chief, we had a little lovers' spat. That's all it amounted to. I didn't even know she got bruised. Wonder Boy here is just jealous because she used to be with him, but he screwed that up and now she's with me and *he* can't deal with it, so what does he do? He comes in with some trumped up bullshit about me beating on her. I mean, come on, Axel. Don't we have more important things to discuss than this?"

Brody placed his hands in front of himself signifying a moment of prayer. "God. Why me? Look...I don't want to hear anymore about what goes on in your personal lives. My good mood is rapidly disappearin'."

Grant was on a roll and the teeter totter of control was slanted in his direction. "I said there were three reasons why Butch is in such a foul mood. Dana Beth was number one." Not giving Brody or Butch an opportunity to speak, he rambled on, "Here's the number two reason. Because of the raid last night over in Sevierville the dog fighting ring had to pack up and git." Grant, bluffing, pressed his luck. "It seems ol' Butch here has from time to time been attending dogfights."

Butch had a stunned look on his face when Brody looked him square in the eye. "The Dana Beth business I can blow off, but now we're gettin' into some serious allegations. I'm only gonna ask you one time, Butch. Have you been to dogfights?"

Butch stammered, "Well, ah...I...you see..."

"eGot dammit!" yelled Brody. "Quit blabberin' and give me a straight answer. Yes or no?"

Butch, suddenly pissed, fired back, "Hell yeah, so I went to a few dogfights. What's the big deal?"

Brody's face was getting redder by the second, "What's the difference? Dog fightin' is a felony. You could be fined and serve time. You're an officer of the law. You're supposed to prevent these type of activities...not support them!"

Butch tried to object. "Look, I only went to some dogfights. I don't own any of the dogs. I don't set up the ring. I don't promote the fights. I just go and place a few bets."

Brody looked toward the ceiling as if he were looking to heaven. "Butch, the more you speak, the more I realize how got damn stupid you are. Just because you don't own the dogs or promote the fights, gets you off the hook. Attendin' a dogfight in this state is still considered a misdemeanor. How can you sit there and claim to be an officer of the law when first of all I find out you're beatin' on your so called girlfriend and then I find out you're attendin' dogfights?"

Butch waved his hand at Brody. "Axel, calm down. You're overreacting."

Brody stood up. "Overreacting my ass! Look here, you're not only an officer on the Townsend Police Force, but my cousin. What you do in this community is a reflection not only on the community but me...the chief of police."

It was time for Grant to get back in the conversation. He had Butch right where he wanted him. He had put him in the coffin with the Dana Beth event, then had closed the lid with the dog fighting and now it was time to nail it shut. Reaching into his pocket he produced the frayed blue dog collar and threw it on the desk. "Better sit back down, Axel, because the third reason is the worst of all."

Brody sat back down and picked up the collar. "What's this?"

"A dog collar," explained Grant. "Dana Beth found it in the backseat of Butch's car."

Brody, not understanding his meaning, held up the collar and shrugged.

"Look at the name on the tag."

Brody read the name out loud, "Prince."

"I called Marge to get a list of the stolen dogs' names. Prince was on the list." Butch looked like he had been hit in the face with a brick. Grant continued, "Why would a collar of one of the stolen dogs be in Butch's backseat?"

Before Brody could answer or react Grant answered the question himself. "I'll tell you why. Butch Miller has been stealing neighborhood dogs and selling them to the dog fighters as bait for their fighting dogs."

The look on Brody's face when he stared directly at Butch made Grant glad his temper at the moment was not directed at him. Brody was so upset he couldn't speak. Grant continued with his explanation, "Chief, do you have any idea what these men who own the fighting ring do with these stolen dogs? I looked it up on the web. It's enough to make you wanna cry. They tie up their back legs and their mouths so they can't defend themselves, then they're tossed into a ring and the fighting dogs are let loose to practice on these defenseless animals. They are literally ripped apart."

Butch was now at the stage of pleading, "Come on Axel, you can't believe this."

Brody shook his head in disgust. "Shut up you asshole! When I think about all the families I had to visit who reported their dogs missin'. When I think about all of the children who asked me to find their pets and bring them back home. You're sick Butch. These dogs you stole were not just *dogs*. They were pets, family members, loved ones and you hauled them off to be brutally butchered."

Standing, Butch, regained his confidence. "Look, I've had enough of this crap. Pointing at Grant, he emphasized, "If poor ol' Grant over here wouldn't have gotten so upset because me and his former girlfriend had a little tiff, none of this would have ever been brought up. It's all bullshit!"

Grant was out of his chair in a second, lunging at Butch knocking him back over his chair. It happened so quick Butch couldn't defend himself. Grant got in three good solid licks to Butch's face before Brody was able to pull him off. Pushing Grant to the other side of the room, he ordered, "Denlinger, get control of yourself...now!"

Grant, leaning against the wall pointed at Butch and sternly warned, "If you ever lay a hand on Dana Beth again, I'll kill you!"

Butch struggled to his feet, but the beating he had received as far as he was concerned had turned things in his favor. Wiping blood from the side of his mouth he demanded, "Axel, you saw what he did. That's the second time he's punched me in the office. What are you going to do about it?"

Making sure Grant had calmed down Brody walked toward Butch and calmly answered, "I'll tell you what I'm goin' to do. You're suspended for a week,Miller, until I can sort this out. Now, get your ass out of my police station before I finish up what Denlinger here started. I'll call you next Monday to let you know if you still have a job."

Butch looked at Brody, then at Grant. "This isn't over ,Denlinger." With that he stormed out of the office slamming the door behind him.

Brody motioned toward a chair, ordering Grant, "Sit down son." Looking at the chair that was knocked over he looked back at Grant.

"Well, there goes my good mood. I should suspend you as well, but I guess I can understand the way you feel. Besides, I can't afford to lose both of you for a week. Here's what were gonna do. You're gonna get back out on the streets and get back to the business of makin' sure our citizens are safe. I'm goin' to just stay put and sort this crap out. When Kenny gets here later on this afternoon, I'm goin' home and try my best to keep from gettin' drunk. We'll talk tomorrow. One last thing before you go…thanks."

Grant nodded, got up and walked down the hall and out to the cruiser. He couldn't wait until he got home later that evening so he could tell Dana Beth how things had worked out. The one thing that bothered him was what Butch had said about it not being over. He was going to have to tell Dana Beth to be careful. Hell, he was going to have to look over his own shoulder as well. There was no telling what Butch might do.

CHAPTER FOURTEEN

IT WAS A GLORIOUS SUNDAY MORNING. The azure blue sky was dotted with puffy white clouds, the light breeze keeping the temperature in the low seventies. After attending church with Dalton and Greta, Grant drove Dana Beth back to the farm where his mother was planning on having a Sunday afternoon meal: roast beef, mashed potatoes, corn on the cob, fresh baked rolls and of course, pie for desert.

Grant pulled into the driveway, his mother saying dinner would be in about two hours. Dana Beth insisted on helping and suggested the boys just relax and sit out on the porch until dinner was ready.

After changing into more comfortable clothes, Grant found his grandfather already seated on the porch, the Sunday paper spread out across his lap. Reclining in one of two cushioned white wicker chairs, Grant asked, "Anything interesting in there?"

Folding one section and picking up another, Dalton adjusted his reading glasses and answered, "On the bottom of the front page there is a small article that recaps the raid on the dog fighting ring. Basically, what it says is due to a tip from an unknown source, the Sevierville Police working with the state police raided J.J.'s Junk Emporium. There was evidence there had been dog fighting activities on the site recently, but it was to no avail. Apparently the group was tipped and bolted before the authorities showed up. The owner was questioned and said he knew nothing about it. Since they didn't find any dogs on the premises there won't be any charges."

"Do you think the ring will come back?" asked Grant.

"Not for quite some time. They'll move off to another location somewhere else. They don't like attention. It'll be quite awhile before they ever come back here." Looking at Grant, Dalton added, "At least, we don't have to worry about any more missing dogs. There's another article further back in the paper. You know that guy who writes the weekly column: *What's happening in the*

Smokies?"

"Never read it, but yeah I've heard of it."

"His topic this week is, now get this: the *Pittman-Henks Murder Tours.* According to this John, hell, I can't even pronounce his last name...he went on one of the tours. I can't remember which one, no wait. It was the one that runs over to the Henks' place. He writes he was pleasantly surprised at how professional the tour was handled. He goes on to say the property is absolutely beautiful. According to his article once inside the house tourists are shown where Mildred Henks was abducted, or possibly killed. They've got certain areas roped off like in the living room where there is a slit open fifty pound dog food bag, dog food spread across the carpet, china bowls filled with water, the china cabinet door is open. A pair of white fur lined slippers are positioned on the floor apparently where she was attacked. A large dog cage is positioned at the edge of the carpet where the marks in the floor appear. The tubs, shampoo bottles and the hose connected to the sink are exactly where they were found. After the tour of the house tourists are invited for a light lunch out by the pond at picnic tables they have set up. You can also go in the barn where the dogs were kept. He said that was the part of the tour he really didn't care for. Despite the fact they had tried to clean up the barn, it still had an odor to it. All in all, he said the tours are rapidly becoming a must see in the Townsend area."

"It's amazing," commented Grant, "how people can figure out a way to make money off of almost anything. Five months ago both Asa Pittman and Mildred Henks were walking the streets of Townsend. They were both murdered...I mean brutally murdered, and yet people seem to make light of it. I remember when we went over to The Mountain View Stables when we first got wind of the tours. Brody was so confident he was going to shut them down. But, between Merle Pittman and Franklin Barrett, well let's just say they were way ahead of the curve. They dotted their I's and crossed their T's, everything was done legally. Before I left that day Barrett had a conversation with me about how these tours would bring in a lot of tourists." Shrugging his shoulders, Grant half laughed, "I guess he was right."

Dalton changed the subject. "It's been what...the better part of a week since Brody gave Butch the heave ho. Have you heard anything more or seen Butch around town?"

"Brody has been really quiet. He hasn't said a word about Butch. I haven't seen hide nor hair of Miller all week. Tomorrow, Monday, is the day Brody is supposed to give him a call and either tell him to come back to work, or I guess maybe let him go."

Dalton pushed the rest of the paper to the side. "I find it hard to believe Brody actually suspended Miller, but then again what choice did Axel have. He isn't going to jeopardize his own career for the sake of his *law breaking cousin.* Brody is no doubt looking down the road. If Miller was found guilty and convicted of not only attending dogfights, but stealing those dogs, which he won't be because there really is no proof that will stand up, Brody would want to distance himself from Butch."

Grant shook his head in agreement. "It has been an odd week. Brody hasn't uttered an unkind word to anyone. Even when I told him about the tobacco I had found at Asa and Mildred's place, he just examined the bag and asked me some questions. I thought for sure he was going to rip my head off."

Dalton crossed his legs and looked up at the bright sun which had just crept out from behind a large cloud. "So what do you think? Come tomorrow do you think Brody will give Miller the axe?"

"If he's got a brain in his head...he will. But then again, we're talking about Axel Brody here. I can't imagine him letting Butch slide by, but I guess we'll just have to wait and see."

Dalton smiled at Grant. "I guess you and Dana Beth are back on line."

"Come on, Dalton, it's only been a week."

"Maybe so, but I've seen the way you two look at and act around each other. It's like you're getting a second chance." Hesitating, he then continued, "When are you going to pop the question?"

Grant looked in the window and then at the screen door, then leaned toward his grandfather. "Look, I haven't told anyone this...so you never heard me say anything. Next Wednesday I've asked Dana Beth to go to the movies and dinner over in Pigeon Forge. I'm going to ask her then...for the second time in my life."

"How do you think it'll go?" asked Dalton.

"I'm feeling pretty confident. Next week this time I should be engaged."

Dana Beth was just finishing drying the last of the dishes and

Greta was busying herself with putting up leftovers. Dalton, patting his stomach commented, "Now that was one good meal." Walking to the hall closet he opened the door and removed his favorite hat. "I've got to head on into the chamber office. We've got a short meeting at five o'clock. Not sure what time I'll be getting back."

Grant, wiping down the dining room table, draped the washcloth over his shoulder and entered the kitchen. "Dana Beth, if you're about ready to go, I'll run you home."

Greta jumped in on the conversation. "Not before we enjoy some pie out on the porch."

Dalton opened the front door and shouted back into the house, "Make sure you save me a slice."

It was just after five-thirty when Grant watched Dana Beth wave goodbye to him from her front porch. Professor Pearl was walking toward their garage. He had just finished mowing their yard. Pulling out of the driveway Grant felt good about the way things were going, at least in his personal life. He was looking forward to Wednesday, which was four days off. During dinner, he would lay the engagement ring she had sent back to him two years ago in front of her and ask her to marry him. He just knew she would say yes.

Passing the police station on his way back home, he noticed Brody's pickup truck parked in its usual spot out front. Tomorrow, Brody was going to have to make a decision on Butch. He wondered what Brody was thinking. He wondered what Butch was thinking.

Butch Miller sat up, looked around the expansive lake then opened his cooler. Popping the top of his eighth beer of the afternoon, he threw the tab into the water and laid back, his head resting on his lifejacket that he seldom wore. Laying his left leg over the side of the small fishing boat he took a sip and watched a flock of geese in their familiar V formation fly overhead, an occasional honk resonating across the lake. Closing his eyes he smiled, the late afternoon sun caressing his face. His smiling didn't have anything to do with the way he felt about himself. It was a direct result of drinking too much. He was drunk again. It had been nine days since Brody had suspended him and each day he had spent on Laurel Lake, floating and drifting about from one side to the other drinking one beer after another.

Watching a plane fly over, Butch reviewed the day Brody had suspended him, just like he had done everyday for the past week. Taking another large swig, he thought about the fact that any hope of being with Dana Beth had gone by the wayside. Hell, she had broken up with him before the dog fighting and dog stealing issues were brought up. With those two things hanging over his head his chances of ever getting back with her now seemed impossible. But that was the least of his problems. If he was convicted of attending dogfights, more than likely he would just get fined on a misdemeanor charge. If he was convicted on the theft of the dogs and they proved he had supplied the dog fighters with them that would directly tie him in with their illegal activities, which meant not only a stiff fine, but jail time. But, since the raid on J.J.'s turned out to be a bust the authorities really didn't have anything to use against him. He felt there was a good chance he would walk away from the accusations. What he wasn't sure of was what his older cousin, Axel would do. Axel had always been in his corner, but now he wasn't so sure of where he stood with the chief.

Finishing up the beer he tossed the can up toward the front of the boat, sat up and reached for the cooler again. Opening another beer he looked back toward the shore where his truck was parked. There was a man hooking his boat up to the rear of a truck and two women walking along the edge of the water. Lying back down in the boat again he thought about ten weeks ago when Mildred Henks' body had been found on the far side of the lake. Sipping on his beer, he thought about Mildred. He never liked her. She was always speeding around the county in that Thunderbird she drove. She thought she was hot stuff. He recalled one time, about a year ago, when he had pulled her over for speeding. Wearing that stupid long white scarf of hers, she had given him a rash of crap about pulling her over. Didn't he realize who she was? She was the top real estate agent in the area, a woman who knew important people. When she had asked him who in the hell he thought he was, he answered comically by saying, 'No one important. Jus' sum dumb ass hick givin' ya a ticket ma'am. Ya all com back an' see us sum time, heah.' Butch smiled to himself. She was just one of those people the town was better off without; her *and* Asa Pittman.

Pittman, he remembered was an uncouth, uneducated type while Henks was educated and successful but still a pain in the ass. They were both what he had considered big mouths and now someone had taken them both out. *Good riddance,* he thought. Taking two long swigs of beer he laid back and closed his eyes. At the moment he didn't give a shit about anybody or anything.

An hour later Butch woke up. The sun had disappeared behind the mountains to the west and in thirty minutes it would be dark. Sitting up he looked back at the shore where he had parked his truck. It was the only vehicle left. Everyone was gone. There was not a single boat on the water. He turned in every direction. Not a soul. A small flock of ducks floated peacefully on the serene water thirty yards to his left. Moving to the rear of the boat he adjusted the choke, then hit the electric starter. The fifty horsepower Evinrude outboard motor sputtered but then started as Butch guided the boat in a circle then headed for shore.

When he approached the shoreline it was getting dark quickly. He noticed a set of headlights; someone was driving across the empty, dirt parking area. The vehicle stopped twenty yards down from where he ran up on shore. The lights went dim.

Stepping out of the boat he looked in the direction of the vehicle that appeared as nothing more than an opaque shadow. Suddenly, a small light flickered through the driver's side window. *Someone lighting up a smoke,* thought Butch. It would be pitch black before long. Butch, still half drunk, stumbled the few yards to where his truck was parked and opened the passenger side door to get the flashlight he kept in the glove compartment. Grabbing the flashlight, he stood back up and was instantly drug backwards as he felt a smelly rag being pressed against his face. He tried to struggle free but his strength had been weakened by the alcohol coursing through his veins. He felt himself slipping away, his last thought, *What's happening to me?*

Forty-five minutes later he was starting to come around, the drug was wearing off, his senses acclimating themselves to his surroundings. He could see he was in total darkness, hear the steady hum of an engine and felt every bump in the road. He could smell a sweet aroma. Trying to move his arms, then his legs he realized he was bound. The sense of fear he was feeling erased his previous feeling of drunkenness. He wanted to yell out for help but the duct tape across his mouth prevented him from doing so. Suddenly he was pitched to the side, his body rolling up against something that crinkled beneath the weight of his body. Trying his best to relax he was rolled to the left, over the crinkling hard floor. He got the feeling he was bound up in some sort of a ball. A short glare of light penetrated the darkness but then quickly disappeared. He heard what he thought was the sound of passing cars. Turning his head slightly he saw a grouping of small yellow numbers in the darkness. Suddenly he realized he was looking at gauges. He was in some sort of a vehicle, like a truck or a van. Another glare of light filled the back of the vehicle, but then went away as a car going in the opposite direction passed.

Concentrating he tried to recall what had happened. He had been getting his flashlight out of the truck, then there was a rag, then everything went blank. The vehicle came to a stop, his body rolling toward the front, hitting what he thought was the seat. Then he heard a voice, "I see you're coming around, Mr. Miller."

Looking up he saw a shadow of a man, someone who was obviously driving the vehicle. The voice continued, "I apologize for any inconvenience you may be feeling at the moment..." The man was interrupted, a greenish light filtering back through the vehicle as it moved forward causing Butch to roll toward the back. Then, it came to him. *A green light,* he thought. The vehicle had stopped, but was now on the move again.

The man spoke again, but louder so he could be heard over the sound of the motor. "Just hold tight...we should be arriving at our destination in about ten minutes."

Butch struggled to release his arms from the bindings but it was useless. He rolled from side to side, forward and backwards, the vehicle going around curves, stopping on occasion then moving on again. Rolling hard to the left he was bounced up and down. The vehicle was no longer on a smooth surface but what felt like a bumpy road.

After what seemed like a minute the vehicle slowed and turned to the right, then stopped. Looking toward the front of the vehicle Butch, confused, watched. The dash lights were turned off. He was now in total darkness. Through the darkness came the voice again, "We're here, Butch." The next thing he heard was a door slam shut then there was silence. Within a few seconds the back of the vehicle was opened and Butch could see the shadow of the man outlined by a nearby light of some sort. The man pointed a flashlight directly at Butch and flipped it on. The light blinded Butch from seeing the man's face. The man sat a lantern on the floor near the back of the vehicle and turned it on, at which point the flashlight was turned off. Butch, looking around discovered he was in the back of a paneled van. It was strange. The interior was lined with clear plastic secured to the sides with duct tape.

Climbing up into the back, the man shoved and pushed Butch up against the left side of the van. Hanging the lantern on a hook the man was now in full view. Sitting against the opposite side of the van he spoke, "Sorry for my strange dress attire but it is necessary for this type of work." Pointing at his black ski mask, he explained, "I normally wouldn't wear one of these but we have met a couple of times in the past and I'm not quite ready to allow you to know who I am. When you find out, I have no doubt you'll be surprised. You gave me a speeding ticket about two years ago. Your abduction has nothing to do with that particular incident. I was speeding and you were just doing your job."

Pulling a pipe out of his coveralls, he laid it on the floor then removed a pouch of tobacco. He picked up the pipe, filled the bowl with tobacco, lit it, took three puffs then commented, "I'd offer you a smoke, but I know you don't smoke a pipe." Taking another puff he held the pipe up in front of himself as he examined it then remarked, "Smoking a pipe is almost becoming a lost art."

Looking at Butch, he thought for a moment, then said, "Now where were we? Ah, yes. I was saying you were just doing your job." Pointing the pipe at Butch the man emphasized, "Being an officer of the law is an important occupation. People in Townsend and in the surrounding county, not to mention a great number of visitors that come here for vacation, depend on you to not only uphold the law, but to be an example to all of us…as in doing what's right."

He shifted his weight to get more comfortable the man continued, "For a young man with his whole life ahead of him, you strike me as rather stupid. Why on earth would an officer of the law attend dog fighting, unless it was to arrest those involved? In your case it was to watch this horrible spectacle and to place a few bets. And then there's the missing dogs we have experienced recently in our area. I have been observing you for the past couple of months.

Even though there seems to be no proof you did actually steal these dogs, I know for a fact you did. Therein lies the problem. The dogs you stole were sold to the dog fighters. Most people are not aware dog fighters not only have fighting dogs, but they need dogs for opponents to keep their fighting dogs…let's say on the edge. I've done my research, Butch. I know what they do with the neighborhood dogs they are supplied with. These pets that are for the most part non-violent, are thrown into the ring against dogs that are trained to kill. Now, one would think a family pet would have little chance in surviving when pitted against a trained killer. But still, for some reason these men who run these fighting rings have devised a method to ensure their dogs will not get injured during these training periods. The dogs that are stolen have their back legs taped so they cannot maneuver and their mouths are taped shut so they cannot defend themselves. They are simply tossed into a ring and the fighting dogs are allowed to tear them apart. I for one cannot imagine a worse death."

Getting up on one knee, the man laid his pipe down. "Here I am going on and on about something you already know. This must be very boring for you. Tell you what. Let's get into something a little more interesting."

He reached toward the front of the van and grabbed a black bag and dragged it across the floor. Unzipping the bag, suddenly something he thought of made him laugh. "Do you remember the movie Scarface? I think it was out back in the early eighties." Snapping his fingers, the man put his hand to his forehead. "Sorry, that was before your time. Anyway, in this movie there is a scene where the main character is preparing for his house to be assaulted by his enemies. Well, they break in the front door and there he is waiting for them with this M-16 assault rifle as he shouts at them, 'Say hello to my little friend.' That line has become one of the most famous movie lines of all times *and* I think it's the perfect line for the situation we have here."

Reaching into the bag he slowly removed a set of lopping shears. Smiling at Butch he tapped the shears in his hand twice. "Say hello to *my* little friend!" Leaning the shears up against the side of the van he reached into the bag again this time removing a pair of white plastic gloves. Snapping the first glove on his right hand he nodded toward the shears. "I just had these sharpened last week." Snapping on the second glove he explained, "I've been using them quite a bit over the past few months." Picking up the shears he touched Butch's fingers with the edge. "Been amputating a lot of toes and fingers lately."

Butch suddenly realized he was face to face with the man who had killed Asa Pittman and Mildred Henks. Squirming, he tried to back away but there was nowhere to go. His heart was pounding, the sense of what might happen to him started to sink in.

The man looked closely at Butch's eyes, then spoke, "I can see from the fear in your eyes you've figured out who I am. Well, I stand corrected. You don't know who I am…but you do know what I've done."

Picking up the bag, the man crawled out of the back of the van still holding the shears in his hand. "Be right back…I've just got to get a few things done." From the dim light of the nearby fixture, Butch watched the man approach a tall chain link fence. Bending down he placed the bag on the ground, then proceeded to cut the fencing near the bottom in a fashion so it could be pushed inward. Next the man removed a small piece of paper from the bag and secured it with duct tape a few feet above the cut fencing. Closing up the bag the man walked back to the van, opened the door and threw the bag on the passenger seat.

Back at the rear of the van he once again threw the shears onto the floor and crawled back in. "Here's the way it's going to go, Butch. Those dogs you stole were family pets…well taken care of. I suppose most of them were groomed from time to time, especially their nails." Pointing the shears at Butch the man explained, "When cutting a dog's nails you have to be extremely careful not to cut too far back or you'll cut the quick and thus cause not only bleeding but pain for the animal. I've tried to cut our dog's nails and I really don't have the patience for it, so we usually take our dog to the vet. Now, I'm going to attempt to cut your nails but I'm going to need your cooperation during the process. If you move or jerk your hands I may cut your finger by mistake and we wouldn't want that to happen now would we?"

He closed the van door and wedged Butch in the corner. Butch, knowing what was coming turned his head violently from side to side, trying to scream. Slapping Butch strongly across the face the man spoke firmly, "Settle down!" Grabbing Butch's right hand he snapped off the first finger, a small amount of blood spurted out onto the floor. Butch let out a low muffled scream while the man sat back against the side of the van. "I'm so sorry, I guess I cut back a little too far. I told you, I was going to need your help in this. If you keep jerking around this is going to get messy."

Reaching out he took Butch's hand again and snapped the shears, another finger falling to the floor of the van. Butch watched in horror, the blood from his finger squirted out and splattered the side of the lantern. The intense pain from the first two cuts was excruciating. He clenched his teeth, the sound of the sharp blades penetrating the skin and bone equally as frightening as the pain he felt. He felt like he was going to pass out.

The man grabbed a third finger, commenting, "Eventually I think I'll get the hang of this." Cutting off two more fingers and then the thumb without the slightest hesitation, the man leaned the shears against the side of the van and reached for a bottle of water setting behind the front seat. Drinking nearly half of the bottle, he gathered up the four fingers and thumb lying on the floor and placed them in the opposite corner, then asked Butch, "Is it hot in here or is it just me?"

Finishing off the water, he pitched the empty bottle up over the seat, picked up the shears and moved close to Butch again. "I'm really sorry you didn't get the luxury of having your hands numbed like the other two, but after what happened to those dogs as a result of your stealing them I felt it was important you feel the pain they must have endured."

Butch tried to kick his legs out but it was impossible, the duct tape holding firmly. The man looked into his eyes and smiled. "The look in your eyes tells me you're a fighter. Well, Butch this is a ten round fight, and we've only gone five rounds and you've lost every one so far." Holding up his hand in a make believe fashion he pumped it up and down like he was ringing a bell. "Ding ding, sixth round. Here we go!" Two more bloody fingers fell to the floor. The man could see Butch was once again on the verge of passing out from the incredible pain. Grabbing another bottle of water the man opened it and poured it over Butch's head and then slapped him. "We're almost finished here. Just three more to go. You can do it. Come on."

Cutting the remaining two fingers and thumb off the man rambled on, "We've got to step things up a bit." Snap! "I've already been here too long." Snap! "I was planning on cutting the toes also but we're running short on time." Snap! Sweating profusely the man sat back and took a deep breath. "All done."

Butch's body was drenched in sweat, his eyes filled with tears, his breath labored, his heart beating rapidly. His muffled screaming was now reduced to a pathetic whining.

Getting up, the man slowly opened the van's back door and peered out. Satisfied no one was around he jumped down to the ground, grabbed Butch by the hair and pulled him to the edge and allowed his bound body to slam down on the dirt. Next he leaned the shears up against one of the rear tires, and began to gather up and unfasten the plastic inside the van. He then grabbed the lantern from the hook and the two empty water bottles and threw them onto the bloody plastic.

Butch watched the man drag the plastic to an ugly green dumpster next to the chain link fence opened it, and stuff the plastic inside. Returning to Butch he dragged him by his hair over to the fence. Butch was able to see beyond the fencing. The dim lights displayed row upon row of junk cars, piles of old tires and automobile parts. The man went to the van, opened the driver's side door and extracted a bottle. Walking back to Butch he opened the bottle and said, "And now for the magic ingredient." Pouring the light brown liquid over Butch's arms and face, he identified the substance. "Chicken gravy. Perfect for your soon-to-be visitors." Walking back to the van he gathered up the ten fingers he had placed on the ground and walked back to the fence. Tossing the eight fingers toward the top of the fence, he then duct taped the two thumbs to the note he had hung on the fence. Hesitating for a moment to get his breath, the man removed the ski mask and looked down at Butch. Butch, looking up at the familiar face couldn't believe who it was. The man smiled. "Told ya you'd be surprised."

Pulling Butch in front of the area of the fence he had cut, he forced Butch through the opening, the cut jagged edges of the fencing digging into Butch's arms. Next the man picked up an old piece of lumber lying next to the road. Slowly he pushed Butch six feet further into the confines of the junk yard. Pitching the lumber back toward the weeds, he walked over and picked up his lopping shears and wiped them on his coveralls. He placed the shears on the front seat then took off the coveralls, ski mask and work boots he was wearing and threw them all into the dumpster.

After placing a pair of sneakers on his feet he walked back to the fence making sure he didn't step in any blood. Leaning against the fence he lit his pipe and looked up at the starry sky. "Nice evening out."

Pointing the pipe at Butch, who was facing him, the man spoke, "Your demise will be somewhat different than the others. More than likely they bled out before any critters could get to them. But that won't be the case with you. In the next minute or so you will experience what those dogs you stole experienced. Unbelievable fright and pain. You have been bound just like one of those poor defenseless dogs." Looking off into the distance past the rows of cars, he went on, "This is quite a large junk facility. Over there on the other side somewhere there lurks three of the meanest junkyard dogs you would ever want to lay eyes on." He walked down the fence line and picked up two old rusted hubcaps from a pile of junk. "When I start banging these together, they'll come a runnin'. At first you'll hear them barking as they get closer. You won't be able to see them coming because of the way you're facing. When they arrive, between the smell of blood and that gravy, well, it won't be very pleasant. Those dogs are trained to kill and or maim anything that gets inside this fence during the off hours. The first thing you'll feel will be their teeth sinking into your skin. Then and only then will you realize what you did to all those dogs you stole."

Butch's heart was racing as he watched the man hold up two hubcaps. "On the count of three," the man said. "One...two...three..." With that he started banging the metal discs together, a clanging sound filling the quiet night. Stopping for a moment he heard the barking of the dogs. "They're on their way." Banging the hubcaps together a few more times he tossed them over the fence, removed his gloves and pitched them in the dumpster then walked back to the van, climbed in and started the engine. Backing up he drove to where he was directly sitting on the opposite side of the fence where Butch was laying. Rolling down the passenger side window, the man leaned over and looked at Butch. Taking a puff on his pipe he quoted, "Everything in life is permissible, but not everything is beneficial or constructive. What goes around...comes around."

Just then the first of the dogs appeared; a large black mixed breed who, without the slightest hesitation, pounced on Butch and bit into his arm. The two others, dark in color joined the first, ripping and tearing at Butch. Putting the van in gear the man slowly pulled away. Stopping at the end of the dirt road, before turning onto the highway he heard a horrible scream. The duct tape had been ripped from Butch's mouth by one of the dogs. Placing his pipe in the ashtray beneath the dashboard, the man turned on the radio and thought to himself, *I'm going to have to start buying a better quality duct tape.*

CHAPTER FIFTEEN

J.J. PICKLER OPENED THE DOOR of the rusty green trailer he called home. Still wearing the soiled undershirt and ragged jeans that he had on since Thursday, he scratched his belly and stretched his arms over his head. He made a face when he got a whiff of his own armpits.

He stepped down two wobbly steps and walked a few feet and entered the chain-link fence enclosure attached to the side of the trailer. He turned on the water spigot and filled two dented buckets with water, then opened a thirty-gallon drum and poured a large cupful of dog food into each of the three bowls scattered around the pen. Just a cup, no more, no less. He had to keep his guard dogs on the hungry side, on edge, so that they remained mean. Banging on the side of the fence it only took a few seconds before they appeared. They kept their heads down as they sulked toward him and took their place in front of their bowls. He had taught them well. He was their master. Everyone else was their enemy. Pouring water into their water bowls he noticed something strange about the dogs. "Hey, what the hell did you guys kill last night? You got blood all over your faces and feet. I reckon you been tearing into those rats back near the big shed. That's good." he said, closing and locking the door to the pen. "You keep those sons a bitches out of here."

Following the same routine everyday, his next chore was to unlock the main gate to the junkyard and turn the CLOSED sign to OPEN. An oversized padlock hung from the heavy chain securing the sliding gate to a thick metal post. He pulled out a large key ring from his back pocket, unlocked the gate and pushed back the two-panel barricade that would allow customers to enter the yard.

He sauntered back to the trailer. Once inside, he pushed an open loaf of bread to the side of the cluttered counter and plugged in the coffee pot. Sitting down in a tattered brown chair he reached forward and turned on a small television setting on a three-legged

end table. Just as he lit his first cigarette of the day, the phone rang.
Reaching for the phone on the coffee table he knocked a stack of
papers on the floor. "Hello," he said gruffly. After listening for a
moment, he grumbled, "Yeah, I already told you that." Taking a
drag on his smoke he continued talking, "I told you those tires
would be waiting for you, so you better get your ass over here and
pick 'em up before I start dealing with someone else!" There was
another pause, then J.J. answered, "I don't know. Give me a few
minutes to drink my coffee and I'll go over to the office and see how
many I've got written down. It's on my desk somewhere." Hanging
up the phone, he grabbed the remote and flipped through the
channels until he got the weather report.

The trailer he used for the office was in worse shape than the one
he lived in. He unlocked the padlock and pushed the crooked door
inward. It caught on the floor just like always so he gave it a hard
kick. Walking to an old marred wood desk he sifted through a stack
of papers. Unable to locate the count of the tires he had out back, he
threw down the papers and went back outside. He had been doing
business with Lee Blitzer for a long time. He knew how ol' Lee
worked. He would load up thirty tires and then tell him he only got
twenty. J.J. had learned from years of experience to put the tires in
stacks of five to make sure Lee didn't cheat him. He was going to
have to go all the way out back and check on the stacks again.

Walking around to the other side of the , he climbed into a faded
white and green golf cart. He pushed aside some small auto parts on
the seat and hit the electric start. The motor sputtered, made a
grinding sound then started. Turning left he drove down the rutted
dirt lane through a maze of old cars and trucks, row after row of
mounds of exhaust pipes, mufflers and automobile frames forming
sculptures of rusty metal.

He swatted at a bee that tried to hitch a ride and cursed, almost
running into an old school bus. *Damn,* he thought to himself, *I'm
tired of this business.* If he could have just squeezed out a few more
weeks of dog fighting and some well placed bets on some of the
matches he would have had enough money to spend a couple of
weeks in Florida. Due to a tip, the ring had pulled out hours before
the raid. They were probably already set up somewhere else in
Tennessee or maybe out of state. He had been questioned when
evidence that fights had been staged in his back shed had been

discovered, but because no dogs were found he managed to get off with a severe warning. The dog fighters were off somewhere else making money and he was still stuck in Sevierville until he figured a way to get his hands on some extra cash. The market for old cars and auto parts was drying up; most of his inventory was becoming unusable from sitting out in the weather year after year.

Pulling the cart up in front of where he kept the used tires he got out and looked at the back row. He walked to the fence and started counting. When he reached the end of the second row he noticed something hanging on the fence, it was a white piece of paper held in place with duct tape. He pulled the paper down, the duct tape remained attached to the fence. The sun was shining brightly. He squinted his eyes in an effort to read what was written on the paper: *Pickler. You're next!*

What the hell, he thought, rereading the note again. He pulled down the duct tape from the fence as he noticed two blood-stained thumbs attached to the tape. He yelled and dropped them to the ground, then whirled around looking in every direction. *Was someone watching him?* Suddenly he was sweating, saliva ran down the side of his mouth. *Someone is after me! What does it mean... You're next?*

Running back to the golf cart he jumped in and hit the starter. It sputtered then stopped. "Got damn, come on, dammit!" He tried the starter again. Nothing! The motor was dead.

He had to get back to the safety of the trailer. Beating on the dash he jumped out and ran back up the lane but almost immediately slowed to a trot. He was grossly out of shape. Not even thirty yards up the lane he was out of breath. Bending over he placed his hands on his knees as he panted heavily. He felt like he was going to be sick. He realized that he needed to calm down. Looking back down the lane he whispered to himself, "God, whose thumbs were those?"

Starting up the lane once again he tried to compose himself, but then he saw something that shouldn't have been there—something underneath the rusted bumper of an old Buick. He approached the odd looking object slowly, but then much to his horror he discovered what it was. The mangled remains of a body lying in a pool of dried black blood, the face half eaten away, one of the arms missing. He couldn't believe what he was seeing. He wanted to scream but nothing came out of his mouth. Then he remembered. *The dogs! That's why they were bloody. They had torn the body apart.* Backing away from the body, he knew this was the first time his dogs had ever killed anyone. He turned and ran up the lane all the while thinking, *How did the person get in? Were they put inside the fence? The note said I'm going to be next!*

By the time he reached the trailer fear had completely consumed his emotions, tears running down the side of his face, his heart pounding. Opening the door, he staggered up into the trailer, his side throbbing with the pain of running. He pulled back a filthy curtain and peered out a small window, his eyes darting from the left to the right, looking for any signs of movement.

Seeing nothing, he turned on the faucet and splashed water across his sweaty face, neck and arms. Pouring himself a glass of water from the sink, he drank it slowly and looked out the window again. *Maybe I should let the dogs out? If someone is out there and they are after me, those dogs will tear them apart.*

Drying his face with a dirty towel, he slumped down in the chair as he finished the water. *Calm down,* he thought, *just calm down!* After three deep, long breaths he looked at himself in the floor length door mirror. *I've got to get out of here...now!*

He tossed the plastic cup toward the sink and walked to the hall closet. Opening the metal door he went down on one knee and turned the dial of the Honeywell safe. His hands were shaking and he passed the correct last number twice. Finally, on the third attempt the thick heavy metal door opened. He removed two stacks of money bound by rubber bands, a forty-five revolver and a box of shells. He laid the money and the shells on top of the safe and flipped open the cylinder of the gun checking to see if he had a full load. Satisfied, he stuffed the gun in his pants, placed the money in an envelope and picked up the shells. Then, he heard the sounds of the dogs barking. *The killer was out there waiting for him! There was no time!* Busting through the trailer door, he ran toward his green Cadillac parked in front of the trailer. He had a habit of leaving the keys in the ignition and today he was glad he did. Without looking to the right or left he sprinted to the car, opened the door, threw the money and the shells on the passenger seat, started the car, stomped the gas pedal and spun out knocking over two empty fifty-five gallon drums of trash, speeding toward the main entrance, a cloud of dust trailing him.

Lee Blitzer pulled his old white pickup through the main gate and drove the short distance to the office trailer. He honked the horn, waited a few seconds then honked again. Lee laughed, knowing that honking always pissed J.J. off. When J.J. didn't appear at the door, Lee thought to himself, the *ol' buzzard must be in a good mood this morning.*

Lee climbed out of his truck and walked to the office door, which was standing wide open. He entered the crammed office almost expecting to be cussed out by J.J. for honking his horn. He was greeted by an empty room. Walking to the back of the trailer, he yelled, "Yo, J.J. You in the john?" No answer.

Back to the front of the office, Lee sat on the corner of the desk. Picking up a two-year-old copy of *Car and Mechanic* magazine he flipped through the pages. Minutes later, tired of waiting, he walked back out into the yard. Then, he stopped. He wanted to make absolutely sure where J.J.'s dogs were. He yelled and then whistled, which set off the dogs barking. He walked toward the other trailer and looked toward the pen where the dogs were kept during business hours. There they were, lined up against the fence snarling and growling.

Crossing the yard to the trailer, the dogs began to bark louder. He hated the dogs and was always worried that someday they would break out of their pen and come after him. A frightening thought. J.J. was always teasing him telling him the dogs were out in the yard lurking somewhere and Lee would always curse and refuse to get out of his truck. Today he was in a hurry. He needed to pick up the tires and get home. Knocking on the trailer door, Lee yelled, "J.J., you in there? Come on, I'm in a hurry." Again, no answer. He opened the door slightly and yelled, "Damn it! Where in the hell are you? You knew I was coming!" Pushing the door open even wider he yelled into the trailer, "I'm going out back and get the tires myself. I'll let you know how many I take...like always." He chuckled. This would get a rise out of J.J.

Guiding his truck down the narrow lanes, he had to stop on occasion and back up to make sure his truck would squeeze through a tight fit. Coming to a sharp turn, Lee climbed out of the truck and picked up an old bumper partially blocking him from moving forward. Kicking away some loose trash in the road he noticed something that stood out like a sore thumb. Surrounded by various shades of rust covered cars and parts, he saw something that looked like a pile of bloody rags. At first it was indescribable but on closer examination he discovered it was a body. Whoever it was, they were definitely dead. Insects had begun to crawl over the body. It was almost like the body had been turned inside out. Lee placed his hand over his mouth trying not to throw up. *What or who could have done this?* he thought. *Oh, my God. Maybe the dogs did this.*

Backing up without taking his eyes from the horrific sight, he climbed back into the truck, jammed the gearshift in reverse and backed up. He heard the sound of scraping metal on the side of the truck but at the moment he could have cared less. He'd never seen anything like this in his life. He had to get back to the office and call the police. When he got back maybe J.J. would be there.

Minutes later he pulled up in front of the office and leaving his truck running, he bolted in the office door. It was still empty. He ran across the yard to the other trailer. The dogs were barking wildly. He noticed their blood-stained faces. *Where did that blood come from? Maybe they killed the person. Maybe it was J.J.*

Looking around the filthy trailer he spotted the phone on the chipped kitchen counter. Frantically, he dialed 911 and waited. After an operator answered, Lee blurted out, "This is Lee Blitzer. I'm over at J.J.'s Junk Emporium out on Route 66. There's a body out in the back of the yard. You have to send someone out here…right away!"

The operator, used to panic calls of all sorts calmly replied, "Would you please give me your name again, sir?"

"Blitzer…Lee Blitzer."

"Has there been an accident sir?"

"Accident, no! Someone was killed. Looks like the guard dogs out here killed somebody and ate half of 'im. It might be J.J. the owner. I can't tell. Get some help out here now!"

"Mr. Blitzer. Stay put. We'll have some officers there in a few minutes. Are the dogs loose?"

"No, they're locked up. Hurry!"

Hanging the phone up, Lee sat down on the chair, thinking to himself, *Where is J.J.?* The thought that the body out there in the junkyard might just be J.J. was too much for Lee to think about. *This is bad,* he thought. *Real bad!* Remembering J.J. always kept a well stocked refrigerator when it came to beer he got up and opened the fridge. Sure enough there was row after row of cans and bottles of beer. Without even hesitating he grabbed a can, popped the top and drank half of it without taking a breath. Then he thought, *I can't smell like I've been drinking when the police get here.* Dumping the rest of the beer down the drain he threw the can in an overflowing trash receptacle next to the chair and walked out the front door to wait for the police. Pacing back and forth across the yard in front of the trailer, he went over in his mind what he would tell them when they arrived. He wasn't sure what they would ask or how he would answer. "Just tell the truth," he said out loud to himself.

In the distance he heard the approaching sirens. He climbed up into his truck and turned off the ignition. The dogs were still barking. It seemed like they would go on forever. In the next minute he saw the red and blue flashing lights of a cruiser entering through the main gate, followed by an ambulance.

Getting out of his truck Lee watched the cruiser come to a stop. Two officers climbed out, one looking over at the dogs the other focused on him. The officer who was paying attention to the dogs unstrapped his revolver, his hand resting on its handle. The other officer approached, asking, "You Mr. Blitzer?"

Lee felt better now that the police were there. "Yes, I'm Mr. Blitzer."

Looking at the trailer, then back toward the mountains of rusted junk the officer introduced himself, "Officer Ron Hall, Sevierville Police. Now, what have we got here? Something about a body?"

Leaning up against the hood of his truck, Lee tried to compose himself. "I came out here to pick up some tires just like always. I couldn't find J.J. He's the owner. So I decided to go on out back and load them up myself and that's when I discovered the body. It's just plain awful! I was in Viet Nam, ya know. I've seen men get shot, blown up...that sort of thing. You expect that in war, but not here in the middle of civilization." Looking past the officer at the ambulance he remarked, "You sure won't be needing that. Whoever that person is, they're dead."

"Yes sir," said the officer. "Can you show us where the body is?"

"I can tell you where it is, but I'm not going back out there again." Pointing past the trailer down the lane Lee gave the officer directions, "You go down that lane a couple hundred yards. Make a right at an old school bus, then maybe twenty yards or so down on the right you'll come to a rusted shell of a Buick. You can't miss it. The backseat has been torn out and is setting in the front seat. The body is right under the frame."

The officer remained polite but firm, motioning toward the cruiser, "Sir, it's not a request…it's an order. You need to go with us."

Climbing into the back of the cruiser, Lee felt odd. No door locks or inside handles, a heavy metal screen separating him from the officers. Looking out the rear window, he noticed the ambulance slowly follow the cruiser down the lane. Leaning up to speak with the two officers Lee suggested, "You won't be able to get this cruiser down right next to the body. The lanes back in there aren't wide enough." Pointing ahead he stated, "See that school bus coming up on the right? If you stop there we can walk back to where the body is."

The officer in the passenger seat didn't speak but did acknowledge, nodding his head in understanding. As they approached the bus, Lee said, "Right here will be close enough." Stepping out of the cruiser after the door was opened Lee started up the lane. "Follow me, the body is just up here a few yards."

The officers, followed by two paramedics walked behind Lee and approached the Buick. Pointing beneath the frame, Lee indicated, "There it is…right there."

The officer who had identified himself as Ron knelt down on his haunches, removed his sunglasses and looked at the ghastly sight. After a few seconds he commented, "Looks like there are signs of duct tape wrapped around the torso and legs." Turning to the other officer he ordered, "Cletus, you need to call the homicide unit up here. Tell them to bring the coroner along, too."

Officer Hall stood as the other officer walked back to the cruiser. "Mr. Blitzer, I need you to step over to the side away from the body. I need to ask you a few questions."

Following the officer across the narrow lane they stopped next to what looked like an old delivery truck of some sort. The officer took a pad out of his shirt pocket, clicked an ink pen, then asked, "So you came out here to get some tires? Did you see Mr. Pickler when you got here?"

"No, sir," said Lee. "He wasn't anywhere around. His car isn't even here and that's odd because I had just called him and told him I was coming by."

"Was anybody else in the lot when you arrived?"

"No. There wasn't a sign of anybody. Listen, I know for a fact J.J. was here this morning. Besides talking to him on the phone he has to come in early and put the guard dogs up before he can open the gates for business."

Closing the notepad, the officer smiled at Lee. "I believe that will be all for now, Mr. Blitzer."

"Then I can go?" asked Lee.

"No, you better stick around. The homicide detectives will be here any minute. They might have some questions for you. You just need to wait up there by the cruiser and try to stay out of the way."

Waiting by the cruiser Lee thought it was an odd sight. The two officers and the paramedics stood in a group smoking and talking about everything but the victim. Lee guessed they were used to this sort of thing. It was their job.

Fifteen minutes passed when two cruisers, an unmarked police vehicle and the coroner's van filed down the lane. A total of seven men climbed out of the small caravan and walked toward the school bus: four uniformed officers, two men dressed in suits and a man who was slipping on a pair of plastic gloves, no doubt the coroner. No one paid any attention to Lee. They passed by him and joined the four men who were already standing by the body.

After greeting one another the coroner, who Lee had heard addressed as Alan, bent down and removed a piece of blue material from the body as Ron Hall filled him in on what they knew so far. There was a lot of conversation going on and Lee edged closer so he could hear what was being said.

The coroner stepped out into the lane and pointed to a trail of blood, commenting that it appeared the body had been drug from place to place. Placing the blue material under his nose, he remarked, "There is a brown stain on this material. Smells like some sort of gravy." Looking back at the body he continued, "The victim didn't walk in here on his own two feet. His legs appear to have been taped and there is still some tape on his ankle. This is definitely a homicide. Most of his face is gone but we should be able to identify him from dental records." Speaking directly to the paramedics he ordered, "Let's get the body bagged up so I can get it back to the morgue for further observation."

"That's fine, Alan," said one of the detectives who everyone called Joe. Turning to the six officers he ordered them, "All right I need you boys to spread out. See what you can find, especially over there by the fence line. We're looking for a ladder, a point of forced entry anything that looks out of the ordinary."

The coroner added, "By the way if anyone finds the other arm, I'm going to need it."

The other detective noticed Lee standing off to the side. Approaching him he offered his hand. "I don't believe we've met. Detective Ralph Burns...homicide. Officer Hall said you were the one who placed the call?"

"That's right," said Lee.

"So, what do you think happened here?"

"What do I think? I think Pickler's dogs ripped that body over there to shreds."

"How do you know the body isn't Pickler?"

"That's easy," answered Lee. "The dogs have been put up. Nobody could have come in here and caged those dogs up except J.J. himself." Looking past the detective, Lee shook his head. "I don't know who that is over there but I know it's not J.J. Pickler."

"You might just be right about those dogs. There are streaks of blood and drag marks all the way down the lane to the fence. They must have dragged and tugged on the body during or after the killing..."

The conversation was interrupted when one of the officers by the fence line yelled, "I think I found the arm, or what's left of it."

Alan, helping to place the bagged body into the back of the van, grabbed a larger bag and started down the lane toward the fence.

Turning back to Lee, Burns stated, "Let me see if Joe has any questions for you. If he doesn't, you'll be able to leave."

Arriving at the fence, Alan leaned down and looked at the mangled arm. "Yep that'd be it." Placing the bag over the arm, he carefully turned the bag over allowing the arm to slide inside.

One of the other officers down the fence line a few yards shouted, "Joe...check this out. Looks like the fence was cut, pushed in and then put back in place." Pointing to the other side of the fence he pointed, "There's blood all over the place on the other side."

Joe, bent down and examined the cut fencing. "Yeah, look at this. There's blood on the edges of where the fence was cut." Addressing three of the officers Joe ordered, "Go back up there and get Detective Burns to drive you around to the other side of the fence."

It took nearly ten minutes to maneuver the vehicles around to where one of the cruisers could get back up the lane out the front gate and down the side road that ran next to the junkyard. Getting out of the cruiser Burns instructed the officers, "Be careful where you step. This could be part of the crime scene."

By this time Lee decided to leave. He'd had enough. If they had any more questions for him they knew where to contact him.

The next few minutes resembled a bizarre Easter egg hunt. Everywhere they looked they discovered evidence. There were footprints in a muddy area in the middle of the road, tire tracks that had gone over some blood, a large sheet of bloody plastic, blood splattered coveralls, shoes, gloves, plastic bottles, a ski mask and a lantern stuffed in the dumpster by the fence. A blood stained two by four was found in the weeds on the side of the road.

Alan, who joined the group, was busy instructing the officers on how to bag up what they were finding, when one of the officers discovered a brown wallet lying next to the fence. "Ralph, look here…a wallet."

Ralph carefully picked the wallet up and opened the blood splattered brown flap. He stared at the photo ID and the badge on the opposite flap: Robert Butch Miller. "Well, I'll be damned!" said Ralph. "Butch Miller. He's one of Chief Brody's officers over in Townsend."

Joe, on the inside of the fence, looked at Ralph. "Our victim might be Butch Miller."

"Maybe…maybe not," said Ralph. "This is getting stranger by the second. I have a friend of mine who works for Sheriff Grimes over in Maryville. Ran into him earlier in the week. He was telling me Miller had been suspended by Brody until he got things figured out over there. Said Miller had attended dogfights right here at J.J.'s and he could be the person or one of the people who has been stealing dogs and selling them to the dog ring. The body we found could very well be Miller or maybe he was involved in all of this somehow. We all thought it was strange how the dog fighters were tipped just before they were raided. And another thing. Where in the hell is J.J. Pickler?"

Ralph handed the wallet to Alan who bagged it then spoke to Joe, "Guess I'll give Chief Brody a call and let him know about his officer's wallet being found over here at the crime scene."

Joe looked down at the ground and noticed a piece of duct tape lying in the weeds. "Alan, got another piece of duct tape over here. Bring me one of those bags."

As Alan handed a bag through the fence, Joe picked up the duct tape and remarked loudly, "Son of a bitch! Look at this." Holding up the tape there were two severed thumbs attached to it.

Just then, from the other side of the fence out by the dumpster, one of the officers yelled, "Got what looks like a finger over here."

Placing the thumbs and the duct tape into the bag, Joe asked Alan, "Before you bagged up the body did you notice anything strange about the hands?"

"Really couldn't tell," said Alan. "They were pretty mangled. When I get the body cleaned up I'll probably be able to see more. Why do you ask?"

Looking through the fence Joe spoke to the officer who had located the finger. "Bring that finger over here." The bagged finger was handed to Alan who held it up next to the bag containing the two thumbs.

Answering Alan's question, Joe looked at the two bags, then at Ralph. "You're right Ralph. This is getting stranger by the second. A man has eight fingers and two thumbs. So far we've found one finger and both thumbs. Look at all of the blood we discovered on the side of the fence opposite of where the body was found, not to mention the bloody plastic, coveralls, shoes and section of wood. The victim may have been dead before the body was placed on this side of the fence. The point is, that leaves seven missing fingers. I bet when it's all said and done the body, after being further examined, will be missing all ten. Remember last April when they found that guy up on Thunderhead trail with his fingers cut off, then in June they found that lady up near Laurel Lake with her fingers and toes cut off? Those two murders are still unsolved and from what I've heard folks over Townsend way are of the opinion that they have a serial killer on their hands. So, we either have a copycat killer on *our hands* or the Townsend killer has come to Sevierville."

CHAPTER SIXTEEN

BRODY SLAMMED THE PHONE DOWN, pushing himself back from his desk. "Got dammit! Marge, where in the hell is Miller?"

Marge, carrying a cup of fresh coffee walked into Brody's office. After working for the chief for thirteen years she had grown accustomed to his occasional fits of rage. "Now, what makes you think that I would know the whereabouts of Butch Miller?"

Pounding his fist on the desk, Brody exclaimed, "He knew I was goin' to call him this mornin'. I can't believe he's not at home. This is his job we're talkin' about here."

"Axel," Marge said calmly, setting the cup on the corner of the desk. "Have a cup of coffee and try to relax. I don't have to tell you Butch has a mind of his own."

Reaching for the coffee Brody took a drink. Sitting back in his chair he began to calm down. "Marge, let me ask you somethin? Three years ago when I hired Butch, I recall it was you who told me to really think about what I was doin'. You even apologized to me sayin' you knew he was my cousin but regardless he had always been a troublemaker. Myself, I really thought he had changed and deserved a chance to make somethin' of himself. Over the past three years I realize he has been a tad bit lazy at times and his mouth, well, he can be a smart ass. Did I make a mistake in hirin' him to be an officer here in town?"

"Back then, when you first hired him I had my doubts. But, despite his shortcomings, I've always felt he did a fair job. But, none of that makes any difference now. How could he ever function like an officer of the law when you consider his recent actions." Marge, taking a seat looked Brody in the eye. "Axel, you haven't told me what your decision on Butch is, but I can tell you this. If you retain him it will not only be a reflection on The Townsend Police, but you as the chief of police. Now I know you are not all that concerned about the fact he mistreated Dana Beth Pearl, pushing her around and bruising her, but you've got to remember I'm a woman so I guess I look at that particular situation differently than you. Then there's the fact that he attended dogfights. The worst thing of all is he could very well have stolen those dogs and sold them to the dog fighters." Pointing her finger, she informed Brody, "Listen here, Axel Brody, I can't and won't interfere and tell you what to do, but if you do not fire that young man, then you are not the man I thought you were and you might just have to find someone to replace me!"

Brody looked at Marge and smiled, "Marge, I can assure you I had every intention of firin' Miller this mornin'. He is officially no longer on the force. You know it, I know it, now all I have to do is contact Butch and tell him that!"

The phone rang interrupting their conversation. "Chief Brody, Townsend Police Department." There was silence then Brody spoke again, "I see, the north side of the lake. I'll send one of my officers up there right away."

Hanging up the phone, he asked Marge, "Who's on patrol now?"

Marge got up as she answered, "Grant. Kenny won't be in until later this afternoon."

Walking toward the front door, Brody waved his hand, "Get Denlinger on the horn. Have him meet me on the north side of Laurel Lake where they put in the boats. Somebody called in a suspicious vehicle near the lake. Said it looked kind of strange. Probably just abandoned. Tell him to meet me up there."

Grant turned left off a neighborhood street into the parking lot of an elementary school. Pulling up next to the fenced playground he watched a group of young boys playing kick ball. Relaxing in the seat, he thought about the upcoming Wednesday which was just two days off when he and Dana Beth had a date to go to Pigeon Forge for dinner and a movie. Over dinner he planned on asking her to marry him. He hadn't spent much time going over what he was going to say, because he had asked her to marry him almost four years ago. She had said yes then, so why would she refuse him now? Reaching over he opened the glove compartment and removed the small box containing the ring. Opening the box he took out the ring and held it up. He looked at it closely, then smiling, placed the ring back in the box. By Wednesday evening Dana Beth would be wearing it once again.

A call coming in on his radio got his attention. "Grant…this is Marge. Come in."

"This is Grant. What's up?"

"Brody wants you to head on up to Laurel Lake. He's going to meet you up there. Someone called in an abandoned vehicle."

"On my way," said Grant.

He turned out of the lot, drove one block, made a right onto the parkway and then turned left on Old Tuckaleechee Road. Marge hadn't given any indication that the call was an emergency so Grant drove the speed limit. Turning onto Laurel Lake Road he remembered the last time he had been called to the Laurel Lake area. Mildred Henks' body had been discovered. He was convinced the same person murdered both Mildred and Asa. What other logical reason could there be for the tobacco found at both homes? Aside from the fact that Asa was sweet on Mildred, the tobacco was the only solid clue they had. Sure, they had reason, according to the county coroner, to believe both victims had fingers cut off by some sort of tool, but what kind of tool? Both victims had been left where they would be found. But why? Both victims had traces of some sort of chloroform and Novocaine in their system. The cause of death of both victims had been that they had bled out before any animals had gotten to them. The killer had an agenda or motive…but what was it? Turning onto a dirt road marked **LAUREL LAKE** he hoped this visit to the lake wouldn't turn out to be another murder.

Passing a three-way sign that read **Boat dock—Swimming area—Picnic Area,** he veered to the left toward the boat dock. A few minutes later after the dirt road cut through the tall pines he emerged from the forest, the crystal clear lake spread out before him. Stopping in the middle of the quarter mile stretch of dirt that formed the north shore Grant looked to the right where there were two people putting their boats in the water, a woman walking a dog and three joggers. To the left there were a couple of people walking and a small group of younger people who, upon seeing the police cruiser, signaled by waving their hands.

Guiding the cruiser along the shoreline Grant stopped a few feet from where the group stood. One of them, a young boy about eighteen approached Grant just as he stopped the cruiser. When Grant stepped out, the boy spoke, "Good morning officer. Me and my friends are the ones who called." Pointing his thumb back over his shoulder, he explained, "We found a truck over there with one of the doors open and then a little further up the shore we found a boat. It looked sort of strange so we thought we better contact the police."

Not sure what he was going to be facing, Grant grabbed a pair of plastic gloves out of the console, a pen and his blue notebook. Walking next to the lake Grant asked, "What's your name, son?"

The boy seemed nervous as he answered, "Tim...Tim Stark."

Snapping on the gloves Grant asked his next question. "Are you from around here, Mr. Stark?"

"Yes, I'm from over in Alcoa." Gesturing toward his five friends who were standing next to a truck with its passenger door wide open, he went on, "Those are some of my friends. They drove down from New York to spend the week with me...and my parents. We were going to hike around the lake and then have a picnic when we noticed this truck here. We're not in any trouble...are we?"

"No, you're not in any trouble, but I'll have to ask you and your friends to move back a few yards until we've finished up here. We might have some questions for you."

Just then Brody sped onto the dirt shoreline, a cloud of road dust trailing him. Stopping next to Grant's cruiser, he got out and walked briskly toward Grant, "What we got, Denlinger?"

Grant, signaling for Tim and his friends to move back farther, turned when Brody approached. "Don't know yet, Chief. I just got here myself."

Nodding at the group of young people Brody asked, "Who are they and what are they doin' here?"

"Apparently they are the ones who called it in."

"Did you tell them to hang around?"

"Yes, sir."

"Good, let's see what we can find." Stepping close to the truck, Brody commented, "This truck looks familiar. I've seen it somewhere before."

Walking around to the open door Grant looked down at the dirt. "Someone left a flashlight on the ground. That's odd. Why would someone get a flashlight out during the day time? This truck may have been here all night." Being careful where he stepped he also pointed out, "The dirt here next to the door seems to have been disturbed, like maybe there was a scuffle." Pointing with his boot, he continued, "And look at those drag marks leading up the shore. Something or someone was dragged in that direction."

Brody, at the rear of the truck was making his own observations. "Passenger door left open, tailgate down...doesn't make much sense." Walking up to the driver's side he looked in the window. "No keys in the ignition."

Grant opened the glove box and after sorting through a variety of candy bar wrappers, ink pens and old Lotto tickets, he pulled out a small bent folder. "Let's see what we've got in here." Pulling out various papers he explained what each one represented: "Owner's manual, Tennessee map, receipts for oil changes, a year old receipt for new tires, ah, here we go...a registration." Unfolding the blue document his mouth dropped open. He remained silent.

Brody, who was listening intently, hesitated, and then asked, "Who's the owner?"

Handing the registration across the seat to Brody, Grant said, "Here, you read it."

Brody looked at the document, then at Grant. "Butch Miller."

Grant stood with his hands on his hips. "I didn't know Butch owned a truck."

"Yeah, he does. And that's where I've seen it before. He drove it to work once in awhile but most of the time he drove his Chevy. He only used this truck to hack around in. Like comin' up here to the lake to fish." Looking a few yards up the shoreline Brody looked closely at the boat that was still half in the water. "That's Butch's boat."

"How can you be so sure?"

Walking toward the boat, Brody replied, "I didn't pay much attention to the boat when I first got here, but I know it's his. I should know. I sold it to him about two years ago when I got my new one."

Placing his boot on the side of the boat, Grant looked down inside. "Looks pretty normal." Bending down he picked up a fishing pole. "You said Butch liked to come up here to fish?"

"Yeah," said Brody. "He told me he spent a lot of time up here on the lake."

Grant leaned the pole up against the side of the boat. "Well, he might have come up here quite a bit to fish but that wasn't why he was here today...or last night...or whenever he was last here."

"What are you drivin' at?" asked Brody skeptically. "Of course he was up here to fish. You've got his pole right there."

Picking the pole up once again, Grant pointed out, "Look, if he was up here fishing there would probably be a lead sinker attached to the line." Putting the pole back down he went on, "Also, where is his tackle box and the cooler for any fish he caught?" Reaching down he opened a small cooler. "This cooler was used simply for beverages, beer it appears." Taking out one of three beers, he tossed it to Brody. "The ice has melted to lukewarm water. He hasn't been here for awhile."

Brody walked around the side of the boat and dropped the beer back into the cooler then nodded toward the front of the boat where there were a number of empty beer cans. "You're probably right. Looks like he was just up here drinkin'." He walked to the edge of the water and looked out across the lake. "Where in the hell could he be?"

Grant picked up the lifejacket, suggesting, "Since his jacket is here and he isn't, there is always the possibility he drowned, but I'm more inclined to think he was dragged off. At least that's what those marks along the shoreline indicate."

Brody started back toward the truck, "Let's have another gander at those marks."

Throwing the jacket back into the boat, Grant followed.

They stopped next to the truck where the drag marks began and followed them up the shore where they stopped after twenty yards. Looking out across the lake again Brody rubbed his hand across his face. "Whatever or whoever was drug over here was more than likely loaded up into somethin'…probably a vehicle." Examining the surrounding ground, the dirt was crisscrossed with a number of tire tracks. Brody shook his head. "Let's not jump to any conclusions just yet. Hell, this whole thing might have been staged when you consider the hot water Butch is in."

Grant made a face. "So you think Butch would stage his death or abduction so he could skip town?"

"I doubt it," said Brody. "But then again, who knows what goes on in his dumb ass brain." He looked over at the group of young people. "Did they have much to say?"

"No, not really," answered Grant. "They're just up here for a hike and then a picnic. Saw the boat and truck. Thought it looked strange, so they gave us a call."

Walking toward his truck Brody ordered, "Tell them to get the hell away from here. I'm goin' to head back to the station and continue to try and contact Butch. You need to stay here and keep an eye on things until I can get a tow truck up here. We'll haul the truck and boat back to the station." Climbing into his truck, Brody lit up a cigar and said, "Should have the tow truck up here within an hour. See ya later."

Grant stood and watched as Brody's truck disappeared up the road into the trees in a cloud of dust. Walking back to Butch's truck he shouted at the teenagers, "You can go on now...and thanks."

Moving his cruiser between Butch's truck and boat Grant got out and opened the trunk. He had decided after the murder of Mildred Henks to start carrying a camera with him while on duty. A camera was a valuable tool, especially at a crime scene. A good set of eyes according to what he had learned in school was important, but the human brain when remembering what one saw was not always accurate. A photograph was permanent, the facts of what were on it could not be argued. It was there right in front of your eyes.

Checking to see if he had film in the camera he walked to the boat and clicked off three shots; two of the interior and one of the outside. He took four shots of the surrounding ground then walked to the truck. He snapped off one shot of the open tailgate, then one of the open door and one of the flashlight still lying on the ground. Pitching the flashlight into the front seat he closed the door, then started to take shots of the area where there appeared to have been a scuffle. Finally he took a couple of shots of the drag marks. His concentration on the ground where the marks stopped was interrupted by a voice, "Hello there."

Turning, Grant saw a middle-aged man dressed in waders and a fishing vest, over top of jeans and a flannel shirt. Placing his fishing rod over his shoulder, the man removed a hat that was decorated with various lures. Looking up at the late morning sun he wiped his brow with the back of his hand then replaced the hat, asking, "You up here because of that truck?"

Grant closed the lens cap on the camera while looking the man up and down. "Some kids reported the truck and boat over there as suspicious so we came up here to investigate."

The man snapped his fingers then pointed at Grant. "I remember you from the Henks' murder over at the golf course."

Grant was confused, "Pardon?"

"You wouldn't remember me. I was one of the golfers they kicked off the course. I watched everything from the balcony over at the club. I remember seeing you there. I knew Mildred Henks. We were good friends. We worked together at Tri-County Realtors for years. She was one tough cookie, that Mildred. I attended many a party at her home. Now, they've got those damn tours running through there. Can't the police do something about that?"

"Actually no," responded Grant. "It's all legal."

"Well, all I can say is it's a damn shame." Changing the subject the man nodded toward Butch's truck. "That truck and the boat has been up here everyday for I guess almost a week or so. I'm on vacation this week so I'm getting my fill of fishing in. Been up here daily for the past few days. Everyday some young fella., I reckon about your age, drives in here, parks, unhooks that boat and heads out on the lake until it gets dark. Then he hooks up the boat and leaves for the day. I don't think he caught a single fish the entire time he was here. Last night when I was leaving the truck sat there just like you see it with the tailgate down and the door open. I just figured he was around here somewhere, ya know maybe off in the woods taking a piss." Squinting at Grant the man asked, "Is there a problem?"

"We don't know yet. Right now the man is just missing."

"Hope it's not another murder. Folks are getting kind of antsy around these parts." With that the man saluted and moved on up the shore.

Up until that very moment Grant hadn't even considered the fact Butch might have been murdered. Walking back to the cruiser he put the camera back in the trunk and walked to the edge of the forest where he sat on one of the many benches scattered around the lake next to the hiking trail.

Sitting there peacefully, Grant looked out across the lake, the last statement the man had made still on his mind: a third murder. The more he thought about it the more he suspected foul play. The clues they had found were red flags; the tailgate had been left down and the side door of the truck was left open. And what about the flashlight lying on the ground near where the disturbed dirt indicated a possible struggle? The most convincing clue as far as Grant was concerned was the drag marks. He was not buying into Brody's philosophy that the whole thing might have been staged to give Butch a chance to skip town in order to beat any charges brought against him. Besides, why would Butch wait until the last day before Brody was to call him before he decided to leave town. He could have left earlier in the week and no one would have known.

The whole situation seemed odd. It was like a giant puzzle with a vital piece missing. If Butch was abducted—or murdered—why? Maybe it had something to do with the people who ran the dogfights.

Getting up from the bench he walked to the cruiser to check the time. It seemed like the tow truck should be arriving soon. He leaned on the hood and watched a fisherman cast his line from a boat out into the water. He thought about Butch again and why anyone would want to murder him—if in fact that is what happened. Maybe it was because he had stolen all those dogs and as a result what had happened to them. The fact those dogs had been bound and thrown into a ring with trained killers probably didn't set well with their owners. Would someone kill another person for treating a dog in that manner? *Maybe they would,* he thought. Someone had killed Asa Pittman, a man who hunted illegally, skinned animals, shot a neighbor's dog. Someone had killed Mildred Henks, a woman who bred dogs but treated them horribly. All this time he and everyone else had been trying to figure out why Asa and Mildred had been killed. Maybe the killer was an animal lover. Then again, there were a lot of animal lovers in the world, but not a lot of people who would kill others because of their stance on how animals should be treated. Just then he heard the honking of a horn as a tow truck rumbled onto the dirt area along the shore.

Twenty minutes later, Butch's truck and boat were hooked up to the tow truck. The driver pulled out and Grant took one last look out at the surrounding woods and the lake. He had the strangest feeling. Getting into the cruiser he backed up, turned to the right and followed the tow truck.

Grant pulled up in front of the station as the tow truck disappeared around the side of the building. Looking at the dash clock it was just after one o'clock in the afternoon. He hadn't had anything to eat so he decided to check in, then grab a bite. Entering the reception office he came to a dead stop when he noticed Marge sitting at her desk dabbing at her tear stained face, Kenny standing over her, his hand on her shoulder. Grant, concerned walked to the desk. "Marge…are you all right…what's wrong?"

Looking up at Grant she tried to speak but just broke down in tears, then buried her face with the Kleenex. Looking to Kenny for an answer, Kenny shook his head, then spoke almost reverently,

"You better go in and see the Chief. He's in his office."

Walking quickly down the hall he stopped in the doorway. Brody was sitting at his desk, his head in both of his hands. "Chief, they told me I needed to see you. What's going on?"

Brody looked up, his face red with tears. Nodding at a chair he said softly, "Sit down, Grant."

Grant seated himself and waited patiently for an explanation. Brody stared at the desktop for a few seconds which seemed like an eternity. Finally, he looked across the desk at Grant and spoke in a low tone, "Butch is dead."

Grant couldn't believe what he was hearing. "What do you mean, dead?"

Pounding his fist on the desk, Brody answered loudly, "D-E-A-D ...dead! What other kind of dead is there?"

"How?" asked Grant. "What happened?"

Brody pulled open his bottom desk drawer and sat a bottle of whiskey on the desk along with two shot glasses. Pouring himself a full measure, he downed the drink in one swallow, then wiped his eyes. He offered the bottle to Grant but he refused, "No thanks."

Placing the bottle back in the desk, Brody started to regain his composure. "We just got a call from the chief of police over in Sevierville. Came in about ten minutes ago. They found a body over at J.J.'s Junk Emporium. The body was, well, he said it was like a ball of raw meat. It looks like the guard dogs had a go at it..." Brody started to choke up again.

Grant remained silent, but then asked, "How do they know it was Butch?"

"They found his wallet at the scene. It was blood stained. They also found a finger and two thumbs...severed."

"Oh, God," said Grant. After a few seconds of silence he asked, "Are they sure that the body is Butch?"

Brody sniffed and wiped his eyes again. "They were able to pull prints from the thumbs. Came up as Butch."

Grant wanted to talk about the severed fingers, but at the moment it seemed inappropriate. Instead he tried his best to console Brody. "Axel, I'm really sorry about Butch. I know he was your cousin."

Getting up, Brody walked to the small window at the back of his office and looked out. The tow truck was pulling away. He stared at Butch's truck and boat for a second, turned and walked back to his desk. "Butch always ran on the edge on the cliff, even when he was younger. Always gettin' into trouble, pushin' everyone's buttons. He drove his parents nuts." Sitting back down at the desk he folded his hands and commented, "Well, I guess he pissed off the wrong person this time. And the way it looks so far with the severed fingers it could very well be the same person who killed Asa Pittman and Mildred Henks. Three murders in a little over five months."

Now that Brody had opened up the can of worms Grant felt a little more comfortable talking about a third murder. "After you left I ran into a local who was fishing up at the lake. He told me Butch's truck and boat had been up there this past week. He saw Butch up there everyday arriving, putting the boat in the water, then leaving just before dark. He told me that last night the truck was sitting there just the way we found it. He didn't think anything about it. He thought the owner was around there somewhere."

Brody, not paying any attention to what Grant was saying, stood up. "Listen we have to get our act together around here. The chief and one of the detectives who was on the scene from Sevierville are meetin' here with Sheriff Grimes about two o'clock. You need to be here. I'm gonna run home and freshen up some. You might wanna grab a bite. I have no idea how long they'll be here. Could be a long afternoon."

Sitting near the back of Lily's Café, Grant stared at the hot roast beef sandwich and gravy he had ordered. Suddenly he wasn't hungry but he knew he needed to get something in his stomach. Every table in the small restaurant was taken and a few customers stood in line. Looking around Grant didn't recognize one person he knew. He assumed most or maybe all of the customers were out of towners. A couple near the front window, apparently finished with their meal stood up and walked to the register. Grant couldn't help but notice they were wearing what were becoming popular t-shirts: Pittman-Henks Murder Tour. Cutting into his sandwich, Grant recalled what the fisherman up at the lake had said. 'The tours are a damn shame.'

Swallowing his first bite, he washed it down with a drink of cold milk, then glanced around the small eatery. People loved to come to Townsend, *The Peaceful Side of the Smokies.* It was a relaxing place, a great place to spend a vacation. The people who lived in

Townsend, the business owners and the chamber had done an admirable job of keeping their heads up; it was business as usual. But he knew different. He realized that beneath the thin veneer of happiness the town displayed there was a time bomb getting ready to explode. The fact that one of their officers had now been murdered, coupled with the two previous murders made for a bad combination. The local residents depended on the police to protect them. But now, one of the local police had been murdered. How would they feel? The town and the surrounding area was like a giant sponge soaking up water, only in the case of the three murders it was blood. How much more could the town endure before the invisible sponge was saturated?

Before he realized it a woman holding onto a child with each hand approached. Stopping in front of his table, she spoke, "Excuse me, sir. Are you one of the officers with the Townsend Police?"

Grant, laying down his fork answered politely, "Yes I am. What can I do for you?"

"My name is Roberta Lewis and these are my two daughters, Deborah and Denise. My husband Ronald is over there paying for our meal. We're from Virginia on vacation. We heard so much about Townsend and we just had to come visit. I just wanted to thank you for the absolutely wonderful community you have here and for sharing it with the rest of the world."

Grant wasn't sure how he should answer so he simply replied, "You're welcome."

Looking down at his plate he was no longer hungry. Glancing around the crowded restaurant he wondered how many of the people seated at the tables knew about the horrible murders that had descended on Townsend over the past year. Even worse, if they knew one of the town's officers had been murdered how could they possibly feel safe? It was like walking a tightrope without a safety net.

He arrived back at the station at ten minutes to two. Brody's truck was parked in front. Entering the main office, Marge seemed to be in better spirits. "Marge I'm really sorry about Butch. Are you going to be all right?"

"I'll be fine. It's just…the other two murders, well, even though they were bad…this one hits close to home." Changing the subject she nodded toward Brody's office. "The Chief told me to tell you when you got back to head on into his office. Kenny is out on patrol. Our visitors should be arriving soon."

Grant shook his head in confusion. "Why is it so important I attend this meeting?"

"Don't know," said Marge, "but you best get in there."

Just as Grant was turning to walk down the hall, Sheriff Grimes walked in the door followed by two men Grant had never met before. Almost bumping into Grant, Grimes reached out shaking his hand. "Why, hello there, Grant." Before Grant could say a word Grimes introduced the two men with him: "Grant, this is Sam Levering, the Chief of Police in Sevierville and one of his homicide detectives, Joe DiMarco. Joe, Sam, this is officer Denlinger of the Townsend Police." Detective DiMarco shook hands with Grant and gave him the strangest look.

Hearing all of the conversation out in the hall Brody stuck his head out the doorway and spoke, "Gentlemen, please come back."

Grant led the way, the three others following. Grant, feeling he was the one in the room with the least amount of clout, took a seat in the corner. Bert sat against the wall and Joe and Sam sat directly across from Brody.

After everyone was seated Bert was the first to speak. "I don't think we have to tell you how sorry we are for the loss of one of your officers, Axel."

Sam and Joe nodded in agreement.

Brody raised his hand in a sign of thanks then asked, "So, what do we have so far?"

Motioning to Joe, Sam jumped in on the conversation, "I think Detective DiMarco is best suited to fill you in on where we stand, since he was at the crime scene."

DiMarco scooted forward on his chair. "The body was found at J.J.'s Junk Emporium jammed up underneath one of the cars. The body was in a condition well beyond recognition. The coroner is still working on it but right now it looks like the guard dogs inside the fenced area chewed on the victim. It appears the body was shoved through the fence by means of a section of lumber we found outside the yard. There was a large amount of blood on the side of the road and where the body had been dragged to the fence. In a large dumpster next to the fence we discovered a large section of clear plastic splattered and soaked with blood in certain areas. Also, in the dumpster we found a pair of bloody coveralls, a pair of blood-stained gloves, a pair of work boots and a ski mask, a lantern and some plastic bottles. There were also tire marks where the vehicle traveled over the blood. We found one severed finger on the outside of the fence and two severed thumbs on the inside."

Sitting back in the chair, he continued with the rundown. "Now here is where it starts to get strange. Even though the body was pretty mangled there was evidence the legs and arms were strapped back with duct tape. There were also traces of duct tape around the mouth area. This resembles the way dogs used as bait for fighting dogs are thrown in the ring. A horrible death. When you consider there was a recent raid over at J.J.'s and that J.J. Pickler, the owner, has disappeared, well, things just don't add up."

Sheriff Grimes seeing Joe was finished at least for the moment spoke up, "I was just telling Sam and Joe on the way over here that you had recently suspended Mr. Miller for not only attending dogfights but he was suspected of stealing dogs and selling them to the dog fighters. I also told them you decided to terminate Mr. Miller from the force but you couldn't get hold of him, despite numerous calls to his home."

Chief Levering was the next to speak, "The main reason for us coming over here to meet with you aside from the fact one of your officers has been murdered, is this case seems to be strangely similar to the Pittman and Henks murders. That being, the body found over in Sevierville had the fingers severed just like Pittman and Henks." Looking around the room at everyone, he emphasized, "If, up to this point, you were not convinced that we have a serial killer on the loose in the area, you can now be sure we do!"

Brody, shifted in his chair and addressed the entire group. "I guess we've all been thinkin' along those lines but no one wanted to admit it. Now, it seems so obvious." Looking at Grimes he went on, "Bert, we really didn't have a chance to let you in on what we discovered this mornin'. It's a case that seems to still be unfoldin'. We were called up to Laurel Lake about an abandoned truck. When we got up there we found out it belonged to Miller. There was also a boat up there that belonged to him. The whole thing just didn't look right. There were signs of a scuffle, the truck door was left open, and the tailgate was left down. There was a flashlight layin' on the lot and marks leadin' down the shore like someone or somethin' had been dragged. I am now convinced this is where Miller was abducted."

Detective DiMarco spoke up again, turning to Grant. "Officer Denlinger. You're probably sitting there wondering why you were included in this meeting. In a conversation Chief Brody had with Sheriff Grimes last week it has been reported you and Miller didn't get along all that well. That you two had come to blows twice here at the station and after popping him in the mouth right here in this office you threatened him by saying if he ever touched a girl by the name of Dana Beth again...you would kill him!" Looking directly at Grant, DiMarco asked, "Is this a true statement?"

Grant suddenly realized why he had been invited to the meeting. "Now just hold on a minute! Sure I said I'd kill him. But that was nothing more than a colorful metaphor, something people say all the time. Just because I said it doesn't mean I did it!"

DiMarco, who seemed quite adept at doing his job, slid forward on his chair in an intimidating fashion. "Sure, we've probably all said that at one time or another in our life, but the person we've said it to doesn't wind up dead within a few days. And there's the difference. You said you'd kill him *and now* he is dead!"

Grimes, seeing things were getting a bit out of hand spoke up, "Hold on, detective. Officer Denlinger is a fine officer. He was at both murder scenes we've had over here and has been quite helpful. I can assure you, Grant Denlinger did not kill Butch Miller."

"I never said he did kill Miller," argued DiMarco. "All I'm saying is he is a suspect at this time...a person of interest."

Grant stood up. "Don't give me that person of interest bullshit! I didn't just fall off the turnip truck. I know what it means and I don't like being accused of killing Butch Miller. Sure we had our differences but that's as far as it went."

DiMarco stood and took a step toward Grant. "A lot of folks have differences but they don't punch them in the mouth and then indicate verbally they're going to kill them."

Grant had never been pushed this hard in his life. He clenched his fists, trying to keep DiMarco from pushing his buttons.

Looking down at Grant's fists, DiMarco moved closer. "You'd like to take a swing at me right now...wouldn't you?"

Grimes, astonished at the way Detective DiMarco was verbally pushing Grant stepped in between the two as he looked at Brody. By this time Brody was out of his chair, his face turning red, "Back off, detective. That's one of my men you're talkin' to." Turning to Grant, he ordered him, "Take it easy, Denlinger. Everyone just needs to chill."

Following a few seconds of sour looks, everyone was seated. Brody, looking at Grant spoke firmly but softly, "Grant, here's what we're gonna do. I want you to take two weeks off."

Grant objected. "You're suspending me?"

"No, I'm not suspendin' you. You've got two weeks of paid vacation comin' and I think you need to take them. I'm sorry, but you need some time off. Hell, we all need some time off. These murders have thrown everythin' and everybody out of whack. Now, don't say another word. Get out of here and I'll see you in two weeks."

Grant was so upset he couldn't have said anything if he had wanted to. Getting up from his chair he shot Detective DiMarco a hard look then turned and walked down the hall. As he opened the door to the parking lot he waved at Marge then commented sarcastically, "See ya in two weeks. I'm on vacation!"

CHAPTER SEVENTEEN

GRANT PULLED THE JEEP into Dana Beth's driveway and looked at his watch. It was exactly seven thirty in the evening. Reaching into his pocket one more time, he ran his hand over the top of the velvet ring box. He ambled up the paved driveway and quickly took the seven steps up the porch. How many times had he done this very same thing in the past? One thing had always been the same. When he reached the door and got ready to ring the bell, she had always opened the door and said, "Hi!" He grinned when he thought about all those times and wondered if it would happen tonight. Even though it had been quite some time, sure enough, when he put his finger on the doorbell, she flung the door open. "Hi!" she said, displaying a wide smile.

She looked great, her slim figure encased in a snug fitting black dress with a neckline just low enough to be interesting. Her hair looked radiant in the light of the hallway as she escorted him in. Grant was glad he had decided to wear a suit even though Dalton said he looked like he was going to a funeral, but tonight he wanted to be serious and what could be more serious than a dark blue suit.

"You're right on time," said Dana Beth. "Mom and Dad want to say hello, then we can go." Leading the way down the hall she was much taller in three-inch heels, which she seldom wore.

Professor Pearl, sitting in the den put down his paper and offered his hand to Grant. "Grant, good to see you. It's a pleasure to have you in our home again."

Dana Beth's mother, Ruth, came around the corner from the kitchen her arms extended. "Come here and give me a hug, Mr. Denlinger." Throwing her arms around his neck she kissed him on the cheek. "I can't tell you how so very glad I am that you are back in Dana Beth's life." Looking at her husband, she went on, "Conrad always said I was very partial toward you and that I was devastated when you two broke up." Folding her hands in front of her in a prim and proper manner she looked at the grandfather clock in the corner.

"Now, you two better run along if you want to make your eight o'clock reservation."

Practically running across the porch, down the steps and driveway, they stopped next to the Jeep, Dana Beth asking, "So, where are you taking me to dinner? I just want to let you know I'm starving, so you better be prepared."

Opening the door for her, Grant smiled then joked, "Let me check my wallet. I don't know how anyone so small can have such a big appetite."

Grant jumped into the driver's seat and turned the ignition, Dana Beth continuing their conversation, "I'm trying to make up for all those months I was so miserable without you." Placing the back of her hand against her forehead she sank back in the seat, giving her best southern belle rendition complete with accent: "My lands, ya'll know I just couldn't eat a solitary bite without you around."

Grant laughed and pulled out of the driveway. "Yeah right, like you'd miss a meal because I'm not around."

Lightly punching him on the arm, she jokingly scolded him, "You're going to pay big time...buddy boy." Looking out the side window, she was suddenly silent for a moment then turned back to him. "Grant, I'm so sorry about all the mess going on with your job, but let's try and forget about all that for awhile. I've gone over and over Butch's murder in my head and I still can't make any sense of it. Even though I was really mad at him, I didn't want him dead."

"I know, neither did I."

Wanting to change the subject, she asked, "What are you going to do with all your unscheduled time off?"

Making a left hand turn onto Wears Valley Road, Grant winked at her, "Catch up on some much needed sleep, help my grandfather and mother around the farm, try to figure out what's going on with these murders." He stopped then added, "And, oh yeah, I might try to squeeze in some time with you."

"You better!"

Twenty minutes later, Grant pulled the Jeep into the parking lot of the Park Grill. Dana Beth let out a squeal. "You're kidding me! I haven't eaten here since the night following high school graduation when you proposed to me. I love this place."

Walking around the front of the Jeep, he opened her door. "Yeah, the last time I brought you here I had to save up for two months in order to be able to afford dinner, but tonight…you can have one of everything on the menu."

Their waiter escorted them to a table Grant had requested which was directly in front of the fireplace. After getting settled in, Grant ordered a bottle of wine while they mulled over the extensive menu. He couldn't concentrate on what he wanted to eat because he was concerned about going through with the planned proposal. He just wasn't sure with the recent death of Butch that the time was right. Even though he had never been fond of Miller, still, he had worked side by side with the man for the last year or so.

Although Dana Beth had broken things off with him, it almost seemed like it was just too soon for them to move on with their lives.

He knew he couldn't shield his doubt for long so after they ordered their meals, he nervously blurted out, "Look, I was going to give this to you later, but I can't wait a minute longer." Digging into his suit coat pocket he pulled out the ring box and slid it across the table. Then he thought to himself, *That wasn't very suave.*

At first Dana Beth just looked at the small box, but then she reached down and slowly opened it. She stared at the ring she had worn on her finger for just over two years. Looking across the table at Grant she spoke softly, "You kept my ring all this time?"

The horse was out of the barn. It was obvious what he was supposed to do next, but he was frozen. He just sat there thinking, *Ask her you idiot! Ask her.*

Before he could form the words, she tilted the box. "I love this ring."

Grant took a deep breath. *Here goes!* "I screwed this up the first time and I feel like I'm getting ready to fumble the ball here, but if I were to ask you to marry me for the second time, would you wear that ring?"

She leaned across the table and kissed him. "Of course, I'll marry you, Grant. I've never stopped loving you."

Grant removed the ring from the box, took her hand and slipped it on her finger. Holding her hand so the firelight reflected off of the ring, Dana Beth spoke sincerely, "I love you, Grant."

He wanted to take her in his arms, realizing that the hole in his life had been filled, but he would have to wait as plates of medium-rare steaks, baked potatoes and pan-seared vegetables arrived at their table. "Damn," said Grant jokingly. "I knew I should have waited until after our food arrived. The food has arrived and the mood is gone."

Examining her ring once again, Dana Beth picked up her fork and pointed it at Grant. "I'm glad you didn't wait until after dinner. Now, my nerves are calmed down and I can eat even more."

Grant took her hands in his. "Let's bless the food and our upcoming marriage."

The blessing complete, Dana Beth took a drink of wine. "I consider myself blessed to be here tonight with you. I was such a fool to ever let you go. I never really took the time to see things your way. I do now and I want you to know how sorry I am for being so stupid. I thought after making such a dumb mistake by dating Butch you would never forgive me."

"Don't ever call yourself stupid. I was the dumb one. I should have come up to your school and carried you off and married you. Instead I just limped away and let you go."

She held up her glass. "A toast to the two dumbest people in the world."

Grant cut into his steak, then reached for a bottle of steak sauce. "I suppose your mother will be planning a big wedding as soon as you tell her?"

"Probably, but to tell you the truth, I wish she wouldn't. I'm kind of worried about my father and I know if there are wedding plans he'll want to be right in the middle of things. He hasn't been feeling well for quite some time. He keeps telling my mother everything will be fine…that he's fine. Just last week she was telling me she feels he is keeping whatever illness or sickness he has away from us."

"I'm sorry to hear that. Well, maybe your mother would settle for a smaller or medium-sized wedding."

For the next hour they enjoyed their meal and finished up with a chocolate mousse concoction they shared but could not finish. They sat and talked and polished off the wine taking the last two glassfuls with them out onto the balcony of the restaurant. There was a bit of a nip in the air. Dana Beth wrapped her lightweight jacket around her shoulders and cuddled close to Grant. "This seems so normal," she said. "I could stay right here forever." Walking toward the balcony railing she took a drink, then turned. "I have an idea. You have another week and a half off and if I pulled a few strings I could get some time off, too." Walking back to Grant she touched his arm. "Why don't we get married Saturday?"

Grant, a little shocked, asked, "Saturday...what Saturday?"

"The one coming up...you know, Thursday, Friday, Saturday."

Grant, stunned, downed the last of his wine. "You're serious. You want to get married in three days?"

Setting her glass on a small table she answered, "Why not. I don't ever want to lose you again. I want to support you through all of the turmoil you're going through at work. I hate not being with you all the time. We can get a license and get married at the Mountain Valley Chapel in Gatlinburg and then spend the night at the Eagle Ridge Resort. Then, the next morning we can take off on a trip somewhere. You know...like a real honeymoon."

Grant just stood there with his mouth wide open not sure what to say. He had been confident she would accept his proposal, but to get married in three days. It was crazy!

Tears welled up in Dana Beth's eyes. "I've never been more sure about anything in my life, but I understand if you need time to think about all this."

"No, I don't need time, are you sure? It's...it's just so sudden."

Reaching out and holding his hand, Dana Beth looked into his eyes. "It's not sudden, Grant. It's long overdue. We love each other so why should we wait any longer?"

Grant didn't respond.

Dana Beth stepped back, placing her hands on her hips. "What's wrong? Are you changing your mind about marrying me? I know you Grant Denlinger. Did you think you could propose to me tonight then wait for my mother to start making wedding plans? Sure, we could just go back to work and start saving money, maybe pick a day next spring. If we did that we'd just be putting things on hold again. I can see your clinical mind at work. For once in our lives let's just do something spontaneous, just for us. I'm going to put everything in my heart and soul into our marriage because I believe in us. And no matter what happens in the months or years to come I know we'll be strong enough to handle it."

Grant put his empty glass down on a nearby chair, walked over to Dana Beth and placed his hands on her shoulders, looking her square in the eye. Picking her up, he swung her around showering her face with kisses. "I love you...I love you...I love you! What the hell! Let's just get married tonight!"

They hugged as Dana Beth joked, "Now who's pushing things? I think this Saturday will be fine."

On the drive back to Townsend they talked about what to say to their parents. Grant knew Greta would be pleased and Dalton, well he was expecting Grant to ask her to marry him. Dana Beth felt her folks would be thrilled. Grant brought up the matter of asking Professor Pearl for her hand in marriage. Dana Beth said it would be overkill as Grant had already asked her father if he could marry her once before. Why would he feel any different now?

When they arrived at her house all of the lights were out except for the hall entry. Standing on the porch at the front door Dana Beth said, "They must be in bed. I'll tell them tomorrow before I leave for work. It'll make for an interesting breakfast." Turning she kissed him on the cheek. "The next time I'll see you will be Saturday morning. That'll give me two days to get ready."

Starting down the steps Grant stopped. "Wait, we have to decide where we're going to go on our honeymoon. I mean we need to know what kind of clothes to pack...what the weather will be like...things like that. Actually, I'd like to get as far away from here as possible."

Dana Beth looked up at the bright moon. "How about New York State or maybe California?"

"Too many people," said Grant. "Let's go someplace where it's quiet and there aren't so many tourists running around, like it used to be here in Townsend when I was a little kid."

Dana Beth thought for a moment then snapped her fingers. "Hey, I've got an idea. I've told you about this before, but you've probably forgotten. When I was much younger my family took a trip every year up to Itasca State Park in Northern Minnesota. It's beautiful up there. There are about a hundred lakes and it's the headwaters of the Mississippi. You can hold my hand and we can walk across it. They have rustic cabins tucked back in the woods, small quaint restaurants with great food, lots of fishing and hiking and not near the amount of people there are here in the Smokies. In fact, by the time we get there they may have even had a frost. I can remember waking up in the morning to the sound of the Loons paddling across the lake. I would be all wrapped up in blankets while looking out the cabin window at the mist on the lake. My father was always up early. He took his fishing gear and headed out the door before the sun was up. Hours later he would return with a line of fish. It was great. We swam and had bonfires at night. If you think the pine trees are tall here, wait until you see the ones up north. They are huge. What do you think?"

"I'll tell you what I think. I think you should work for a travel bureau. You sold me. After we tie the knot on Saturday we'll drive up there. How far is it?"

"I'll check but I think it's about an eighteen hour drive."

Grant groaned, "Whew! Well, sounds to me like you'd really like to go there. It's worth it and so are you." Bounding down the steps he said, "I'm outta here."

"Hey," said Dana Beth. "Don't forget to bring some warm clothes and your fishing gear."

The next morning over breakfast Grant told his mother and grandfather about the plans he and Dana Beth had made the previous evening. Grant mentioned they might live on the farm for awhile if it was all right. Greta agreed, saying there was plenty of room. Dalton was also excited about the prospect of having his grandson and wife live with them. Grant spent the next two days helping Dalton prepare the summer house for the newlyweds upon their return from the trip up to Minnesota. Friday evening Grant took a walk back through the woods out behind the farm. For the moment the tragedy of the three murders took a backseat to what was about to happen in his young life. Tomorrow he would be a married man.

Dana Beth wore a pale blue dress and Grant wore his funeral suit once again as they walked up the path that led to the Mountain Valley Chapel. It was a short ceremony. Grant placed the silver band on Dana Beth's finger, and she slipped the matching ring on his. They were pronounced man and wife, they kissed, and the minister's wife threw confetti over them. Outside, the ceremony complete, Grant stared at his left hand. He was now married.

Too excited about their trip up north, they decided to forgo the night at the resort and take off on the long trek to Minnesota. Stopping six hours later in Northern Kentucky, they spent the night in a Holiday Inn. The next morning they awoke, enjoyed a continental breakfast then hit the road. At seven o'clock, Sunday night they arrived at the Brookside Resort and following a few formalities and some minor paperwork they settled into a cabin tucked away in a grove of trees next to the lake. It had been a long trip. They were exhausted. They slept for thirteen hours, waking up on Monday morning.

"Morning, sleepy head," Dana Beth said, laying her head on Grant's back. "We need to get up and go to town and get some supplies. We need fishing licenses and food…and more food."

Grant rolled over and took her in his arms. Maybe we oughta just grab a stick and some string and go catch breakfast."

Dana Beth jumped out of bed. "I don't think so. I want sausage and eggs and toast and coffee. Lots of coffee."

Grant sat on the edge of the bed and ran his hands over his face. "The trip up here really wore me out. Just let me grab a quick shower then we can head down to the office and find out where everything is around here."

Stepping into the small closet Dana Beth yelled back at him, "I already know where to go. While you were busy getting our bags out of the Jeep when we first arrived I talked with the lady at the front desk. I asked her if the country store on the other side of the lake was still there. When my folks used to bring me up here for vacation I remembered there was a store on the lake my father always took us to. It's a great little place. They have a great breakfast there. If you want you can sit right out on a deck facing the lake."

"Great," shouted back Grant. "Soon as I get my shower we'll drive over."

Sticking her head out the closet door, she corrected him, "You don't drive to this place. That's what's so neat about it. We have to rent a boat and cross the lake."

"A boat!" exclaimed Grant.

"Don't worry. We'll work up a good appetite."

Entering the main cabin where the front desk was located, Dana Beth couldn't believe her eyes. "Mrs. Rodell, I can't believe after all these years you're still here." Turning to Grant she made the introductions, "Grant, this is Mrs. Rodell. She and her husband own and run Brookside. They were always so nice to me when my parents brought me up here for vacation when I was younger. Mrs. Rodell, this is my husband…actually my new husband. We've only been married for two days."

Mrs. Rodell removed her reading glasses from her face. "Well, congratulations. So, I can no longer refer to you as Miss Pearl. You are now?"

"Mrs. Denlinger," answered Dana Beth.

"Many a couple over the years have come to Brookside for their honeymoon. What are you planning on doing during your stay?"

"First of all, we're going to get stocked up with some food. Thought we'd take a boat over to the country store they used to have on the other side of the lake. I hope it's still there."

"It is still there *and* they still serve the best breakfast around these parts. Tell you what, with it being your honeymoon and all the boat's on the house for today." Rubbing her chin, Mrs. Rodell looked Dana Beth up and down. "Well, you've certainly blossomed into an attractive young woman. How many years has it been since you've been up here?"

Dana Beth thought for a moment then answered, "I think the last time I was here I was twelve. That makes it about ten years."

"The first week of October is just around the corner." Looking at a large calendar hanging on the wall, Mrs. Rodell commented, "That's about five weeks away. Your father will be coming just like he does every year for a week on the lake."

Grant had a look of confusion on his face as Dana Beth explained, "When I turned twelve my mother and I opted to go to the shore rather than coming up here, so for the past ten years my father has been taking us on our yearly vacation down to the Gulf Shores to spend a week on the beach. However, he just loves it up here, so every October he takes a week off and comes up here by himself to fish and relax."

Another couple walked in the front door. Mrs. Rodell pointed in the direction of the lake. "The boats are kept down by the dock. There should be five of them down there right now. Take your choice. When you get in the water go right staying close to the shoreline and follow it around for about two miles. You'll eventually come to a sign that's anchored in the water that reads: Gas and Bait. You can't miss it. Enjoy yourselves."

After Dana Beth was seated in the green flat bottomed boat, Grant pushed the small motorboat away from the dock jumping in and rocking it from side to side. Dana Beth laughed. "Only been married two days and I'm on the verge of drowning!"

"Ha, ha," remarked Grant, pulling the starter cord. "I hope this place isn't too far. What did she say…two miles?"

"Yep, two miles," said Dana Beth, putting on a bright orange life jacket. "I know we're not going to be that far out on the lake but you strike me as a land lubber. Have you even ever been in a boat before?"

"Not for some time, but I think I'll be able to handle it. The last time I was in a boat was back in boy scouts quite a few years back. Now you just settle in and enjoy the ride." Turning the boat to the right he headed up the shoreline.

Laying back in the boat Dana Beth struck a pose. "This is so romantic. Just like in the movies."

Ten minutes later after staying clear of low hanging branches and rocks, Grant maneuvered the boat around a small cove. Stopping he wiped his brow. "Guess I wouldn't make a very good sailor."

Dana Beth chuckled, "Hey no breaks there, me swabby. Ya got a new wife over here who at the moment is starving. Heave ho mate!"

For the next forty minutes Grant continued guiding the boat along the shoreline. They enjoyed the color of the fall leaves and the peaceful morning on the lake. They talked about how their parents had reacted to the suddenness of their wedding. Grant said his mother didn't have a problem with the way they had gone about things. After all, he was a man and capable of making his own decisions. Dana Beth on the other hand said her mother had been slightly upset since she was her only daughter and, as a mother, she looked forward to the day she got married. Her father really didn't seem to care about a big wedding, he was just glad Dana Beth and Grant had not only gotten back together but had married. Grant suggested maybe in the future they could have another ceremony for the benefit of Dana Beth's mother. Dana Beth said that might be a possibility but for right now she was just glad to be with Grant and she didn't want to think about anything else.

Grant slowed the boat when Dana Beth shouted and pointed. "There it is! The sign. Doesn't say anything about food. I guess when you're out on the lake fishing, gas and bait are more important."

The large rustic cabin was another fifty yards across the water. Getting close to the dock Grant turned off the small, five horsepower engine and allowed the boat to drift to the old wooden structure. Jumping out with the towrope, he tied the boat to the pier and helped Dana Beth out and then led her up a dirt path to the log home nestled in a canopy of tall pine trees.

The front porch of the cedar building was lined with fishing poles, nets and tubs of shiners. Two elderly men sat on stools playing checkers on a board painted on top of an old whiskey barrel. Dana Beth and Grant stepped up onto the porch, the two men glancing up at them, nodding and then continued with their game.

Grant opened the screen door which greeted them with the clanging of a bell attached to the inside of the frame. It was dimly lit inside, but the smell of something really good wafted across the room and into their noses. The right side of the store was strictly for fishermen who came to the lake: waders, lures, tackle boxes, poles, hats, and other fishing paraphernalia. The left side of the building was lined with makeshift shelves filled with groceries, a large refrigerated case and a small counter. Across the back of the large room there was a row of five tables with unmatched chairs at each. A red-checkered curtain separated the kitchen from the rest of the room.

Just then a large woman wearing a blue and white apron pushed the curtain aside. Smiling, she said, "Welcome to the Country Store on the Lake. What can I do for you young people?"

Dana Beth took a deep whiff then answered. "Whatever you're cooking, we'll have some of that."

"You sure can, honey," the woman laughed, placing her hands on her hips. "Got me a batch of corn muffins just about ready to come out of the oven."

"Can we get anything else...like eggs, sausage, toast and coffee?"

"You just plop right down there at one of those tables and I'll get you a couple of menus."

Grant pulled out a chair for Dana Beth, then walked around the table and took a seat himself. The woman returned with the menus, two mugs and a pot of coffee. "My name is Hilda." Pouring coffee into the mugs she commented, "Can't have breakfast without coffee. Now, whenever you two are ready to order just let me know. Those muffins will be out in a minute."

Two minutes later Hilda returned with a basket of warm muffins and a small dish of apple butter along with an assortment of butter and jellies. As she was refilling Grant's cup, Dana Beth spoke up,

"I think I'm ready to order."

Pulling an order pad out of her apron, Hilda removed a pen from behind her ear and smiled pleasantly, "The sooner you place your order the sooner you'll be eating."

Dana Beth pointed at the menu. "I'll have two eggs over easy, sausage links, pancakes and a large orange juice."

Grant chimed in with his order, "Eggs scrambled, bacon on the crisp side, toast and some hash browns. I think I'll have orange juice also."

"Very good," said Hilda. "I'll have your food out here in about ten minutes." Before she turned to walk through the curtain she asked, "Haven't seen you around here before. Where are you from?"

Handing both menus back to Hilda, Grant answered, "Townsend, Tennessee."

"We get folks up here from Tennessee once in a while. Do you know a professor Conrad Pearl by any chance?"

Dana Beth smiled and excitedly responded, "Conrad is my father! It's a small world. I can't believe you know him. He used to bring my mother and me up here on vacation, but that was years ago. Now, he comes up here every fall to enjoy some time away from school and to get some serious fishing in."

"You must be Dana Beth. He talks about you all the time. I know your father quite well. He eats breakfast every morning while he's up here. It is a small world. Well, let me get busy with your orders."

The sound of the bell announced the entrance of another customer as a middle-aged man wearing a tan uniform, brimmed hat and black boots opened the screen door and walked to a stool next to the counter. Hilda walked over and poured him a cup of coffee. "Rubin, those folks are from Townsend. They know Conrad. That young lady is his daughter."

Dana Beth spoke up, "And we're up here on our honeymoon. Just got hitched two days ago."

Rubin, with a look of amazement on his face got up and took a chair at the table next to them, then said, "So you guys are from the Great Smoky Mountains. Nice place to live. I love that part of the country what with the mountains and all. You sure traveled a long way to get here, especially when you consider you have mountains and lakes right in your own backyard." Taking a sip of coffee he further explained, "Most of the folks who come up here are fisherman or folks on vacation. They normally stay at one of the lodges on the lake. Not much happening on this side of the lake especially with fall setting in with the cooler weather." Suddenly, he changed the subject and he became somewhat serious. "Too bad about those murders you have going on down there in the Smokies. I saw it on television."

Grant shot Dana Beth a look as if to say, *Good grief. I drove eleven hundred miles and still can't get away from the murders!*

Scooting his stool closer, Rubin remarked, "Course, we've got our own mystery going on up here in the north. I guess the news people don't think it rates much coverage, but I guarantee you, if it happens again this year, they better do something about it."

Grant had no idea what Rubin was talking about and wasn't sure he wanted to ask. There just seemed to be something strange about the man.

Rubin was getting ready to say something when he was interrupted by Hilda who returned with hot plates of food. Standing back she inspected the table. "If you need anything just give me a shout. Enjoy your breakfast." She refilled everyone's coffee then disappeared back behind the curtain.

Rubin scooted closer to the table. "You folks mind if I join you?"

Grant was surprised at the brashness of the man and there was just something about him he couldn't quite put his finger on. Dana Beth answered Rubin. "Of course you can join us. Care for a muffin?"

"No thanks," said Rubin, holding up his hand. "I already ate breakfast." Putting his cup on the edge of the table, he went on, "I'm the Fish and Game Warden on this arm of the lake. If you folks are going to be doing any fishing you'll need to pick up a license." Smiling, he stated, "I'd hate to give you young folks a ticket." He laughed and took a sip of coffee.

Grant stabbed a slice of bacon. "We're planning on getting our license when we finish eating." Reaching across the table, Grant offered his hand. "My name is Grant Denlinger and this is my wife Dana Beth. *That sounded strange,* he thought. *It was the first time he had said that to anyone.*

Rubin smiled at Dana Beth, then commented, "I sure do like your accent. I know your father quite well. You favor him." Grant was getting the strangest feeling Rubin had taken a shining to his new wife for some reason.

Rubin, who had just moments earlier refused a muffin, picked one up out of the basket, split it open and applied a pad of butter. "You know from time to time we have hunting accidents up here. Up until ten years ago we had maybe, one or two in the entire state. Hell, we had more reports of injuries from hunters falling out of their tree stands than we did fatal accidents. The first couple of weeks of hunting season are the worst. We get a lot of so-called hunters up here who have never even held a gun in their hand before. They walk around in the woods using their gun as a pointing stick. And then there are those who shoot at anything that moves. They don't care if it's a cow, a goat or even a person. The worst ones are the ones who get drunk and stumble around in the woods."

Fingering the rim of his cup, Rubin looked out the front window with a look of sadness on his face, then he continued, "Ten years ago, the first week of November three people right here in the Itasca Forest were shot. Two were injured and the third killed. The ballistics report showed all three were shot with the same gun. There was an investigation but eventually it was recorded in the county records as a hunting accident. Then the next two years during the same week in November two more hunters were killed. Ballistics showed the guns were different than the first killing, so two more hunting accidents went in the books.

The authorities around here: the local police, the state police, the park police, all were starting to think that maybe we had a killer on the loose, but then the next year no one was shot during hunting season. The only accident was a hunter who was found at the bottom of a ravine. The coroner said the man died of a heart attack. Since no one was shot that year everyone just sort of forgot the whole thing and the idea of a local killer was put to bed. The next year when hunting season rolled around it was business as usual until the first week of November when two hunters were found shot to death in their tent. Everyone got up in arms again and there was an investigation, but nothing ever came to the surface. The next year a hunter was found who had been mauled by a bear, but the coroner found a bullet hole in his stomach. The local police came up with some cock and bull story about how he must have shot himself while he was fighting off the bear. The last four years just like clockwork a hunter has been shot. It's strange though. None of the ballistics match up."

Taking his final swig of coffee, Rubin gestured with his hand. "I've been down to the Park Headquarters in Park Rapids trying to convince them that all of these killings are related. I think they already know, but without a weapon or a witness they refuse to close the park the first week of November. You just watch. When November rolls around this year it'll happen again. It's the same thing you've got going on down there in the Smokies. You've got a killer who has struck in the spring, summer and fall. Come this winter I bet he'll strike again."

Dana Beth, finished with her breakfast and tired of the one-sided conversation stood. "I'll leave you boys to discuss the murders. I'm going to start gathering up some groceries."

Grant was impressed with Rubin's knowledge and his interest in the murders. Pushing his plate to the side he said, "Rubin, I'm a police officer in Townsend and I think I know what you're going through. I'm worried about the upcoming winter and the fact the killer in the Smokies might kill again. Just like the problem you have up here, I don't know what to do either." Reaching into his wallet Grant pulled out one of his business cards and handed it to Rubin. "Here, take one of my cards. I'd like to know what happens this year up here in November. I'd appreciate it."

Putting the card in his shirt pocket, Rubin stood. "You're the first person I've talked to about this in some time. Most people don't care to talk about the killings. Any more it seems most of the hunters stay out of the forest the first week of November. They do most of their hunting on private land. I wish the rest of them would do the same."

He walked to the door and waved at Dana Beth. "Didn't mean to bend your ear so long. I best be getting back out on the lake. You be careful up here, you hear."

Grant joined Dana Beth and her collection of needed groceries at the counter. Pulling out his wallet he said, "We need to pay for our breakfast, these groceries and we need two fishing licenses"

Hilda reached under the counter and grabbed a ragged green folder and leafed through the pages until she found two license forms. Handing the forms to Dana Beth she explained, "Here, just fill these out and by the way, don't pay too much attention to Rubin. He's a little slow if you know what I mean. He's border-line retarded. He's highly functional...more so than most in his condition. It's like he's just a beat off. He has to really think about what he's doing or saying, except if it's something he knows about. Then it's hard to keep him quiet. Like those killings we've had around here. He knows more about them than anybody else." Taking two twenties out of his wallet Grant handed them to her. She opened the cash register, made change then handed it to him, all the while talking, "Rubin is not really the Fish and Game Warden. It's just an honorary degree the park police gave him because he's been up here everyday for the past twenty-five years patrolling the lake. He's really harmless. Just likes to run his mouth."

Signing the forms Dana Beth filled out Hilda tore off the bottom copies and handed her two small registration tags. "There you go. Now, you can fish legally."

Placing his wallet back into his pocket, Grant asked, "Is Rubin correct about all those murders in the past ten years?"

"Oh yeah. Everything he told you is true. There have been eleven people killed over the past ten years. Every year the first week of November we lose somebody. Now, whether they were murdered...that's never been proven. Like he said, it's a mystery. Myself, I don't pay much attention to what goes on out in the woods. I mind my own business and stay on the lake."

"Thanks for the breakfast. We're staying up here for a week. We'll no doubt drop by again."

"Have a nice honeymoon," said Hilda.

After loading up their groceries, Grant helped Dana Beth back in the boat, then started the journey to the other side of the lake. They were no more than a few minutes out when Dana Beth looked at Grant. "No more talk about murders...okay husband?"

"I promise," said Grant. "No more talk of murders...wife."

Five glorious days and nights in the Itasca State Park gave Grant a sense of relief. The crisp fall air and the unending blue sky seemed to renew his energy. He and Dana Beth spent the semi-warm afternoons on the lake and the chilly evenings wrapped in each other's arms. Between Dana Beth's cooking and her cuddling up close to him every night he thought this was a life he could get used to.

On the last night at the cabin he walked out to the lake and thought about how they would now be returning to the reality of everyday living. Dana Beth would return to her job at the hospital and he would once again be patrolling the streets of Townsend. He was going to have to decide if he even wanted to work for Brody any longer.   To think he was even considered a suspect in the murder of Butch Miller pissed him off to no end.   Maybe he'd contact Sheriff Grimes about the offer he had made him months ago. Maybe not.   He had the strangest feeling the killer was about to strike again.

CHAPTER EIGHTEEN

WHAT IS OUTWARDLY NORMAL to some is completely the opposite to others. Although it had been six weeks since the last murder, Townsend was not experiencing a typical fall. There was a new presence in town that hadn't been there the previous year or any year for as far back as folks could remember.

In a building down the street from the Townsend Police Department the FBI had set up what they called a "temporary office." Two federal agents and a government assigned secretary manned and worked out of the office from eight to five, Monday through Friday. They ate in the local restaurants, and had taken up residence at the Richmond Inn on Winterberry Lane, an upscale Bed and Breakfast on the outskirts of town. They spent each day questioning locals and going to various locations to follow up on an occasional tip. They were a constant reminder that the people of Townsend and the surrounding area were being observed, not only by the agents, but also by a serial killer who could very well be living amongst them.

The one thing the FBI did manage to accomplish, much to the satisfaction of many residents and the disdain of some of the local businesses, was the temporary closing of the Pittman-Henks Murder Tours. Franklin Barrett was irate when an agent approached him at the Mountain View Stables and informed him all tours in regard to the unsolved murders were being temporarily halted.

It was the end of October, the busiest season for Townsend when the changing leaves were at their peak. People from every corner of the country in cars, vans and busloads made the drive over to Townsend to view and enjoy the stunning color of the fall leaves in the surrounding mountains. Franklin Barrett found out rather quickly the power he had always enjoyed and wielded in and around Blount County quickly went by the wayside when he tried to butt heads with the federal government. The agent simply informed him, unless the tours stopped immediately all of his businesses would be shut down, he would be fined and, because of his lack of cooperation, he could serve time in prison since he was interfering with a murder investigation.

Franklin was also informed, despite the fact he owned the Henks' property it was being temporarily impounded by the federal government and they would be sending in a team of crime scene investigators to go over the property until they were satisfied they had discovered all the evidence available.

Merle Pittman was contacted as well about the halt to the tours and the fact that the same status held true for the Asa Pittman farm. It was off-limits until the investigation was concluded. The very afternoon Merle received notice about the Feds invading his life he stormed into Mayor Fleming's office carrying the briefcase full of the documentation he had dazzled Chief Brody with. The mayor listened to Merle go on and on about his rights and how he was a business owner and how the government had no right to interfere, the brief meeting ending with the mayor explaining to Merle that this was the FBI who held the power to do whatever they felt was necessary. It was out of his hands. It was at that point, people began to realize the power the FBI carried. In restaurants, at work, in church and meeting places, local residents were careful about what they said. There was no more joking about how someone should be shot or about someone they hated.

The hardware store advertised low prices on padlocks, deadbolts and security lights and usually sold out right after they received a shipment. Editorials in the local paper by concerned citizens stated that no one should allow a killer to intimidate them and control their lives by means of fear. The articles in the paper only quelled the fear of the locals for a short time. People who had lived in Townsend for a number of years knew better. Daylight was a respite which allowed people to go about their business, but when darkness descended on the community even a cat or a raccoon knocking over a trashcan would invite a call to the police. With three unsolved murders on the books in the past seven months the word was out: the killer was an animal lover. The veterinarian business in and around Townsend was booming. People flocked to get their pets vaccinated or treated for the most minor injury. Folks were extra careful to make sure their window was cracked if they left a pet in the car for any length of time. No one complained about their neighbor's dog. Adoptions were way up at the Humane Society in Maryville. People wanted it known they were concerned over unwanted animals in the area. Money was coming in from all over the county to support and feed homeless animals. In the eyes of most folks Townsend was under the microscope of not only the FBI, but an unknown killer. A shroud of suspicion settled in over the normally peaceful mountain community.

Walking through the door of Lily's Café, Grant saw Doug Eland seated at a corner table. Doug looked just the way he had when he first met him back in April: neatly trimmed goatee, friendly eyes, camouflaged pants tucked into heavy-duty hiking boots, khaki safari shirt, and a small camera hanging from his neck. As Grant approached the table, Doug pushed his empty breakfast dishes to the side as he stood and offered his hand. "Grant, it's good to see you again."

"You too, Doug," said Grant, pulling out a chair.

Sitting back down Doug offered, "Care for some breakfast…maybe some coffee?"

"Just coffee," answered Grant. "Had a big breakfast out at the farm."

Raising his hand Doug signaled for the waitress. "He'd like a cup of coffee, please. I'll just have a refill and my friend here will have…" Hesitating he looked at Grant.

Grant chimed in, "Make mine decaf, sugar, no cream."

Turning his attention back to Grant, Doug folded his hands on the table. "Well, I guess a lot has happened since we met back in April."

Grant nodded and responded, "A lot has happened since we talked on the phone back in June."

Doug was about to say something when the waitress returned with their coffee. He stopped talking until she walked away from their table. Grant noticed his reluctance to speak about the past murders in front of others. "You don't have to tread lightly around here when it comes to the murders. Everyone knows what's going on. They just don't know who's doing it."

"That makes sense," said Doug. "The news about the local murders down here is already common knowledge up in Louisville. I mean it's not the main topic or on everyone's lips but people have heard about what's going on here. Three murders in seven months in Louisville would be considered by many as normal. I know that sounds tacky but after a while people get conditioned to rapes, murders, fires…things they hear or read about on a daily basis. I realize down here in a small town, murders, especially three in a row committed by the same individual are not the norm. I can imagine how upset the locals must be."

"Upset isn't the word for it. It's like a spreading disease. It all started back in April when you were down here. When the word got out about Asa Pittman's brutal murder it was the talk of the town, the talk of the county. By the time June rolled around people had pretty much put his murder on the back burner. It seemed like the wound the town had received from a local murder had almost completely healed. Then, in mid-June we find Mildred Henks up by Laurel Lake stuffed in a dog cage, her fingers and toes cut off. We started to think it was the same killer. The second murder reopened the wound and people around town were beginning to question Chief Brody's ability to be on top of things. Then we had a rash of dognappings in and around the area. Turns out Butch Miller was not only attending dogfights but supplying them with neighborhood dogs for training purposes. Ten weeks went by and folks were starting to calm down some when Butch winds up murdered over in Sevierville. That really set people back on their heels. To think, one of our officers right here in town was murdered."

Stirring his coffee, Doug tasted it then dumped another spoonful of sugar in. "Sounds like doom and gloom to me. Is there any good news to report?"

"As far as the murders are concerned…no. But there is some good news. Like I told you over the phone when we talked last week, I got married a few weeks ago. It's the best thing that ever happened to me. We're living with my mother and grandfather over at the farm."

Doug, drinking his coffee commented, "Never had a desire to get married myself. I've always been too obsessed with my work, I guess. Over the years I've dated once in awhile, but I've never been able to connect with anyone." Taking another sip of coffee, he corrected himself, "Well, until just recently anyway. I met a woman up in Louisville. She's a career woman…a lawyer. She loves my work and doesn't mind me traveling all of the time. She's involved in corporate law so she's on the road more than I am. We don't see each other much but it seems to work out just fine."

Grant smiled. "There is nothing quite like being married. I

mean, I'm no expert. Hell, I've only been married for six weeks, but I've got to say, being married has changed the way I look at things now. I'm not so stressed at work. I've got more to live for than just myself."

Doug changed the subject. "You said you were free all day, right?"

"Well, I'm supposed to be home tonight for supper at five." Looking at his watch, Grant confirmed, "That gives us nine hours."

Doug stood and finished his coffee. "Let's roll. Like I told you over the phone, I've got someone I would like you to meet." Throwing a five-dollar bill on the table, he explained, "We're going to drive over to Cherokee. There is a friend of mine over there who I think just might be able to help you with these murders."

Out in the parking lot, Doug motioned toward his car. "I'll drive."

Pulling out of the lot, Doug flipped down the sun visor, "So tell me about this girl you married?"

For the next forty minutes Grant told Doug how he had met Dana Beth in high school, they dated for two years then, they became engaged, and after two more years had a falling out. She, believe it or not, had started seeing Butch Miller. He and Butch had a couple of scuffs regarding her. She eventually broke up with Miller. The following week Butch was found murdered. Grant himself, because he had threatened Miller winds up being a suspect and is ordered to take a two week vacation. He goes to dinner with Dana Beth and asked her to marry him, she accepts and three days later they are married.

At Newfound Gap on Rt. 441 Doug laughed, "Sounds like a soap opera!"

Grant, looking out the side window at a group of tourists asked, "So who is it you are taking me to see?"

Doug guiding his car around a sharp curve explained, "He's an old college buddy of mine. He's a full blooded Cherokee Indian, has a degree in Criminology and Psychology *and* is the chief of police over in Cherokee, North Carolina. His birth name is Billy Blue Smoke or as the Cherokee pronounce it Sha-co-na-te. He was the first Indian from his family to attend college. He changed his name to William Blue in order to get along in the white man's world. William is one of the sharpest, most perceptive people I have ever met. Between his innate foresight as a Cherokee Indian and his background in criminology he's quite the profiler. I've been coming over here to Cherokee every fall for the last ten years to do some wildlife shoots. Over the years William and I have remained the best of friends. We call each other just about every week. He has been keeping me up to date with the murders down here. Just last week he told me he wanted to meet you and get the inside scoop on what's going on. He said he might be able to give you a hand in the investigation, but he would have to meet you first."

Grant turned sideways in the seat with a confused look on his face. "You said something I don't quite understand. You said he was the chief of police and he had degrees in criminology and psychology and he was a profiler. I understand all that. What I don't understand is what you said about his innate foresight as an Indian. What does that mean? Is he some sort of a medicine man or what?"

Doug laughed, negotiating another sharp turn. "Look, I can't explain the way he goes about things. All I can tell you is he is very good at what he does." Nodding at the road ahead he gestured, "We'll be there in less than ten minutes then you can ask him."

The last few miles of Route 441 was level with wide sweeping curves and long straight stretches, both sides of the road surrounded with gently rising hills covered with pine trees. Breaking out of the forest they found themselves once again surrounded by signs of civilization, signs advertising Cherokee, North Carolina's restaurants, hotels, businesses and places of interest. It reminded Grant of a smaller version of Gatlinburg and Pigeon Forge. Entering the town limits the place looked the same as when he had last been there, which was five years ago. Stopping at a red light on the Trail Road which was actually called Main Street, Grant scanned both sides of the street, one shop crammed in next to the other advertising Indian knives, moccasins, jewelry, quilts, baskets, pottery and of course T-shirts.

On the opposite side of town they turned onto Wilber Sequoyah Road, drove a short distance and turned into the Cherokee Police Station. If Grant remembered correctly the town of Cherokee was an actual Indian Reservation. The biggest percentage of the local residents was Cherokee. But, nonetheless, it was still a tourist trap. The Indians had learned well from the white man. They had taken their way of life and turned it into a way to generate a ton of money, nearly four million people a year visited the small community.

The police station reminded Grant of the station they had in Townsend. One story, small parking lot, two police vehicles parked in the front. Entering the station, Doug approached a young woman seated behind a neatly kept counter. "May I help you, gentlemen?" she politely asked.

"Yes you may," answered Doug. "My name is Doug Eland and this is Grant Denlinger. We're here to see Chief Blue." Looking at a circular clock on the wall, Doug pointed out, "We actually have an appointment at ten o'clock. Looks like we're about ten minutes early."

Excusing herself, the woman said, "I think he's in his office. Just let me check. I'll be right back."

It wasn't even fifteen seconds when she returned and opened a half counter door. "Second door on the left. He's expecting you."

Doug led the way into the room which, in Grant's opinion, was much neater than Brody's disorganized mess of an office. The walls were tastefully decorated with photographs of various waterfalls and framed commendations. A potted fig tree sat next to a row of file cabinets. A desk centered toward the back of the room was spotless, the only thing on its top was a phone which sat on the left hand corner. Behind the desk sat William Blue, the Cherokee Chief of Police. William stood and walked around the desk before Doug was even halfway across the room. "Doug! Welcome to Cherokee." Shaking hands he looked past Doug and noticed Grant. "And this young man must be Grant Denlinger?"

William gave Grant a firm handshake and he introduced himself, "William Blue, Police Chief in these parts." William Blue was definitely a full blooded Cherokee: reddish-brown complexion, chiseled face, keen eyes, six-foot in height. His long dark hair was fashioned in a ponytail secured by a braided, leather one-inch band. His stocky body was framed in a light brown suit over top of a collarless light blue shirt complete with a Native American turquoise bolo tie. The most amazing part of his dress attire was a pair of what appeared to be authentic Indian moccasins.

Offering his two guests seats he asked, "Would you care for some coffee?"

Doug, who was seating himself declined, "No thanks, I'm coffee'd out for the day."

"Me, too," said Grant.

Seated once again, Chief Blue looked directly at Grant. "We've met before. You probably don't remember. That was nearly eleven years ago. I was fresh out of college. Had just joined the force here in Cherokee. I attended a seminar over in Gatlinburg for new officers. Your grandfather, Dalton, was one of the speakers. He talked about patience. I was quite impressed. I learned quite a bit from him. You just happened to be with him." Shaking his head in approval he stated, "For a white man your grandfather has some deep wisdom. That day I shook your hand and you told me some day you were planning on being a policeman just like your grandfather. Looks like you're well on your way."

Grant, humbled, answered, "I've got a long way to travel before I measure up to Dalton."

Gesturing toward Doug, William continued speaking to Grant, "Doug here tells me you're up to your backside in alligators over there in Townsend with these murders."

"To say the least. Since the first victim back in April, which, by the way, I'm sure you already know about, Doug discovered, we've experienced two more murders: the second in Townsend and the third over in Sevierville. We really don't have much to go on. We know, or at least think, it's the same person doing the killings. There are always signs of duct tape being used, all three of the victims have had their fingers or toes cut off, and all three have been left where animals could get to them. We think the killer may smoke a pipe. We found the same kind of tobacco at two different crime scenes. They've brought the FBI in but at least for now they seem to be stonewalled. Everyone, especially Chief Brody, thinks I'm nuts when I start talking about how I feel the killer will strike again...probably soon."

Pointing at Doug, William spoke, "Doug and I have kept in contact about these murders. The reason he brought you over here to see me is because I think I might be able to assist you in the investigation. I've got an extensive background in criminology and psychology."

Grant scooted forward on his chair. "Doug was telling me on the way over here about your qualifications. He said something I don't quite understand." Looking at Doug for verification he went on, "I believe he put it like this, you possess some sort of innate Cherokee foresight. For the life of me I can't even begin to imagine what that means."

Getting up, William walked around to the front of the desk and leaned against it, then began his explanation. "Innate foresight goes beyond what a normal criminal profiler would be capable of. But, before I explain how it works I think it's important you understand how a profiler works. Criminal profiling is a method of utilizing psychological and criminal principles to create profiles of offenders. We then can use these profiles to locate the person responsible for the crime. Criminal profiling has been around for nearly a hundred years, but it really was not all that effective until around the '60s and the '70s when the FBI developed a step by step process to use profiling to apprehend criminals."

Folding his hands at his waist William continued, "First of all we need to examine all of the evidence from the crime scene, including photographs, sketches, witness testimonies, autopsy results and anything else relevant. After all of the pertinent information is gathered, then we begin to ask questions: Was the crime premeditated? What was the killer's motivation? How was the victim, or in this case, victims killed? Was there any damage inflicted to the body after death?

"After we come up with the questions we want answered, we then begin answering the questions based on the evidence found. The answers we come up with will allow us to put together a criminal profile based on how, when and where the crime was committed. Most of the time criminals are grouped into two very distinct categories: organized and disorganized based upon the way the crime was committed. An organized criminal always plans ahead, brings his own, for lack of a better phrase, supplies and sticks to his or her plan. A disorganized criminal who acts without a plan more than likely lives somewhat of a chaotic life."

Walking to a water dispenser, William drew a paper cupful, drank it, then turned back to finish his definition of criminal profiling. "I could go on talking about this for hours, but what it boils down to are five steps: Starting to create a profile; examining the crime's elements; reconstructing the crime; establishing a profile and then using the information. By following this process of criminal profiling many serial killers have been stopped. Some of the more well known ones are the Son of Sam, the Green River Killer and Ted Bundy."

Throwing the now empty paper cup into a trashcan, William smiled at his small audience. "Now that I have bored you to death with the history of criminal profiling I'll answer the question of the innate foresight of the Cherokee Indian. The Cherokee Indian has a more definite sense of the surroundings at a crime scene than, let's say the typical white man." Using Doug and Grant as examples William emphasized, "You white men, look at things, but the Cherokee *sees things!* The white men touches things, but the Cherokee *feels things!* The white man hears things, but the Cherokee *listens!* In short, the Cherokee is more in tune with mother nature: the weather, the trees, the grass, the animals and so on. This innate foresight added to the more modern philosophy of criminal profiling makes for a powerful combination."

Finished, William looked at both Doug and Grant who just looked at each other in total amazement. "All right, I realize that was a lot for you to absorb," said William. "Here's what we're going to do. I've already taken the liberty to contact the Feds over in Townsend earlier this morning. I've worked with Agent Gephart a few times before. I asked him if he could use my help and he said at this point they would welcome any help they could get. We'll meet bright and early at seven o'clock at the Hearth and Kettle in Townsend for breakfast with Gephart where we'll set up a plan for the day. We'll have a four-man team: Gephart, myself, and both of you. Doug will be filming anything of interest and you, Grant, will be helping to bag up anything we find and taking notes. Any questions?"

Grant spoke up immediately, "This all sounds good, but I've got a problem. Chief Brody. I doubt very seriously if he's just gonna let me skip off for a day with the Feds."

"That's already been handled. Gephart said he was quite familiar with Brody and he would give him a call informing him that tomorrow you will be working directly with the FBI. End of story!" Clapping his hands together, William said, "How about if I treat you white fellas to an authentic Cherokee lunch?"

CHAPTER NINETEEN

GRANT WALKED INTO The Hearth and Kettle at 6:55 the next morning only to find he was the last to arrive. William and Doug were there along with Ralph Gephart, one of the two agents assigned to the Townsend area. They were already seated around a circular table. Doug stood and signaled to Grant, pointing toward the buffet table. "Grab a plate and fill 'er up. I'm buyin'."

Not one to turn down food, Grant followed orders and walked down the long steam table piling bacon, scrambled eggs, biscuits and gravy, and toast on his plate. Grabbing a set of silverware and a cup of coffee he joined the group. "Mornin', gents."

Gephart was the first to respond, standing and shaking Grant's hand. "Glad to have you on the team."

Pointing at Grant's plate, William suggested, "Better lay in a good base. This might be the only meal you get today at least until later tonight. It's going to be a long day."

Pulling out a chair, Grant sat, took a drink of coffee then spoke to Gephart, "I assume you cleared all this with Brody?"

Biting into a slice of toast, Gephart answered, "If you're referring to my request that your presence has been requested on the team…yes."

Grant was surprised. "He didn't give you any crap?"

"I didn't say that. He gave me plenty of crap and it wasn't just about you. He said he didn't need some damn out of state, wanna be Cherokee Indian combination chief of police and medicine man runnin' around over here on his turf. He also said he couldn't see what you could possibly contribute to any further investigation. I got tired of listening to him so I simply told him that's the way it was going to go." Everyone laughed.

Changing gears, Gephart asked William, "So, what's the game plan for the day?"

William pushed his plate to the side, placed his hands on his stomach and let out a deep breath. "Mighty good eatin'. I thought what we would do is go to each crime scene location in the order they happened. Grant, you've been to most of them so what order should we use?"

Grant, surprised William was asking for his opinion answered quickly, "Well, let's see, I think we should go up to Pittman's farm first since we believe that is where he was kidnapped, then we can go on up to Thunderhead Trail where he was murdered. I guess after that we need to head on over to the Henks' place where it is thought Mildred Henks was abducted, then over to Laurel Lake where we discovered her body. While we're up at the lake the next stop will be on the other side where we found Butch's abandoned truck and boat. If we make it that far and still have enough light we'll finish up over in Sevierville at J.J.'s Junkyard. That should just about do it."

Doug, stuffing the last bite of sausage in his mouth commented, "That's a lot of territory to cover in just one day. I mean, even if we spend an hour at each location that's six hours and when you consider driving time from one to another we probably won't get any farther than Laurel Lake. We could be looking at two days to completely examine all six locations."

Gephart took a swig of coffee and corrected Doug. "That's if we were driving, which we are not. We're flying!"

Doug gave Gephart a strange look. "Flying…you said flying?"

"That's right." Looking at his watch Gephart suggested, "You better eat up fellas. Just so happens there is a helicopter coming in from Knoxville this morning. Scheduled to arrive over at the park at eight o'clock sharp. That's in thirty minutes."

Grant, not all that enthused about flying, especially in a helicopter asked, "How big is this copter?"

Gephart finished up his coffee. "Four seater."

Pushing himself back from the table, Doug asked, "How's that going to work? There's four of us on the team. When you consider the pilot that makes five. It's going to be a little bit crowded."

The pilot flying the copter down is an agent. After he lands he'll be driving my car back to the Townsend office to fill in for me."

"But then we don't have anyone to fly the copter," said Grant.

Gephart stood. "Yeah we do…me! I flew them when I was in the Air Force. Now, we better get moving if we want to be at the park on time."

Twenty minutes later the group stood near a gazebo at the park when they first heard the whomp, whomp, whomp of the blades and then eventually spotted the copter. It flew over the park, circled around, and hovered for a few seconds then landed a few yards away. Following the group toward the copter Grant was starting to feel queasy. He'd never flown in a helicopter before. He was starting to get the same uneasy feeling he always got in the pit of his stomach when he reluctantly climbed onto the Ferris wheel or the roller coaster at the county fair.

The pilot climbed out, shook Gephart's hand, took the car keys from him and drove off. Ralph signaled for everyone to get in. Grant took a seat in the back wishing now he wouldn't have had such a large breakfast. Doug sat next to him, William next to Gephart, who after checking to see that everyone was buckled in, pulled back the stick, the copter rising straight up then banking sharply to the right out over the park and the Little River. Grant sat back in the seat and closed his eyes thinking if he could not see how high up they were he'd be all right.

Gephart interrupted Grant's concentration on not getting sick as he turned and shouted over the noise of the spinning blades, "Grant, which way to the Pittman farm?"

Grant opened his eyes and looked out the side of the glass-encased cockpit, watching trees and buildings race by below. Taking a deep breath he answered, "Follow the parkway until you see the entrance to the National Park. Turn right and follow the Laurel Creek Road until we are over Cades Cove. Then go right again. The farm is located next to a large field separated by a grove of trees. If you see Laurel Lake then you've gone too far."

Just then the copter banked to the right, Gephart commenting, "We are now following Laurel Creek Road."

Grant closed his eyes and sank back in the seat trying his best to control his stomach. It wasn't even five minutes when Gephart shouted, "That must be the field. I'm taking her down."

The next thing Grant felt was the slight thud when the copter touched down on the field. Stepping out of the copter, William took a deep knee bend and glanced around the large weed covered field. "Which way to the farm?"

Grant, who was glad he was standing on solid ground again answered, "North, which ever way that is. I'm all twisted around."

William looked at the sun, then pointed over his shoulder. "This way. Spread out. Whoever finds the farm first give a shout."

Crossing the field and stepping over some barbed wire Grant entered the forest. The wind had picked up blowing the colorful fall leaves in every direction. Five minutes into the woods Grant turned and looked back toward the field now completely shielded from view by the thick trees and vegetation. Finally he came to a dirt road where the old rusted cattle gate was located. He knew the farm was just up ahead. Starting up the road he heard Doug shout, "Over here…I found the farm." By the time Grant walked the rest of the way up the road everyone had congregated in front of the old cabin.

William motioned everyone to the front porch as Gephart asked, "What's the plan, Mr. Blue?"

"When we get inside I must have complete silence, unless I speak or ask someone a question," said William. "Doug, you need to take any photographs of anything I point out and Grant needs to take exact notes. Mr. Gephart, you're here mainly to observe and oversee. Let's go inside gentlemen."

Gephart unlocked the front door and switched on a hallway light, which didn't do much to illuminate the interior. William pulled out a flashlight and turned it on. Making his way down the hall, the group followed. Grant, who was bringing up the rear thought the place looked like it had when he had been here months earlier: spooky. The only difference seemed to be that Merle and Barrett had roped off all of the rooms so the tourists could walk down the hall, but not enter the actual rooms.

Entering the living room, William carefully stepped over the rope and told everyone to stay back. Looking over the room slowly he moved the light from right to left, then sat in one of the chairs, placing his hands on the armrest and taking in a long deep breath. After a few seconds he stood and smelled the back of the chair. Pointing at various items in the room he snapped his fingers indicating that Doug take photos. Next he went into the bedroom, lay on the bed and smelled the bed coverings and pillows. After he left the room he told Doug to take pictures of the bed, the magazines and the closet, which was a shambles. Next came the bathroom where he sat on the commode and opened the medicine cabinet, which he had Doug take a photo of. They finished up in the kitchen, William asking Grant where he found the tobacco. Sitting at the kitchen table where Grant found the substance, William looked around the room while running his hand across the top of the table. The last thing he had Doug take a photo of was the kitchen cabinets.

Outside they walked to the barn, which was also roped off. William and Doug entered the barn, while Grant and Gephart remained out in the yard. Photos were taken of the still, the traps, the loft and the barrels of animal bones and skins. William spent more time in the barn than he did in the cabin, touching and smelling various items. The last thing he did was to walk the perimeter of the property. Thirty minutes later he returned and told everyone to gather on the porch.

Sitting on the front steps, William pointed at Grant. "Time for you to start taking notes. I'm going to go pretty fast. If you miss something I say, don't worry. We'll go over everything at the end of the day." Standing, he started across the front yard. "Come on, I'll fill all of you in on what we discovered on the way back to the copter." Turning one last time before entering the tree line, he looked back at the farm then started through the woods. "We found out quite a bit about our first victim, Asa Pittman, and one possible very important clue about our killer. Despite the fact there have been hundreds of tourists in the house, they have been kept mainly in the hallway, which means the rest of the house is full of clues. Asa Pittman lived alone in his home. He was not what one would call a very clean man. The furniture and his clothing reek of body odor. He was a man who was celibate. There are no traces of any sexual activity in the house for many years. He was a man who loved guns, and had no respect for animals. While walking the perimeter of his property I discovered no traces of animals on or near his farm. They can sense death…and danger. From the condition of Asa's house it's easy to see he was a very disorganized and untidy person." Entering the field William finished up his prognosis. "Now, about our killer. Grant, you said you found traces of pipe tobacco on the kitchen table. First of all Asa did not smoke. There were no traces of anyone smoking for a prolonged period of time in the house. It could very well be the killer sat at the kitchen table and smoked a pipe and while sitting there noticed Mr. Pittman's disorganized cabinets." Pointing at Doug he went on, "When you get those pictures developed note the one taken of the bottles and containers of spices. You'll notice when looking at the photo that the spices are lined up alphabetically. This is out of context with the way Mr. Pittman kept his house. Our killer is very organized and might be obsessed with neatness. So, while sitting in the kitchen smoking his pipe he may have decided to arrange the spices in order."

Stepping up into the copter, William asked, "How far is our next stop?"

Grant, dreading yet another copter ride answered, "That would be Thunderhead Trail. We'll be landing at Spence Field which is just a couple of hundred yards from where Asa Pittman was murdered."

Fortunately for Grant's stomach it wasn't even five minutes until they were landing on the open area of Spence Field. Getting out of the copter, Grant bumped Doug on his arm. "Bring back any memories?"

Doug checked his camera then responded, "This place gives me the creeps. I'll never forget what the body looked like."

William bowed, then gestured to Doug. "Lead the way, my friend."

Minutes later they entered the area just off the trail. Walking to the spot where Asa's body had been found, Doug turned in a circle, displaying the surrounding forest. "This is the place."

William joined Doug and told him to return to where the rest of the group was standing. He then told the group to stand out by the trail because he was going to need maybe a half hour or even more to get the feel of the immediate area. Silently Ralph, Doug and Grant watched William start his process. First he walked to the tree where Asa had been bound, circled the tree then bent down and ran his hand over the grass and weeds growing near the base of the tree. Next he closely examined the base of the tree then stood up and went to the back rubbing his hand lightly over the bark, hesitating in three different areas. For the next ten minutes he walked around the surrounding area looking up at branches and moving clumps of weeds with his foot. Then he moved out farther from the crime scene and circled the area. Another ten minutes passed when he signaled the group to come over to the tree.

Bending down he pointed with a two foot section of branch at the ground near the base of the tree. Looking up at the group who had surrounded him he addressed Grant, "Now if I remember correctly, yesterday over in Cherokee when we went out for lunch you said there were a couple of things about this crime scene, I think you referred to them as loose ends that had to be tied up. One of the things you mentioned was that it was thought Mr. Pittman had been tied or secured to the tree. I believe you said it was also thought he had been duct taped to the tree. You then said it was still undetermined if he died from bleeding out or at the hands of the local wildlife." Standing up he motioned to the group with the branch. "If you'll please step back a bit I can explain or demonstrate to you what transpired."

Laying the branch on the ground he stood with his back to the tree and explained, "This is the position Mr. Pittman was secured in. His hands were duct taped in a fashion that allowed the killer to freely cut the fingers off, hence the blood dripped down onto the ground near the base of the tree." Pointing at the ground nearest his feet he wiggled his fingers to get their attention. "The ground indicates the largest blood loss was at the base of the tree. Even though there are traces of blood further out, there is evidence he bled out while still on the tree."

He stepped away from the tree, bending down and ran his hand over the tall weeds. "See how the weeds and the grass in this section are more healthy looking. That is because of all the blood absorbed into the ground at the victim's feet. The iron and the nutrients in the blood caused the vegetation to be more fertilized." Pointing at the bottom of the tree trunk, he went on, "See those two marks on the bottom of the tree. These were not caused by any animal or by anything Mother Nature would have caused. What we are looking at are heel marks from the back of boots or some sort of shoes. See how the marks have been dug into the bark from movement. They were caused from the victim struggling to get loose or from the pain inflicted upon him."

Standing, William said, "One more thing that verifies Pittman was secured to this tree." Walking around to the backside of the tree he ran his hands over the bark, then lined himself up with the tree and explained, "There are three areas where a thin layer of bark has been peeled away from the tree. These marred sections are approximately two inches wide and are at three different levels." Demonstrating with his hand he pointed at his chest, then just above his knees and finally at his ankles." This is proof he was secured to the tree with some sort of tape...not rope. Duct tape would be my guess. Masking or packing tape wouldn't have been strong enough."

Grant walked next to the tree and looked at the bark. "I can't see where the bark has been, as you say...marred."

"You can't see it. You can only feel it."

"Where?" asked Grant.

Pointing at a section on the tree, William stated, "Right there."

Grant ran his hand across the bark twice and then commented, "I can't feel any difference."

William laughed, "Remember what I said when you were over in Cherokee? The white man touches but the Indian feels!"

Not waiting for a response William stepped around to the front of the tree, picked up the small section of branch he had before and looked up at the branches just above their heads. Reaching up he pulled down a branch and pointed to the end where it had been cut. "This branch was not destroyed due to Mother Nature. As you can see…it was clearly cut." Pulling it down so they could see the end, he tapped the end of the branch with the section he held in his hand. If this section of branch would have been a result of anything nature would be capable of doling out the break would be more jagged, not smooth like it appears. Notice the cut has no saw marks so that means the branch was taken off with some other sort of man made tool. A garden tool, I would say. Maybe a set of lopping shears or maybe a tree pruner." Turning the section of branch he was holding around so it matched up he said, "And this is the section that was cut off." Using the branch as a pointer he explained, "I found this over there in the weeds where it had been tossed after it was used…*and* it was used." Displaying the branch he stated, "There are traces of blood on the end and the side of the branch and I also might add a few stray human hairs. This was probably used to beat Mr. Pittman over the head although I doubt if this was the main cause of death. If you will match up Pittman's DNA with the blood and hairs on this branch, you'll get a match." Handing the stick to Grant, he ordered, "You need to bag this up."

Walking out to the trail, he announced, "And one final thing I noticed." Pulling down another low hanging branch he broke off a smaller branch. "There are traces of human hair on this branch where possibly someone may have bumped their head. If you'll run the DNA on this hair you might have a sample of the killer's hair or then again it just might be someone who was out here hiking around or on one of the tours." Handing the small branch to Grant, he gave more orders, "Grant, you need to take some notes. Doug I need you to take a few photos."

Ten minutes later they were once again airborne, this time on a longer flight over to Mildred Henks' place. As they flew over the Little River, William turned in his seat and addressed the group, "So far I haven't been able to establish the killer's motive. Normally, a person who kills multiple people is classified under one of three categories: mass murderer, spree killer or serial killer. Once we determine if the murders were sexually motivated or based on financial or emotional reasons, we'll know more as the investigation continues. At this point it's hard to say if the killer knew Mr. Pittman or not. A lot of facial injuries usually indicate that the killer knew his victim. But from what Grant has told me Pittman's face was practically eaten away so whether the killer knew Pittman or not still remains a mystery."

Suddenly the copter took a sharp downward movement to the left. "There's the Henks' place," said Gephart. "I'll just set the copter down in the backyard."

Grant was the last one to climb out of the copter. Stepping down onto the well-mowed grass his stomach felt better than on the first two short flights. Gephart removed the keys to the house from his pocket. "We'll go in the house first. From what we have so far it looks like that is where Henks was grabbed."

Walking around the side of the house and up the driveway, William stopped, noticing something on the driveway, but then quickly followed the others. Once inside the house he placed his hands on his hips, scanning the large living room. "Well, I must say Mildred Henks kept a better looking house than Asa Pittman." Ducking beneath the rope he walked over to the fireplace, stopped, turned and looked at the dog food that had been placed on the floor for the benefit of the tourists. "Grant, you and Sheriff Grimes were the first to arrive at the house after Henks was discovered up at Laurel Lake. Is that correct?"

"Yes...that's correct," answered Grant. "We drove up here right after she was loaded up by the coroner."

"The way everything is set up for the tour, is that just about the way it was when you first got here?"

Grant walked to the edge of the rope, glancing around the room. "Well, let's see. The dog food was spread across the carpet just like it appears now except it seems to be neater than when I was here before. It looks like it was carefully placed there. Before it was thrown across the carpet haphazardly. And that dog food bag was leaning up against the fireplace. If I remember correctly, it was cut down the back, not evenly across the top. We still have the original bag. It was bagged as evidence."

"What about the water bowls?"

"Those bowls look like the same ones." Pointing at the open door of the china cabinet, Grant explained, "When we got here there were bowls just like those on the floor filled with drinking water for the dogs. We found a number of broken plates that matched the bowls in the trashcan in the kitchen. Along the edge of the carpet we found a few small fragments of broken china. We assumed at some point some china was broken. Now, whether it was broken while the killer was here we can't say for sure. The remaining fragments along the edge of the carpet signify at some point someone swept or cleaned up the broken china. That could have happened before the killer got here."

Nodding his head in an affirmative manner William walked around the living room, stooping down, smelling stains on the carpet, then walking into both bedrooms and the downstairs bath, and eventually into the kitchen. He had Doug snap off shots of the stains, the china cabinet, the dog food and the tubs in the middle of the floor. He only spent a short time upstairs, saying nothing happened in that part of the house as far as the abduction was concerned.

Outside they walked the perimeter of the property and finally entered the barn, William having Doug take a number of photos. Back on the porch William talked with Grant extensively about the marks on the floor and the porch. He told William the marks on the floor were the same measurement as the cage they found Mildred in. Grant also told William the marks were evident in the gravel that led around the side of the house stopping in the middle of the driveway. They already had photos of the marks but the actual marks could no longer be seen due to the heavy tourist traffic over the past months.

William put his arm around Gephart as he walked him to the corner of the porch. "We're going to have to take some carpet samples. I hope this isn't a problem?"

"Not for me," answered Ralph. "Might be a problem for Barrett Franklin, the owner, but if you think it's necessary, then go ahead. We can always reimburse him for the carpet."

Turning to Grant, William ordered, "Follow me and bring along five or six evidence bags. The rest of you wait here."

Inside, William walked to the fireplace where he removed a

heavy-duty pocketknife from his pocket and pointed it at a stain on the floor. "There appears to be four different varieties of stains on the floor." Reaching down he sliced the carpet then proceeded to remove a three-inch by three inch section which he handed to Grant to be bagged. He then went about the process of repeating the cutting, taking three more sections of carpet, two from where the dog food was located and one by the couch. "Mark the bags, one, two, three and four," said William as he took one final look around the living room, then motioned toward the back door. "There's one more thing I'd like to take a look at outside. Come on."

William stopped at the bottom of the porch and pointed at the marks where the cage had been dragged down over the steps. "At some point after she was more than likely stuffed inside the cage she was dragged across the floor, then across the porch and down these steps." Inspecting the driveway William began to walk around the side of the house all the while looking down at the gravel. "You told me earlier pictures were taken of drag marks leading around to the side of the house. About where did the marks stop?"

Grant, following William could only estimate as he stopped next to the large stone chimney attached to the house. "I guess about right here."

Bending down William drew a circle in the gravel with his index finger surrounding a gray, faded stain. Next, he lay in a prone position and smelled the spot. "Just like I thought. I noticed this spot when we first arrived and blew it off as insignificant but when you consider the marks stopped somewhere in this area this spot might be a clue. It has an aroma that resembles motor oil…I'd say probably 10W30, or 40. Someone, in the past parked a vehicle here that had an oil leak." Getting up, he asked, "Do we know where Mildred Henks normally parked her vehicle?"

Grant shrugged. "When we got here her Thunderbird was parked out front."

"And where did you and Grimes park?"

"Out by the fountain."

Walking to the front of the house, William yelled to Doug and Gephart who were standing by the copter that they would be along soon then directed his next remark to Grant, "Show me where her car was parked."

Stopping at a three-car wide paved area, Grant pointed at the space nearest the house. "Right there."

"Notice any oil leak marks on the pavement?" asked William.

"No…looks clean."

"That's right," said William. "Mildred's car didn't have an oil leak, but someone's vehicle did *and* they parked it on the side of the house. This is really a long shot. The oil leak could have come from one of the tour buses or maybe from a vehicle Barrett Franklin drove in here or just maybe it was a leak that came from the vehicle Henks was loaded into. I say that, because if the drag marks stopped somewhere in the vicinity of the chimney, which is were the oil spot is, then maybe, just maybe the oil spot is from the killer's vehicle."

Doug was at their side, asking, "You guys find something else, cause if you haven't we better get moving. We've been here for almost two hours."

Walking back around the side of the house, William ordered, "Doug, I need you to get a shot of that oil stain. Grant you need to bag up the stained gravel, then we're out of here."

Minutes later they were in the air again headed for Laurel Lake. Gephart, curious, asked, "What's with the carpet samples?"

"Glad you asked," said William. "We took four carpet samples that are stained. Despite the fact the carpet has been vacuumed and the stains were altered by some sort of spot remover, by taking samples we can therefore smell the back of the carpet and make a determination what caused the stain. On the underside the odor will still be prevalent." Turning in the seat, facing Grant he inquired, "Hand me those four bags with the carpet samples."

Placing the bags on his lap he held up the first bag. "Bag marked #1. When I smelled the underside of this section of carpet it reminded me of feces, probably dog feces." Holding up the second bag, he went on, "The second sample smells like urine, probably from one of the dogs. The third sample gives off an odor resembling vomit. Now whether it was from one of the dogs or from a human might be hard to figure out. But the fourth bag is very interesting. This sample carries an odor that does not fall in line with the other samples. It has a strong medicine smell to it, not to mention it was located next to the couch. This may have been where Mildred was actually drugged. What we have in our hands here might just be a sample of chloroform."

Gephart interrupted William when the copter came to a halt. Pointing downward he announced, "We're right over the middle of Laurel Lake. Where do we want to land?"

Grant leaned up between the seats as he suggested, "If you'll circle the lake you'll see the edge of the Laurel Hills Golf Course. They have an overflow parking lot that's seldom used. It's out past the regular parking lot next to the clubhouse. You should have plenty of room to set down there."

Within minutes, Gephart located the parking lot and went about the process of landing the copter in the far corner of the lot. They no sooner touched down and had stepped out of the copter when Bob, the manager of the club, riding in a golf cart, approached them. Another cart trailed him across the lot. "Afternoon, been expecting you. When Ralph called us and told us this morning you'd be dropping by we let all the golfers know the ninth green might be shut down for awhile." Gesturing toward the carts, Bob offered, "No sense in walking all the way. Hop in."

When they arrived at the ninth green Bob asked about how long they would be. William estimated about an hour and apologized for holding up play on the course. Bob said it wasn't a problem and the golfers could wait or play through.

For the next fifteen minutes, William walked around the green asking Grant questions and having Doug snap off a few photos. Finished up on the green, Grant led the group back into the trees where they had found Mildred's body. Following another ten minutes William said there wasn't much left in the area as far as clues were concerned. The grass, once again, where the body bled out was higher than the rest of the surrounding vegetation, just like up on Thunderhead Trail. Grant leading the group up the path toward the parking area explained they found where the cage had been dragged on the path from the lot. When they arrived at the cracked and uneven pavement, William immediately displayed interest as he bent down, looking closely at what appeared to be an oil stain. "Remember what I said about the oil stain back at the Henks' place being a long shot? Well, the fact that there is one here *and* the fact it appears to be an old stain means it could be from the same vehicle. It's still a shot in the dark. This stain could be from anyone's car, but then again it might be from the killer's vehicle. Doug, snap a shot of the stain." Looking out across the lake, William asked, "Where did they find Miller's boat and truck?"

Grant walked to the edge of the water and pointed north. "On the other side."

"Can we get there by walking around the lake?"

"Sure, but it's gonna take about an hour to get there. We'd be better off going back to the copter and flying over. It'll only take us a few minutes. We can land on the shoreline. There's plenty of room."

Three and a half hours later the four men wound up exactly where they had started the day, The Hearth and Kettle. Seated at the same table they sat at earlier at breakfast, the waitress took their drink orders and said she would be right back. Gephart announced he was buying. Dinner was on the Federal Government. After everyone ordered and their meals were set in front of them, Ralph stood and proposed a toast. "I just want to thank all of you for your efforts today. I think it was a good day and I feel we have made some headway."

Cutting into his steak, William agreed, "Indeed we have." Stuffing a large bite into his mouth he explained, "After Doug gets all the photos he took today developed and Grant gets all of his notes organized our next step is to combine what we discovered today with the evidence previously collected so we can begin to create a profile on our killer." Taking a long drink of ice water he continued, "However, based upon just what we discovered today we already have the makings of a profile. The most important thing we ran across today was the oil leaks. When I first saw the leak out at the Henks' place you'll recall I said it was a long shot. But then when we found a leak out at the parking lot just down from where Mildred Henks was murdered, the leak back at her home becomes a little more important...but, still a long shot. To find oil leaks like we did on the other side of the lake where Butch might have been abducted and then just outside the fence at the junkyard over in Sevierville is too coincidental. I think it's safe to say our killer just might be driving a vehicle with an oil leak."

Doug spoke up, "But those leaks could be from anybody's vehicle...probably more than likely from a number of different vehicles. How can we be sure they are all from the same vehicle?"

"We can't be sure," said William. "But that's the process. We collect anything and everything that looks suspicious. Just like the spices that were all lined up alphabetically at Pittman's place. It might not mean anything but then again it might be important. It's not just the collecting of the evidence...but the using of it to create a profile." Sitting up straight and using his hands he gestured, "It's like this, you take all of the evidence significant or not and place it in a large hopper, then shake it up and out of the bottom something always comes out giving us a profile of the killer."

Grant jumped in on the conversation. "I thought another great clue we got today was what the sheriff from Sevierville said about J.J. Pickler. Remember how everyone thought when Pickler disappeared he was a suspect? He was almost gone for a month but then he came back to Sevierville and went to the police showing them the note he claimed was left for him: *You're next!* I can't blame him for getting out of town. Can you imagine seeing Butch's mangled body and then that note attached to the fence? I don't think I would have hung around either."

Buttering a hot roll, Grant looked at William. "So tell me William, how does your innate Cherokee foresight play into all of this?"

Pouring some ice water from a pitcher into his glass, William answered, "It's a form of wisdom that goes well beyond modern police techniques. It's a feeling one gets at a crime scene. It's something that lingers long after a crime has been committed."

Grant, interested, probed, "And what does this lingering feeling tell you about our killer?"

"Actually, quite a bit," said William. "Our killer is well organized. He picked out each one of the three victims specifically and had a plan for their demise. These killings were not spur of the moment. They were well thought out...and then executed. Our killer has been experiencing some sort of pain and he has felt this way for many years. Something happened to him sometime in the past. He never forgot it...he could never put it behind him. But he was patient. He knew over the years, when he finally struck it would be with violence. He had to wait until something else happened in his life that convinced him to move ahead with the murders. Our killer is not what you would want to refer to as mental or nuts. He is very normal and what he has done is pictured as justified in his own mind. There is definitely a connection between all three of his victims. Asa Pittman, a man who was a poacher at times, hunted out of season, skinned animals, shot local critters just for the fun of it. The there's Mildred Henks, a woman who ran a puppy mill and treated the dogs she owned horribly. Finally Butch Miller, a man who stole local dogs and sold them to dog fighters for training purposes. If you take the time to think about it our killer is making sure animals have a part in the murders. Pittman, even though dead was mauled and practically eaten by coyotes. Henks, once again assumed dead was attacked by raccoons and who knows what else. Miller probably died the most violent death at the hands of those guard dogs. Our killer is getting even with people who treat animals badly and he wants the public to know it." Holding up a fork he pointed at the other three at the table. "You can be sure of one thing. He's far from done. So far he has killed in the spring, the summer and the fall. Winter is just around the corner. Get ready gentlemen. He'll strike again. He probably already has his next victim picked out. He's just waiting for the right moment."

CHAPTER TWENTY

"GOOD MORNING FOLKS. Looks like we're going to have a few more days of unseasonably cold weather here in the Smoky Mountains Region. Old Man Winter is coming at us in full force. The temperature in the next few days will hover in the low teens with a chance of snow flurries. Stay warm."

Charley Droxler flipped off his old transistor radio and got up from his kitchen table. Walking to the window he pushed back the dirty curtains and gazed out across the open fields behind his farm, thinking: *Snow. Dammit, I hate snow! Better make sure I've got enough supplies.* Crossing the small kitchen he opened the cabinets above the sink. *Let's see, what do I need?* Moving to the cabinets next to his ancient stove he peered inside inspecting the contents. *I need some sugar, bread, soup, hmm...that should do it.* Closing the cabinet door he chuckled as he remembered, *Crap! Can't forget a fifth of Ol' Grand Dad.*

Charley walked into the back bedroom and sat on the edge of the unmade bed, pushing his feet into his hunting boots. After lacing up the boots he picked up his wallet from the dresser and grabbed his old gray parka slipping it over his skinny shoulders. Hesitating at the front door he adjusted the thermostat and spoke under his breath, *Damn cold weather!*

Pushing open the door he was met with a stiff blast of icy wind. After he closed and locked the door he crossed the yard to his truck, looking at the distant mountains. He shivered. It was probably ten degrees colder up there. A few small flakes of snow wafted through the air. Unlocking the truck he climbed in and started the engine, the old truck instantly springing to life, the sound of the engine was like the voice of an old friend. Adjusting the heater to high, he sat back in the seat and blew a warm breath into his cupped hands, waiting for the defroster to drive away the condensation that had formed on the windshield. Not a very patient man he ducked down and peered through a small spot that was free of frost. He put the truck in gear and started down the dirt lane.

Passing the split rail fence that sectioned off the pasture he glared at the herd of horses huddled together by the fence. *Damn horses,* he thought. *I hope you all just go ahead and die! And damn you Mildred Henks! I should have known better than to get involved with the likes of you.*

Turning onto Banks Road he was glad his house was off the beaten path. Unless someone was coming to specifically pay him a visit there was no reason for anyone to be on the road. Opening the glove compartment he removed a tin of chewing tobacco and took out a pinch, which he stuck under his tongue up against his right cheek. Heading up the road that led to Alcoa he thought about Mildred Henks again. What an idiot he had been for hooking up with her.

He remembered the first night he had run into her. He had been minding his own business at a corner table at Hooters enjoying a plate of wings and slowly nursing a pitcher of beer when someone had called his name. Looking up, he saw Mildred Henks, of all people approaching his table. She had been dressed to the nines: black, tight pants, a white, low-cut sweater and that white scarf she always wore draped around her neck. He remembered thinking how surprised he was she even knew his name. She plopped down at his table, reached over and helped herself to a wing as she ordered another pitcher of beer. They talked for nearly two hours. She ordered another dozen wings and they put away a third pitcher. He always heard she was such a bitch, but he found her really easy to talk with. When she got ready to leave she had asked him not to mention to any of the boys, his pals over in Townsend, that they had dinner together. She was afraid of their gossiping tongues as her divorce was not finalized.

It had been hard for him not to say anything to Asa, and the others about his evening at Hooters with Mildred Henks. He wanted to bust into the Parkway Grocery and rub Asa's nose right in it. But he had promised Mildred he wouldn't say anything to his friends and besides that she was on the verge of getting divorced. He thought maybe he had a chance with her. Asa would have been so pissed if he knew he had spent some time with Mildred. Asa was the one who was always saying he wanted to bed her, but she would never have anything to do with him. Now, looking back, it seemed so strange. Both Asa and Mildred had been murdered. It was just as well no one knew he and Mildred had been chummy. With both of them being murdered he might be considered a suspect.

Daydreaming, his truck veered into the opposite lane. He had to swerve at the last second to avoid a head on collision with a logging truck. Quickly steering his truck back into his own lane he mumbled a long string of profanity thinking to himself, *God, that was close! I've got to pay better attention to what I'm doing.*

The truck under control, he started to think again about Mildred Henks. He couldn't help remembering how excited he had been when she called him and invited him over to her place for dinner. He wondered why someone like her would even give him a second look. He was overweight, almost bald and didn't have a whole lot to show for himself. Except for his job at the gas station, he was still living on the money his parents left him when they died. He always got a lot of ribbing from his pals for being fifty-five years old and living at home, but now he lived alone in the house where he had been born and the thought that Mildred had any interest in him had just been hard to believe.

The night he went to her house for dinner, he had been like a kid going to the circus. He always heard her home was a real showpiece. He had not only been curious but full of anticipation. When she answered the door he forgot all about her glamorous home. There she stood in that teal blue dress and white heels. Suddenly he hadn't cared about the house any longer.

She prepared a wonderful meal for him of pan-fried chicken, mashed potatoes, gravy and corn. After dinner they sat in front of the fireplace and knocked off a bottle and a half of expensive wine. Around midnight she sat close to him on her white couch and he recalled trying to remain calm and not jump the gun.

His concentration suddenly returned to the road, stopping at a stop sign before making a right hand turn. On the move again he remembered everything about that night at Mildred's earlier in the year. He beat his hand on the steering wheel thinking how stupid he had been to even think she had any interest in him.

Sipping on her glass of wine she proceeded to explain that she had a business offer to propose to him. He hadn't planned on talking about business, but had thought the evening was going to be the beginning of something good finally happening in his life; a relationship. Politely he sat on the couch and listened, Mildred telling him about a herd of horses she could purchase really cheap and then resell them to the local riding stables in the area. They were good quality stock and belonged to a man whose house she had just recently sold. He was moving north and getting out of the horse business. She could buy the herd for a song. The only problem was she had nowhere to keep the horses. She had the money to purchase them, and he, Charley had the land to house them. Together they could realize a big profit. She played him like a fine fiddle. She knew he had pastureland. He tried to discourage her by telling her he didn't have a barn he could put the horses in, but she said that didn't make any difference. It would only be for a short time. The night was heading in a much different direction than what he had figured. He felt like running out the door, but with her leg touching his and her hand on his shoulder combined with all of the wine he had consumed, he fell victim to her request. When he said yes, she jumped up and kissed him on the cheek. Twenty minutes later she said she was really getting tired and she had a meeting to go to early the next morning so they had better call it a night. Walking him to the door she kissed him on the cheek once again and thanked him and said she would be in touch soon.

Charley had no idea that soon meant three days later when he got a call from Mildred telling him to expect delivery the next afternoon. He also had no idea there were thirty-one horses involved in the deal. It took three large horse trailers to deliver the herd. He didn't even like horses, in fact he didn't like animals period. It was too late for him to do anything about it, and since he had plenty of grass in the pasture and a small pond for drinking water he figured if there was anything else they needed it would be provided by Mildred.

Two weeks went by and he hadn't received a single call from his so-called business partner, Mildred. He lived up to his end of the bargain and housed the horses. Now it was up to her to start selling the stock and splitting the profits with him. Everything had come to a standstill. He wanted those damn horses off of his land.

He tried to call Mildred a number of times and she always brushed him off telling him the market was not good for horses right now or that they were not the quality the stables were looking for. Finally, he called her and informed her if she didn't get them off of his property he was going to shoot every last one. She whimpered and begged him to hold on for a bit longer. Two weeks later one of the horses died. He'd be damned if he was going to bury it. To have it hauled off would cost well over a hundred dollars so he took the easy way out, poured gasoline over the dead animal and burned it.

By the end of spring he threatened to tell everyone about the horses, and that she owned them and was not supplying them with what they needed to survive. He told her she needed to get them moved, and now! But then, Mildred was murdered. Just his luck! He had no bill of sale for the horses or anything showing where he had gotten them. Who would believe they belonged to Mildred Henks? He was stuck with thirty, under nourished horses and he didn't care. He hoped they all died.

When fall rolled around most of the grass in the pasture was gone, but the horses held on. They were a sickly looking bunch and he couldn't believe more of them hadn't died. He called several rendering companies that would be glad to take them off his hands but they required a bill of sale proving they belonged to him.

A week later, two of the horses went down from weakness in the field. He had no choice. He had to shoot them. Using his old tractor he tied a rope to their feet and dragged them to a ravine. He left their carcasses there to be eaten by coyotes and turkey vultures. Now wintertime was upon him and the horses had no grass to graze on, no shelter and very little water. Within a couple of months they would all die and be stinking up his place. He didn't have any idea what he was going to do. He could shoot them all but then what about all the work involved in dragging them down to the ravine. He wished now he would have never gone to Mildred's house and agreed to her crazy scheme. Of course, he could call someone like the humane society and explain what had happened. They would know what to do. But then, if he did that everyone would know what a fool he had been. No, he couldn't look like a fool.

Turning down Banks Road, he pulled his truck into Food City. The parking lot was jammed. Everyone was stocking up at the prospect of bad weather. He could get everything he needed here, except for his Ol' Grand Dad. He had to drive into Townsend for that. What the hell. What else did he have to do?

Two hours later he was back on the road heading home to Alcoa. The roads were covered with a dusting of snow. He was glad he was going to be back home before the roads got too bad. He wasn't concerned. With food and booze in the house he was in good shape unless the television went out.

Turning onto his drive, he noticed a number of tire tracks in the now, one inch snow. He must have had a visitor. Strange, no one ever came out to see him. The tire marks went around to the back of the house. It appeared from the marks the vehicle had come and gone at least twice. There were no footprints in the snow leading up to the front door so he figured whoever it was had turned around and drove off.

Parking his truck in front of the house, he carried his sack of groceries inside, bumped up the thermostat to seventy, tossed his parka on the couch, kicked off his boots and began to put away his supplies. He was starving. He hadn't had any breakfast, just some morning coffee. Heating up a bowl of chili, he made himself a bologna and onion sandwich, which he polished off with a cold beer and a shot of whiskey as he watched television. Finishing off the last gulp of whiskey, he felt tired. Time for his afternoon nap. He pulled back the lever on his worn easy chair, propped up his feet and dozed off.

Charley awoke with a jolt. For a moment he didn't know where he was. He couldn't see, his body was rigid, something was wrong! He tried to move but his feet and hands were bound tightly. He wiggled around wildly in the chair until his body weight tipped the chair over onto its side. He shouted out in frustration, "Got Dammit!" He pushed himself to a sitting position on the floor and tried to remove the blindfold with his forearms, but he was unsuccessful. He yelled again, "What's happening? Is anybody here?" Then, another sensation hit him. Except for his boxer shorts he was totally unclothed.

His struggling was halted by the sound of a pleasant voice, "Good afternoon, Charley. Did you have a nice nap?" It sounded like the voice was coming from the couch.

Looking to the right, then the left Charley bellowed out, "Who is it? What do you want? I don't have any money in the house, but I can go to the bank."

"No need for that," the voice said. "I'm not after your money."

Squirming on the floor Charley demanded, "Who are you? Take this damn blindfold off of me. How did I get like this?"

The voice responded, "Not quite yet, Charley. We need to talk first. Actually, I'm going to talk and you're going to listen. It's amazing what a small amount of chloroform can do. It knocked you right out. Of course, I know your routine. You eat a late lunch every day then take a two hour nap after throwing down a shot of whiskey. It was easy to get in your house. You should put a better lock on your backdoor."

There was a moment of silence but then the voice spoke again, "I want to talk with you about the horses, Charley. You know they're starving and most of them will freeze to death before the week is out. Let's just say I have come to their rescue. You would think folks in these parts would start to get the idea; the idea of what happens to people that mistreat animals. People like Asa Pittman, Mildred Henks and Butch Miller."

Charley yelled, "No, no, I'm not like them! I know who you are. You're the killer! Oh God, please! I'll go out and feed them and..."

The voice ordered, "Shut up! It's too late for all that, Charley. I had to sit by and watch those poor horses suffer longer than I wanted, hoping you would redeem yourself. You didn't *and* now it's too late."

Charley began to sob, tears streamed down his face. Pulling his knees up against his chest he pleaded, "Oh God, I don't want to die. Please."

The voice remained unsympathetic. "I know you don't want to die, but those horses didn't want to remain outside in the heat of summer and have their bodies eaten by horseflies. They didn't want to live on grass that gave them bloat and diarrhea. They needed someone to shave down their hooves to keep them from splitting and cracking, but you stood by and did nothing. We all have to pay for the mistakes we make in life. When it comes to those horses out in your pasture the decisions you made or the decisions you didn't make have caused me to be with you here at this moment. It's time to pay up."

There was silence then Charley could hear whoever was in the room with him walk across the floor in his direction. Not knowing what to expect he raised his taped hands up in front of his face. His hands were pushed to the side as a piece of duct tape was plastered across his mouth. The blindfold was removed. Charley's eyes widened as he stared at his visitor shaking his head in disbelief. The man who stood over him wore a dark blue, long, wool parka, black rubber boots and cheap brown gloves.

"Surprised?" said the man. "Now, I want you to remain quiet and try not to upset me. If you do irritate me, I may have to alter my plan, and trust me, that would makes things a lot worse for you. I want you to stand up Charley and don't make any sudden moves or attempts at escaping." Reaching into his parka pocket he pulled out a pocketknife and opened it displaying a six-inch blade. "This knife is extremely sharp, so don't make me use it. I don't want to get blood all over your house."

Almost choking on his tears, Charley rolled over onto his side, and then got to his knees and then his feet, wobbling from side to side. His legs were shaking and he bumped into the overturned chair and nearly toppled over but the man reached out to steady him. "Whoa, hold on there. Steady, partner."

Removing the tape from his legs he took him by the arm and led him down the hallway. Pushing open the bathroom door, the man shoved Charley in ahead of him and ordered him to step into the moldy tub. Charley was resistant but only for a second when the man placed the blade at his throat and said calmly, "Move."

Reaching up the man turned on the cold water and stated, "Just a little cold shower. It'll make you feel better." A blast of frigid cold water sprayed out and over Charley's naked body soaking his boxer shorts. The initial shock of the cold water caused him to cower up against the sidewall, but the man quickly directed the spray in his direction. "You'll be out of there in about a minute or so. I just want to make sure you're nice and wet before we venture out back."

By the time the man turned the water off, Charley was shivering. Helping Charley back out of the tub he was led back down the hallway where they stopped. The man picked up the bottle of Ol' Grand Dad that was setting on an end table. Picking up his black bag he prodded Charley with the pocket knife as he held up the bottle. "You're probably going to need this."

Stumbling through the kitchen, Charley balked at the backdoor. Placing the knife near his throat the man ordered, "Keep moving."

Stepping outside, Charley shivered. The man looked up at the grey snow-dotted sky. "Sure is a cold one today. Feels like maybe what…nineteen, twenty degrees out here? Glad I wore this warm coat and my boots." Pushing Charley forward he pointed out, "I want to show you something."

Charley could barely walk. His body was shaking so hard it was difficult to keep his balance. The snow on the ground stuck to his damp feet causing him to walk in an awkward marching gait. Fifty feet out from the house he stumbled and fell to his knees. "Now, now," said the man. "None of this. Get up!" Charley just lay there shivering. The sharp prick from the pocketknife in the calf of his leg caused him to struggle to his feet. Ten yards further on they stopped and the man pushed Charley up against a wooden fencepost. The horses noticing someone had approached the back fence worked their way around to the back pasture where they now stood staring at the two humans by the fence.

Spinning Charley around so he was face to face with the horses, the man spoke roughly, "Take a real good look at them, Charley. Their eyelids are so full of frost they can't even blink. Look at their feet. See how they are trying to shift their weight to keep the pain away. Count their ribs Charley and tell me you did the best you could."

He dropped the black bag to the ground and opened it. Turning Charley back around, he duct taped him to the post at the chest, waist and ankles. Testing the tape to make sure it was secure the man looked Charley in the eyes. "You're getting off easy. I hear hypothermia is a pretty easy way to die. I also know alcohol dilates the blood vessels close to the skin and speeds up the process, so I think you need to take a few drinks. Unscrewing the bottle, the man ripped the duct tape from Charley's mouth and forced his head back and shoved the bottle into his already blue lips. Charley tried to speak but could only let out a gurgle as the man tipped the bottle up, the whiskey pouring down his throat. "Enjoy it," said the man. "Take a couple of gulps. You'll be glad you did." Gagging and choking, Charley swallowed what he could, the rest running down the front of his stomach and bare legs.

Retaping Charley's mouth the man reached into the bag and removed a set of lopping shears and held them up in front of Charley's face. Charley struggled but his bonds were tight. His eyes grew wide with fear. Ten seconds later his first two blood-stained fingers laid at his feet,the white snow turning to a crimson red. Charley tried to scream but at best his feeble cry could only be heard a mere ten yards away. "Scream all you want, Charley. No one will hear you except the horses. Now, I'm going up to the house where it's nice and warm. I might even check your refrigerator and see if you've got anything good to eat. I'm famished. I'll be back down to check on you in about ten minutes. If you're not conscious

I'll bring you back around."

Ten minutes later, as promised, the man walked out of the house to the fence carrying a mug of hot chocolate and a donut. "I did find something up there to eat. This is just a snack. I'm warming up some soup on the stove." Looking down at Charley's feet he saw the blood stained area in the snow growing larger. Picking up the shears the man commented, "You're tougher than I thought. With that he cut off two more fingers, this time blood squirting out further making a grotesque design in the white snow. Charley tried to scream again when the man tapped him on the nose with the shears. "Break time again. I've got to go check on my soup. I hope you have crackers. I hate soup without crackers. Be back in ten."

Charley watched the man walk back to the house. He stared down at his feet, the dripping blood from his severed fingers creating crimson red holes in the snow. He shivered. It started to sleet, the tiny windswept particles of ice stinging his bare skin. The pain in his throbbing hands was excruciating. Sweat had broken out on his face but quickly evaporated from the low temperature. Behind him he could hear the horses, stomping on the ground, followed by an occasional nay. Turning his head to the side he could see some of the horses standing farther down the fence line, their warm breath escaping their nostrils then slowly dissipating. In between the shots of pain he thought about what he had heard about the three murders. About how they had their fingers and Mildred had her toes as well cut off. How they had bled out. That's how his life was going to end. The slow loss of blood was making him even colder than he already was, his teeth chattering uncontrollably.

Another ten minutes passed when the man appeared again at the back of the house making his way across the yard. Walking to the fence, he reached up and patted three of the horses on their noses. The other horses, anticipating they would be fed, congregated across from where the man stood. Walking down to where Charley was he said, "Soup's cooling off. Should be ready when I go back up to the house." Looking off into the distance the man remarked, "This is what I call soup weather." Reaching for the lopping shears he continued with his explanation, lopping off two more fingers. "For some reason soup always tastes better when it's cold outside. The colder it is the better the soup tastes." Charley tried to scream but his strength was dwindling rapidly.

Leaning the shears up against the fence, the man looked at the horses, then commented, "I think the herd would enjoy something good to eat also." Holding up his index finger he said, "Be right back." Walking to his white van parked at the back of the house, he opened the rear door and removed five large bales of hay and three large bags of oats. Charley watched the man make eight trips back and forth from the van to the fence line, dragging and carrying the hay and oats. Next the man went about the process of cutting the twine on the bales and systematically throwing large handfuls over the fence which the horses ate with what could only be described as great joy. Seeing the herd was enjoying the hay, he split open the bags of oats and dumped the contents along the fence line. Standing back he smiled at the sight of the horses getting something to eat rather than grass and weeds. "Does my heart good to see them eat like that," said the man. He then turned and walked back to the house where he located a garden hose and hooked it up to an outdoor spigot on the side of the house. Turning on the water, he walked back to the fence, laid the hose on the ground and grabbed the duct tape from his black bag. Placing the hose on top of the fence he tightly wrapped it with duct tape so the water flowed up over top of the fence like a makeshift water fountain. It didn't take more than a few seconds for the horses to figure out how to lap at the water. Saluting at Charley, the man said, "Gotta get back inside and have that soup. See ya in another ten minutes."

The pain from his severed fingers had grown worse but suddenly seemed to be subsiding. Charley realized he was becoming delirious not only from the loss of blood but from the numbing cold. Hanging his head he imagined that his body was involved in a bizarre race between bleeding out and freezing to death. Whichever form of death arrived first he was still going to lose. He looked off in the distance at the Smoky Mountains. He had lived here all his life. He loved the mountains. He was starting to pass out, but one of the horses bumped into the fence bringing him back.

Apparently another ten minutes had passed and the man approached him again, this time puffing away on a pipe. Pointing the pipe at Charley, the man asked, "You don't smoke do you Charley?" Admiring the pipe, he held it up. "I really don't smoke much myself, but I do have to say I truly do enjoy my pipe."

Clenching the pipe in his teeth he picked up the shears. "Gotta move things along." Snapping a finger off he kept right on talking, "It seems to me in life there are certain things as a man, you just can't do much about. Like cruelty to animals for instance. It's so widespread and common it's hard to imagine anything that one could do to improve things for animals. *Snap!* Another finger fell to the ground. "That being said, I feel one man can make a difference. I mean, I feel I've put, if nothing else, a miniscule dent in cruelty toward animals in the area. Due to the death of Asa a few less bears will be killed this year and a few less coyotes will meet a terrible death. The birds, squirrels and chipmunks around his farm will now have a fighting chance at life. And because Mildred is no longer walking the face of the earth, those dogs she held captive for years all now have homes where they are loved and cared for, not to mention those wonderful pups I rescued."

Snap! A thumb fell to the ground followed by a trail of blood. "Then there's ol' Butch Miller. A awful man who attended dogfights and stole neighborhood dogs for dog fighting purposes. Because he no longer exists there will be far fewer dogs missing in the area. And I might mention the dog fighters took off in the middle of the night because of the action I decided to take. So, you see, I have made a difference."

Snap! The last thumb fell into the bloody snow. Finished, the man stood up straight and took a puff on his pipe. "You see, Charley, what it amounts to is this. I've done what a lot of people, animal lovers, would like to do to people like you, Asa, Mildred and Butch. The only problem is most people don't have the nerve to take action. I know most folks around here are of the opinion, the killer...me, is a sadistic maniac. But what they won't tell you is secretly, if they really knew why I have done the things I have, they would approve. Like it says in the Bible: When justice is done, it brings joy to the righteous but torment to evildoers."

Charley's head sank to his chest. Holding Charley's chin up, the man looked deep into his eyes then felt the weak pulse in his wrist. "Won't be long now, Charley. Another ten to fifteen minutes should do it for you. I'm going to start packing things up, maybe go back inside for a few minutes and warm up, then I'll come back down." Picking up his shears he cleaned them off with snow then placed them and the duct tape inside the bag, walked to the van and tossed the bag in the back and closed the door.

Going back inside the house the man located some paper and a pen. Sitting at the kitchen table he jotted down a note: *Please take care of these horses. Thank you!*

Rereading the note to make sure it said what he wanted it to, he reached into his pocket and removed his tobacco pouch and refilled the bowl of his pipe. Lighting the pipe he sat back down taking a few long puffs then got up and walked to the kitchen window. Across the yard he viewed what was an odd sight. Charley Droxler, attached to the fence, more than likely close to death and behind him stood the horses munching away on hay and oats. They were still alive and soon their lives would be better.

Waiting for a few more minutes the man decided to give Charley his final inspection before he made the call to Alcoa. Walking across the snow covered yard he noticed Charley wasn't moving. His head was down on his chest, his arms hung at his sides. He looked dead—frozen. Checking his pulse, not once, but twice the man looked at the horses and said, "Well, that's it then…he's gone." Just to make sure he would not be revived somehow he took the hose down from the fence and doused Charley's head with a good soaking. A final shock to his body. Pitching the hose down on the ground, he sliced a small section of duct tape from the side of the post and attached the note at the top of the post just above Charley's head. Standing back he took a moment to make sure everything was the way he wanted it to appear. Satisfied he walked back to the house for the last time. Picking up the phone in the living room he dialed 911.

The Alcoa operator answered the call at 4:20 in the afternoon. In an almost inaudible voice, the caller said, "Help me, I'm having a heart attack. Charley Droxler, Route 23, off Banks Road. Last mailbox on the left."

The operator responded, "We're on our way, Mr. Droxler."

Nine miles down the road at Kresges Gas Station the man placed the nozzle in the tank of his white van as the white and yellow emergency paramedic van, its lights flashing, its siren blaring sped by the station. The man smiled to himself: *Right on time.*

CHAPTER TWENTY-ONE

CHIEF ROY CHAPMAN looked up from his desk as Nadene Parks stuck her head in his office. "Chief, you've got a call on line two. It's the Rural Metro Ambulance Service. Sounds like an emergency. Said they wanted to talk directly to you."

"Thanks," said Roy, picking up the receiver. "Chief Roy Chapman, Alcoa Police Department."

"Roy! This is Earl with the ambulance service. We're out here at Charley Droxler's place off Banks Road. We received a call from him not twenty minutes ago. Said he was having a heart attack. When we got out here we found him dead."

Roy cut Earl off before he was finished speaking. "Earl, why are you calling me because ol' Charley Droxler keeled over from heart failure?"

"That's just the thing, Chief," said Earl. "He didn't exactly keel over and it appears that he didn't die from heart failure. He was murdered. We found him strapped practically naked to a fence. Looks like he froze to death and one other thing. All of his fingers have been cut off. Besides freezing to death it looks like he bled out. Either way…he's dead."

Roy stared at the phone but remained silent.

"Roy…are you still on the line?"

"Yeah, I'm still with ya. I was just talking with Charley not two days ago up town."

"Look, you need to get up here, Chief before we can touch anything. We took his pulse… that's all. The body is a mess. To tell you the truth what with the fingers being cut off and all I'd say our killer has struck again."

Roy stood, the phone still at his ear. "Call the coroner. I'm on my way!"

Grabbing his hat he walked into the front office and ordered Nadene, "I'm heading up to Charlie Droxler's place. Looks like he's been murdered. Fingers cut off just like the others. I need you to call Sheriff Grimes over in Maryville and then Chief Brody in Townsend. Tell them we've got another possible murder on our hands and they need to meet me up there. You might have to give them directions."

Brody was just about to call it a day when Marge stopped him as he was climbing in his truck. "Axel! We just got a call from the Alcoa Police Department. Charley Droxler has been murdered. They said for you to meet them over there...right away!"

Standing next to his truck Brody looked toward the sky then at Marge. "This shit's never goin' to en, is it? How do they know he was murdered?"

"They didn't say much, Chief, just that his fingers had been cut off. Said you needed to head on up there."

"Hell, I don't even know where Charley lives. Somewhere outside of Alcoa."

Marge handed him a slip of paper. "Here, they gave me directions."

Climbing in his truck, Brody took the paper and looked at it. Rolling down the window he backed out, ordering Marge, "Give Denlinger a call. Have him meet me there."

Grant was in the process of filling up his cruiser when the call came through: "Grant, come in...it's Marge."

Reaching in the open window Grant grabbed the radio. "Marge...Grant here...what's up?"

"Brody just took off outta here like the blazes. He told me to call you and have you meet him at Charley Droxler's over in Alcoa. We just got a call from their police department. Looks like Charley's been murdered."

"God!" said Grant. "Did they give you any details?"

"Nope, just that he was found dead, and oh yeah, his fingers were cut off. Said you need to get up there. Do you know where Charley's place is?"

Removing the nozzle from his gas tank, Grant answered, "Not really."

"Banks Road...a few miles out from Alcoa. Last mailbox of the left."

"I know where Banks Road is. I'm on my way!"

Closing the gas cap, Grant jumped in his cruiser and sped out of the station, flipping on his overhead lights and siren. Watching snow flurries start to fall, he thought, *Another murder.* William Blue had been right. It had been three weeks since he, Doug, Gephart and Chief Blue had visited all of the crime scenes. Blue was right on the money when he summed things up by stating the killer was not done and there would be more killings. Since the killer had murdered someone in the spring, summer and fall, it was almost a given he would strike in the winter. Here it was November, a week before Thanksgiving and they were faced with the fourth murder of the year. Blue had firmly established something Grant had already suspected, that the killer was an animal lover and was making a point to the public by killing people who were unkind to animals, but why Charley Droxler? He was just an old man who didn't bother anyone. Sure he owned a small farm but as far as Grant knew it was just an old farm house and an abandoned barn that was about to collapse. At least that's what Asa and the rest of the fellas at the Parkway Grocery had talked about earlier in the year.

Grant remembered the conversation back in January. Asa had given Charley a hard time saying his place could hardly be referred to as a farm. There wasn't one single animal on the place, not a cow, pig, chicken, dog or even a barn cat. Hell, Charley didn't even grow any crops, not even a small garden. What could Charley have possibly done to cause him to be the killer's fourth victim?

The more Grant thought about it the weirder it seemed to get. It had been Charley who told him Asa had been sweet on Mildred Henks, but that she wanted nothing to do with him. And it had also been Charley who seemed to hold no mercy for Asa even after his death, saying something else would soon come along that would turn things upside down and make Asa's murder seem insignificant. Little did Charley realize it at the time, but besides the murders of Mildred Henks and Butch Miller, his own death would be part of the reason why Asa's death was taking a back burner position. It just seemed strange; out of the five old friends that met every Monday, Wednesday and Friday, two of them had been murdered. Grant was missing something. The puzzle just wasn't coming together. There were too many pieces out of place.

Suddenly, it hit Grant as he entered the Alcoa town limits. Charley was the one who had called him and tipped him to the dogfights over in Sevierville. Could it be that's why he was killed? Maybe he ticked off the wrong person. After all, the dog fighting ring had to pack up in the middle of the night and scoot. Besides skipping town in the nick of time, they had probably lost money.

Making a right hand turn at the square in Alcoa Grant drove south where he knew Banks Road intersected with Route 23. He had only been out Banks Road once before and that was years ago when he was in the Boy Scouts. He and seventeen other scouts and their scout master had been driven out to the end of Banks Road in a school bus and dumped off where they hiked up into the foothills for a weekend of camping.

The snow was picking up when he left the outskirts of Alcoa. His thoughts shifted once again to Chief Blue and the observations he had made about the killer. Things like, he was not crazy, but very organized, a person who specifically picked out his victims. Despite the fact he was on his way to yet another murder scene, Grant smiled, thinking about how Chief Brody didn't see eye to eye with William Blue. For one thing Brody didn't like anybody superseding his authority and when it came to Townsend he tried his best to keep a tight reign on the power his badge carried. But it was more than just the fact another law officer was treading on his territory. Brody didn't like the fact he wasn't even from Tennessee, but over in North Carolina.

Arriving at Banks Road, he took a right turn, the cruiser sliding toward the side of the road. Grant turned the steering wheel in the opposite direction correcting the slide as he continued up the country road, realizing the roads were getting bad from the falling snow, that was coming down in heavy, large flakes sticking to his windshield. Turning the wipers on HIGH, he recalled what Marge had said, 'Last mailbox on the left.'

Banks Road was only about two miles long and before he knew it he saw the old black mailbox: Droxler. Turning into the snow covered drive, that was marked by various tire tracks he saw the flashing blue lights on top of Brody's truck, which was parked, next to the barn. Passing the house and driving around to the side he saw police cruisers from Alcoa and Maryville, an ambulance and the county coroner's van.

Parking next to Brody's truck he got out and walked across the backyard to where it seemed all of the activity was taking place. It was an odd scene, a herd of horses standing by the fence as they observed the group of men who had congregated nearby, Roy Chapman talked with Chief Grimes, Jeff Bookman was having a conversation with the paramedics from the ambulance service, and Brody had his foot propped up on the fence as he tied his shoe.

Jeff was the first to notice Grant walking toward the fence. "Grant...we meet again...unfortunately. We were just about to cut down the victim." Stepping to the side he gestured toward Charley Droxler's body and remarked, "You might want to take a look at the body before we remove it."

Brody shook his head in disgust, thinking the county coroner had more faith in one of his officers than himself.

It was a ghastly sight that interrupted the peacefulness of the falling snow and the backdrop of the horses. Charley's head was lowered to his chest. His boxer shorts, which were the only clothing he had on were soaked with a yellow stain where he had urinated himself. His eyes were wide open and held a look of hopelessness. His bare skin had taken on a shade of blue, his lips almost black. The top of his head and shoulders were covered with snow. His arms hung limply at his sides, the remaining blood on the stumps of his hands had coagulated and had become crusted. At his bare feet laid his severed fingers, some covered by the snow. Blood was splattered down both of his legs and in the snow. At his feet there were ten evenly spaced red holes in the snow where the blood from the cuts had slowly, drip by drip, penetrated the snow making it appear like grotesque art.

Grant, realizing he was the lowest ranking officer at the scene, remained humble, but commented, "William Blue was right about our killer. He said he would strike during the winter." Raising his hands to display the surrounding snow and the victim, he emphasized, "It's definitely winter *and* we have our fourth victim."

"Speaking of Chief Blue," said Jeff. "Did anyone think to call him? I mean, at this point he's just as much a part of the investigation as any of us, especially since he hooked up with the Feds."

Grimes jumped in on the conversation, "I gave Blue a call on my way up here. He said he'd be here as soon as he could. But with the snow it's going to be slow going coming over the mountain from Cherokee. I also called the Feds in Townsend but they took a few days off for the upcoming holiday and went back to Knoxville. I gave their office up there a call. They're on their way as we speak."

Turning to the paramedics Bookman ordered, "Let's get him down from the fence, then we'll load him up. Bag up all the duct tape and the fingers."

Brody, who had remained quiet joined the group. Standing next to Grant, he remarked sarcastically, "This is really goin' to screw up the holidays. Thanksgivin' is in a week. It's always been my favorite time of the year. Folks gettin' together, sharin' food and friendship, thankin' the Good Lord for all their blessin's. It all seems so strange. Asa Pittman, Mildred Henks, Butch, my cousin,; and now Charley Droxler…all murdered. I gotta tell ya, it's gonna be hard to be thankful for anythin' this year."

Bookman agreed, then cut into the duct tape. "Crime never takes a holiday."

It was then Grant noticed the attached note on the fence. Pointing he asked, "What's that?"

Chapman tapped the edge of the note with a pen he had in his hand. "We think it was left by the killer."

Cutting the tape from Charley's legs, the paramedics held him in place as Bookman nodded toward the note. "We'll know more when they match up the handwriting with the note left over at J.J.'s. I have a strange feeling they are going to match."

Stepping forward Grant read the note then repeated what was written: "Please take care of these horses. Thank you!" Walking to the fence he reached up and patted the nose of a nearby horse, three other horses approaching for some attention. Looking at the half-starved animals, he commented, "These horses look near dead. Look at their ribs and their feet." Turning back to the group, he stated, "It was common knowledge Charley didn't have any animals of any kind on his so called farm. Where on earth did these horses come from?"

"At this point," said Chapman, "no one seems to know the answer."

Grimes started to walk toward his cruiser. "I guess I better get the humane society over here. These animals are going to not only need shelter, but food and water. It's going to be a big job to get them hauled out of here."

Grant walked down the fence line to where the three empty fifty pound bags of oats laid. He noticed small traces of scattered hay on the opposite side of the fence. "Someone fed them recently." Walking back across the yard he followed a trail of more scattered hay which stopped next to the house. "Looks like someone dragged some hay from here to over by the fence." Bending down he noticed something. An oil stain partially covered with snow. He recalled what William Blue had said about the killer driving a vehicle with an oil leak. Since he was the only one present on the four man investigating team Gephart had headed up, Grant decided to keep the discovery of the leak to himself until Chief Blue was on the scene.

Walking back to the fence Grant watched as Charley was loaded up in the coroner's van. Approaching Grimes he suggested, "Listen, I've got an idea. I'm sure the humane society doesn't have the facilities to house all of the horses. When you contact them why don't you have them give Franklin Barrett over in Townsend a call. He owns two riding stables over there where they could be kept and besides, he has horse trailers they could be hauled in. The vets can work on getting the horses back in condition over at his place."

"Sounds good," said Grimes. "I'll have Helen give Barrett a call. If he's not interested I'm sure one of the other local stables will be..."

Brody overhearing their conversation interrupted, "Barrett, you gotta be kiddin' me. He's an asshole!"

Grimes didn't say anything but looked at Brody like he was nuts.

Grant, on the other hand calmly stated, "Look, Chief, just because you don't get along with Barrett doesn't mean he won't be willing to pitch in and help us out."

Placing his hands on his hips Brody looked first at Grant, then at Grimes. "Do what you want. I think it's a mistake bringin' in the likes of Barrett."

Grimes was about to say something when he noticed a light green sedan and another police cruiser pull up next to the house. Chief Blue stepped out of the cruiser, shaking hands with Ralph Gephart and Harold Green as the coroner's van backed up, then pulled down the drive. Grimes approached and extended his hand in welcome. Nodding toward the van that was now turning onto Banks Road he commented, "You just missed the victim."

As the foursome walked toward the fence Chief Blue asked, "What was the vic's name?"

"Charley Droxler. Lived here alone on this farm. Pretty much stuck to himself."

Stopping next to the fence, Grimes made the introductions, "Chief Chapman from Alcoa, this is Chief Blue from over in Cherokee and these two gentlemen, Ralph Gephart and Harold

Green are with the FBI. I believe you've all met Chief Brody from Townsend." Everyone shook hands except for Brody who gave Chief Blue a nasty look. Grimes finished up the introductions and gestured toward Grant. "I believe you already know Grant."

Gephart brushed past Brody and shook Grant's hand. "Yes, Grant was the fourth man on our investigative team I headed up a few weeks back. He was quite helpful."

Grimes turned to Chapman, suggesting, "Roy, since this is your jurisdiction why don't you fill in Chief Blue and the agents on what we have so far."

Roy cleared his throat then motioned the group to the blood-stained snow just below where Charley had been found. "We got a call about an hour or so ago from the Metro Ambulance Service in regard to a call they responded to. Apparently Charley Droxler, the victim, called in that he was having a heart attack. I guess it took them about twenty minutes to get up here. They found Droxler duct taped to the fence in nothing more than a pair of boxer shorts. All of his fingers had been cut off and it looked like he froze to death." Handing the note they had found to Chief Blue, Chapman continued, "We found this attached to the fence just above the victim's head. We plan on seeing if the handwriting is a match to the note left at J.J.'s."

Chief Blue read the note out loud, "Please take care of these horses. Thank you." Handing the note back to Chapman, William walked to the fence and surveyed the horses. "They look in pretty bad shape. I think our killer made it pretty clear Droxler was killed because of the condition of these animals. It's the same M.O. as the other murders. The killer continues to send us a stern message. He or she or whoever it may be will not stand by and put up with the mistreatment of animals."

Brody pissed that Chief Blue seemed to be taking over the crime scene, started to walk toward the house. "I think we should head on up to the house and see what we can find."

Gephart touched Brody on the arm. "Hold up, Axel. Remember, this is still a federal case. I'm in charge." Looking toward the house he went on, "You're right. We should go up to the house. But, we're not going to go in there like a stampeding herd of buffalo. Chief Blue will enter first and we will all follow. From the short time I have spent with Chief Blue I have learned he has the ability to see clues we would overlook."

Brody placed his hands on his large hips. "So, what you're saying is the rest of us are a bunch of dumb asses!"

"No, that's not what I'm saying. What I am saying is Chief Blue has proven beyond any doubt he can detect things we may not see. Until he joined forces with us we didn't have a clue as to what type of an individual we were dealing with. Thanks to his ability to find additional clues we now know the killer is an animal lover who is very organized and will no doubt kill again. After we conducted a tour of the other crime scenes it was Chief Blue who told us the killer would strike this winter." Nodding toward the bloody snow, Gephart finished up, "And the killer has struck again...just like Chief Blue said he would. End of conversation. Chief Blue goes in first and we follow." Gephart gave Brody a firm stare which resulted in Axel rolling his eyes.

Sheriff Grimes agreed. "I concur with agent Gephart. William goes in first."

Chief Chapman nodded in agreement. "No problem here."

Brody turned and started for his truck. "Screw all of you. I'm goin' back to Townsend. I don't know why you called me over here in the first place. I'll be damned if I'm goin' to hang around while some medicine man from over the mountain comes over here and takes over!" Hesitating for a moment he looked directly at Grant. "Well, Denlinger are you comin' or not?"

Grant looked at Gephart then responded, "Reckon not, Chief. Sorry, but as long as I'm on Gephart's team, I'll go with what he says."

Shaking his head in disgust Brody turned and stomped off.

No one said a word when the group started toward the house. Stopping just short of the back porch Grimes watched Brody back up, then spin his tires and speed away from the barn. Placing his arm around Grant's shoulder, he whispered, "Ya know, that offer for a position in Maryville still stands."

Grant shook his head in wonder, and then spoke, "I might just be talking to you...real soon."

Chief Blue who had completely ignored Brody's uncalled for outburst addressed the group. "Did anyone think to bring a camera along?"

Snapping his fingers, Grant answered, "Yep, got one in my cruiser. Be right back."

Walking back to his cruiser Grant thought about Brody's actions and what an embarrassment he was as a representative of the Townsend Police Department. He had a lot of thinking to do. Did he really want to work for Axel Brody and continue to put up with his crude mannerisms and methods? Maybe after the first of the year he'd go and speak with Grimes about his offer. Grabbing his camera out of the glove compartment, he checked it to make sure it had enough film then walked back toward the porch. Holding up the camera he announced, "Loaded and ready to go."

"All right then," said William. "I'll go in first. Grant needs to be directly behind me so he can snap off any necessary photos. The rest of you will follow Grant but stay back a few feet."

Chief Blue no sooner opened the screen door than he held up his hand for the group to stop. Pointing at the worn linoleum flooring he spoke, "Grant, snap a few shots of those wet footprints. They probably belong to our killer since Charley wasn't wearing any shoes." While Grant was adjusting his camera William looked around the back porch area. The screened-in porch was crammed with old furniture and boxes leaving only a narrow three foot wide path leading to the kitchen. Satisfied nothing significant happened on the porch he carefully opened the wooden door and looked around the kitchen.

The wet footprints continued into the kitchen. Chief Blue signaled for Grant to take a number of photos of the kitchen floor. As Grant was taking the photos William explained, "The killer entered the house from the back porch a number of times, I'd say at least…three or four times which the wet boot prints indicate." Pointing around the kitchen he went on, "Once in the kitchen the wet prints tell us the killer went to the refrigerator, the cabinets, the sink, the stove and to the table. The fact the floor is still wet from his walking around in here tells us it wasn't that long ago."

When Grant was finished taking pictures William invited the group into the kitchen. Sitting down at the kitchen table William nodded at an empty bowl that contained the remains of what appeared to be tomato soup and a spoon. To the left of the bowl sat an open box of crackers. Noticing an empty can of tomato soup setting on the counter William got up, walked over, opened the microwave, stuck his hand inside and commented, "The microwave is still a little warm which indicates it was used within the last hour and the person who used it was most definitely not Charley Droxler who according to the coroner had to have been outside secured to the fence for nearly two hours. The killer at some point more than likely made some soup and heated it up in the microwave."

Pointing to Grant he ordered, "Take a few shots of the microwave, the empty can and the bowl on the table." He then turned to Gephart. "After the pictures are taken you need to bag up the can, bowl, spoon and box of crackers. Later on we might want to dust for prints although it will probably turn up nothing. I have no doubt the killer wore gloves."

Entering the living room, William smiled and touched the edge of the over turned chair. "There was some sort of a struggle in here. This may have been the room where Charley was abducted." Sitting on an old couch William noticed something on the coffee table. "Grant, didn't you find some sort of tobacco at both the Pittman farm and out at the Henks' residence?"

After snapping a quick photo of the over turned chair, Grant responded, "Yes I did. The owner of a tobacco shop over in Gatlinburg identified it. It's Peach Brandy."

Rubbing his hand over the coffee table then taking his fingers to his nose William spoke again, "There are traces of what I think may be tobacco on this table." Motioning Grant to the table, William offered, "Take a whiff of this and tell me what you think."

Grant, picking up a few granules, placed them beneath his nose. "Yep, same thing...Peach Brandy."

"Bag it up," said William.

Getting up and walking to the bathroom, William signaled Grant to follow. Looking in the door William said, "From the looks of all the water sprayed on the walls and the floor I'd say something unusual happened in here. Not to mention the carpet leading from the bathroom is wet. Charley Droxler may have indeed died out there on the fence, but the whole process started in the house." Looking at the stairs leading to the second floor William suggested, "Let's go upstairs and see what we can find."

Fifteen minutes later the six men gathered back down in the living room. Grimes looked out the front window and asked William, "Well, Chief Blue. What do you think?"

William leaned up against a well-used fireplace. "To begin with if we expect to catch this killer we have to stop focusing on what we think. We have to take what we know and go from there. Thinking is merely based on pure speculation while knowing is based on facts. So what do we know? We know the same person killed all four of the victims. He is trying to tell us in his own bizarre way he will not stand by while animals are mistreated." Giving Gephart the respect he deserved as the agent who was heading up the investigation, William asked, "What's our next move...what's the plan? What do you want to do now, since we have a fourth murder dumped in our laps?"

Gephart sat on one of the kitchen chairs and looked around the room. "You were right, Chief Blue, when you told us the killer would strike again and it would be in the winter. If he continues with the pattern he has followed so far that means he won't strike again until next spring, which is what...four to five months off? That gives us some breathing room. I think a week or so after Thanksgiving we need to get together and really start to focus in on all of the clues we have. I feel we have everything we need in our possession to catch this killer. With Chief Blue's assistance I think we can put together a profile. We already know he is an animal lover and he smokes a pipe. He may live right here in Blount County."

Grimes jumped in on the conversation. "We need to start talking to people in the area that are known animal lovers. For instance, we can talk with people at the various animal clinics in the area. Have they heard anyone speaking about the killer in a favorable way or is there someone who has mentioned the killer is doing the right thing. We can talk with any animal activist groups in the area. We can place adds in the local papers asking if anyone has heard anything or seen anything no matter how insignificant it may seem to contact us."

Grant added a thought of his own. "Maybe we should talk with J.J. Riddick again. It's strange he received that note the night Butch was murdered, especially if the handwriting matches the note found here."

Chapman gestured toward the group. "Does that about wrap things up around here?"

Grimes started for the backdoor. "Believe it does. You all need to get out of here and go on home. Try to have a nice Thanksgiving. Roy and I are going to hang here until we can get some officers up here to tape off the crime scene and blockade the driveway. I'm going to post a couple of officers up here for the next week. When the news about this gets out it'll be a madhouse in Alcoa. We'll have to schedule a press conference for the media. I have a feeling with this fourth murder the news is going to gain national attention."

Standing in the snow just off the back porch, Gephart and Green shook hands with the others, Gephart telling the group he would notify them when the next meeting would take place. Grimes and Chapman walked to the fence and continued to talk about the murder. Grant walked with Chief Blue toward their vehicles. When they were a distance away from the others, Grant stopped William. "Chief Blue. Look, I found something I didn't mention to the others. I wanted to wait until you got here. I just didn't have an opportunity to bring it up." Walking to the spot where he had noticed the oil stain he knelt down and pointed at the black stain in the white snow. "Looks like an oil stain to me. What do you think?"

William knelt down and closely examined the stain. "Yep, that's what it looks like. If you weren't convinced before the killer is driving a vehicle with an oil leak, you should be convinced now. Let's get this stain bagged up. I'll bring it with me to our next meeting." Standing, William looked at the horses. "Think I'll come back over here tomorrow by myself and have another look see. I'm sure there are some things around here we missed." Reaching for Grant's hand, William smiled. "Have a great Thanksgiving. In the next few weeks we're really going to dive into all of this. We'll nail this killer. It's just a matter of time. Gephart's right. We have everything we need to catch him. We just need to figure it all out."

Grant stood and watched Chief Blue climb in his car and drive off down the lane. Turning, Grant looked back at the blood-stained snow where Charley Droxler had faced the killer. Getting in his jeep he thought back to what Dalton had told him the night after Asa Pittman had been murdered: It'll take some time, but sooner or later we'll know who killed Pittman and why. Three murders later and they were still in the dark. How much time would pass? How many others would be murdered before they caught the killer?

CHAPTER TWENTY-TWO

GRANT SAT ON THE BED waiting patiently for Dana Beth. He glanced at his watch. They were already late. Laying back, placing his hands behind his head, he thought about the past week. It had been seven days since the murder of Charley Droxler. The very next day following the murder the media had descended on the town of Alcoa like ants on a leftover piece of cake at a summer picnic. The four murders in the past year had attracted not only the attention of the state, but was now rapidly becoming national news. There was a serial killer on the loose in Blount County, Tennessee, a killer who eliminated those who mistreated animals. While taking the law into one's own hands was against the law, many of the local residents voiced their opinion in favor of this unknown killer saying he was a vigilante of sorts. Finally, someone was setting things right as far as animals were concerned, even though they were doing it in a very brutal way. Someone was doing what a lot of folks just simply talked about: justice for animals.

The last thing Gephart had said to him when they had left Droxler's place was to try and have a nice Thanksgiving and within the next two weeks he, Grant, Chief Blue and Sheriff Grimes would be getting together and discuss everything they had accumulated on the murders. The FBI was working diligently on the case, so along with their help, Gephart expected to solve the murders as quick as possible. He felt the pattern of the killings led him to believe the killer would not strike again until next spring…four to five months away. They had everything they needed to catch the killer. They just had to figure out how to put all of the pieces together and get to him before he killed again.

Getting out of the bed, Grant looked at his watch again. There was no way they were going to get to Dana Beth's parents' house on time. Yelling toward the bathroom door, Grant asked, "How are you doing in there, Babe? Can I get you anything?"

Dana Beth opened the door, holding a wet washcloth on her

forehead. "I'm trying my best to get ready, but I just keep getting sick."

Walking to the bed she sat and laid her head on his shoulder. "I think we're going to have to tell our parents today. If I go to my mom's and she sees me picking at her Thanksgiving dinner, she'll start to worry. She's got enough on her mind with dad not feeling well."

Grant grinned. "Hey, that's fine with me. I can't wait for them to hear the news."

From the bottom of the stairs Dalton's voice boomed, "Grant, we're leaving. We have the pies in the van already. Your mother and I will meet you over at the Pearls. You two better get moving!"

Dana Beth stood up and walked to a large walk-in closet. "Dalton's right. We better get a move on." Removing a soft green dress from a hanger she stated hopelessly, "I thought morning sickness was just...in the morning...not the entire day. I can't wait for this sickness to be over. I can't imagine ever feeling good again."

Grant kissed her on the forehead. "This will all pass and soon you'll be back to your old self. You haven't been much fun to be around lately." He ducked as she slung the washcloth at him.

Dana Beth slipped into a pair of beige shoes, checked her hair in the mirror and then sprayed some perfume on her wrists and neck, turned and said, "Let's hit it!"

Five minutes later Grant pulled the front door shut and locked it. Walking down the steps to the jeep he stopped and asked, "Do you think we need to take a bowl or maybe a bucket along in case you get sick on the way?"

"I think I'm fine now," she answered, climbing into the jeep. "I guess you know next time this year you'll probably be driving a mini van."

The gray overcast morning shielded the sun during the short drive to Dana Beth's parents' house for their first Thanksgiving dinner as a married couple. Looking out the passenger side window, Dana Beth smiled. "I remember when I was younger, one year my father drove us up to Lake Itaska for Thanksgiving. That was before he started working for the university. It was just the three of us. He told us the couple who owned the lodge had invited us up. They really put on a feast. Every year it was a tradition for some of the folks who live on the lake to go to the lodge for Thanksgiving. There were kids running around everywhere. We would go outside and have giant snowball fights and go sledding. We would stuff ourselves with turkey and then sit around the big fireplace eating pie and roasting marshmallows." Just then she turned to Grant and remembered something else. "Remember Rubin, the man we met at the cabin on the lake when we had breakfast up there?"

Grant looked across the seat at her, then answered, "Yeah, I remember him. That lady, Hilda, told us he was on the slow side. Something about how he really wasn't a park ranger, but they had given him a make believe title anyway. What about him?"

"I just remembered he was there that year. He was in charge of making the sticks for the marshmallows. For some reason my father really took a liking to him. He was an odd person, but he had a good sense of humor."

"Well, that's just Conrad. Seems to me he's always been nice to folks. Sounds to me like the folks up at Itaska have a great tradition going on. As time goes by we'll no doubt start some of our own."

Dana Beth was quiet for a moment, watching the scenery of bare trees and brown fields pass by. Touching Grant's knee she spoke, "I would like to ask you a favor before we get to mom and dads."

"Sure, anything…just ask." said Grant.

"Is there anyway we can stay completely away from talking about the murders? I know somebody just might bring it up, but I would really like this to be a day without thinking about all the awful things that have happened this year."

"That'll be easy. Why, with the good news we have to share we won't have any time to think about the murders. I know I need a break from it." Reaching over he placed his hand on hers. "I promise. No talk of murder today."

"Well, it's about time you two got here," said Ruth, opening the front door adorned with a huge fall wreath. "I hope you don't mind I invited Uncle Bill and Aunt Betty and the Colson's from across the street." Cupping her hands around her mouth she leaned forward. "You know, they don't have any family anymore."

Entering the living room Dana Beth was greeted by the wonderful aromas of her mother's cooking. The house smelled of cinnamon and roast turkey. The house had already been decorated for Christmas with a ceramic Nativity scene arranged on the mantle of the fireplace, a strand of garland and hanging green and red satin balls graced the staircase, a seven foot tree sat in the corner, the tinsel and various decorations glimmering from the white and blue lights. Her mother loved the holidays.

Ruth took their coats and hung them in the hall closet as Conrad approached. Kissing his daughter he reached out and shook Grant's hand. "Welcome to our home. Happy Thanksgiving."

Accepting a glass of wine, Grant sat in a chair next to a large picture window and looked around the room. Uncle Bill, Mr. Colson and Dalton were consumed with the highlights of an upcoming football game on the television while Greta, Aunt Betty and Mrs. Colson busied themselves with setting the table. Ruth had pulled out all the stops. She was using her best crystal, china and silverware. Dana Beth asked her mother if she needed anything done. Ruth responded by telling her she could mash the potatoes if she cared to.

Conrad seated himself next to Grant, taking a sip of wine. "So, tell me, Grant. What ever happened to all those horses at the Droxler place? I hoped they were all rescued."

Grant's promise of not talking about the murders hadn't lasted long and Dana Beth had been right that someone would bring the topic up. Not wishing to be rude Grant answered the question, "Franklin Barrett took them in at one of his stables. The humane society reports they'll all survive." Before Conrad could ask another question Grant leaned forward and whispered to his father-in-law. "I promised your daughter we wouldn't talk about the murders today."

Conrad was apologetic, placing his hand on Grant's shoulder. "Of course…let's just concentrate on having a great Thanksgiving."

For the next thirty minutes Grant and Conrad had a number of conversations ranging from how beautiful the fall leaves had been to how his job at the university was going to when the city was going to repair the sidewalks along the parkway. Grant couldn't help noticing the professor looked gaunt and on the pale side. He appeared to have lost a lot of weight lately. Dana Beth had told him her mother was concerned about his health, and now seated across from his father-in-law, Grant could understand why. Finally, their discussion was interrupted as Ruth announced, "If everyone would take a seat at the table dinner will be served."

Conrad and Ruth sat at either end of the table, the Colson's, Uncle Bill, Aunt Betty, Greta, Dalton, Grant and Dana Beth across from each other. The twenty-five pound turkey centered on a sterling silver serving tray was the last item to be placed on the table. Seating herself, Ruth examined the table: homemade stuffing, mashed potatoes, green bean casserole, relish and cheese tray, creamed corn, fresh sliced tomatoes, cranberry salad and hot rolls. Conrad lit the two candles then asked everyone if they would bow their heads while he blessed the food. The blessing complete, he then stood and raised his glass of wine. "I would like to propose a toast. Here is to our new extended family. Dalton, Greta, Grant. We are overjoyed to have you as part of our family. Drink up everyone."

Grant tapped his now empty glass with a spoon and stood, "Dana Beth and I would like to make an announcement before we eat."

Ruth let a loud squeal. "Oh, my goodness, Dana Beth...you're pregnant!"

Dana Beth smiled and nodded, looking at Grant who simply shrugged, realizing Ruth had stolen his thunder.

"I knew it, I just knew it," said Ruth. "I saw you when you pretended to drink your wine and your cheeks are so rosy. There just seems to be a glow about you. I can't believe it. I'm going to be a grandmother!" Looking down the table at her husband she grinned. "Did you hear that, Conrad? Dana Beth is going to have a baby."

"Of course I heard it." Standing he extended his hand to Grant. "Congratulations, you two."

Dalton suddenly blurted out, "I'm going to be a great-grandfather! Seems to me I'm too young for that, but I'll take it."

It was a joyous dinner, everyone consuming lots of great food, except for Dana Beth whose meal consisted of mashed potatoes and a roll. The conversation around the table was equally joyous, topics ranging from how far along Dana Beth was, who her doctor was, did they want a boy or a girl, how big of a family were they planning on in the future.

An hour later, Grant pushed himself away from the table, placing his hands on his over stuffed stomach. "Ruth, the meal was delicious and I can't eat another bite." Ruth smiled and Dana Beth could tell how happy her mother was to be entertaining guests again.

It had been a long time.

Grant stood. "I'm starting a new Thanksgiving tradition. I'm going to help with the dishes." Picking up his plate, then Conrad's, he dropped two forks to the floor.

Ruth started laughing, "Oh, no you don't! You men are too clumsy. Give me my china. You can start a new tradition in your own home. But here today, you're our guests, however since you are offering your services I do have a small chore you can do for me. I have some cans of vegetables and fruit in the kitchen we didn't use. They need to be taken out to the pantry in the garage." Staring at her valuable china he was holding, she emphasized, "I think I can trust you with some cans." Everyone laughed.

Following Ruth to the kitchen, she piled six cans in his arms and turned him toward the side door that led out to the detached three-car garage. Opening the door for him, Ruth smiled. "Now, try not to drop any of those."

Grant backed out the door and took the two steps down to the side driveway. Walking the short distance to the garage he noticed it was starting to spit snow. He balanced five of the cans in his left arm and placed the remaining can under his neck. Opening the garage door he entered and dropped one of the cans which began to roll across the cement floor. Placing the cans on a workbench he flipped on the light and saw the runaway can disappear beneath a large black tarp that ran the length of the garage. Opening the pantry he deposited the cans and started across the garage to collect the can.

Picking up the bottom of the heavy tarp, he reached under trying to grab the can of pumpkin filling but it was no use. The can had rolled further than what he thought. Stooping down, he ducked under the tarp. Standing up he noticed a large object that consumed most of the room. His eyes slowly adjusted to a dim beam of light, filtering down through a small window near the top of the garage. The object slowly started to come into focus. It was a van...a white van. *Strange,* he thought. He never knew the Pearls owned a van. Maybe the professor used it to drive back and forth from Knoxville.

Going down on his knee he looked under the van to see where the can had rolled to, but it was too dark. Then, he remembered a flashlight he had seen on the workbench. Walking back out to the main part of the garage he grabbed the light and turned it on. Grant ducked back under the tarp and went down on his knee again and shined the light under the van. The can had rolled to the other side, but the beam of light displayed something that piqued his interest: an oil stain. *Interesting,* he thought. *An oil stain!* The fact they had found oil stains at Mildred Henks' place, Laurel Lake, J.J.'s junkyard and at Charley's was one of the most important clues they had found. The sight of the oil stain had simply triggered his mind into thinking about the murders. *Just a coincidence.*

Walking around to the back of the van to get to the other side, the beam of light fell on the rear bumper where there was an old sticker: **WILL BRAKE FOR ANIMALS.** Staring at the bumper sticker he recalled seeing that very sticker on the back of a white van twice in the past year. Thinking back, he remembered the night of Asa Pittman's murder he had seen a white van at The Parkway Grocery. He recalled how he could barely see the driver through the rain who had filled up the van and had thrown a bundle of something away in the trash. He had also seen a van with that same bumper sticker again later in the year pulling out of Arby's. *Another coincidence,* he thought.

Grant walked to the other side of the van and shone the light on the floor. The can had rolled all the way to the wall. He picked it up and slowly walked to the front of the van. Stopping at the passenger side window the light illuminated the interior of the van. The familiar aroma of Peach Brandy grabbed his attention. The beam of light fell on a pipe in the console ashtray next to a pouch of tobacco. Then he remembered the night following Asa's murder how he had pulled out behind the van when he had left the Parkway Grocery. The van had pulled over due to the incessant rain. He recalled how he had looked over and saw the opaque image of a man, as he lit a pipe. He was starting to get the strangest feeling.

Opening the van door, the aroma of Peach Brandy hit him again. The same aroma he had smelled at Asa's farm, Mildred's house and Charley's place. Climbing in, he sat back in the seat. What he was thinking just couldn't be true! There had to be a reasonable explanation for all of this.

Turning, he shined the light in the back of the van which illuminated a black gym bag. Further back into the rear of the van something else caught his eye, small pieces of hay scattered on the floor. The sight of the hay caused him to think about the traces of hay he had found at Charley's. Realizing his imagination was starting to get the best of him, he started to turn back around when the circle of light exposed what looked like the corner of a business card stuck to the bottom of the bag. Crawling into the back he grabbed the bag and sat it on the driver's seat, then removed the card from the bottom. It was stained with what appeared to be blood but he could still read it. He read the card aloud:

MILDRED HENKS
REALTOR
1-645-555-9000
593 Old Chilhowee Road
Townsend, Tennessee

Now things were really starting to get strange. What was one of Mildred Henks' business cards, a blood stained card at that, doing in a van in the Pearls' garage? He started to unzip the bag but then pulled his hand back. If what he was thinking, which seemed absurd to him, was true, then he was screwing up evidence. He needed to get some plastic gloves and evidence bags he kept in his jeep and also his camera. Getting out of the van he walked around and ducked under the tarp, realizing he had taken too much time to simply put six cans away in the pantry. He needed to go back inside before he did anything else.

Opening the door leading to the kitchen Grant was instantly questioned by Ruth. "What took you so long? We were beginning to worry."

"I was just getting some air. Actually I think I'm going to grab my coat and take a short walk. I need to walk off some of this food."

Walking into the living room, Ruth's voice sounded behind him, "Don't be too long. We'll be serving pie and ice cream shortly."

Just as he opened the closet door to get his coat, he noticed Conrad was nowhere in sight. Uncle Bill, Mr. Colson and Dalton were all piled up in front of the television watching a game. Grant, concerned that Conrad might go out to the garage asked, "Where is Conrad?"

Dalton, without looking up answered, "Said he wasn't feeling well. Said he was going upstairs to lay down for an hour or so."

Grant grabbed his coat from the closet and walked back into the kitchen. Dana Beth who was placing leftover potatoes into a container asked, "Are you feeling all right?"

"Fine, just fine," said Grant. "Just gonna talk a short walk. I think I ate too much. I'll be back in around fifteen to twenty minutes." Pointing at three pies setting on the counter, he remarked, "Make sure you save me a slice of blueberry."

Outside, he walked to the garage then checked to see if anyone was watching. He quickly went to the front of the house and climbed into the jeep. After removing a pair of plastic gloves, his blue notebook and camera from the glove box he made his way back to the garage.

Grant grabbed the flashlight and ducked beneath the tarp and turned on the light shining it into the front seat where he had left the bag. He walked around the front of the van to the opposite side, opened the door and sat in the passenger seat. Slipping on the gloves, he drew in a deep breath, and then started to unzip the bag. Aiming the flashlight into the bag the beam of light exposed a set of lopping shears with razor sharp edges. *Oh, God, no,* he thought. *Please tell me it's not true!*

Placing the shears on the seat next to the bag, he then discovered a roll of duct tape, a hypodermic needle, a pair of gloves, several large plastic bags, a pocketknife and an unmarked small bottle of clear liquid. Unscrewing the cap on the bottle he took a short whiff. He jerked his head back quickly, the strong odor making his dizzy. *Chloroform,* he guessed. Removing everything from the bag, he shined the light on the canvas interior. It was stained in two different areas with a dark brownish red stain. *Were they old blood stains?* He knew the answer to his own question.

He looked around the van and took a deep breath. Picking up the tobacco pouch he opened it and took a few granules between his fingers. Taking them to his nose there was no mistake. The aroma was identical to the scent he had discovered at Asa, Mildred and Charley's place. Closing the bag he returned it to the console. *There's no way,* he thought. *Professor Pearl is a sweet, gentle man. There has to be some mistake or maybe even a logical explanation. The evidence is all here. The lopping shears, duct tape, hypodermic needle, bottle of chloroform, probable blood stains inside the bag, and most important of all, one of Mildred Henks' business cards which appeared to be blood stained. Then there's the pipe and the tobacco...not to mention the oil stain.*

He needed answers. Opening the glove compartment he rifled through a small stack of papers. Finally he came to what he was searching for. Slowly he unfolded the vehicle registration form. The owner of the vehicle was Conrad Pearl. Realizing he had to get back to the house before they sent someone to look for him, he replaced the documents back where he found them and closed the glove compartment. Placing everything back inside the bag, including the pipe he turned off the flashlight. He got out of the van and took the bag with him back out to the main part of the garage. He glanced at the house to make sure no one was watching as he walked quickly to the jeep where he slid the bag under an old quilt he kept in the back.

Back at the side door of the house he took several deep breaths trying to control himself. When he got back inside he couldn't let on he had experienced anything other than a brisk walk. Opening the door, he smiled and announced, "I'm back."

"About time," said Dalton who was standing next to the pies. "If I don't get a piece of pie soon I'll have withdrawals."

"Just let me hang up my coat up and use the little boy's room then we can dig in."

Inside the bathroom, Grant looked around for something that would have Conrad's fingerprints on it. It was the downstairs bath, probably seldom used by the family. There were no toothbrushes, combs, brushes…nothing except guest towels, a scented candle and bowl of colorful marbles. Then he remembered: *Conrad's wine glass!*

Flushing the commode, he turned on the faucet to make it sound good, waited a few seconds then walked back into the living room. Dalton was still in the kitchen with all of the women, Uncle Bill and Mr. Colson had their backs to him as they concentrated on the television. Looking at the coffee table situated in front of where Conrad had been seated Grant said silently to himself, "Thank goodness, the wine glass is still there."

Nonchalantly, he walked to the table, making sure no one was looking in his direction. He picked up the glass and walked to the closet. It only took a few seconds for him to open the closet door and deposit the glass inside his coat pocket. Closing the closet door now all he had to do was figure out how to smuggle the glass out to the jeep. Checking again, everyone's attention was either on the television or on the kitchen. He could be out to the jeep and back in less than a minute. He walked to the front door, opened it, crossed the porch and down the steps to his jeep parked in the drive.

Opening the rear door he placed the glass beneath the old quilt, closed the door and returned to the house. Climbing the porch steps he thought, *That was easy.*

When he reached for the doorknob on the front door he was interrupted by a voice, "Grant, come join me."

Turning, Grant saw Conrad wrapped in an afghan sitting on a rocking chair at the end of the porch. In his hand he held a steaming cup of hot chocolate. Grant, taken by surprise thought, *Did he see me take the glass to the jeep? If he did, how am I going to explain my actions?* Grant walked across the porch trying to act as if nothing had happened. "Conrad, I thought you went upstairs to lay down for awhile."

"Changed my mind. I thought I'd just sit out here for a spell." Gesturing at the large trees in the front yard he explained, "I've always enjoyed sitting out here, especially the fall. It's my favorite time of the year." Pointing toward a chair, Conrad suggested, "Have a seat. I'd like to talk with you about something."

Grant's mind was racing as he sat down. *What does Conrad want to speak to me about? His favorite time of the year, the great dinner we had, the weather, Dana Beth's pregnancy ...or his observation of his new son-in-law stealing one of his wife's crystal wine glasses?* Trying his best to avoid having the dreaded wine glass discussion, Grant looked out at the huge maple trees in the front yard as he commented, "The leaves were really awesome this year, but they are almost all down now." He could feel his insides shaking, but he had to remain calm.

Conrad took a sip of his chocolate, then coughed getting Grant's attention. "Grant, if I've learned anything over the years, especially as a college professor, it's just this: things are not always as they appear. Just because you see something...unusual, doesn't give a person the right to assume anything. It's always important to ask questions first, to collect all of the information available before coming to a conclusion." Looking out at Grant's jeep, he had a strange look on his face, then continued, "I just saw you do something a minute ago that I don't quite understand."

Grant remained quiet, not quite sure what Conrad was getting at.

Setting the hot chocolate on a small table, Conrad hesitated, but then asked, "Why would you be putting one of my wife's wine glasses in the back of your jeep? I'm sure there's a logical explanation. It's just rather strange."

There was no way Grant could explain away what Conrad had witnessed. He had planned on taking the glass to the station the following day and run fingerprints from the glass and compare them to those that he might find on any of the evidence he had found in the garage. If the prints matched he was going to take a few days and sort things out before he approached Conrad, but that was not the way things were working out. It was only ten minutes ago that he had been in the garage and now here he was—facing Conrad Pearl, his father-in-law, possibly the killer they were looking for. There was nothing Grant could do but be completely honest.

"You're right, Conrad. Things are not always as they appear. I did take one of your wife's wine glasses. It's the one you drank from and before I assume anything I have to ask you some questions, collect all the information as you say before coming to a conclusion."

Grant hesitated; realizing that what he was about to do wasn't going to be easy. What if he was wrong? Maybe someone else drove the van. Maybe there was something he was missing. He had found all of the pieces of the puzzle, but the one piece that just didn't seem to fit was the fact that Conrad Pearl was the killer.

Conrad shifted in his chair making himself more comfortable. Just as Grant was about to speak, Conrad held up his hand, stopping him. "You seem uncomfortable...sort of on edge. You see, I already know why you took the glass." Looking back out at the trees in the front yard, then at Grant's jeep, he continued, "You want to see if my fingerprints match up with the items you found in the gym bag from the garage."

Grant's mouth dropped open. He was completely taken off guard. He felt like he was out of his league. How could he possibly converse with Conrad about the fact that the clues he had discovered pointed toward him as the killer? He was just a high school graduate, a young man who hadn't even finished college yet. Conrad was a successful professor at a well-known university, a man who was used to dealing with people Grant's age. He stumbled for the right thing to say, "Look, Conrad, I...well...you see..."

Conrad interrupted his feeble attempt to communicate. "I saw you not only place the wine glass in the back of your vehicle but also the gym bag. You didn't see me looking out the upstairs window. Your mind must be filled with questions that you need answers for. A few moments ago you agreed with me saying it was important to collect all information available before assuming anything. So, what would you like to ask me? Am I a murderer? I was quite clever, don't you agree? Four murders and not one of you, not even the FBI could solve the cases. Oh yes, I planned them well." He stopped for a moment. "You're looking at me as if I were insane, Grant. I am you know. Have been for years. I had quite a bit of therapy in my younger years, but I was finally able to control my psychosis. At times it would flare up and I would have to go away by myself on a fishing trip for awhile to allow it to pass." A strange smirk crossed his face.

Grant took a deep breath, realizing that once he crossed this bridge there would be no turning back. "Conrad, as your son-in-law I feel guilty about the way I feel after finding certain things out there in the garage, but then again as an officer of the law, I hope you understand I have to do my job. I just can't sidestep the things I discovered." He was too nervous to remain seated, so he stood and walked to the porch railing. "When Ruth sent me out to the garage with those cans, I dropped one of them. It rolled under that tarp you have out there. I discovered a white van, which at first really didn't ring a bell for me. But then, when I knelt down to retrieve the can I noticed and oil stain under the van. It got me to thinking about the fact we found oil stains at Mildred Henks place, Laurel Lake, J.J.'s Junk Emporium and then at Charley Droxler's. I blew it off as a coincidence. Then I saw the bumper sticker on the back of the van: WILL BRAKE FOR ANIMALS. I recalled how the night following Asa Pittman's death I saw a white van with that very sticker over at the Parkway Grocery. The driver threw a bundle of some sort into the trash, then lit up a pipe. I saw the van again later in the year pulling out of a fast food place. I just thought it was another coincidence."

Looking out at the falling leaves, Grant, without facing Conrad continued with what he had discovered, "Walking around to the other side of the van to get the can I passed the passenger side window which just happened to be rolled down. An aroma that I have become quite familiar with came from inside the van: Peach Brandy smoking tobacco. The reason I have become familiar with this brand of tobacco is because we found traces of it in Asa Pittman's kitchen, Mildred Henks' living room and Charley Droxler's kitchen. It became very obvious to us the killer smokes a pipe and that his tobacco of choice is Peach Brandy."

Grant turned back facing Conrad. "I don't know what caused me to climb into the van, but I did. I saw a pipe and a pouch of tobacco. I shined the flashlight I had around in the back of the van and discovered some loose hay. Things just started to add up. We found traces of hay where bales had been dragged across the snow to feed the horses up at Charley's place the day he had been murdered. I also found an old gym bag. I opened it and found a set of lopping shears, some gloves, duct tape, a knife, a hypodermic needle and a small bottle of what smelled like chloroform. On the bottom of the bag I found one of Mildred Henks' business cards. The fact that the card was blood stained really got me to thinking so I went through the glove compartment to see who owned the van. I really prayed the vehicle was not yours, that maybe you were just renting space in the garage to the owner, but the registration confirmed that you own the van. I took the bag along with the wine glass to see if the fingerprints matched." Grant was feeling uneasy with what he had indicated. He returned to the chair, sat and asked, "Conrad, please tell me that the fingerprints won't match."

"I can't tell you that," said Conrad, "but I do want to share a very interesting story with you. A little over forty years ago when I was ten years old, my brother and I, who was eight at the time lived with our folks over in Johnson County in the eastern part of the state. We lived in the middle of nowhere up in the Iron Mountains, about twelve miles from Mountain City. My father, Millard Pender and his wife Etta were tough mountain people. My father worked out of an old barn. He was a self-taught mechanic of sorts and was known throughout the region as a man who could fix anything that had an engine. He also made the best moonshine in that part of the country. My mother made homemade elixirs from herbs and roots, which she took to town to sell. We didn't have much, but we got by. The year I was ten, my brother and I were up in a fort we had built in a big oak tree that stood at the corner of my father's property."

A stiff breeze blew across the porch, Conrad pulling the afghan up around his neck as he continued, "We were just sitting up there in that tree talking about this and that when we heard voices. It was a nasty November day during hunting season as I recall: windy and cold, not to mention the rain and sleet. Well, we look down and we see four hunters approaching. They were talking and laughing loud. That didn't make any sense if you wanted to bag a deer. The least little bit of noise will spook a deer and send him off running.

"When they were directly under the tree, we could hear every word they were saying. They were talking about what a lousy day it had turned out to be. The weather was horrible and they hadn't even seen a single deer. The more they talked the more they got upset and it was then that we realized they were drunk. They were acting stupid, pushing each other around and almost falling over which was something my brother and I were used to seeing. Our father was drunk most of the time. He beat our mother and was always knocking us around. He could be quite violent and even when he was sober he didn't take any crap from anyone. He was a mean son of a gun. My brother and I hated our parents. My mom would always stick up for my father no matter how much he beat on us and she took food away from us when we didn't do exactly what they wanted. I guess that's why my brother and I loved our animals so much.

"Anyway, the four men walk up to the corner of our father's property which he had fenced off with barbed wire. That particular corner of our property is where my father pitched everything he had no use for. He had an old school bus, a rusted out dump truck and a bunch of old dilapidated cars he had hauled down there. There were a number of old appliances, some old furniture and a large number of cans and bottles scattered around. Before you know it one of the hunters started to take pot shots at the school bus. In a matter of seconds all four of the men were shooting at my father's junk pile. They were laughing as they passed a bottle of some sort of alcohol around. Each time a gun went off, we could hear glass shattering and the ricochet of bullets off the bus.

"Suddenly, from out of nowhere our father pops out of the forest with our three hunting dogs. My father raised his shotgun and fired over their heads and ordered them to get away from his land as it was posted as No Hunting. The men argued with him saying that they were not shooting at any game, just a bunch of junk. My father informed them the junk they were shooting at belonged to him and that they best move along before he turned the dogs loose. They continued to argue with him and then he let loose with another blast from the shotgun that hit right in front of the men. My father then explained to them that they had no right to come up onto this side of the mountain, it was private property. He told them that he had his own brand of justice and if they didn't hightail it out of there they'd be shot and dragged off to some ravine where they would never be found. Three of the men continued to yell at my father but the fourth man who didn't seem to be drinking as much convinced the others they should leave. Following a lot of cursing and obscene gestures the men walked down the fence line. By that time we had climbed down from the tree, ran down the fence line and climbed another tree."

Grant, sitting there, started to wonder if this story was going anywhere, but then remembered what they had taught him at school in Connecticut: *Your ears are one of the most important tools that you possess...so listen carefully.*

Conrad rambled on as if what he was explaining was happening now...not forty years in the past, but now. "The men stopped right under the tree we had climbed at the opposite end of our property. They were still cursing my father and complaining to one another how horrible the day had turned out when the skies opened up and a freezing rain set in, which only made things worse. We had a pen near the edge of the property where we were raising two fawns whose mother had been killed by hunters. The men no sooner came up on the pen than one of the men raised his rifle and shot one of the fawns. The first fawn no sooner dropped than the second was shot by one of the other men. It was so senseless and cruel. They were laughing and pointing at those innocent animals, all except for the one man who seemed stunned by what they had done. Tears came to my eyes as I hopelessly watched from the tree. We had raised those fawns. My brother and I had sat up at night trying to keep them warm and feeding them with a bottle. Then, things got worse as the man who shot the first fawn, just kept reloading and shooting at everything in sight. He took aim and shot our horse that was grazing nearby. About this time my father comes running out of the trees. He never said a word. He just drew a bead on one of the men and shot him in the arm. His second shot grazed one of the others in the lower left leg and then all hell broke loose. The hunters panicked and reacted as they shot back at my father. He never even had a chance to reload. They killed him where he stood and when the dogs came running at them they shot all three a number of times. My mother hearing all the commotion came running down from the house, screaming. She bent down by my father and picked up his gun and aimed at the man. In the next second she grabbed her chest and fell to the ground shot right through the heart. My brother and I were frozen up in the tree, afraid to make a move. After a few seconds the men realized what they had done. They began to argue with each other, one saying that it was an accident, another agreeing saying that they had no choice; the old man was going to kill them. One of the men said they should contact the police. The two men who had been shot were not in agreement pointing out that they were in the middle of nowhere and they had to get the hell out of there. The last thing were heard them say as they were leaving was that they were not going to the police and they would never speak of this again. After they left my brother and me stayed up in that tree all night in the freezing rain. We were just too scared to climb down. We thought we would freeze to death but we made it through the night. The next morning we ran four miles down to the nearest neighbor and told them what had happened.

"An hour or so later the local police from Mountain City came up and drove us back to our place. We really didn't want to go but they said we had to. They asked us to identify the men but all we could tell them was they were dressed as hunters. They all wore dark tan coveralls and tan hunting jackets. They all had hats, with the earflaps down, covering most of their faces.

"We didn't have any kin that we knew of so we stayed with a widow lady down near town. There was an investigation but with all the hunters running around the area the law came up empty handed. Two months later, the widow lady died and we went to an orphanage that was in Mountain City. We stayed there for about two years when a couple by the name of Pearl finally adopted us and took us to live in Knoxville.

"The Pearl's were nice folks and we lived with them for years, however, I never forgot what those men had done to our family, especially the animals. I vowed that some day I was going to get even with people who mistreated animals. Eventually, I graduated from high school and went to college and got a degree in teaching. I met Ruth in college, we got married, then years later I acquired a job as a professor in Knoxville." Conrad shivered as he coughed three times in a row, then took a drink of the chocolate.

Grant waited for his father-in-law to say something else but Conrad remained quiet as he stared out at the yard. Finally, Grant spoke, "That's quite a story. I'm not really sure why you told it to me. You said you never forgot what those men did to your family and that you had vowed to get even with people who mistreat animals. I guess my question is, did you in fact get even by committing the four murders we've had this past year, and why now after all these years?"

"There's more to the story," said Conrad. "Back about a year and a half I went to a friend of mine who is a doctor in Knoxville. I hadn't been feeling well for some time. I was diagnosed with pancreatic cancer; third stage. My friend informed me that with radiation and specialized treatment my life could be extended, but the cancer would more than likely not be stopped but slowed down. He told me I had about a year, maybe two years to live. I declined treatment and never said a word to Ruth or Dana Beth about my illness. With the short time I had left I decided to live up to what I had promised myself. So, this past year, I guess you could say that I have struck a blow for animals. So, to answer your question, did I commit the four murders this past year? Let me put it this way. I've got maybe a month to live...maybe less. When I die the murders will stop...there will be no more murders."

Grant sat in silence, not quite sure what he was supposed to say.

Conrad reached over and touched Grant on the knee. "I know this must be difficult for you. Your silence is an indication that you don't know how to react to what I have told you. You really don't need to say anything else, but you do have to decide what it is that you are going to do now. You can report what you have discovered here today to the proper authorities tomorrow morning at which point they'll come to my home, arrest me and haul me off to jail.

"Chances are I won't serve much time, if any at all. With each day that passes I get weaker. Who knows, my incarceration may be in a hospital bed while I'm under guard until I fade away. Whatever happens to me now, well, it doesn't make much of a difference. But you, young man...you've got a choice to make."

Grant moved forward on his chair. "A choice you say. What choice do I have? I, along with everyone else who has been involved in this case, have been struggling to solve the murders. Today out there in that garage I had all the clues that are needed to wind this thing up dumped right in my lap. When you combine that with what you have told me...what choice do I have? I'm an officer of the law and I took an oath to do my job to the best of my ability. I don't see where I have a choice."

"It's simple, Grant. You can walk in the Townsend Police Station tomorrow armed with all of the clues that you need to solve the case. You'll be a hero in the eyes of everyone in town, in the county, the state. Why hell…you'll probably get national attention. It'll be great for your future career. But, are you willing to ruin other people's lives in doing so?"

Grant shook his head in confusion. "All right, now you've lost me, Conrad."

"Think about it. What is going to happen to my wife, Ruth and then there's Dana Beth. How will they be able to live with what I have done hanging over their heads for the rest of their lives? Then there's Dana's pregnancy. How will the news affect her? You also have to consider your future children. Do you want them to go through life knowing that their grandfather was a killer?"

Grant thought for a moment, then spoke, "What other choice do I have. I have sworn to uphold the law."

"And I admire you for that," said Conrad, "but once again is it worth it to hurt those you love?"

With a look of amazement on his face Grant responded, "Maybe you should have thought of that before you went ahead with the murders."

"I thought about it plenty of times, but with the way I felt it was difficult to lead what most folks would describe as a normal life. Somehow I always managed to hide my feelings of revenge from my wife and daughter. Like I said earlier, whenever my feelings started to flare up I'd go away on a fishing trip and then it would pass. It was on my last trip that I started to pick my victims and plan their murders. Grant, it's hard to explain. It's something that's been eating away at me for over forty years. Actually, I'm at peace with what I have done. I'm sure with your police training that you're familiar with the term psychopath. Some people say you are born with it, others say it stems from a traumatic occurrence in your life. Either way, I fit the pattern. Psychopaths can lead a normal most of the time. I love my family and I would never hurt them, but I have very little empathy for most people, especially those who are cruel to animals. Trust me, Grant, I held my illness at bay as long as I cared to."

Grant rubbed his hand across his forehead. "Earlier you said I had a choice. What other choice do I have other than to report what I have discovered? You need help, Conrad. Serious help."

"It's too late for that," remarked Conrad. "You can just let things play out. I'll be dead in a month or so, the murders will stop and

Ruth and Dana Beth will never know the truth. As far as the murders are concerned they will just remain unsolved."

Grant got up and walked to the porch railing. "I've got to tell you, Conrad. That's a lot to drop on a person. It's a lot to ask. You're suggesting that I compromise my integrity for the sake of your wife and daughter. I mean, if I do what you are suggesting, I'll have to live with what I've done,for the rest of my life."

Conrad stood and folded the afghan and picked up his mug of hot chocolate. "Either way, it's your decision. All I can say is whatever your decision turns out to be, it'll be okay with me. You have to decide what's right for all involved, then move on with your life." Placing his hand on Grant's shoulder Conrad spoke softly, "Thank you for marrying my daughter. I believe you are a good man and I can go to my grave knowing that she will be well taken care of. Thanks for coming by for Thanksgiving. I'm not feeling very well at all. Think I'll go up and lay down for a bit."

Grant stood and watched Conrad walk back inside the house. Through the front window he saw Conrad climb the stairs to the bedroom. Turning he looked back out across the yard. He had some serious thinking to do before tomorrow morning. What was he going to do? He was stunned. *Dammit, Conrad Pearl. I hate you for what you have done to your family and me. You're a cold-blooded killer and now I bear that burden on my shoulders and you're telling me thanks for coming to your home for Thanksgiving. You are a psychopath.* He was shaking all over, his fists were clenched and he wanted to run upstairs and drag Conrad out of bed and tell everyone what he had done. He knew one thing. He had to get Dana Beth and head on home. He wasn't going to be able to hang around the house much longer. He knew someone would eventually realize he was acting strange.

Walking back into the house he entered the kitchen trying to sound as casual as possible. "Ya know what folks? I hate to be a party pooper, but I think I'll take my lovely wife home."

"But Grant," said Ruth in a disappointed tone, "It's still early. You haven't even had pie."

Grant lied, "My stomach is a little upset…that's all. I'd like to have a slice of pie, but the way I feel I really don't think I'd enjoy it. How about if I come by tomorrow and have a piece of all three?"

There was a moment of silence. Grant thought to himself: *Am I sounding convincing? What I'd really like to do is run upstairs and ring Conrad's neck. No, stay calm. Just get out of the house!*

Dana Beth came to his rescue, remarking, "I'm feeling kind of tired myself, Mom. I think I'd just like to go home and put my pajamas on and slip into bed. I hope you don't mind."

"Well, I suppose if that's what you want," said Ruth, looking into the living room where Uncle Bill and Mr. Colson had fallen asleep in front of the television. "Looks like everyone is ready for bed."

Grant turned to get their coats when Dalton commented, "I'm not budging from this kitchen. I for one am wide awake and ready for pie!"

Returning with the coats Grant helped Dana Beth into hers as she spoke to her mother, "Tell dad we said good bye and I love him."

CHAPTER TWENTY-THREE

IN THE JEEP, Dana Beth laid her head back and yawned. "I'm really tired. I'm glad we're going home." Fastening her seatbelt she asked, "Grant, are you upset with me for some reason? You haven't said a word to me since we left the house."

"Heck no," said Grant. "I could never be mad at you. I was just thinking about the baby. Your parents seemed quite pleased. And Dalton, well his reaction was more than I expected. My mom surprised me though. She didn't have all that much to say."

"She already knew," remarked Dana Beth as she reached for a Kleenex from her purse. "Last week she asked me if I was pregnant. I couldn't shield my excitement. She promised she wouldn't let on until we decided to make the announcement."

Changing the subject, Grant wanted to find exactly what Dana Beth knew about her father. "I didn't know your family owned a van. When I went out to the garage I dropped a can of pumpkin filling and it rolled under that tarp. I saw the van that's parked out there."

"Oh, that old thing. My father has had it for years. I've only been in it a few times and that was years ago when I was younger. My mother has never driven it. I can't even remember the last she rode in it. My dad uses it to run errands and stuff like that. Every year when he makes his fishing trip up to Lake Itaska he drives the van. To tell you the truth, I forgot it was even out there in the garage."

Turning onto the driveway to the farm, Grant parked the jeep in front of the house. Getting out he opened the door and commented, "I'm going to take something for my stomach and then I might watch T.V. for awhile."

Dana Beth climbed out of the car, yawning. "Like I said, I'm going to turn in."

Ten minutes later, Dana Beth snuggled in bed, Grant tucked her in and kissed her on the cheek. "Listen, I'm going downstairs. Might make myself a cup of coffee. I'll be up in about an hour. Good night."

Downstairs in the kitchen, he dumped a small of amount of coffee into the coffee maker, then added water, and sat down at the table. He felt guilty for lying to not only his wife but to Ruth as well. There was no way with what he knew about Conrad that for at least the moment, he could be honest with them. It was turning out to be a very unusual Thanksgiving. He imagined most people were with their families eating dessert and watching football, but yet, here he was sitting alone in his grandfather's kitchen trying to convince himself that what he had discovered just couldn't be true. But it was true. Conrad, in so many words, in a round about way had confessed to the murders. To even think Conrad had killed Asa Pittman, Mildred Henks, Butch Miller and Charley Droxler was hard to imagine.

Getting up he checked the coffee, but it wasn't ready. He walked to the window and noticed large flakes of snow starting to fall. Staring out the window Grant knew that Conrad had to be more than just mentally unbalanced; he was a psychopath. As he stood there he recalled how the victims had been murdered. It had been brutal. Conrad had to be sick and the sickness went far beyond the fact that he had cancer. How could a rational man, a man in his right frame of mind commit such heinous murders? If what Conrad told him was true, about what he and his younger brother had witnessed from up in that tree forty years in the past, Grant could understand how they had been affected. Both of their parents shot and killed right before their very eyes, not to mention the two fawns, their horse and three dogs, which they obviously loved more than their parents. What was it Conrad said? He and his brother had stayed up in that tree all night in the freezing rain ,scared to death.

He thought about the fact that Butch and Dana Beth had dated. He had no idea of what Conrad thought about Miller. But, even if he didn't approve of him, to think that the professor had cut his fingers off and then left him behind to be mutilated by the junkyard dogs. Grant felt a shiver go through him. He thought about ol' Charley Droxler and how he looked hanging on that fence. He started to think about Asa when a buzzer sounded on the coffee maker indicating that the brew was ready. Removing a mug from the cupboard he poured himself a cupful, added sugar then walked into the living room.

Sitting on the couch in the dark, Grant remembered what his professors in school taught him about solving a crime; about how when everything came together and a case was solved what a great sense of accomplishment there was. He had, for some reason, just simply stumbled on a number of clues that indicated who the killer was. Conrad, himself, had admitted to the murders. He had, in essence solved the murders but there was no sense of accomplishment. There was only deep sadness and the burden of what he should do next.

He sipped at the coffee but it was too hot. He thought about what Chief Blue said about the killer. He was not a maniac, but a person who was well organized and felt that he was justified in killing those who mistreated animals. William had also stated that something had happened to the killer sometime in the past...something the killer could not get past...would not forget. He also said the killer had waited until something happened in his life that caused him to finally act.

William's profile fit Conrad perfectly. He was definitely an organized individual and seemed perfectly sane. In Conrad's mind, based upon what he had witnessed as a child, those he had killed deserved to die. The unfortunate invasion of cancer in his life had been the catalyst that spurred him to finally take action. To think that Conrad, hours earlier, had shaken hands with him, the same hands that had wielded those lopping shears, the same hands that had stuffed Mildred Henks into that dog cage, the hands that had tortured Asa Pittman and had thrown Butch into the junkyard sent a chill through his body. The more he thought about it the more squeamish he became. Conrad Pearl, the killer, had hugged his daughter and congratulated them on their upcoming child. Dalton's headlights coming down the drive distracted his pattern of thinking. He really didn't want to talk with his mother or Dalton. He was too upset. His mother, especially, would notice that something was wrong and he didn't feel like lying to anyone else.

Dana Beth was fast asleep when he entered the bedroom. Mentally, he was drained. He turned on a small table light and sat in the recliner next to the window and stared at his sleeping wife. How would he ever be able to break the news to her that her father was the killer? Opening his Bible, he only managed to get through three pages as he struggled with what he would do the next morning.

Closing the Bible he closed his eyes and prayed, *Dear Lord, I have no idea what I'm going to do. Give me a sign.* He was so tired, he couldn't think straight. Finally, minutes later his eyes succumbed to the need for rest.

It was five-forty-five in the morning and Grant was nowhere close to making a decision on what he should do than what he was the night before. He felt so stiff. Sleeping in the old recliner was the worst thing he could have done. Even the hot shower he had taken didn't seem to ease the pain in his neck and right side.

Tapping his fingers on the kitchen table he stared at the cup of coffee sitting in front of him. Taking a sip, he made a face. It had grown cold. Walking to the sink he dumped out the cold liquid and poured himself a fresh cup. Standing at the kitchen window he looked out at the darkness of the early morning. He thought about the past year and how he had been running around like a chicken with its head cut off looking for the killer, and later on in the day it would all finally come to an end. The only problem was he didn't know which ending it would be because he still hadn't made his decision. He just couldn't make up his mind as to what he should do. He had considered talking the whole thing over with Dalton, but then he would be getting someone else involved in a decision that he and he alone had to make. He thought about all the people involved in the murders and their efforts to locate the killer. He remembered what Jeff Bookman had said to him up at Laurel Lake after they had discovered Mildred Henks' body. Jeff had told him he knew that Grant would do everything he could to catch the killer *and now* here he was Grant Denlinger, the most unimportant person involved in the case. He possessed proof beyond doubt that Conrad Pearl was the killer. Chief Brody, Sheriff Grimes, the park police, the state police, the Feds, even Chief Blue had struggled to piece the puzzle of the four murders together. He had discovered the missing pieces and had in all actuality solved the case. Now, all he had to do was turn over what he had discovered to Brody or the FBI.

Taking a drink of coffee he realized it wasn't as easy as it sounded. How could he ever live with himself if he turned in Conrad? Would Dana Beth ever forgive him or would she agree with him? Her father was a cold-blooded killer. It would kill Ruth to know the truth. It was easy to see the way they acted around each other that she dearly loved the man after thirty years of marriage.

And then there was the new baby who would have to grow up with the stigma that his or her grandfather was a serial killer. Everyone Conrad had killed probably deserved to die, at least as far as animal lovers were concerned, but who made Conrad judge and jury?

Realizing he wasn't getting anything accomplished standing in the kitchen, he headed back to the summerhouse. Tiptoeing into the bedroom he pulled back the covers and kissed Dana Beth on her cheek. Turning, he walked out of the room thinking that this might be the last time he ever saw her that peaceful. The future of his wife, his mother-in-law, his new baby, Townsend and the surrounding area—even his own future rested on the decision he had to make.

Townsend was asleep. The stoplight at Wears Valley Road blinked yellow: on and off. It was just starting to rain. The stores were not open yet, their neon lights of red, blue and green cast an eerie glow out onto the damp street. It was Black Friday, normally a quiet day in Townsend when most of the locals would be driving over to Gatlinburg or Pigeon Forge for great deals and specials on holiday gifts. In just a few hours tourists and locals alike would be up and ready to enjoy the biggest shopping day of the year.

It really was a black Friday for Grant. Today his life was going to change forever. He had made his decision on the way into town. He was an officer of the law. He had sworn his duty to protect the citizens of Townsend. He had taken an oath. Sure, it would be easy to turn his back and not report what he had discovered about Conrad, but how could he live with himself?

Turning down Tiger Street, he glanced to the left, viewing the Townsend Police Station and a few buildings down the street on the right sat the building where the FBI had set up their temporary headquarters. Stopping in the middle of the street he stared at both buildings. Bowing his head, he was having second thoughts about turning Conrad in. He mumbled a short prayer: *"Lord, if you're listening to me...give me a sign. Show me what I must do."*

Pulling into the station lot, he couldn't imagine Chief Brody displaying any type of sympathy for the situation Grant found himself in. He could just see it. If he reported to Brody that Conrad was the killer, Brody, after spewing out his usual line of profanity would run out of the office, jump in his truck, turn on his flashing, lights, hit the siren and speed directly to the Pearl residence where after knocking loudly on the front door would cuff Conrad and haul him off leaving Ruth wondering what was going on.

The FBI would be much more professional. He could see them walking up to the house, ringing the bell. When someone answered the door they would flip out their badges. He could image what they would say: 'Conrad Pearl...you're under arrest for suspicion of four counts of murder.' Sitting in his jeep the very thought of what would happen was making him sick to his stomach. He felt like he was going to throw up.

Brody wasn't even in yet. It was way too early. Getting out of the jeep, he decided to take a walk up through the main part of town. It would be another hour before the station was open. He wondered if Dana Beth was up yet. She and his mother had planned on going into Pigeon Forge for a day of shopping. Would she wonder where he had gone so early? He had left her a note saying that he had to run an errand. What else could he say? Good morning sweetness. I love you. I'm on my way to turn your father in. He's the killer!

He remembered her horror when she read about each one of the murders. She had even remarked how she couldn't understand how anyone could be so cruel to another human being. If the killer wanted them dead, then why didn't they just shoot them instead of all the torture? Maybe that was a question she would have to ask her father. And what about her pregnancy? What kind of trauma would the news about her father have on her health—and the baby?

Grant hadn't realized how far he had walked. He was soaked from the rain. Turning around to head back to the station he noticed a small parade of cars heading out for a day of shopping. Soon he found himself standing in front of the police station, Brody's truck parked in front. It was then that he decided. He would report everything that he had discovered or knew to the Feds. Walking a half block he stood in front of the FBI Headquarters. Gephart's green sedan was parked on the side of the building. Stopping at the front door Grant took a deep breath and reached for the doorknob when his cell phone rang.

Pulling his phone from his pocket he looked at the glowing screen. It was Dana Beth.

"Hello, Dana Beth?"

There was silence, then his wife's voice, "Grant."

Grant could tell she was upset...crying. "What's wrong Dana Beth?"

"Grant, my mother just called. My father suffered a heart attack. He...died...about an hour...ago. Please come home. We need to get over to my parents' house."

Grant removed his hand from the doorknob. "On my way."

Running down the street, he climbed into the jeep, but then it hit him. He had asked the Lord to give him a sign. Conrad Pearl had died. The murders were now going to stop. There just didn't seem to be much sense in turning in Conrad now. He was gone and Dana Beth, Ruth and their new baby would never have to live with the fact that Conrad was the killer. Time would heal the wounds of the citizens of Townsend. When spring came and there were no more murders, the last year would just be something that they would talk about for a long time, but at least never have to experience again. Turning on the windshield wipers he thought, *The Lord works in mysterious ways. He had been given the sign he asked for.*

About the Authors

Originally from St. Louis, Marlene makes her home in Kentucky now. A mother and grandmother, Marlene has a wide range of interests including watercolor and oil painting, yet writing has always been her passion. That comes through loud and clear in her wonderful novels!

These novels reflect a genuine sincerity with very strong characters to which her readers can relate. To quote Marlene: "It took me a long time to start writing, but now I can't stop. The stories just keep on coming."

Gary Yeagle was born and raised in Williamsport, Pa., the birthplace of Little League Baseball. He grew up living just down the street from the site of the very first Little League game, played in 1939.

He currently resides in Louisville, Kentucky, with his wife and four cats. He is the proud grandparent of three and is an active member of the Jeffersontown United Methodist Church. Gary is a Civil War buff, and enjoys swimming, spending time at the beach, model railroading, reading and writing.

Excerpt from Echoes of Death:

THREE DAYS AFTER THANKSGIVING, Conrad Pearl was put to rest in the Bethel Cemetery in Townsend, Tennessee. Under a grey, overcast sky, the six pallbearers carried his coffin from the hearse to the gravesite.

Grant exited the limousine and helped Dana Beth and Ruth from the backseat. He put his arms around both of them as they climbed the small grassy slope surrounded by pine trees. He didn't remember much about the funeral, except that he was amazed at the great number of people filling the church. He had no idea how popular Conrad had been. The last three days his mind had been filled with the circumstances surrounding Conrad's death. Dealing with the grief of Ruth and Dana Beth hadn't made things any easier. He was still torn over his decision regarding the killer's identity.

Passing a large oak tree, he noticed a man standing next to the tree. He was dressed in black, loose fitting clothes, with a black knit cap pulled down over his ears. The man seemed out of place, as everyone else was congregating down by the gravesite. Maybe he was one of the grave diggers or just a passerby. Grant couldn't make out his face, but at the moment he really didn't care.

He looked around the gathering of people under the canopy protecting the open grave. Some were sitting, others stood, but they were all solemn, remembering a pillar of the community. They were his neighbors and his friends, his students and fellow professors, his beloved wife and daughter.

Those living in Townsend and the surrounding area still had to deal with the fact that there was a serial killer running loose and waiting to strike again.

Grant heard the minister say "Amen." Hugging his wife, Grant noticed that the man who had been standing next to the tree was gone. Suddenly, a strange sensation gripped his body as he thought he smelled the aroma of Peach Brandy tobacco.

coming from BlackWyrm in 2011

Also from Marlene and Gary...

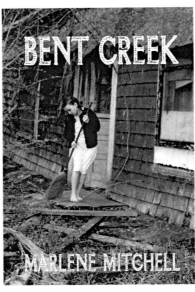

at www.blackwyrm.com

CPSIA information can be obtained at www.ICGtesting.com
Printed in the USA
239954LV00003B/3/P